What Empty Things Are These

JL Crozier

Regal House Publishing

Published by
Regal House Publishing, LLC
Raleigh 27612

Printed in the United States of America

ISBN -13 (paperback): 978-1-947548-12-1
ISBN -13 (epub): 978-1-947548-13-8
Library of Congress Control Number: 2018941143

Cover design by Lafayette & Greene
lafayetteandgreene.com
Cover Photos: Pierre-Louis Pierson (French, 1860s)
Metropolitan Museum of Art, Creative Commons (CCO)
and Abigail210986/Shutterstock

Regal House Publishing, LLC
https://regalhousepublishing.com

To my sons Tom and Alan Bell, who have lived with me
and these Victorians for a very long time.

My heart is like a singing bird
Whose nest is in a watered shoot;
My heart is like an apple tree
Whose boughs are bent with thickset fruit...

Christina Rossetti, 'A Birthday'
November 18th, 1857

Part One:

In which George suffers apoplexy, and Adelaide and Sobriety are left to discover their circumstances

Chapter One

Much later, I thought how Mr Hadley and I had both seemed suspended in that very long moment. Frozen, wild-eyed, as though we illustrated some penny-dreadful sold at railway stations.

There was George Hadley's arm stretched up, in his hand the cane with the chased-silver knob (very fine and an heirloom). His dark frock coat—he had not been home five minutes—swept wide like the wing of doom. Beneath were his sombre cravat and the subtle brocade of his grey waistcoat, which spoke of his authority and his impeccable choice of tailor. The angry pink of his face glowed under the sudden tossed halo of his white hair and whiskers.

Jehovah, I thought, breathless, perhaps in this way distracting myself from the matter at hand. I waited in a partially crouching form, watching first the anger flush and then the cane descend.

The suspense of the moment was broken; the cane thumped against my side as it would a stuffed cushion.

We both, he and I, grunted with the impact.

Time burst back into itself. I began to think quickly, once again, how best to deal with this in order to stop him: *Shall I whimper and apologise? Is it best this time to be stoic?* I heard his wheeze and gasp and then that heavy collapse as of something large dropped from a height, as of something felled. I'd had my head averted and protective hand raised, and now, after a beat of silence, I opened my eyes. He had caught the edge of *The Illustrated London News* with his cane as it swooped, and the pages, at first airborne—sea birds in a wind—were sinking to the ground. Printed ladies in the latest fashions of Paris sighed to a stop across the mound of his waistcoat. He lay still as the newspaper settled, there, just inside the entry to our parlour.

I had been reading the first volume of Mr Collins's *The Woman in White* when Mr Hadley had come home, had reached the part where the young Mr Hartright observed, to his perturbation, that the lovely Laura bore such a resemblance to that lunatic wanderer, the woman in white. I was engrossed in this excellent tale, speeding my way to the chapter's end with my breath anticipatory, my finger wetted to turn the page…and so was startled at the clunk of the front door and Mr Hadley's steps in the hall. I had neglected to hide the volume. Under a cushion would have done—such a simple thing—before his entrance into the room and into his rage.

Now I nearly dropped my novel, the cause of all this choler and collapse—though I did not, for the moment, rush to him. I was, frankly, much too surprised. The choleric moment that was so present—was just as quickly gone. In the silence the clock ticked stout and polished on the mantel; the plum velvet curtains hung as if carved; the crystal vase was bright and sharp on the lace reaching to the floor on either side of the coffee table.

Yet there he lay, and something must be done.

My mind filled with fog.

'Ma'am,' came from the open doorway. Sobriety, my lady's maid—my dear, dear Sobriety Mullins—stood, feather duster in hand, fresh from straightening my room, her eyes wide in a pale face.

Thank God, not Cissy or Mrs Staynes.

I felt my shoulders cringe immeasurably against the breath of humiliation. To have attention drawn so to myself, who must be at fault as the cause, or at least for having no notion what to do, and certainly for my leading role in this unwarranted drama in the midst of sober and respectable domesticity. I had *so* enraged my husband that… And in any case, here was undoubtedly a task, and here my duty to undertake it.

In a moment of pure absurdity, I fancied a crowd of lorgnettes

3

turned as one in my direction.

'Ma'am,' Sobriety said. 'You make him comfortable and I will fetch the doctor.'

'Yes, yes. Do. I shall.' Here was the relief of duty. I thought, *I shall loosen his cravat.* 'Be quick,' I said, but Sobriety's footsteps had already padded downstairs, and the front door slammed.

I sank, with adjustments and rustling. The careful lift to govern the tilt of crinoline and skirt was necessarily awkward, since the book was still in my hand and I must close it, with nothing to mark the place I had read to.

A base thought, how base—it came to me—*how could this cross my mind?*

I put the book down, with no marker, and leaned in with fingers poised while my husband breathed, badly but evidently. I looked at the knot on the cravat to see where would be best to tug to undo it. This was a thing I had never done before. There was a pin with a small sapphire set in silver, which I removed delicately. I myself was not breathing, absolutely intent as I traced the convolutions of the knot, until I pulled at the correct point and it slid apart. I undid his topmost shirt button, took a breath and let it out, then sat back on my folded legs.

At last, achievement. *What next?*

A head lying in that way upon the hard floor, and turned oddly as it was, could not be comfortable. I cast my eyes around the room from where I sat. Most of the embroidered cushions were much too large and stuffed. But the small blue satin cushion that had bolstered his back in times of strain—this was in its place on the divan. I rustled and teetered to my feet and fetched it, lifted his head very gently, and placed the cushion beneath it. When I leant over him there was an ache at my side, bruised now, and pressed hard as it was by stays.

At the time of his last chastisement, we had been visiting his sister, Mrs Courtney. We stood on the steps of the house, awaiting Mr Brent and the carriage—with all the world walking or trotting past in the street—and I had had to stay his hand with: 'Mister Hadley, we are in public!' I have no memory of what my infraction had been. And so he saved his task for home, struck me almost without anger, and his cane left a pattern for days on my ribs where it had struck across whalebone and stitching.

I supposed he was as comfortable, there on the floor, as I could make him. Adjusting myself to rise, I noticed the newspaper, still with its sheets splayed. I reached, shook and folded it carefully, before lurching to my feet once more, hand against the doorjamb both for balance and to achieve a tilt that would not hurt my bruised ribs.

I went to sit on the side chair by the mantel and fireplace—that chair with its cameo rose tapestry so entirely pristine and formal, so very rarely sat upon. I myself had never sat on it before that day. It did, at least, face where he lay. I could keep watch while his mounded waistcoat rose, hovered, and fell, and his head lay wild and white against his cushion. I perched there, skirt spread and hitched a little at the back to allow for sitting, very straight with my hands in my lap. Watched him and listened to the silence—a silence of aftermath reflected from the walls and the paintings in their gilt frames of varying sizes, from heavy mahogany legs and clawed feet to the arched tapestried backs of chairs and settee and the polished pianoforte with its stool tucked beneath; all rich and heavy and voiceless. At the window and between the heavy falls of velvet, a fragile light from the innocent day reached through the shower of lace.

Into the silence the clock ticked, then chimed briefly. It was eleven in the morning. Outside, a horse clattered past in   counterpoint. *The many minor noises that make up silence*, I thought, and again became aware of the rough drag of Mr Hadley's breathing.

And then knew a distant clamour behind that fog in my mind that was a tiny voice insisting: *I am responsible, I am not responsible, I am…* As I sat perfectly still and perfectly erect, the voice joined with a nausea of terror to become a distant chorus: *What if I am responsible?* His chest rose and fell as my own ribs pushed against corset and chemise and bodice and the very air of this suddenly stifling room.

Tugging at my own mind to make it listen to the clock as it ticked—to calm all this turmoil that I felt—I thought, *He might die,* and broke into a sudden perspiration, a light damp sheen over hot cheeks. There was elation, sheer joy, and then panic.

To think that!

But I was reduced, made abject, packed. I could see myself: a whirling figure seeking escape, turning and turning in the fog, grey skirt swaying as a bell tolling without sound. I could not begin to parse this feeling, to separate one pain from another, perhaps because I was quite simply not brave enough.

Simply not brave enough. My lack of courage settled over me in a pall, drab indeed.

I sat there and tiny tears pricked. Outside, a cloud crossed the sun; the light dimmed a moment and returned.

Neither Mr Hadley nor I had moved (though his mouth sagged open and his breathing was rough, like something dragged across rocky ground) when the door opened just as the clock chimed the half hour. Sobriety entered with the doctor and his big Gladstone bag, and the doctor's 'boy'—a large man in an ill-fitting coat who exuded a musky dampness, a stale sweat that billowed across the room. Like fingers clicked in my face, the odour caused me to rear back, its hulking maleness shouting of life and death, both. The others seemed unaware of my little movement. Perhaps I had only thought I moved.

Rising to my feet, I remembered on my way to greet the doctor that I still held newspaper and book. I left them on the bureau and reached to shake Doctor McGuiness's hand. A small man, he moved in an open-legged manner that had the effect of clearing a space before him and gave a firmness to his presence.

'Ah, Mrs Hadley, a sad business. I shall test his vital signs a moment before we convey him upstairs.' Doctor McGuiness was curt, though his face, in its frame of tight springing grey curls, creased just enough to demonstrate sympathy.

My husband, I noticed, had wet his trousers at some time during his apoplectic fit. There was a wetness the size of a hand unfolding there. As the doctor opened his bag and listened to Mr Hadley's heart with an instrument, bent an ear to listen to the labouring of Mr Hadley's lungs, I was riveted by this growing stain. Both startled and confused to be so suddenly suffused with pity for my husband—whose toilette was the concentrated ritual of an hour every morning before his meeting with the day—I was then washed over with needle-pricks of mortification and had to turn away. I possessed an acute desire to apologise or to rush some covering over Mr Hadley, and neither of these things was possible since either would attract attention to his shame. Still, I looked about covertly for something that might serve, though there was nothing. I made to stand as near as possible to hide the damp patch from view, but this created only awkwardness with everybody standing about so close on the landing or in the doorway: There was Sobriety, small and alert for some direction; the doctor's boy, shambling and odorous (like Bottom on the India rug, holding his cap in big red hands); the doctor, crouched over my husband who lay in shadow cast by the crowd; and myself, by now pacing about behind them.

Doctor McGuiness picked up the cane from where it had fallen and handed it to Sobriety, who took it downstairs to place it in the umbrella stand, where it stood next to the feather duster. This seemed odd to me, suddenly. Sobriety must have thrown the duster there, in her haste to fetch the doctor. I thought, *That speaks of crisis. What else would a duster in the umbrella stand signify?* Then I blinked away this distraction. Sobriety rustled quickly back up to the small crowd upon the landing.

'Madam, shall I fetch Cissy to prepare Mr Hadley's bed?'

'Yes, yes.' The agony of uselessness lifted. 'And…and perhaps she should light his fire. Perhaps a hot bottle, too. And Mrs Staynes will have suggestions to make. And Albert to help carry—' There seemed little time for much of this just now, for almost as soon as Sobriety had trotted back down the carpeted stairs, Doctor McGuiness gestured to his boy. They grasped Mr Hadley's arms and legs, lifted and, remarkably gently, bore him up upwards, the lumbering doctor's boy checking his way behind him all the difficult way.

I rushed into my husband's chamber ahead of these men with their burden. Mr Hadley's sheet and counterpane must be pulled back in readiness, which I did, though it was by myself. All that heaving and heavy breathing—and the air loaded with the sweat of the doctor's boy—while Cissy, breathless, was by now a-tremble and fumbling to begin her work at the grate, and Albert loitered bewildered at the door, waiting for his turn to deal somehow with the question of Mr Hadley's clothing.

But when they had placed my husband on the bed, the doctor turned and said, 'Mrs Hadley, there is no need for you to stay. We will attend to him. My boy and Mr Hadley's man will change him into nightclothes. I will speak to you after a more thorough examination.'

This was undoubtedly dismissal. I said, 'Oh, oh yes, of course', and left too quickly for real dignity, with Cissy scraping desperately with matches, so that she could leave too and run for the hot water bottle Mrs Staynes must by now be preparing in the kitchen.

Thus I found myself again in the silence of the drawing room, on the tapestried side chair, with a muted squeak of floorboards from above. My eyes closed for just a moment, and I thought of Mama saying so often 'Take three breaths,' and I dutifully did so. I tried to imagine what might be needed next (*beef broth…?*), and was calmed a little. My mind drifted.

I began to muse upon the cut and expense of widow's weeds and how, if one were not too pale, these could be becoming on a blonde woman, especially one still young. I had seen instances where the effect was appealing, fragile and dramatic all at once. The widow— *Oh Lord.* The room blurred about me; I felt a tear travel over the curve of my cheekbone.

Such ungovernable thoughts. Such a contemptible woman.

I brushed the tear away.

Chapter Two

When I, Mrs George Hadley, was the very small and whispering Adelaide Broom, perhaps five years old, I would be called to sit upon my father's knee on evenings when there were guests. I tipped my oft-patted faery-white curls to one side, gazed out of my glass-blue eyes (so noted by my elders), and hid my face in Papa's shoulder if his friends spoke directly to me. Sometimes I must present my face so that my cheek might be pinched, then caressed by fingers yellowed with tobacco.

My sister Gwendolyn, older than me by a decade and the eldest of we younger Brooms, might play a popular piece on the piano-forte, adequately enough. She would then sit for a decent interval before slipping away (always unsmiling and straight as a dowager-in-waiting, careful of her dignity and that it not be questioned), perhaps for chess with my older brother Harry. Dickie, aged between Harry and me, yet closest to Harry, would stay to be chaffed by the men, his face patched florid with pleasure at their attention. When Nanny tapped at the door at bedtime, I got up with a jump of many inches to the floor, curtseyed, and kissed my papa on his cheek. I left the room wrapped in the approval of Papa and his friends, knowing that their gaze followed me to the door.

The passage of a very few years would see the visitation of my siblings' own families, a seeming crowd of nannies and babies accompanied by quarrels and crying. But there were still those other masculine evenings, when I visited with Papa and his friends, all bewhiskered and grey, before my supper and Nanny's summons. I sat silent and flounced, as golden in my prettiness as my own precious porcelain *poupeé*, while men such as Mr Hadley smelt of whisky and cigars, and spoke of business and trade, of the escalation of crime, sometimes of discoveries in foreign parts, of politics and capital and power. Mr Hadley and Papa spoke of their adventures in investment and of their plans for partnership.

They toyed with my curls as I bade them goodnight.

My father's estate beckoned children to play in its vast spaces; crafted, as it was, at great expense with a rolling grassy slope and a small, reflective lake next to trees. I would climb high to hide among the shivering leaves. It was a game I held to myself, for otherwise there were those of my brothers', where I might be obliged to play the soldier to Harry's General and Dickie's Colonel, or the prisoner to their pirates. I could see for a very great distance from these branches, and could not myself be seen. My favourite tree was very old, I believed, and an elm; it cupped me within its boughs. Harry and Dickie were glad enough to be off by themselves to play at their boys' games, and none of we three ever told that I was thus left unaccompanied for hours.

When there was little else to do on days of inclement weather (and there was often little to do, for my very few friends lived too far for easy visiting; Gwendolyn was so often improving herself somewhere in the library or the sewing room; and Harry and Dickie tended more toward wrestling and bickering when it rained, and were to be avoided) I would wander throughout the great house where we Brooms lived at some distance from London, down the long corridors dark with doors and aged timbered floors worn into grooves. The world through the windows was blurred with wind and rain. Inside, I imagined, the very shadows breathed their boredom, and the very fringes of our elderly oriental carpets were limp with it.

'These carpets were swept from the East by an earlier Broom,' Mama would say frequently with her half-smile, a play that I did not yet fully understand though believed very clever. Mama found it amusing not merely to toy with words but also to tease Papa. 'So many Brooms for one house!' she would murmur behind her tucked smile, and I always laughed with her.

Up the stairs I went, until these narrowed from a wide sweep with an intricate banister to a steep and narrow tripway for maids at the end of their day. I peeked sometimes into the two rooms newly built at the top of these stairs, large enough only for a tiny bed and a clothes-horse under a sloping ceiling, chill and damp in winter and hot as Cook's kitchen in summer. These rooms were always empty with the maids off working, except for the time when I had forgotten or had not known that Ida was ill, and found the girl trembling with an ague, clutching a thin blanket with a shawl spread over the blanket up to her chin and the snow eddying and silent beyond the window.

'Leave me be, Miss, please,' Ida said and I, caught out, ran off, *tap-tap-tap-tap* down the little steep stairs, embarrassed from the surprise but also with a tight envy in my chest, of Ida, who had a space of her very own, just my size.

The envy—and it was some time before I confessed it to be unreasonable—stayed throughout my bedtime in my own room and all its bustle, where Becky had been to turn down the bedclothes, light the fire, and draw the curtains; Nanny had come with hot cocoa, taken my clothes for airing, and shaken out my nightdress; Mama had entered for the goodnight kiss and to read a story. It lasted, my envy, until the morning, when Nanny swept open the curtains to a day like a sudden, too-bright pearl.

For some days, then, I searched for and tried out cupboards and wardrobes for myself, *tap-tap-tapping* along floorboards, with muted footfalls along the old carpets. I looked for dark-timbered spaces breathing a history back to the earliest Broom of all, even beyond the history of Papa and his importation of Indian silks (Mama referred to 'new Brooms of Empire', smirking lightly into her embroidery when Papa, in irritation, snapped the pages of his journal).

I was intent on finding a small, dark space with a smell of dry dust and the faintest line of light at the crack of the door. Here, I could close my eyes in the silence and fancy ancient footsteps beyond the panel, a rustle or a clatter as of some awkward thing being dragged.

Perhaps (I imagined) there was once the body of some sad young man, dead in his doublet, slain in a duel by another in hose, both consumed by an urgent passion for ladies in farthingales; such ladies themselves wilting for love behind the disguise of their jewelled masks.

Both the notion itself, and the fact that I had invented it myself, sent a frisson of excitement racing through my veins. Here were worlds to anticipate, worlds where the whispers were of my praises.

Hush! For it is she: Miss Adelaide, the brave...

I found a space under the stairs and Ida swept it clear of spiders.

My Lord of Rothesay, my father would never allow this marriage, for I am betrothed to another... I began there in the near-dark, and continued in this way for hours, alone (for Ida had left to carry out polishing).

I collected candle stubs and matches, snippets of wool and material from Mama's sewing box, and clothes' pegs that I turned into well-dressed dolls, pasted with flour-and-water stirred together in the kitchen. They wore tiny curling feathers in their headdresses. There were books, borrowed from —and, usually, returned to—tables and shelves in the big house; scraps of paper, with a small pot borrowed from the kitchen for paints and my brush; and a much-sharpened pencil for short tales of heart-rushing heroism (*My Lord of Rothesay*...I wrote).

Dickie was invited, on occasion, for songs and recitations

especially learned for the performance, for he was my most precious brother and I yearned toward him. For his sake, I had even learned to adore his toy soldiers and to tell the difference between the ranks. In return, I think, he indulged me, and sat for perhaps half an hour at a time on a tiny stool as I performed, and even clapped, before declaring that that was enough and returning to his own pastimes.

Here under the stairs, I began years of musings and misspellings into writing journals that I kept in an old hatbox of Mama's under my bed. The short, childish tales became longer stories of mystery or love or daring, revolution sometimes, and once a tale of a lady spy who faced the guillotine. I read these tales in instalments aloud to Ida right up until the first of my coming out parties.

After which there was little time to write of adventure, what with hours of standing straight, withstanding the pinpricks of the dress-maker who circled and circled, adjusting and tweaking, forever glanc-ing at the clock—for she had, as she often muttered, a great crowd of young ladies awaiting her skills.

'Oh, my admirable Adelaide,' Mama whispered in my ear. 'What a new Broom is this, who will sweep all before her!' I giggled, which loosened pins at my waist and caused the seamstress to snort and tut.

And there was no time and there were few words to describe the nausea of anxiety that was anticipation of my first great ball, to which I travelled with Mama on the one side and Dickie on the other. Mama pinched my cheeks, for, she said, they had turned a pale green from fear. That first time, I trembled as I danced and dizzied at the swirl of movement about me, the golden twinkle of jewels in the glare of gaslight, the heat, the twittering of voices as in an aviary, behind which beat music, music, music, and the heavy sweep of skirts a-swing over their layers of petticoat and frame. Such a weight was fashion then!

I grew braver, of course, and nights grew longer; each begun with two hours of preparation—Ida dithering at the side of the woman Mama had hired for her experience in these things—and ended with the dawn faint above the chimneys. We stayed for the time being at Harry's house in London, yet—the hours being what they were— often did not see him or his wife from one evening to the next.

The looking glass told how the hectic pace of it all now made me both pale and pink. I whispered to various of my new and glittering circle—girls who swam in giddiness as I did, whose love for each other was ecstatic, for the moment—that I would kiss a certain boy who was tall, with dark falling curls, and whose full mouth spoke (metaphorically) of fruit and poetry. And I did so, truly, and was thus short of breath behind a column in a darkened corner of the hall, my pulse pattering and my cheeks hot. His hands, and the hands of others, were at my waist; his mouth, and those of others, murmured in my ear as I danced, and society and all its lights swung about me.

But then it was that both mood and tone altered, oddly, and I found myself at dinner, not once but several times, seated next to Mr Hadley. He took my arm into and out of these dining halls. I listened from my bedchamber to the raised voices of my mama and my papa, who had unaccountably arrived to stay some days.

There was a scene where little was said directly, and little under-stood—by me, at any rate. I was called to Harry's drawing room and told to sit, and Papa, as if continuing some thread of conversation that I should, surely, have noticed, said, 'Mr Hadley, as you know, is my oldest friend and business confidant. He will elevate you greatly in life.'

I must have seemed very stupid indeed, looking from one parent to the other. My mind was full, still, of young men with soft, direct eyes and whose hands I imagined about my waist. Each night I looked about myself as I entered another ballroom, and all around were young women and young men, looking about themselves.

Mr Hadley, let it be said, was the furthest possible thing from my thoughts.

After a silence, Mama said, 'You will have children and your own house,' though she did not look at her daughter. At me. She put her hand to her side, for she was to bear another child and had been quite unwell. Since my own birth, Mama had not borne another that could continue more than a few days alive.

All of a sudden, I was affianced to the old man, and bewildered at how it had come about, at what had been in my hands that had shone and promised breathless mystery in worlds beyond my own, and which now had been pulled away. All that brightness, all the breathless anticipation of every twinkling, dancing evening, circling and circling within the arms of young men…all receding pell-mell into darkness, the music fading with it as it took all my friends away.

Some of this I had written down, though it was difficult to find the words, and these scraps stayed in the dark of my space beneath the stairs, forgotten, and no doubt were lying there still when Mr Hadley, years later, wheezed and waned on the floor of his grand house, far away at London's comfortable centre.

Chapter Three

This house, that I now decided I had never felt to be mine, loomed heavy about me. It sat, that great weight of bricks, loaded and draped with velvet and tapestry, its carved banisters like forearms; a dozen precious, ugly objects crouched on every mantel. Its clocks ticked, endlessly through all the man-made segments of Time, all separate from sun or season. I was compressed by it; there was not enough air about me. My stays creaked as my lungs filled. Wandering from room to room, I felt myself a child again, examining the spaces about me and imagining their history, though there was no history here save that of a loveless marriage.

Doctor McGuiness gave his orders. And so I spent hours on duty in the sickroom, staring at the disorder of Mr Hadley's white hair, the pleats and folds gathering now about his emptying face, the eyes gone moist, yellow, resting fractionally open yet unknowing; the man himself, mute and shadowed in the half-light. His brocade bed-jacket was wet at the neck from dribble; his breath had begun to smell of rot; his lungs laboured on like sodden bellows.

I gazed at him—interested that I could do so in so nearly a disinterested manner—and began to think. Had he breathed in that way, with the whisky blowing in gusts, while I listened in the dark to thumps and short, wordless cries, and muffled, urgent clattering in Sobriety's room, directly above my own? That clattering that resolved into a rhythm like aggression (the bed, I knew, rammed again and again and again against the wall, a declaration to me and to Sobriety both). Then the great shout of his climactic triumph; then a brief pause; then the slam of a door and his steps down the narrow stairs. A long, long moment of silence before the creak of movement from the room above.

I remembered thinking, lying and listening that night in my bed as he lay claim to and outraged my Sobriety, of the visit made once with my husband to the National Gallery—because one is seen to visit the National Gallery now and then—and the viewing of *The Rape of the Sabine Women*, how celebration was made in this painting of the seizing of women's flesh against their will. I looked long, wondering that such celebration could be made of violence against those who did not even take up arms, whose pain, somehow, was their tormentors' triumph. I wondered what was to be attained by this subjugation, this usage of women. Mr Hadley, bored, sauntered away to gaze elsewhere.

Here, in this house (I thought to myself that night beneath my coverlet, listening to Mr Hadley's assault of my maid), was no splash of colour or vibration from sensual flesh and drapery; here were but one man and two women in the dark, one of whom struggled while the other heard it.

There followed at least a week, I fancied, where the three of us moved in different parts of the house, we women avoiding not only Mr Hadley but also each other. Our eyes did not meet; we barely stirred the air about each other. I made my choice of dress in the quiet of my bed before rising to wash at the basin, and to powder; Sobriety, in silence, passed drawers (with myself so sensitive to the presence of Sobriety's fingers, her arms rising and falling with the lifting and folding, the busy swing of her skirt), which I slipped on beneath my nightdress, and my under-petticoat. She hooked up the corset over the chemise; she tied at my waist the tapes of the steel-hooped crinoline; she passed the flounced petticoat with the daily flurry over my head.

At night were the undressings, without a word between us two.

Sobriety flitted, when these duties were finished, from my bedchamber, head bowed, and somehow very small indeed.

Mr Hadley's breath whistled infinitesimally. I moved to sit by the window and look out, the lace pulled a little to one side. The small fire in the grate snapped from time to time; the room was too warm and dim.

On the wall behind Mr Hadley's bed, Rosetti's *Lady Lilith* stared down, all lushness and spreading hair and fur and glowing wantonness, and I, as I had when he first bought the painting and had it raised onto the wall, avoided the woman's eyes.

Once again, the thought occurred: *The painter is so forthright, his statement of licentiousness so plain, yet his sister the poetess is so troubled and questing...*

I knew my embarrassment to be humiliation in itself.

I looked back to the window.

In the street outside, hansoms passed from time to time, the cabbies wrapped to their red noses against the cold.

I rested my hand against my side.

Cissy placed a small table, brought up from the morning room, by the window in Mr Hadley's room. It had struck me that this little table could have more uses at last than the merely decorative. On my finest notepaper, I wrote notes to relatives and to my husband's business associates:

> *Mr George Hadley suffered an apoplexy this Tuesday last and, while he is with us still, he recognises no one and his physician is not encouraging of an eventual recovery.*

I paused before dipping the nib again into the inkwell.

Of a sudden, there reared the appalling possibility of a stream of frock-coated gentlemen come calling, grey whiskers well-kempt and on display, perhaps in company with wives whose faces had settled long ago into unsmiling dourness, all of whom I may have met briefly and by whom I had, often, been chilled into silence. Mr Hadley would be entirely unaware of their visit, while I would shrivel under their superior gazes, the arrogance of their sympathetic duty. Perhaps there would be pity (which I doubted would be sincere). I would read into those faces—whose expression was all of one controlled kind, that of very little expression at all—that I now lacked or would soon lack position, and they would no longer consider me as anybody of moment.

Might I hold them at bay?

My hand not altogether steady, I put pen back to paper, my cheeks heated at what was, I knew, my cowardly stretching of the truth:

> *While I assume of course your very best wishes toward him, visiting is not advisable.*

To my son's headmaster I added:

> *We feel that Toby ought not to come home as yet, since it is not known how long the illness will continue. Michaelmas is not far, when he is in any case expected here. I shall write to him myself…*

I paused again with my child in my mind, straight-backed as was his habitual stance, cool with a child's contempt and his father's hand on his shoulder, turned away as if I was of no account. As if I was not there.

Neither was I prepared for that.

> *…in a few days.*

And at the last, for I had put off the writing of one note until all others had been done, and while I considered, indeed, whether I would write it at all, I dipped my pen once more into the ink.

Dear Mrs Charles,
It is my sad duty to inform you…

Mrs Charles, to whom my husband would bow his lowest and smile his widest. She would turn her head, elegant with its streaks of smoke and silver and altogether assembled like an item of great value, to regard me as if I were rather ordinary china or, if we were out of the house, as if I trailed Mr Hadley like some puppy at heel. It was so the very first time she and I met, when Mr Hadley had taken me to promenade one Sunday in Hyde Park, with Toby, our very new baby, muffled up in his carriage and pushed by Nanny. We were all paraded thus, though I was weak still, and slow, and very conscious of it, and folding and refolding my shawl about me the whole afternoon.

We did not promenade often in those days (and hardly at all since) and it was evident to me we had only done so then to add to Mr Hadley's social advancement and to demonstrate the arrival of his heir. There were indeed those who bowed to Mr Hadley, simpered at me, and bent to look at the child. But before Toby's arrival, when we had been on promenade, my husband had not been at all pleased that young men too frequently settled their eyes on me. It was a parade to mortify both man and wife.

Then had come the meeting with Mrs Charles and I had felt myself placed aside in my youth and my illness, which was somehow shameful. I had torn so during the birth and bled still, and must focus my mind even to stand without tottering, or to walk with some grace; I felt myself to be of no consequence. I knew my body would never quite be set to rights again. *A puppy that can no longer breed*, was what I told myself. I was young; I was silly; I was clumsy and had nothing to say.

Mr and Mrs Hadley soon ceased these Hyde Park perambulations, to our mutual relief. And, in any case, Mrs Charles was not always promenading.

Still, here is one who might grieve over George Hadley. I pressed my lips together over the thought. I had long known—with the knowledge gained from my careful observation of every glance between them— Mrs Charles's relationship with Mr Hadley. I stilled, uncertain, my pen in my hand, and then: *I will be honourable, and tell her.*

I folded my notes into envelopes. *I have been honourable, and I have been kind.*

Glancing over at Mr Hadley, slumped where he had been propped there in the gloom, with his chest moving slow and shallow, I stared a moment and thought: *Ah, husband, see how I am a child still with all of this, affrighted of everyone.* I closed my eyes and opened them again. *Even of my own son.* I took a long breath and let it out. What I told him thus in my mind, I realised, was no more than the truth. *Still*—and here I passed a hand against a damp cheek—*I may at least cause some delay.*

I looked at the topmost note. It seemed doubtful they would *all* keep away. Delay, I knew, was the best I could hope for.

Then for a time, I read Mr Collins's book—the second volume now, which Sobriety had fetched for me from Mr Mudie's library, that excellent establishment. When I thought every now and then to look toward Mr Hadley, I saw how he sagged.

It is as if he is a sack with the stitching gone.

I must not think these things.

A cloth, soggy now from his incontinent dribbling, had been tucked around his neck and over the collar of his jacket. I took a deep breath to test the sensitivity of the bruise that pressed against my stays.

In Mr Collins's distressing tale, Mr Hartright and Laura had been separated cruelly despite their love for one another. Laura was obliged to marry the odious Sir Percival Glyde, who had shut Ann (the woman in white) up in an asylum. Laura's half-sister, Marian, was convinced there was evil about that vile and clever Sir Percival.

I turned a page of my book and felt a sudden fanfare through all of my nerves. A complex of sensations, I thought, like so many notes from so many instruments, like a band just arrived from far away, blaring with all its notes and all its instruments, a noise of sensations to overwhelm all else. These sensations had whispered ever since Mr Hadley fell insensible; they clamoured now, so loud and crowding. I sought to define them, searching through phrases and terms that might fit—*Is this threat, as for Laura or Marian? A dark inkling? Terror? Perhaps a little terror. Constrained, yes, bound but more than that*—desperate to dispel panic that existed, I felt, because I could not so define them.

And then I recognised *rebellion* and was surprised, and then was shocked as if I had been caught out once again, appalled. And thus began another jumble of reactions to…to…my *rebellion*—yes, my *rebellion*!—all marching through my blood like a brass band until I had to fill my lungs, as I had sat without breathing at all, apparently, for many minutes. I looked at that man lying in his bed.

There lay he who had raised his voice at the notion of women reading sensation, at this literature's stirring of imagination among the weak, at the distraction from duty, at the wanton tempted away from their virtues . . .

A book, Mr George Hadley. A book, read by respectable people. And I find comfort in books.

How is this wrong?

Does not Mrs Charles read novels such as these? Or do you not feel the need to direct her thus?

I thought, as I had often thought before, how Mr Hadley was angriest when my mind lay furthest from his direction.

He pays me no mind, yet when I wander in my own garden of imaginings…

Yet there was guilt, still, at the reading of a novel, this novel—the cause of my chastisement, and my husband's collapse during that chastisement. My guilt was palpable, tumerous, sitting next to the feeble voice that sought to justify myself, and next, again, to the Adelaide of my mind who stamped her childish feet, and then felt guilt for doing so…

I was recovered (though enervated somehow, as if I had exerted myself up a mountainside, though this was only the Montblanc of the mind) and ready to hold Mr Hadley's head more or less erect when Mrs Staynes, pale as damp clay, arrived with Cook's broths to spoon into his unresponsive mouth. These were concoctions we three, Cook and Mrs Staynes and I, had discussed together and experimented upon, with boilings and mashings and infusions and tales of family recipes and disasters. Silent and listening, as we women talked, the child Cissy had rubbed at silverware at the other end of the great table, while Sobriety pressed at lace with the iron, and tested for heat with a tiny *tsst* of spit at her finger.

I lost track of time, until a Thursday came and Cissy was at her weekly polishing of wood and brass throughout the house; I rustled past to the morning room to fetch a pen and paper or my book. I had left the sampler on the armchair, half-finished in its frame. My attempts at embroidery had always been half-hearted, taken up only because Mr Hadley's sister, Mrs Edith Courtney, pressed upon me the virtue of framed mottoes—*Bless this House*, and *Speak Not to Deceive, Listen Not to Betray* were both hung upon the wall in Edith's front hall; such improving thoughts to greet visitors. Now, I stopped to glance at my poor sampler, noticed my neat rose, uncertain, unfinished, declaring *Bless this H…* to the world.

My own meals were often taken at the small table that now stood by the window in Mr Hadley's room. And then there were his meals, with me and sometimes Cissy, sometimes Mrs Staynes, our mouths compressed, wiping some moist mess into him. Scooping, wiping, pressing. In my mind was the chant: *One is right to do this. This is what a wife does.*

Yet hovering too, and plucking at my sleeve in imagination, was a contrariness that Mrs Ellis—that mistress of modern manners whose book was given to the young Adelaide as to all young girls— had insisted one must not consider:

> "What shall I do to gratify myself—to be admired—or
> to vary the tenor of my existence?" are not the questions
> which a woman of right feelings asks on first awaking to
> the avocations of the day.

I wished with a guilty wail in the depths of my soul—which must be very dark indeed, surely—absolutely and fundamentally to vary the tenor of my existence.

Beneath Mr Hadley, Mrs Staynes had folded sheets into padding, and another around his loins, and these were changed every morning and afternoon and evening. We women bent with our faces averted from each other and from the stench (for he had lost all control of his bodily functions) and from the urge always to cringe from this now-cold evidence of human frailty and weakness, yet dogged in the face of it and barely aware of our mouths tugged down at their corners. Cissy reached beneath our arms, as we trembled from the effort of holding his flaccid, hanging weight, and fetched away the sodden cloths.

Visitors left their cards and did not stay. One of them had been Mrs Charles. I read the names and wrote short notes of thanks. Sometimes I looked idly through the lace curtains. An old cart in the street bore an ancient iron bed, bound and rattling, and an old man

25

sat atop it, lurching along in counterpoint, sometimes poking the tired nag that dragged them all. Two gentlemen walked fast along, swinging their walking canes. One of them checked his watch.

Later, it rained. The sound whispered from the world into the house, and every window looked onto streaming water that stirred the light when I inched back the lace to see. Drops spit and spattered and trickled down the glass in runnels that raced, joined, and zig-zagged to the edge of the pane. In Mr Collins's book, Marian clung, whipped by rain and wind, to the very narrow gutter, the better to spy on the plottings of his lordship, Sir Percival, and the Italian count.

I put my hand on the page lest I lose my place. The house stood silent and a little cold as the rain washed against its walls and windows. Into all the whispering and moaning of the weather, I mused to myself: *Is all movement here, in the house, for me, slowed now? Slowed, until it ceases altogether? Do I follow George into stillness and silence?*

side a little before bowing it again.

I considered myself and Mr Hadley. I searched about for some sense of loss—for some reflection of the loneliness and rush of cold after the death of my mama; of that anguish, wilder and more chaotic than grief, when my papa had fallen from his horse, struck his head, and died. The breeze puffed at his thinning hair as his eyes stared sightless at the sky.

I had been surprised—deep in a still, quiet corner of my mind— that my grief for my father should be so powerful, as if I were shaken in the grip of a huge, choleric fist. So many hours spent clinging to Sobriety's hand, my maid (truly my only friend) crooning to me as if I were a child, until I settled, finally, into a near-silent contemplation of everything—daily events and all the domestic comings and goings—as if I were at one remove, standing watchful, perhaps, on the other side of glass.

Much later, I watched Sobriety's own slide into misery, herself sapped of joy after the cholera had taken her elder sister, her Hope. The loss of love can leave a person folded, packed into a tight, arms-wrapped parcel, rocking with the pain, the repetition of movement mesmerizing, almost liturgical. There was my Sobriety alone with all of this; for no matter how bright the sunshine casting its lace-dappled light, or how crowded the room, it was as if she were abandoned alone in a darkened place, steeped in grief left uncomforted by her family's Methodism and its many dictates on sin, by the ungentleness of her father's lay-preaching.

'For Hope,' Sobriety whispered through her weeping, 'was not a sinner and had not deserved to be denied her life.'

'Of course not, of course not.' I held Sobriety and rocked with her. 'Of course not.'

Unhearing, Sobriety twisted like a tortured thing between the memory of her father, that farmer, that thundering lay-preacher, and her uncle. The latter's rare visits shone like relief, I gathered, when he would argue from the depths of his Jacobin zeal that men must believe in their rights, and that the real sin lay with a world based upon injustice and inherited power.

See them, I thought, *leaning forward on their elbows at the table, silent with the frustration of their endless disputation, staring each with an equal, messianic gleam.*

'How did you get your name?' I asked, curious, when Sobriety's tumult at last began to quieten.

'My mother,' she said, 'when expecting my birth, was inspired at one of my father's sermons about the godliness of steadiness and self-discipline, as well as the denial of indulgence.' Sobriety patted back a lock of hair that had come loose. 'And my father approved her choice.' Sobriety's mother had thereupon felt her first pains and the baby arrived soon after to take up her name. 'It was seen as a sign, that I should be named so.' Sobriety's smile was wan and tired, though she seemed to take some strength from the telling of family stories. Hope, she related, had been given the work of carrying the baby for her busy mother, singing to her, changing her soiled wrappings, and teaching the little girl as she grew the prayers that all Mullins children should know.

Before Hope's sad removal from this world, Sobriety and I had spent comfortable hours together exchanging tales of family. Parades of dour farmers and craftsmen; the uncle with his sailor's rolling gait and well-fired Jacobinism; wives of a firm religion and one more given to soothsaying and cards (and condemned thereby for so casting away her grace in God's eyes); all passed through my morning room like ghosts on an animated visitation. I could see, as if I had been there, the yellowing message nailed to the smoked mantel in the dark farm kitchen: 'The Lord God knows ALL.' Sobriety repeated the names of her sisters—Hope, Faith, Charity, Modesty, and Temperance ('Has there not been a repetition there?' I could not help but ask, but Sobriety looked away rather than return the smile)—as well as those of her brothers, Simon and Peter.

But Hope fell to the cholera, and Sobriety's memories set themselves against each other and exhausted her so that, day after day with my arm around her, she would end with a whispered: 'Hope did not deserve this. How can the world be without Hope?' And I would kiss her forehead.

It was right, if odd, to say, 'Hope will always be with you,' to which Sobriety nodded her head several times and replied, 'Yes, yes, yes. 'Tis so.'

Sobriety received long letters from home at this time, at first putting the homilies away, for she was too much in the midst of her grief to accept calls for acceptance. Still, eventually, she came occasionally to say that Hope had had a "holy dying" and was joined with the Lord, as her father had written to her; even though Sobriety spoke still as if she sat alone in shadow, too quiet and with her eyes cast down.

In my stolid Anglican way, I had until then dealt with the Methodist outlandishness of Sobriety's name by use of the usual appellation of "Mary." My maid had, besides, been referred to thus in the original letter of reference from her previous employer, Mrs Hayes, now long ago gone to India with her Colonel husband. But then it seemed to me, with the terrible tale of Hope's dying now told, that Mary was no name for my maid and friend after all, and from that day I called Sobriety by her own name. Which—I confessed it to myself—best suited her in any case. My maid is a most sober person.

Mr Hadley, at this time of Sobriety's greatest grief, was away a fortnight on business; off to Liverpool it had been. Perhaps it was to oversee the arrival of shipments from India (or so I thought, for he did not tell me much of his business except that he would be away).

In any case, I had Sobriety into my morning room most evenings, and read to her sometimes, and sometimes Sobriety read to me. I watched Sobriety's doughtiness stand up, despite her grief, and we learned to speak with each other as friends do.

I sat in the sickroom and my gaze settled back onto my husband: *I am sorry, Mr Hadley. There was never friendship from you and there will not be grief from me. Not from me.*

I wondered if I felt enough to pity him for this.

Chapter Five

Mr Hadley's sister, Mrs Courtney, arrived one Tuesday from the country, with her humid emanations and her tight-bound stoutness. Her bustling, sweeping carelessness threatened the vase from China on its little hall table—it teetered for a breathless moment—as she waved a list of the proper methods for tending patients. She recited these, her handkerchief sprouting from her fist. *At the ready*, I thought, standing by with one hand resting in the other; then, *Poor woman. I must remember compassion;* and with resignation, *Ah, well. She is staying*, as Edith Courtney removed her bonnet and shawl. *It was to be expected*. I was Patience itself.

My sister-in-law continued with a conversation full of woe and exclamation (which was to be expected), and digression (which was habitual) and I watched her face at its expressive exercise. As so often, Mrs Courtney's maid bore the brunt of her complaint.

'My Mary is in a pet, would you credit it!' Mrs Courtney waved her hands in illustration. 'She disapproves of this; she disapproves of that. Oh!' She put her hand to her forehead. 'I am obliged to leave her behind, she is so vexing, at such a time!'

In secret sympathy with Edith's maid, I was taken, of a sudden after all these years, by the smoothness of Edith Courtney's features. This smoothness was only partly due to a general rosy portliness and the lack of any truly defining line to nose or cheek. It was also, I felt, as she bemoaned her wilful Mary who would not approve her every scheme and notion, that the face reflected a mind constantly scrubbed by the owner herself of all intelligent thought.

So that there is nothing left in that mind but the shallow whisperings of a child seeking reassurance. I recognised pity within myself, and was a little taken aback.

When Mr Courtney died, and Edith had begged her brother to tell what she was to do, he replied, 'You will do what you ought,' a phrase borrowed from my own sister Gwendolyn. Thereupon, Edith had subsided, for, of course, what she ought to do was very little indeed, less now even than when Mr Courtney lived.

Mr Hadley, having wrought this stricture upon his sister, moved on, all unthinking, for he viewed her—as he had so often said to me—mostly as an embarrassment. Indeed once, after a visit by Edith, he sat down to his supper, grasped his butter-knife and muttered: 'God save us from the histrionics of middle-aged women, both husband-less and childless.' His eyes flickered over me before turning back to bread and butter, while I thought, *I have one child, at least. Do I therefore outrank Edith?* Though I was uncertain how well this would hold me in good stead in his eyes. If at all.

I now regarded my sister-in-law not just with pity but also with a vague and insinuating dread.

Is Edith Courtney the pattern of things to come?

Edith held Mr Hadley's hand; it lay in her own, limp as an empty glove. She held her kerchief to her mouth, in the manner of the deeply saddened, her head tipped a little to the side and her brows drawn together. Thus, she demonstrated a pitying concern that all would recognise: she did her duty and behaved with commendable womanliness.

What a theatre put on for my benefit. I supressed a sigh, and then from downstairs there came a sharp rap upon the front door. *Who is that?* I wondered, while Edith was herself not to be distracted.

'Oh, my poor George. Tell me, my dear, what are you feeding him?' Edith said this last very nearly as a whispered aside, glancing

around at me with those earnest brows. But I was by then listening out—and for my own part demonstrating thus how distracted
I was from this question that I did not wish to answer (for fear of
eliciting extended advice)—for whatever disturbance the world was
bringing to my front door. This, I could hear, was opened at last and
Gwendolyn's voice drifted to me.

I was able to excuse myself to Mrs Courtney.

My own relations had, evidently, come to visit: my brothers Harry
and Dickie and Dickie's Amanda—Harry alone, since Sarah was herself in confinement with another baby on its way—and Gwendolyn's
daughter, my niece Bella, as ever frail and slight as a twig. Most
significantly, there was also present our family eldest, Gwendolyn
herself, in her widow's layers of black and purple and a veil that,
when she lifted it as I descended the stairs with Edith Courtney
behind me, left her face dough-white, dour, and unsmiling in its
somber framing.

"One does as one ought," Gwendolyn's best-used phrase, was taken
up after a time, as I said, by Mr Hadley, who employed it especially to
check his own sister's querulous uncertainties. Unlike my husband,
however—who perhaps only applied it to others—Gwendolyn
believes firmly in the axiom, and strives to ensure that all about her
did indeed do as they ought. She rules with a thin-boned, nervous
grasp that declares such governance is done in memory of those at
the centre of her life who have passed on and must be reverenced—
her husband, her mother, and her father. Else they would be dishon-
oured, indeed disgraced, as would all in the family, and all forced to
live exiled from society itself. Such an exile would be a terrible thing,
perhaps a little like death. One's place is of and within society; one
certainly does not conceive of a place without it. And more, it is not
to be borne that the family should be noticed, should draw attention,
should be made a spectacle, for that would be to demonstrate an ec-

centricity. Eccentricity itself is not to be countenanced.

Gwendolyn's life has been spent in service of her role, thus—watchful for any straying from invisibility, unless one is to be noticed for doing what one ought—and forceful in her insistence on conformity. We are a family to be noticed only for its conventionality.

Fate is not kind with its coincidences, I thought now as my family crowded into the hall for what would doubtless prove to be a most complicated visit. It was a rare thing indeed for Edith Courtney to be in a room with Gwendolyn, or to be invited to be so. It had never seemed likely to me that the two personalities would rub along at all well. While my sister made to have such a grip on all things about her, Edith Courtney had no such grasp, but babbled and babbled. Perhaps it was indeed as Sobriety had whispered once (and then apologised, unnecessarily, for her opinion) that they were each like a ship headed, however tight or loose the grip about the tiller, for rocks they feared lay in wait somewhere unseen beneath the waves.

I felt a familiar nausea of foreboding. Gwendolyn always aroused such feelings.

Gwendolyn had always been, of we two girls, the more dedicated to the instructions of Mrs Ellis, that author of moral guides. Nanny read for hours to us from Mrs Ellis, instilling her strictures on correct behaviours. Thus, it was made clear to us that:

> A careless or slatternly woman…is one of the most repulsive objects in creation and no power of intellect, or display of learning, can compensate to men, for the want of nicety of neatness in the women with whom they associate in domestic life.

Ostentation, Mrs Ellis advised us all, was near to a sin, and a dreadful example set by women of elevated class for those poorer than themselves. Gwendolyn took to Mrs Ellis's dictates as a pattern for her life. Provided all she did walked in step with the authoress, Gwendolyn could be confident of living in ironclad virtue untouched by the wild winds of contrary opinion, difference, or sensuality. I, on the other hand, struggled with this view of correct behaviour, while at the same time living at all times a little disturbed that I did not play virtue well enough.

In Gwendolyn's presence, it seems to me, there has always been a strong sense of envelopment.

Yet Mama herself had had about her an air of the careless that implied no very deep love of Mrs Ellis. This could be read, perhaps, in her hint of a smile and once, I am certain, in the flick of an eyebrow—even though she durst not speak ill of the authoress when Gwendolyn was in earshot. There was a deal of comfort for me in Mama's unspoken opinion. Now, as then, it made me wish to smile, which itself left me with a little guilt at the temptation to which I had succumbed.

This flock of family entered the drawing room and sat, with much rustling; a subsidence of massive birds, except for Harry who stood behind Gwendolyn's armchair. Here was the patriarch in lieu of our Papa, with Gwendolyn the matriarch in Mama's stead. *Yet more dedicated to the role than Mama ever was*, I thought. Bella sat to the side, her young face set in sulking wilfulness, and her sharp jaw borne very still atop the stalk of her neck.

Gwendolyn glanced a moment at her daughter, my niece, and then settled her gaze back on me. What she lacks of the authority of age—she is in fact barely forty years old—Gwendolyn makes up for in a stately, dragging gravity. To smile in her presence would be a levity and, by and large, we do not smile when Gwendolyn is about.

See, my sister has purpose, I thought. This annoyed me, so that I compressed my lips. I preferred not to know what that purpose might be.

The whole group, once perched, moved eyes to me as a committee might contemplate a problem of public amenity, or might, I thought, attend politely to the stuttering of an underling before declaring all arrangements had, in any case, already been made. But then, I thought it unfair, perhaps, to think of them all so, for there were among them Dickie, my favourite brother, and Amanda, his wife. Yet the group took on its own stern collective personality (*so like a monster with many heads*). While I loved some, truly, still there was a prickling as of the brush of tiny needles, as I knew the whole enfolded me and I absolutely did not wish to be so taken up.

'So kind of you all to come.' I sank (and it felt like a sinking) to the edge of my chair and rang for tea.

'Oh yes, oh yes. Such a time, such a sad, sad time.' Edith Courtney's voice began as ever, in too high a key. 'And so very encouraging that one's family should rally around…' She had set herself down next to me, somehow as if she, too, received these visitors.

Gwendolyn turned her head the merest inch toward Edith, who drifted into silence.

Conversation dwelt heavily on the weather as tea, carried in on its tray by a white-knuckled Cissy, was gathered upon the low table, with the great silver pot central to it all, heavy with carven curlicues and small cupids and laden thus with parloured importance. I lifted its great weight and poured and passed, poured and passed, and indicated a choice of cake or bread-and-butter.

Gwendolyn accepted her own cup and bread-and-butter, placed the plate down, sipped her tea, and stated, 'Bella will have cake.' This was said with finality, and every syllable expressed itself so. But Bella herself—her face small, fleshless, and as if fresh-chiselled at nose and cheek and chin—was silent. Instead of assenting, she regarded the far corner of the room, with its fine and weighty cornice so intricately painted. It was plain she ignored her mother. I was obliged merely to set the cup and plate down before her.

Tea, cake, and bread-and-butter were passed about the siblings and their wives, yet it seemed as if Gwendolyn and Bella sat by themselves in significance. It was as if the air about them carried the clatter of their silent battle. Mother and daughter swung great glinting weapons at each other, to speak in metaphor, even though they sat so still, poised and nearly regal, with the polished surfaces, lace, brocades, velvet and fringes of the room frozen all about them.

I thought: *See how they reflect one another, their heads held so exactly alike in imperiousness, though Bella is so much the smaller version.*

Cissy having departed the room, there was a pause that none could doubt held deep meaning. No one moved, yet it seemed as if all drew away from Gwendolyn and her daughter. Gwendolyn placed her cup back down upon its saucer. All eyes turned to her, while she herself regarded Bella.

'Your cake, my dear.' Gwendolyn placed her gloved hands in her lap, her eyes steady and unblinking upon the girl.

All of a sudden, I was oppressed by this enactment before me—*they do not shout, and yet it is as if they do, and we must all witness it*—and sought some relief in looking about the room. The crystal vase stood on the lacework protecting the pianoforte; Mrs Staynes had done well with maidenhair and white roses, though some drooped.

Moments seemed somehow extended for very long indeed (filled with the faintest sounds of breathing and the heavy ticking of the clock, while Dickie attempted a clearing of the throat). Bella, at last, reached forward and detached the smallest crumb from her slice of cake and placed it in her mouth. Gwendolyn closed her eyes for perhaps three further ticks of the clock, exhaled at length, and turned to me.

'Your notes to us all were brief, Adelaide. Are we to understand Mr Hadley is unlikely to recover?'

Edith took in a sharp breath and whimpered lightly. I knew that Gwendolyn would consider sensitivity in this or similar matters a waste of time. *My sister is brutality itself, wrapped in strait propriety,* I thought, as Edith Courtney began to gust, and her breast to heave accordingly.

While my mind clattered with tactful alternatives that might appease the two at once, I knew from experience that none would serve.

In any case, it was too late.

Gwendolyn glanced at Edith. Her voice came clear and uncompromising. 'A most painful time, I understand, for my sister and for you, Mrs Courtney, but I have always thought it best to call a spade a spade.' The thought glimmered briefly that Gwendolyn had doubtless never actually seen a spade. There was barely time for Edith to clasp her handkerchief to her mouth once more, before Gwendolyn turned back to me.

'Is it so?'

'Oh…' I thought it best, in the absence of any means of curtailing Gwendolyn's more unfeeling approaches, to place my hand on Edith's shoulder and pat it. Edith gave out a long and shuddering breath.

'He is indeed gravely ill and has not recognised anyone since his collapse, I am afraid,' I said.

'It must have been very sudden,' Dickie broke in, flushing as he had always done when speaking of anything at all. It turned my attention to him: he looked, to me, as if he had collapsed a little. He seemed, I thought, to have grown smaller inside his clothes, perhaps (though this was evidently only imagination), since abandoning—after heavy admonition by Gwendolyn—late nights away from home wagering with his wife's money at games and horseracing. A person might indeed shrink when under heavy admonition by Gwendolyn, no matter how deserved.

In days not so long ago, Dickie had been as evasive as quicksilver to any who cared for him, would slide away too fast for outstretched hand—his wife's, or that of any member of his family—to restrain him. He had had a hectic look about his eyes; he laughed too often and at too high a pitch. He began, of course, to draw attention to himself, and important heads turned first toward in curiosity, and then away in ominous judgement. Finally, Gwendolyn (and Harry) called him to a family conference and fixed him with what he ought to do. His own small legacy, and Amanda's money, were turned to better purpose, enabling his subsequent attendance at Pembroke College to do Classics. We all now awaited his ordination into the Church. The public example of Gwendolyn's success, Dickie clearly knew himself to have no defence against the humiliation of reproof and enforced improvement. The murmur of his more elevated detractors ceased, and these dour gentlefolk increasingly made clear that they were 'at home' to Gwendolyn.

'Yes, indeed it was. A great shock.' I bowed my head in agreement. Edith Courtney dipped her own head several times and dabbed at her eyes.

'Oh, my dears—' Amanda's murmur was very quiet. She wore her half-smile upon her small, plump face, as ever; it was meant to speak sympathy and comfort, and it always did so. I suddenly comprehended how great Amanda's own humiliation must have been, both at the hands of her husband and of her sister-in-law.

Gwendolyn cut across her. 'I will send my medical man.'

Dread returned to me with force. 'Doctor McGuiness,' I spoke, perhaps a little too fast, 'has always had our absolute trust, and has attended Mr Hadley for many years—'

'My man is excellent. I will send him to you,' Gwendolyn spoke

41

in answer but did not look at me, instead glancing at her daughter, where the rebellion continued. Bella had taken no more cake than before and at some point had pushed the plate further away; it seemed unlikely she would revisit it. She tilted her own face to one side, so that she might not meet her mother's eyes.

Gwendolyn pressed her lips together.

I was washed over once again with sudden irritation—like a wave of the grittiest of sand—and it made me wish to wring my hands and stamp my feet. The mime of Gwendolyn's feud with Bella played out as if my own humiliation were minor, something secondary. *As if to have my family reach out to govern me was not a humiliation. Which it is, it is.* I breathed against it. *I will imitate Amanda; see, her hands do not clutch each other.*

'That is most kind, Gwendolyn, but Doctor McGuiness may not take kindly—'

'I shall also send you Barker, for the time being. He is strong, and will serve well for heavy tasks.'

'Most practical solution, sister,' came from Harry, who placed his cup down with perhaps too much of a clatter and glanced at the watch hanging on its chain. *The business stated*, I wondered, *he is eager to go?*

It has long been understood that Harry is Gwendolyn's helpmeet in family matters. He comes to stand, at times like these, to lend his presence and his bulk, his tailoring and timbre—he who inherited the great Broom estate, where I as a child had searched out my cupboard. Harry's presence approves Gwendolyn's strictures. Yet there is more to these enactments, I have always thought. What might Mama have said? *He brings a Broomness to every case.* I felt over the tea things now a rise of mild hysteria, which may or may not have been laughter. I took another breath against it.

'It might be so, and my thanks.' My gabbling, I knew, was fed by simple anger borne on a less than simple panic. *She means to take my very house from me! She means to fill it with her myrmidons and spies! She means—*

Slowing and inhaling (*count to three*), I made myself understood. 'And yet we are fending for ourselves quite well.' I could feel my eyes grow round—and I gripped my hands together to steady myself. My hands were damp.

Surely, this is revolution!

Chapter Six

Glancing at Amanda, that model of grace and calm, I bade my-self loosen my hands from their white-knuckled grip on each other.

Gwendolyn's chin rose fractionally. I imagined the temperature close about her fell by degrees. Harry leaned upon the chair's back with one hand and placed the other upon his hip. Here for him was a situation bordering on the disturbing—Harry's acquiescence in Gwendolyn's control of family matters was predicated on an absence of disturbance. He would hold the domestic tiller, provided he need not actually steer; we all well understood it. His energies, in the main, would be spent on mastering his own vessel of business.

There was a stir as they all adjusted and turned, the better to see what I did next. Even Bella's eyes widened a very little, perhaps in surprise that there existed now a battle with her mother that was not her own. Having quelled the urge to titter, I felt myself, curi-ously, rising to meet them, in a manner of speaking, with my smile clenched. *Sometimes, one is most charming when most pressed.* I arranged my hands—one hand atop the other in my lap, rather as Gwendolyn herself was wont to do at points in a difficult conversation. *Ladies are well trained for this.*

'And, of course, Mr Hadley's Albert would very much object. Besides…' I smiled around at my unblinking family. 'With George abed, Albert has little else to do.'

There was a silence. Into this came sounds from the front door: a knocking, a murmuring, the door closing, and someone—perhaps Mrs Staynes or Cissy—stepping back along the hall.

My smile slid into a grimace so that my entire face was stiff with it. I was unable for the moment to tell fright from thrill. To allow

Gwendolyn's infiltration of this household was not to be countenanced (*Not now! Not now! Not…ever!*); neither was the possibility of outraging Doctor McGuiness by doubting his word. I had heard of an instance once, involving another family and another medical man, which had resulted in unseemly offence and public embarrassment. Undoubtedly, I knew, this would be the case here also, followed, quite possibly, by Doctor McGuiness's flouncing out, leaving Gwendolyn's choice in supreme command of the sickroom.

She must not win in this, yet her absolute defeat must be avoided. My thoughts struggled now, almost feverish. Lord knew what Gwendolyn's reaction might be were she to be utterly routed; yet I knew well enough how I might suffer were she absolutely to win. Either eventuality must be avoided. *Else life would be made unendurable.*

I blinked a little over memories of Gwendolyn crossed. It had never been advisable to leave her, even as a girl, in humiliation; something must always be found in amelioration. Once, she had taken to her chamber for days, had accepted only soup on trays, while Mama and Harry whispered downstairs in order to seek to define exactly what had caused her righteous and long-lived indignation; else, of course, a convincing apology could not be made.

'Though I am certain, now I think on it, that your medical man's opinion might be most valuable.'

I leaned forward a little, in the guise of Gwendolyn's younger sister seeking help. Girlish, I tipped my head to the side. 'It would be most kind if you would approach both men for me, for I should be so wary of giving offence.' My smile (I had forced a softening here) remained to help bear the message. 'You know how professional gentlemen do protect their empires.'

'Oh yes, my poor Adelaide. Such a timid thing,' Edith said. 'And these such eminent gentlemen.' I smiled so sweetly on my sister-in-law as to startle the older woman into a blush.

All eyes turned now to Gwendolyn, who was still a moment and then adjusted a sleeve. She arranged her hands in her lap. *She understands I leave the task of confrontation to her, if she must have it so. She knows she cannot have her way without confrontation, which may become a public spectacle.* The clock chimed the hour and somewhere downstairs a door closed.

Gwendolyn lifted her head, her cheeks pink with the perturbation evidently at work in her mind. She looked surprisingly like Dickie when most conscious of himself.

Gwendolyn turned toward where Harry stood behind her, though this only fractionally, as dictated by dignity, and was thus able only to address the air around his elbow. 'Perhaps you, Harry, would be our emissary.'

'Do you intend I should approach the two doctors?'

'Yes, indeed, Harry. Perhaps it might best be done man to man.'

He shifted a little where he stood. By now, all eyes had swung to him. 'As you wish,' he said, with a lack of emphasis that indicated his displeasure at being asked to steer Gwendolyn's ship of morals. He drew out his watch again.

'Oh, thank you both very much,' I said. 'I do not know how I could have managed it.'

My relief gave wings to my performance. There was much I could do, after all, to settle Doctor McGuiness's feathers now that the offence was not to be laid at my door. While it is true that I have never been fond of him, I could, I thought, offer sympathy in this and be absolutely sincere.

Later, as I farewelled my family and poor Mrs Courtney, I glanced at the dish in the hallway. Mrs Charles had left another calling card.

In my morning room after breakfast, I sat with the journals that were still delivered regularly. Daily, Mr Hadley ploughed through *The*

London Times, and later all the various weeklies and monthlies—*The Economist*, *The Illustrated London News*, *Lloyd's Weekly*, and *The Cornhill Magazine* (with whose opinions he disagreed more often than not). For his light relief, the *Archaeological Journal* arrived quarterly. I would have them continued, at least until a time when I might decide otherwise. I would see how they pleased me, though it must be said I looked sidelong and with some suspicion at the *Archaeological Journal*. I smoothed a page of *The Economist*. Indeed, I would read them. What a pile there was! I had never in the past read these journals much—save those parts Mr Hadley indicated I should peruse. Most often, he would read passages to me. For myself, I was permitted the fashion plates of *The Follet* and *The Englishwoman's Domestic Magazine*, which came monthly and took up very little of my time when it did. I was reminded by it far too much of Mrs Ellis. Aside from its fashion plates, *The Englishwoman's Domestic Magazine* might well be discontinued. I would think on it.

Perhaps I might ask my dear Amanda's view on *The Lady's Newspaper and Pictorial Times*, which I had seen on her coffee table once.

Else, without the news of what the world did described and discussed in these sundry periodicals, our planet's achievements and crises would surely recede into a distant wordless murmur while I sat on here in cell-like exile, while the empty days repeated themselves without end.

In any case, there was a certain encouragement in knowing the world carried on with such energy beyond my quiet door. I might find some way of going to meet it; it might sometimes come to me.

It came to me that once, years ago, I had had a friend.

She was Susan, Mrs Ford, whose husband was just then seeking entrée into Mr Hadley's business circles. George twice shook me by the arms as we entered our drawing room after an evening out, because my friend was not graceful, had laughed out loud, had made a spectacle of herself and implicated me, his wife, in this.

Then Mr and Mrs Ford were gone to Edinburgh where there were relatives, it was said, willing to ease their entry into the right circles. The episode of Susan Ford was over, slipped with her husband from Mr Hadley's entourage.

I stretched my arms as wide as the sleeves would permit to open the pages, flicked and struggled with the folding and turning. It was time to take my turn with Mr Hadley and so I read to him for hours of empire and derring-do, of mystery and the desperate endeavours of the criminal classes. There were many histories that were shocking, and then (I discovered) pages and pages where there was nothing of interest at all.

I glanced up and saw that the cloth under his chin needed changing. I replaced it with a dry cloth waiting by the bed, thinking, *There is both more and less to your world, George, than you told me.* And considered also that his reading of passages aloud had left, perhaps, one small memory behind of intimacy between man and wife.

Having read to the end of matters of interest, I took some trouble to fold the journals, and caught through the window a man and a woman, both dressed in their shabby best a little like frayed parcels, engaged in conversation. The woman shook her head several times and he leaned in toward her, glanced around, leaned in again. The woman shook her head once more, most firmly, and the two parted.

After luncheon, I sat at the window in my own room. *There is such a busyness about things back here.* The laneway at the rear of all the large houses was crowded with lurching carts, their ponies bowed down and hauling, their ragged tails limp. I watched a delivery of firewood, and a woman with one hand on her hip, swinging it just a little as she laughed with the man in his kerchief (evidently new, from its brightness) and his old hat, no longer quite black, and his shirt rolled back from thick arms with hair like fur.

I flinched. My memory suddenly filled with the flesh of thick, unfriendly hands beneath the sheets and the heavy, heavy, whiskied, painful, too-large heaving, breaking into my childish body in this, my bed (*without notice, never with any notice*) until I fell pregnant at seventeen and was torn apart, this time by the baby, on this bed, here, to not quite die as my mother had died along with that last, too small, too weak Broom. Knowing, knowing even as I screamed at the overwhelming, ripping outrage that was this childbirth that my mother had, too, been outraged and had screamed unto her very death.

On Sunday, Mr Gordon, Mr Hadley's solicitor, followed up his note of the previous day and came to accompany me to church for, he assured me, he understood entirely how difficult it would have been for me to attend alone. Sobriety and I (for I was not, of course, alone) stood a moment while he bent his long, thin frame to close the door behind us, and I felt on my face a moist and smoky breeze, smelling of horses. My breath condensed in the air.

Chapter Seven

The boy and his father, the one big and white-haired and the other small and tousle-headed, were somehow exactly alike in frock coat and waistcoat: supping together, their spoons rising and falling, rising and falling as one. Their eyes were fixed upon me, who swivelled around them. Swinging around them, but, I realised, also moving away, and now I stood on a small patch of ground while water rose and fell all around me impossibly deep with waves of increasing height. Such dark, dark water.

While they, those two, sat at their distance in the green light, staring, sat at their table with their spoons rising and falling.

Then there was a tickling at my cheek and a heavy, thick and sweet scent as of perfume and powder; and I was a little afraid, for here was that woman, that bejewelled, befurred woman by Mr Rossetti climbing out of her painting and down from Mr Hadley's wall and chuckling low into my ear with the fur tickling and cloying warm. I turned away, perplexed as to how I might run, seeing as my small island would lurch so beneath my feet. Then I realised there was a sound of clanking, and buckets, and decided this sound had been present for some time, however long that might be in a dream. It was indeed a sound of buckets—for Sobriety was mopping, which was odd, for Sobriety never mops—come from where that Rossetti woman had been but was apparently no more, even while I could still feel the fur insinuating sensuality upon my cheek.

Sobriety mopped and cleaned, too busy to look up, or perhaps unwilling to meet my eyes, though I felt her attention and trusted it. Sobriety squeezed out water into her bucket until the water on the floor was all but gone. She propped the mop in the bucket and stepped in her most able, certain way to those two, Mr Hadley and Toby, their spoons poised now while they looked upon her—themselves now uncertain and their eyes wide. Sobriety pulled from her pocket such enormous pearls as I had never seen and cast them at father and son (Does she say they are swine?) so that the pearls bounced all about the table and some fell into the bowls.

And then, while they were occupied in grasping at the pearls and shoving handfuls into their pockets, from under the table Sobriety pulled the large pieces of a box, which she constructed upon the floor and filled with the man and the boy, whom she folded, as unprotesting as a ventriloquist's dolls. Sobriety packed them right away and stood to her small and tidy height, brushed her hands together and said, 'There. I have put them back.'

It had been a disturbed night with little sleep, and had left behind something like befuddlement, yet I was coming to a conclusion. And then another: that I was very much afraid of the first. The skin across my forehead felt both puckered and stretched with worry. Yet there was no way around it, for Mr Gordon the solicitor had come in to morning tea after the service yesterday and given his warning.

'Madam, while Mr Hadley's illness is of course distressing and a great strain upon the household, we can at least be grateful that it does give you time to make preparations for a changed life.'

I looked at him. 'A change. Yes, of course, things will be very changed once he is gone.'

Mr Gordon had leaned over his cup and saucer so as not to scatter a crumb. He had nipped at his slice of fruitcake. His mouth pursed and relaxed in quick succession like a large mouse (*a long, large mouse*, I concluded, despite myself) before he swallowed. I wished that he would clear his throat, unseemly though that would be, and then I realised I had always wished that when he spoke. It was something in his voice.

'It is not so much his absence I speak of, Mrs Hadley, as his Will.'

Mr Gordon put his slice of cake down on its fragile plate and brushed his fingers together. With great deliberation (and apparently he needed me to know how great was his deliberation) he looked into my face. I was suddenly aware (grasping about in my mind, now in uncomfortable prescience, for somewhere else to settle than on the matter of Mr Hadley's Will) of Mr Gordon's stooping height even when seated, of his long, pale fingers, and how he used his black-coated thinness slowly in emphasis of words delivered carefully like parcels. Mr Gordon, unsmiling and crouching, without adornment and fanning his fingers, gazed at me with a look of deep pity at unavoidable Fate. It was as if he had brought this expression in his pocket and put it on especially. A run of cold fear coursed through me, as well as—and this startled me a little—a flash of anger. I did not think my face had changed, fortunately, and he did not seem to have noticed any lapse from a serene (and sad) composure. He licked his lips minutely.

Mr Gordon laid his metaphorical parcels before me and I thought, idiotically: *What empty things they are.*

'It is my melancholy duty to advise you, dear madam, that Mr Hadley's passing will leave you with a small, very small, annuity only.' The lawyer pursed his lips and drew his eyebrows together to indicate pity. 'In my view, this will surely not be enough for the upkeep of the house as it is, with its full complement of servants, even though it is assumed in the Will that the house will be your domicile.'

And who should go? My thoughts whispered in panic. *And would I be the one to tell them? Should we close up rooms? What shall I wear?*

Mr Gordon tipped his head mournfully to one side. While I had no right to sell it, he continued, the house was to be maintained (*but how?*) until my son became of an age to be its owner.

Bypassing me entirely, and resting with Mr Gordon as steward until Toby's majority, would be the country seat, as Mr Hadley had been pleased to call it, the edifice he knew would assure his future, for he had had great plans to make it so. It would labour, this imposing house, very hard toward this end. It was a vessel filled at intervals with parties of minor aristocrats who owed him favours, whose creaking, condescending wives I had often entertained for stiff-backed hours, days and weeks with piquet and parched conversation. The wives and their husbands sailed away at night to the vast and well-appointed rooms Mr Hadley had had carved and draped for them at enormous expense in the hope that this house and its interminable parties would lead to Mr Hadley's reward in that larger, more powerful House.

There had been a time, once, when Sobriety and I were there at the great house, that country seat, a day at least before Mr Hadley and the dragging armada of his guests were due. There was a rushing of servants about the place, and I had given what instructions I could think of—although these were few, for cook and housekeeper knew much more than I what was needed. I was eminently and evidently unnecessary to the running of that hubbub.

Sobriety and I decided upon a walk, despite the dark clouds sagging very low, and we set off in bonnets and shawls, arm in arm. It was a moment I often recalled thereafter. There were we two young women of an age, utterly alone together in an empty terrain—I cannot recall our having been so before—before being plucked apart again when I must play the part of wife to my father's contemporary and all of my husband's contemporary acquaintances, stately and cold, champing and fusty.

But first, there was Sobriety and the bright cold air.

And then the rest of that time alone became momentous, memorable forever. We had perhaps gone four miles, had reached a small rise where trees were few and grassy hills rolled gently to the house, when the wind began a swooping, screaming assault upon us. The very colours of the day changed, darkened, smudged. The little wild flowers shivered and turned grey in the glowering light. The clouds burst free with an angry, sharp rain. We cried out, both in alarm and in exhilaration, as the elements flung at our faces and bodies. I saw her face, as she saw mine, each alive with the wild energies of life itself. We clutched each other beneath that muscular sky, and struggled, gripping our streaming shawls and pressing forward against our slapping, soaked skirts, all the way back to the house.

I glanced at my sleeve as I lowered my cup to its saucer. *A loose thread. I will tell Sobriety when Mr Gordon is gone.* I was, of course, distracting myself from the matter at hand. I looked up at the lawyer, then away.

'Master Toby's schooling and so on, both before and after Mr Hadley's passing,' Mr Gordon whispered on, 'will be provided for, of course, through my own disbursement of the Hadley finances.'

Master Toby, treated as if he had no link to me; as he had been treated when I had known it to be my place to defer to his nurse, who took the new baby off to the nursery, and on occasion thereafter presented him clean and wrapped, his eyes already dispassionate. Ripped by his birth though I was, no one considered I might have need of, indeed deserve, the love of my child. As it was, he grew further from me as I mended, until it seemed we were never to have more than a formal relationship. Certainly, there was no passion there for me, his mother, though I gazed deep in the search for trust, or love, for some pleasure at seeing me. And yet, there had been times when I had pleaded for him, at first, and been rebuffed, for the nurse knew what she did and I did not. Thereafter, I gazed upon my son and heard him as if muffled by distance. It was as if I were trapped in a glass box, my nose pressed to the surface, as I watched my son grow and had no hand in it.

How much, I wondered in the depths of my bruised heart, would he have been disturbed had it been me, and not his father, who lay in bed dying? I closed my eyes for a moment over humiliation and a great irritation, recognising loss—oh, that ever-lurking pain— And still that voice continued relentless. *That uncanny voice, like paper.*

I am unfair. Poor man.

His voice rustles like the paper that fills his life.

I had sat for the most part in silence, utterly unable to look at my husband's legal man. My mind echoed with something like a wind, howling and empty of anything that could comfort or distract, even while I felt as if I were pattering here and there and everywhere in search of comfort and distraction. For I was, henceforth, to be a guest in my own house, this very house. The poor relation conscious of charity as she keeps to her shadowed corner, creeps upstairs, mumbles her food in silence. In this house on sufferance. *I have lost my place*, I thought, and then absurdly, *Like a bookmark*, and again, *Fool! A bookmark? What am I thinking!* My face was hot with the consciousness of being without a place. *Like a very poor person.*

Mr Gordon sipped at his tea, the tip of his nose dipping with the movement of his mouth.

Mouse, I thought.

'After his passing,' he went on, 'there will be sufficient for you to live in modest circumstances, and your son naturally will take responsibility for your welfare when he reaches his majority. It would be advisable that you take, especially...'—His tongue flicked at his lips—'...certain measures concerning the staff. We must remember that additional tax attends male domestics, for example.'

He paused and I bowed my head to indicate that I heeded him, though I was of a sudden conscious of Albert and Mr Brent about the house, unaware of this talk about them. 'And during this period of Mr Hadley's illness—' He gave his rodent's smile. 'That is to say, before the major changes to general circumstances…' He seemed to lean toward me. 'I shall act in his stead, so that you need only apply to me for funds, the payment of accounts, and so on.' His eyes were especially attentive, and I knew by the set of his smile that he meant himself to look kindly, wise, with the emphasis of a dozen crinkles and lines.

These men do set their smiles for the ladies, before they pass onto things of greater moment. I was well schooled to show no expression, and hoped I showed none.

Mr Gordon paused, perhaps for my reaction, though I hardly noticed the silence hovering. I had raised my own cup to my mouth as if I were indeed still attending closely to him, but now there was set up in my mind such a clamouring for him to be gone and take his witnessing presence with him that I had almost believed he must hear the shouting.

'Please feel free to apply to me for anything you may need beyond the usual expenses. You will find me very understanding in this difficult time.'

Yes, yes, yes. Go. Leave me!

Lowering my cup, I placed one gloved hand over the other. *Begone.* 'Thank you very much for your kindness, Mr Gordon. I will consider all this, naturally, and what our needs are. Thank you—' And I rose so that he must rise too, gave him my hand, and rang for Cissy to see Mr Gordon to the door.

Go, go, go!

Chapter Eight

And so to Monday after the longest night of sleeplessness and dreams like hallucinations, and a waking barely less dreamlike. I spent, oh, hours through the day wandering, sometimes, but mainly sitting I hardly knew where. I was caught between fantasies of a rescue bringing a magical showering of wealth, and an intervening sharp awareness of reality, like the periodic slashings of a knife; the reality of a life sunk into muted, stagnant, genteel poverty.

I thought: *I have lost my place.* I was tired. *I am always losing my place.* My gaze sometimes settled into focus on some decorative piece—a vase, a painting, a polished side table—and I was vaguely puzzled to recognise the thing yet understand it to be foreign, or at least myself to be foreign to it. *In any case, in any case,* I thought and believed absolutely and dismally, *this has never been my place. I have no place. I have had no place.* A long beam of evening light reached across the room, touching the Turkey carpet with a patch of gold.

Mrs Staynes rustled through to light a lamp, not knowing how long I would spend unmoving on the settee in the drawing room and no doubt thinking (I knew this somehow, despite my own distraction) she would most likely not be required to light a fire. The circumstance was most unusual, however, and she could not be certain. *This will vex her,* I knew, seeing without seeing the eloquence of the older woman's raised chin and the cross jounce of her skirt as she left the room. Behind her, the door clicked to sharply.

With evening the veiled light from the window faded to a washed violet. Little Cissy drew the curtains together with a clatter and turned up the gas at the wall-lamp, with a hesitation and a glance to where I sat. After all, the use of the lamp in this room, at this time of the day, was not customary.

Cissy left, and I sank with the eventual settling of all the flying nothings of my mind. Within a small clearing space in the fog, a faint voice said, *Money. I must get money.* Then suddenly there was a memory of running in a keen wind sprayed with brine when I was a child at the seaside, shrieking like the gulls with Ida beside me. For that wild excitement was back with me—for a moment, all bonds loosened—until I remembered both the heavy vulgarity of Mammon and that I had in any case no idea how to get it... *Money!*

I could scarcely tell whether my emotions were of excitement or simple terror.

I went down to dinner with chilled feet, shivering a little from having sat so long in the cold. I had headache, and my forehead was actually sore—*extraordinary*, I had felt it with my fingers—from the anxious stretch and pull of skin across it.

Cissy was able, at last, to run back up the stairs to turn down the lamp. I heard her thumping all the way up and then down.

Only much later, long after dinner, when I put down the sewing— *Bless this H . . .* —that I had barely touched with my needle, and rose to climb the stairs to my bed, with Sobriety holding the lamp and our two shadows looming head by head before us, did I remember Mr Hadley, limp and dribbling alone in his room. *Somebody must have sat with him all of this time.* The thought twisted with a pang. Cissy perhaps had done so, poor child, or Albert—if Cook had expelled him from the kitchen, where he mainly spent his newly near-masterless time in sprawling at the table. I had not, for an entire day, held Mr Hadley up and fed him spoons of tasteless mash, nor heaved with Albert or one of the others while Cissy (*poor Cissy*) pulled away his ghastly messes.

Sobriety was talking to me, fingers working in quick twistings at my back, freeing the pearl buttons. *Pearls, oh yes.* I was for a moment bewildered by my dream of the night before, apparently asserting itself here. I blinked the notion away as a mere distraction from my most worrying and very real fiscal predicament. I fingered the adjective in my mind. *Fiscal.* I glanced up at the long mirror and in the dimness lit to the side by the lamp was Sobriety's face behind me, eyes down, a paleness floating somehow, a small, oval, floating sadness even as her unfaltering fingers were busy with unbuttoning. I thought in my confusion: *Does she know? How would she know?* Confusion shook all logic. Was my tragedy, the deep humiliation of my tragedy, laid bare like this before I really knew it myself? I stared at Sobriety's face; my own reflected figure wavered in the mirror like a stranger, inquisitive and out of place.

Sobriety said again, 'I do need some time tomorrow. I am sure I shall not be long, I…' Sobriety's face was still intent on buttons. Such a pale face; so enclosed. Such a small person, such a small face. My thoughts were drawn away from myself. *She hesitates. Whence comes this uncertainty? Should I sense the answer?* Fingers had reached the end of the line of buttons; pushed the bodice forward so that I must hunch up my shoulders to aid the fall of the sleeves; fetched the bodice to lay it on the end of the bed; came back to begin at the laces, tugging loose, pulling. I stared at Sobriety's face and it occurred to me: *We have not spoken in so long.*

'What is it, Sobriety?'

'Nothing, Ma'am. Nothing to concern yourself with. But it is something that needs doing tomorrow.' As if I had raised an argument. 'It cannot wait.'

Sobriety came to the front to loosen laces, head bent so that I stared at the top of her head, where the dark hair was drawn back, divided at the ruler-sharp parting.

'Certainly, Sobriety. Of course,' and then I repeated myself, awkward as 'of course' was spoken over the top of Sobriety's whispered 'thank you,' and my skirt unbuttoned and pulled rustling over my head; and the whole of the undressing and the night-dressing, with the long slow passes of the brush through my hair and Sobriety's folding as I pulled back the sheets and stepped into my bed, all of this done in silence and Sobriety's face still inward, shut up and turned away.

Sobriety left my door ajar so that noise from Mr Hadley's room would be heard during the night; though Albert lay on the divan set up there nightly and only Albert's snoring could be heard. It was a nightly revelation of himself of which nobody spoke. I lay, eyes wide in the dark, hearing him begin. Sobriety was above—a suggestion of footsteps, preparations for sleep, the quiet closing of her door.

My thoughts were much too bright for sleep, bright and ringing with worry. I sent these thoughts to Mr Hadley's room, where he lay in the dark, an insensible mass. *So this is your will for me, is it? Is it? This Will is your declaration?*

When I awoke next morning, slowly, I was aware only of the aching bloatedness of my woman's monthly time. The dull heaviness swinging around again: loaded monthly female secret, messy, odorous; utterly pointless since the ripping catastrophe of Toby's birth.

I rose, fixed into place with tapes an oblong of many-times folded cotton, before Sobriety came through to shake out petticoats for dressing. But as my maid tugged at corset laces and buttoned the close-fitting bodice, I did also think that later I might, perhaps, take myself back to my bed.

I am a pudding, I thought, *a sickly pudding*, and looked around at a room tedious with familiarity. Tossed bedclothes, tilted tall mirror, two fading and sagging armchairs from Mama's sitting room, the flowered jug and basin upon the washstand, all flat, all drained of colour in the light of a dull morning.

Sobriety picked up the nightdress—she would take it to soak away the small patch of blood before it was given to the washerwoman—and said, 'There won't be anything else before I go out?'

Hands against the compressed suet of my waist, I said, 'Oh. No, no. I shall see you later.'

This early, the flow is always heaviest. Without Sobriety to take charge with rinsing water and bucket, I took a small bundle wrapped against recognition in cleaner cloth, to burn at the back of Cook's stove—with Cook herself turned away, stropping knives at the table. Albert was very jocular with someone outside the kitchen door. There was an insolence in his voice, it seemed to me, more evident now that this house was on its way to losing its head—that head lolling up there, insensible on the pillow.

I took myself to the sickroom and waited for Cissy to bring Mr Hadley's milk-softened eggs to me for his morning feeding, conscious of a certain atonement for yesterday's laxity and leaving the door ajar so that—*I am such a child!*—Mrs Staynes might notice that I did my duty. I did this with movements slow as porridge and, for a fleeting moment, a ghastly faintness and skin cold with perspiration. I spooned egg into his mouth, wiped away what escaped almost immediately from between his chapped lips, and thought again that even this was too solid for his capacity to swallow.

At the end of my efforts—even though the bowl was still half full—I sat up and for a moment closed my eyes. Less compressed, I felt my body relax a little. My face was cool now, rather than clammy. When Cissy came for the bowl, cloth, and spoon, I asked her to fetch the new edition of *The Cornhill Magazine* where it lay open at Mrs Oliphant's article, somewhere—in the morning room, most likely.

Though I drew my shawl around me, I did not ask for a fire. I supposed this to be wasteful—time to be mindful of this. Lord!—and Mr Hadley seemed warm enough beneath his heaped blankets, propped in his bedjacket with another of my shawls about his shoulders and a shine of spittle soaking into a cloth under his chin.

Faintly from down in the street outside came occasionally the smart clip of horses drawing carts or carriages; from elsewhere in the house, Mrs Staynes's voice gave some order; once, Cissy's steps thumped unevenly on carpeted stairs, travelling upwards, I knew, with cloth and a tin of polish to rub at banisters on a slow step-by-step trip downward. Mr Hadley's breath strained and whistled. A page scraped as I turned it. I had not read a word.

There was another voice, eventually, and I thought, *Sobriety*. I heard the kitchen door close behind my maid and the suggestion of a step upon the stairs.

My husband's head had tipped to one side as if in sleep—I wondered: *what difference can there be for him, between sleeping and waking?*—and his breathing drew infinitely closer to a snore. I went to the bedroom door, already ajar, and put my head through.

Sobriety stood in mute stillness, while muffled sound floated from elsewhere in the house or from the street. A plate of cold cuts and a hunk of bread on a plate sat on a stair where she had, evidently, just placed it. She herself, one hand gripped at the banister, was bowed over with her back to me and her hand pressed at her waist, to the front.

I rustled from the sickroom across the landing, and down the two steps to Sobriety. I grasped her arm so that she might lean on me and picked up the plate with my other hand.

'Sobriety, are you ill?'

'Yes,' Sobriety paused. 'A little.' Her face was pale, transparent as water, and damp; her eyes were very dark and nearly closed.

Slowly we climbed the stairs, stopping twice to huff in amusement when I, both hands occupied, stepped on the hem I could not hold out of the way. We climbed from carpet to naked timber until we reached Sobriety's chamber door and entered, crowding the tiny, low-ceilinged room with ourselves and the billow of our skirts.

Upon the little bed was the old quilt I had given her years before. I had never visited the room, of course, though I sometimes heard her move about at night or in the mornings. It gave a strange feeling—oddly as though my heart were short of breath—to know that this old familiar had lain here all this time. A hook had been screwed into the back of the door, from which hung Sobriety's few dresses—once again, my own that had travelled up these few steep stairs to live again. At the foot of the bed there was a chest from the Jacobin uncle, very well-made, perhaps by himself—I recalled when it had come, while I had never seen it here in its place. Upon it stood the japanned box as the room's only form of decoration, except for the tract in its plain frame on the wall facing the door that read, in Sobriety's own careful hand:

When from the chambers of the east
His morning race begins,
He never tires, nor stops to rest,
But round the world he shines,

So, like the sun, would I fulfil
The duties of this day,
Begin my work betimes, and still
March on my heavenly day.

'I will help you to bed,' I said as if it were an announcement, and, 'I will help you from your clothes.' Although Sobriety began with, 'No...', I—as if I knew what I was about—placed the plate on the seat of the small chair by the small bed, squinted at the buttons at my maid's back and began the unaccustomed labour of twisting them free. *Through here?* I was not certain, altogether. *No. Yes. Ah.*

Sobriety leaned against the wall until I had finished, slipped out of the dress, waited, pulling slowly at the hooks at the front of her stays while I fussed at draping the dress across the back of the chair (triumphant at my own competence). The petticoat had been patched a little since it had lain in my own chest, yet was of excellent cotton and wearing reasonably well. I untied the tape to release the hoops of the crinoline cage—and then I faltered to a stop.

There was blood, a clarion of blood spreading scarlet through to Sobriety's under-petticoat, an announcement—a warning—of the blood-sodden drawers beneath. A drop fell to the timber floor even as I stood there. A small moan came from Sobriety who, from the set of her shoulders, knew why I had arrested my fumblings but had not turned to see.

'I can finish, madam, thank you so much.' Now she did turn herself a little, made to hold the bloodied patch away from my sight, said, 'I know where my things are, and can find them more easily than you,' addressing somehow the air between the bedroom door and my right shoulder.

I responded to a patch of wall visible beyond the coiled roll of her hair. 'Of course. I shall fetch you tea.'

'Tea?' Sobriety said, voice wavering into a whisper, trembling finger to the wet corner of her eye.

'Yes,' I said, and pressed past my maid (felt her, in that tiny crowded room, so warm and yet faintly trembling) and through the door.

From Mr Hadley's room, I rang for Cissy, and straightened my husband from his slide in my absence to a sidelong heap. Cissy came and I asked for tea, and a sweet biscuit, and went many times from bed to window, window to bed—*Lord, Lord, Lord,* my thoughts chanted—in an agitation thickened by the ache of menses while I waited. I was curt with the child who pouted, cross from the trip to and from the kitchen just as she and Mrs Staynes had begun folding laundry.

Once Cissy was gone back downstairs, I carried the cup rattling on its saucer to Sobriety, now in her chemise under the bedclothes, her face hot and damp. I placed the saucer and cup in the small space beside the plate of food, where it seemed it would stay without falling. We watched it for a moment.

'Drink the tea and eat some food, and sleep,' I said.

Sobriety smiled a little.

I raised my eyebrows and compressed my lips. A little in imitation of Mrs Staynes. 'Don't you laugh at me.' Sobriety gave a weak huff of laughter.

I looked around the room. The bundle of bloodied underclothes was rolled tightly under the bed and I pulled the bundle out while Sobriety's gaze slid away. Holding it to one side, hiding it for the moment behind the bell of my skirt, I said, 'Later, this evening, if you are feeling better, I think we could sit together and I shall read to you.'

Sobriety turned toward me.

'Perhaps the latest piece from Mrs Oliphant.'

Looking at her, I thought: *We will sit in the yellow circle of lamplight, I with Mrs Oliphant in hand, you with needle and lace.*

It had always been in this way, in reading to each other and sewing or undertaking some small task, that we had passed our evenings when Mr Hadley was gone on business.

Sleepily, Sobriety smiled again. I smiled too, for it was a joyous thing, while unaccustomed, to be so evidently trusted.

I took the bundle to the kitchen and burned it while the kitchen was empty, watched as the avid flames embraced it, with Cook below in the coal cellar, with Mrs Staynes and Cissy in the scullery, with the back of Albert's head in the doorway where he sat in half-hearted sunlight, jerking vigorously as he rubbed polish onto his boots.

Part Two:

In which Adelaide and Sobriety, newly become tourists in London, are surprised at what they find

Chapter Nine

Awaiting the seasonal change

By A. Hadley

We have moved beyond the season of mists and into that of fogs and driving rains, an angry season, which leaves us wrapped all the day in shawls, blowing on fingers. The weather vents itself beyond our windows and we remember, and yearn for, a gentler time of softer showers and zephyrs stroking the cheek like the warm breath of babies…

I rolled the blotter over the paper and read again what I had written. *And will it do?* I thought. Was this as young, as foolish as my former childish works on the Lord of Rothesay? My cheeks grew warm. It was carefully done, yes, and ladylike; it would not cause discord. I felt I crept around the edges of the community of writers, very quiet lest I be noticed. *Nay; very quiet lest it be noticed that I have nothing to say.*

What else might I say?

Well. Perhaps I say something, but nothing very well. I smiled sadly at myself and my pretensions.

Picking up my pen wiper and rubbing slowly at the nib, as in meditation, I thought on my use of the name *A. Hadley*. It was both to dash at the thing—actually writing in public—and away from it, perhaps. It was bold in one way, for all those acquainted with me would certainly know this was I. And yet I clung to ambiguity too, just a little. It was done, perhaps, to appear a private person, since I did not state my given name. *As if I might run and hide, at a pinch, I* thought, while I knew this would not be possible. And yet I fancied it, this notion that I stood, in naming myself thus, a little aside, a little in the shadows.

I placed the pen, its wiper, the blotter, and my few pages of writing back in the writing box and closed the lid. At the very least, the taking up occasionally of a little writing task concentrated the mind and was, in its way, soothing. Yet only if it was a privately done thing. What a quandary was this desire to set my opinions in public and yet to stand behind the curtains, at one and the same time.

When my duty in the sick-room was done, I would take my writing box back to my morning room, and Cissy would replace the table by the window.

Mr Hadley's breathing had a faint whistle to it today.

Pressing down between my fingers, wriggling and stretching them, I held my hand out for my inspection. *Yes.* Kidskin gloves, fawn, scallop-edged; a simple three-button length. A favourite pair. And I had on my fine wool paletot, sleek over my gown, my newest bonnet, neat and smart off the face, a veil swept back for now and stirring in the air. I stood at the top of the steps at the front door for Sobriety's return with the umbrella. Mr Brent waited below with the landau, both sections of its roof folded back today; the horses mouthed their bits, shifted with a leathery creaking and snorted in gusts.

I gripped an envelope addressed to Mr Thackeray of *The Cornhill Magazine*, which held the small piece of writing, those elegant few lines about the weather (*it affects us all—who is not interested in it?* I thought, while still my cheek warmed at the very subject) penned just yesterday. I had made a fair copy of it that morning. We would post it while about our business in the city.

Then there was Sobriety, saying, 'My apologies, ma'am, it was Cissy on the stairs with the polish and we would keep moving the same way, like a dance, before I could get past her…' I laughed and we picked up our skirts to *bob-bob* down the steps to where Mr Brent had the carriage door open for us.

We sat, arranged the great whispering piles of our skirts, careful of the metal hoops beneath, which, though between two sets of petticoats each (flounced, in my case), might pinch perhaps or bend a little out of shape with uncareful sitting. I had on my gently figured green, whose colour was reflected in the tartan-style Sobriety was wearing—so well-chosen of her. Hers was my last year's street-wearing best, taken in and taken up invisibly through her inimitable needlework, and made the plainer now with the removal of certain flounces (Sobriety always removes the flounces when a garment is for her own use—such a Methodist!). I myself had worn it only once or twice, and so Sobriety had not sold it on but kept and made it her own, bent closely over the garment for many hours.

We are well-paired.

We brought our veils over our faces, tucked our gloved hands into the sleeves of our paletots.

Mr Brent said, 'Hup!'

The carriage stirred and hesitated, wheels grinding on the grit of the roadway; then it gained pace with that smoothness owed to Mr Brent's daily grease and polish. The horses' hooves *tic-tocked*, their haunches bunched and flexed like well-muscled velvet. The sky was low with cloud, but the great billows glowed white, not grey, with only a tinge of acrid yellow as the city's mark.

I cannot imagine rain today. There will be no rain. I closed my eyes a moment to feel the air move against my face.

It would be such a full day ahead of us. Earlier that morning, I had been unaccountably stirred, impatient with anticipation. Unable to play the serene. Almost, I had been glad of my hour with Mr Hadley, had sat at his bedside with the door ajar, some part of my attention on Sobriety's small thumpings and rustlings nearby as she straightened my room. I sat reading out loud to Mr Hadley—slowly, to quell this nervous buzzing—from journals and newspapers a little as he had, until so recently, read to me, though I now explored the details of these tales and opinions where once he read only what he felt I ought to know. I glanced at his vacant face. *And one reads to him because one might otherwise forget he is there.* The thought crossed my mind with its dreadful admission.

Are you there, Mr Hadley? And then, *Are you there, George?*

Social notes, colonial business of some interest to investors in the City, the theft of a tiny baby from its peaceful home in north London. *His poor mother.* Sipping at coffee, I read until Albert came with his master's shaving bowl, brush, and towel, so that I might at last search out Sobriety for bonnet and gloves and coat.

See how we go to see the world?

'How are you, Sobriety?'

'Very much better, ma'am.'

I felt we smiled like girls with a secret between ourselves, kept behind our veils, as we passed along treed roadways, occasional walled gardens to left and right, and the park receding behind us. Like foreigners, travelling from wealth and unhurried suburban quiet—the *clip-clop* made indolent with birdsong, the shiver of leaves, a wall with a trained spread of late roses—to a place of more urgent energy. The breeze began to carry the smudged smells of a hundred thousand distant lives and occupations.

Houses and places of business soon drew close to the street itself, tall and narrow and pressed together, an occasional figure indistinct in a room beyond a window. Meat hung bloody on a butcher's hooks; further on, hats stood on stands behind mullions. Somewhere behind those houses, a band of brass and wind was playing, creating discord with a man and his barrel organ a-wheezing by the side of the road.

What a clamor! All of this, rubbing together like a file against metal, I thought and was pleased with myself. *A file against metal*.

Women and children with trays called out; an old man cried 'Lucifers!' and rattled a packet. Men with canes halted to consult a paper or a watch. One checked his shoe, with the culprit mongrel, I surmised, in a doorway six steps on scratching its dull fur into a storm of hairs. There was a knot of dusty men with caps or bent toppers cracking with age, their discussion busy with elbows and arms.

The landau jolted over a pothole and the mush of rotted refuse within it. There was a smell of gas—an inkling at first and then altogether present before we passed through this part of the street— from a leakage somewhere.

'What a throng it is, Mr Brent!'

'This is the gentler part of the day, ma'am.' Mr Brent's profile spoke a moment before he turned his head back to the street.

An omnibus passed us, heading back whence we had come, and heads turned toward the landau. My cheeks heated. *Veritable impertinence*. But with a subtle turn of our own veiled faces, Sobriety and I took care not to seem to notice.

It had been an hour perhaps, or it felt so, with progress now slowed markedly and the people poorer, concentrated, and busier; even the children intent somehow on their own survival, brisk on dust-grey legs spindly as birds'.

One boy, carrying brush and woven scoop, ran into the street and among tall grinding wheels, into the mince of horses' legs and their sharp hooves. He was gone from sight for the space of a held breath and then was back to the kerb with his load of fresh manure.

I held my breath at the danger to the child—I went cold for an instant thinking how he might have been crushed. Then I had my hand to my breast as he raised to the street eyes in a face grey and hard as stone, and greasy with ill health. The realization of the boy's inevitable fate came to me: *See how he is aged, as if he had no use for youth here; that he must reach age, then old age, then death quickly, quickly, to get it done...* I wondered what the child's age would be (*Who would know without young pink chubbiness to go by?*) and imagined him of Toby's years; though Toby stood, when I had last seen him, half a head taller than this boy, with hair a soft fall of curls and no broom's head stiffened with lice. This boy's eyes passed across my own and, though he would not have seen my gaze behind the veil, I felt he both saw and hated me. Then I recognized that this was not hatred but an indifference born of distance. I thought, *This child exists so far from cologne and veils and kidskin that they do not exist, that I do not exist*, and recognized in this, after all, something of Toby. *Oh Toby.*

The street boy turned away a fraction, and I saw a small version of himself stood just behind his elbow with a much-buckled bucket, into which was emptied the scoop of manure.

The landau passed the boys by. I turned toward Sobriety to see... *To see what?* To see perhaps if Sobriety had seen, but Sobriety faced away, her veiled profile blurred and shadowed. I fancied there was a breeze-like grief breathing from my maid, from my friend, felt Sobriety had herself gone a distance, perhaps with this boy, or the smaller boy, who might have been like her own if she had not...if George were still...

Surely not. I repeated it to myself. *Surely not.* But then, I knew that if he were capable of smiting, like Jehovah with his hair a white nimbus, or taking possession like...like...there was a confusion in my mind that would not raise a picture beyond a muscled, struggling, sourly-reeking blackness, a panting...then he could indeed cast away, throw away, exile, *condemn my poor, good Sobriety…*

The danger that had faced Sobriety now rushed in all its ice-water reality into my consciousness, and I worked to slow my breathing, shallow and fast now in empathetic fear.

Mrs Lewes, she who wrote as George Eliot, though there was a sympathy for her character who had gone astray—that Hetty in *Adam Bede* (that I had read last year) who caused the death of a living child—understood nothing, *nothing*, I realised then. The woman who is left with a child out of wedlock is left also as bearer of everybody's shame. Everybody else may wash his hands of sin, while the woman is bowed double with it. *See how my Sobriety, in all her Methodist innocence and…and straitness, is threatened and made guilty, and put in danger…*

There was a loud ringing of metal upon metal. I did not see where it came from, and it left its jangling on me for many minutes.

The air was denser with the approach of the river, 'our thick Thames', as George had often called it. His attention had been much attracted to subjects such as the river and effluent, as had everyone else's since The Great Stink, during that stifling summer when Members had fled Parliament itself rather than choke on the river's rising miasma. Sobriety and I raised scented handkerchiefs to our noses. *We should all carry herb-scented pomanders, as the Elizabethans once did*, I fancied…

The breeze blew from the water—there was the river as a darkling suggestion between alleyways, though I could not be certain until the shape of some river craft slid past, like something over oil. There was no avoiding the stench. *I had forgotten this*, I thought, *and yet so far still from the docks.* Craning a little to see if Mr Bazelgette's works were evident at this point on the river, I could see nothing and in any case remembered his sewer building was not planned for, this far down. At least not yet; later, perhaps. I had not paid enough attention to Mr

Hadley's opinions to remember the details.

Perhaps there will be a change in direction of this breeze soon.

In my pocket was the list I had made after the very long talk the household had had together yesterday, and now I pulled it out.

I had known the household meeting would take some time, and had called all of the staff to my morning room. They left the door open and Mr Hadley's too, upstairs, so that we would hear if there were—this seemed most unlikely—an accident, perhaps if he suddenly slid out of bed. I asked them all to sit, with tea for everyone. The two men, creaking from time to time as they shifted, were over-large in their silence.

Cissy giggled, was heady with the excitement of the unusual. She sat at the edge of the footstool I had embroidered myself but used very little (for there were parts where frequent unstitching had weakened the fabric, demonstrating, once again, my lack of diligence in matters of embroidery). Several pastoral scenes—languid, sun-drenched farming, and one of boating—that had belonged to Mama, hung on the wall behind the girl. The thought came to me: *How foreign is a field of corn to this Manchester-bred child.*

Mrs Staynes said, 'Cissy!' The girl stilled her giggles. Instead, she kept up a theatre of sighs and gasps whispered in the background of my description of this house's forthcoming economic state of affairs upon the passing of Mr Hadley. The long discussion that followed was held mostly between me, Mrs Staynes and, occasionally, Sobriety. Cook, Cissy's aunt who nevertheless rarely reproved the child in her frequent excitations, said little and filled the delicate chair by the window with her girth and a sense of kitchen steam—*odd*, I mused, *without her apron or a ladle in those pink hands.*

'Rooms', I had noted, leaning at my small bureau over paper more usually used for letters of invitation than for lists, 'to be closed'. This would save on time spent cleaning, and expense on heating or lighting; though they may have to be reopened when Toby was at home during the term break, if it were needed, though surely this would be rare. Mrs Staynes, who stood at attention throughout the meeting like the seemly sentry that she considered herself to be, crossed her housekeeper's gloved hands in front where the keys hung on their chain. Master Toby's visits were indeed, she agreed, sufficiently infrequent.

I added that the 'Washerwoman should be dispensed with for smaller items', and Mrs Staynes nodded and said she was afraid so. There was a sagging on her face and beneath her eyes that suggested some of these changing circumstances had cost her sleep.

Cissy said 'Oh…' It was clear to all that such washing of smaller items would now fall to the littlest, youngest maid.

'Supplies of non-perishables for the house and kitchen, in the meantime, to be bought in some bulk'. It was agreed very readily, though Mrs Staynes said she would have to consider where these things might be stored. She closed her eyes a long moment. I pressed a blotter to the ink and said that Mrs Staynes should do her considering and would be free, when she was ready, to purchase what she thought best.

'Material for clothing to be bought in bulk, to cover both mourning and general needs into the future, and bedsheets and cloths' was an addition in general thought most practical, and Cissy suggested 'A machine for sewing?' I could not for the moment decide whether this was a practical or an outrageous suggestion, and placed a question mark next to it.

Then there was a pause. Our womanly faces turned first toward, reluctantly, then from the two men, Albert and Mr Brent. I wrestled with what I fancied must be their mortification. This was, it occurred to me, like the embarrassment felt by the fortunate at and for the unfortunate. The men sat awkward together, almost forgotten on the smaller settee, like two looming wanderers mistakenly in this place, teacups scraping against their saucers and incongruous in their big hands. Mr Brent sat square, stolid, his face inanimate as dumpling so that his thoughts could only be surmised, as was ever the case, even while his attention was apparently concentrated upon each of the women as she spoke. I felt a rising anxiety: *Is he angry with us? Is he merely stoical? What are his expectations?*

Albert's legs, meanwhile, were drawn up close. He was a collection of angles, and bound, clearly, not to look at any of the women at all; not, perhaps, to acknowledge any authority in this woman's room. He gazed upward by turns at cornices, curtain rod and chandelier. *He is galled, clearly, and yet this also so clearly concerns him. He knows his employment will cease with his master's demise.* I saw where he looked and felt, in contrariness perhaps, as if I gathered all these oddments to me, claimed them even as he rejected them for their womanliness. *Yes, of all the rooms of this house, it is true, this one is most mine.*

I dipped my nib into the inkwell. We women all agreed (in clumsy bursts, for it was as if the men were eavesdropping, would overhear something that might pain them) that at Mr Hadley's passing the horses and landau should be sold, if possible, and the money could be set aside for general uses; in unanimous chorus, we agreed that Mr Brent should be given most positive letters of recommendation. The chorus added how much we would miss him. And, too, with much nodding, though there was a sense still of afterthought, that Albert should receive letters of recommendation to aid in his seeking new employment upon Mr Hadley's eventual demise.

In any case, there was the tax on male servants to be considered. Mr Gordon's advice whispered and rasped in my head; and I had once heard Mr Hadley berating Albert with this information, when Albert had forgot some duty or other, that he must not only be paid but must also attract additional taxation. And so, I assumed, a first saving would be best made. The thought brought with it an exquisite twist of guilt and I was of a sudden angry with Mr Gordon. *Silly, silly. Not his fault.*

Though I wish I could blame him. Oh, silly.

There was a creak from Mr Brent as he shifted in his seat.

Is he mollified? Have we made this easier for him?

A message was dispatched to Mr Gordon, stating (in general at least) what I intended to purchase immediately. He would not, of course, deem this to be unreasonable, surely, and would, naturally— *and as he had undertaken,* I insisted to myself, *as he had stated, absolutely, would be done for me*—underwrite. I mentioned, too, household changes, and further household purchases, that I felt must be made in due course. This message was written and rewritten three times, for I could not at first achieve the correct tone. I wished not to appear imperious (I thought of Gwendolyn); I wished neither to patronise as one might the servants, nor to cringe, as it were, upon the page. And then, of course, I sat for some time wondering if I had forgotten anything that must be mentioned to him.

'How we must plan like field marshals for the least thing!' I said to Sobriety.

Mr Brent, having committed my letter to the post, was visiting relatives, a cousin and his wife who lived nearby. The horses would by now be mouthing inside their nosebags while waiting for him outside the cousin's dwelling.

Sobriety and I adjusted our attention in the vast emporium lit with windows and lamps hissing in their brackets. Wordless for a stretch of some minutes, we stood and gazed from one end of the space to the other. There were notices and displays and young men and their older supervisors; and women with baskets, fingering lengths of dress material and sturdier material for upholstery and velvet ribbons and satin ribbons and bobbins and cord. There was lace and fabric flowers and trimming frill and naked bonnets awaiting decoration; and netting for the hair, hairpins and hatpins; and buttons and hooks and frogs. We saw lengths for bed sheets and for curtains—plush and brocade as well as plain or flowered prints. Murmurings from customers and assistants, calls and traffic clatter from the street, were all muffled in here, as if bolts of that material had been wound about the head and ears. I had visited here for my marriage, the dress and trousseau, and many items for the decoration of furnishings, but since then had chosen from catalogues, or from samples carried to me by the seamstress.

It was a vaster and busier place than I recalled, in any case. There was so much movement, so much displayed, so many little scenes of transaction, that I forgot entirely what it had been decided, in my meeting with the household, to buy. Sobriety, too, swung her attention this way and that, eyes too wide for her to be of help.

At last, there came to us a young man and his supervisor, smiles fixed and hands gloved; employees of this bewildering establishment. I fetched my list once again from my pocket.

There was indeed on display a machine for sewing, and we had it placed with our parcels, the account to be sent to Mr Gordon (and every argument gathered and detailed, should it be required). *Dear God, what am I doing?* It was the purchase of this machine, perhaps, that set my fingers to trembling. *Ten pounds!* My pulse skipped.

'There will be a man come to show us how to use it,' Sobriety turned to me. 'After all.'

'That is true.'

There was a pause, while we gazed at each other. 'Lord, ma'am,'

Sobriety's breath was a plosive. 'We must never spend like that again, surely!'

'Well, Mrs Staynes might, when she buys for the house.' We each put a hand over our face, and rocked with choked laughter for some minutes, our heads turned away from the other customers.

I have not laughed in this way since Susan Ford, I thought. I put a gloved finger to my eye, and fanned my face a little with my hand, and took a breath to help the laughter subside.

The young man came back from the gathering together of our goods for wrapping and delivery, winding his way with self-conscious grace between the aisles. Sobriety gave the separate addresses for delivery of the purchases and the account—the first to the house and the second to Mr Gordon. I stared, unfocussed, at a display of laces. Thoughts of fleeting friendships had left me pensive, for the moment, I realised.

'Luncheon, I think. Where shall we go?' I said, returning to the present, and Sobriety followed in my billowing wake to the door.

'Mr Brent, it's early yet. I would like to visit Mr Bazelgette's works.' There. It was said.

I had thought of it at luncheon, fork poised over the cake much boasted of in that small, elegant establishment. *We will be much, much too early away home. There is such a bustle here; there's no sign of rain.* At home there were Mr Hadley's sagging cheeks, his fustiness, the phlegm clicking in his throat with every shallow breath. The silence there filled the spaces between the creaking of floorboards. *We should*— I searched in my mind for the means to extend this outing—*visit Mr Bazelgette's works. So many do.* I recalled that Mr Hadley himself had been garrulous on the subject, particularly when the *Illustrated London News* announced in evident relief that 'spade, shovel, and the pick' should at last take 'the place of pens, ink, and debate.' It was a momentous thing, a huge undertaking; it was change brought about by change, by a city bursting with itself.

Mr Brent and Sobriety both looked at me, Mr Brent twisted almost all of the way around in his seat as if he would say something. Though, of course, he did not.

The pause continued until Sobriety said, 'Really?'

Later, I considered that my maid had seemed pale, had been so at luncheon, with a dark smudge at each eye as of weariness and its accompanying despondency. But, I confess it, I was not intent on how Sobriety seemed. Indeed, feeling myself the centre of their combined attentions, the combined bewilderment, the combined disapproval, perhaps, of my own servants, I felt a hot surge over my own face and reached back to bring my veil to the front.

Behind it, I said, 'These are very important works for the City of London. Many, many women will have come to view them with their husbands.' I sat up straight. 'I will view them with you. Hampstead Heath, I think, Mr Brent.'

'Right you are, ma'am,' Mr Brent said. I glanced at the back of his hat. *What is that tone of voice?* He turned to the horses and said, 'Hup!'

Sobriety brought her own veil forward, and the two of us spent ten minutes in silence, heads turned toward the street, while the horses made their contrapuntal clatter through crowds, smells and stenches, catchcries and chatter.

'We see so little of what the world is doing.' I still had my shadowed eyes toward the street.

'True,' Sobriety said, and I put back my veil to turn my head from side to side to view the world, while Sobriety sat back a little, as if to rest her head, though there was no support for it there.

Chapter Ten

The disappointment was vexing. *It is not beautiful,* I thought. Gentlemen tend to describe engineering works as things of beauty, and I leaned forward to see where this might be so. I assumed that the site was up ahead, where there was such concentrated digging. There was a line of men, rising and falling with their picks, tiny in the distance and very rhythmic, a human machine. Their labours had despoiled everything about them, and created great mounds of earth.

We had trotted the horses a very long time up the Haverstock Road to Roslyn Street—to where it became Hampstead's High Street. The town, like a village in its setting of trees and fields, lay northward along the road. We turned, eventually—after consultation with a man in a dray—along Downshire Hill Road until we passed a tavern and the heath came in sight. Up above, ragged clouds scampered across the sky and left streamers behind them.

The works took up a wide swathe of the heath. Beyond the digging, all was green, and treed, the scummed ponds to the southeast a home to weeds, reeds, and hardy fowl. Ahead there were the greys and browns of earthworks, the bluish-red of bricks in serried stacks next to a raw, plainly practical rail line which, it was evident, was the way by which the bricks had come. The landau had, however, to stop at some distance from the works, where a track finally gave way to rutted, undefined space inhabited by two other carriages and horses tugging at grass at its edge.

The clanking of machinery sounded at a distance. I was aware that Mr Brent and Sobriety were waiting; I looked toward the activity and spied a group of frock-coated men, tall hats nodding in conversation. *No ladies.* And now we—Mr Brent, Sobriety, and I—were here, lurking, too shy to see the works of which all the journals had spoken.

'We should walk over there, to where those gentlemen are,' I said, since something must be said. We all looked toward the gentlemen, but remained where we were. *Absurd. I must move.* My cheeks were hot. *What a cowardly baby I am.*

It was Sobriety who broke the silence, of course. 'Mr Brent, would you help us descend?'

The landau lurched with Mr Brent's hop to the ground; the carriage door was opened, the steps let down, and we were out, before more thinking could prevent it. Mr Brent led the horses to where they could pass the time feeding on green tufts of their own and drinking from a trough set up for equine visitors. Sobriety said, 'This ground will not be kind to our skirts,' and we two slipped gloved hands into slits at our waists and tugged on our *porte-jupe* strings to hoist our hems away from mud.

'Mr Brent,' I called, 'if the horses can do without you, might you like to attend us to view the works?' And Mr Brent smiled and said, 'Yes, ma'am, thank you.' *Is he mocking me?* I wondered, and then was cross with myself, once again, for my concern at his opinion of me. We—Sobriety and I—made our way over uneven ground, picking through gravel and around puddles in footwear never meant, heaven knows, for fields or worksites. Mr Brent, hands clasped behind his back, stepped and stopped, stepped and stopped, so as to keep a little behind the ladies. But I glanced back—his gaze was concentrated on the workmen and wisps of steam ahead, and so my cheeks cooled in the breeze. *Poor man. He does not mock me. He would rather goggle at the foundations without us.* I was uncertain if I felt relieved at this, and avoided a small rut. *Men are so taken with concrete.*

One of the frock-coated gentlemen we had spied, on our circuitous route over pocks and gravel and muddied patches, was, evidently, some manner of host to visitors. There was much nodding of his top-hatted head, conversational movements of the shoulder, discursive waving of his hand—there, toward the bricks, and there, following the line of the digging works westward. The other hats nodded more slowly and in unison, and followed the gestures of the hand.

I kicked a small stone away from where it pressed into the ball of my foot even through the sole of my boot. Out here in the open, at this high point on the heath, the breeze had picked up into a light wind, with a cool bite not evident in the city. Our veils streamed behind us; our skirts bobbled and swayed. We each let their arms drop to help weigh down the skirts lest they flip up. *There, is this a natural-seeming stance? I had not considered such a wind!* We, and Mr Brent, stood a few paces from the main group of men, who now raised hands to anchor their hats.

The engineer-host, at last, spied his new visitors, bowed his excuses to the knot of gentlemen and came up to us. He was a short man, his waistcoat stretched across his rounded belly. He bent, causing stress upon the buttons of his waistcoat, and offered his hand to shake mine.

'Madam, welcome. Allow me to introduce myself—Selwyn St George, in charge as overseer of these works at Hampstead under Mr Furness, contracted by Mr Bazalgette of the Metropolitian Board of Works, under direction of Parliament.'

The thought sprang to mind: *He has a longer designation than the average baron.* I introduced myself, along with Sobriety and Mr Brent.

'Please join these gentlemen, Mrs Hadley, to whom I was just explaining…'

Mr St George made summary of his explanations so far, how these works were the beginning of a great network, this section running to Old Ford in Stratford; the tunnels would harness local streams, with cleansing effect; would be dug to a depth of around twenty feet and fall four more per mile; used especially-created bricks (he waved to the piles) called Staffordshire Blues; the cement (Portland cement, also especially produced) was being manufactured at temporary works and brought here (he pointed) by temporary railway line.

After some minutes, Mr St George interrupted himself with a little bow. 'This is no doubt very dry for ladies. Great works are not always graceful.' He gave a waggle of his head and one or two of his male audience tucked in their chins and chuckled down at me.

'Not at all.' I dipped my own head. 'Do go on.' *I have no doubt,* I thought, *he was less circumspect with his descriptions before I arrived. He might even have mentioned the word 'sewer'.*

One of the gentlemen asked a question about depth, and Mr St George returned to his recitation. *How he drones.* My head tipped a little to the side and I looked at Sobriety, whose eyes seemed preternaturally dark with tiredness. Disappointed with the dreariness of this aspect of concrete and bricks and maleness, yet reluctant, still, to end this day's outing, I thought that twenty more minutes would suffice before we made the return journey home. That would be fair. It would answer all needs, I thought, and sighed a little. The breeze, which was overly cool, tilted the cage beneath my skirt and circled my legs. *Perhaps ten minutes.* For the moment, as it blew this way, the breeze also brought with it thumpings and unpretty sounds of work, and a whiff of smoke. Mr St George borrowed a cane from another rounded gentleman, whose whiskers now lifted gently to and fro with the movements of the air. The engineer drew a complicated set of lines in the dirt to illustrate, he said, the conjunction of the various parts of the northern drainage. 'And here...' he said. Everybody bent forward to watch, except me.

What—no, who is that?

I frowned, the better to see. For up ahead, near where the railway embankment was complete over the construction of tunnels, there was a figure, quite alone, making its way in the flapping wind. She—this was a she, with a scarlet skirt dancing in the erratic weather; and a poor person, without bonnet or fashionable shape—was carrying something, clutched close against herself and wrapped tight in blue.

No, no, not quite blue . . . it is that new colour. Purplish, yet . . .

Mr St George was scratching still at the ground, with the gentlemen looking on, and Mr Brent behind them, all bent over in concentration. Sobriety stood a little behind Mr Brent, stretching her head to one side to see past shoulders and elbows. I tapped at her arm and spoke in an undertone into her ear.

'See that strange person yonder, Sobriety. Do you see whatever it is she is carrying? What colour is that called?'

Sobriety looked, squinting a little. 'That is mauve.'

'Oh yes. How odd it is that she should have a thing wrapped in mauve.' While the male murmur nearby estimated numbers of bricks multiplied by distance, I tilted my head at Sobriety. 'I know several young ladies—Mr Hadley's friends' daughters, probably Gwendolyn's girl—no doubt hunting, as we speak, for sufficient yards of mauve silk to carry them through the Season.'

We two began to stroll toward the distant figure. Mr Brent still stood just behind the knot of frock-coated gentlemen (all now gripping their hats), leaning in to their talk while keeping a respectful distance from his social betters, and not noticing, perhaps, that we ladies were slowly moving away from the group. Our veils danced up behind us in paired arabesques; I tugged with each hand at the sides of my skirt, pulling against the efforts of the wind to turn it up like a teacup. Sobriety had brought the umbrella and contrived to hold the material of her own skirt down with it. The wind gusted this way and that, the cages beneath our skirts causing a wobble with each puff. *Punch,* I thought, *would be well-amused at our minor struggles with the elements.*

The two veils pirouetted to the left. There was a sound, a very small sound carried to us, sharply different from the hissings and clankings and thuddings of the works, and the rattle and squeal of the train that had just come to a halt to receive its dirty load. It was a strain to distinguish it, this tiny new sound: *It may have been a bird.* It was, indeed, a faint cheeping between gusts, between bursts of shoutings, impacts, bangings and Mr St George's murmurings. *Or...* Here, in this part of the heath, I could see no birds to speak of. *Or...* There were many birds, of course, dabbling in the ponds at a distance behind us, but they were in the wrong direction for the wind to carry their cries. The tiny cawing came to us again.

'Ma'am! 'Tis a baby! That is a baby that woman is carrying!'

A baby, of course! How many creatures mewl in that fashion... My mouth fell open, such was my surprise.

Chapter Eleven

The figure up ahead broke into a trot, alongside the embankment and heading, it seemed, for an entrance.

'She is a girl, Sobriety, a mere girl.'

The girl's hair broke loose from whatever bound it and blew out in lank, dark streamers.

We stopped still. The men, still discoursing, were some yards behind us. We stared at the girl with her bundle, which, since we were now near enough to see, was moving—*wriggling*, I thought, *rather like a blue caterpillar*—as well as wailing in bursts, between breaths.

I had a creeping realization, my gloved hand to my mouth: *This is a pauper girl heading for empty tunnels with a baby wrapped in a fashionable shawl (those are fringes dangling there, in gold, I think. Yes, and a tassel).* There was a certainty, suddenly, like the brush of a great dark wing, of something very wrong…and then I felt a great lassitude, a reluctance heavy as over-thick custard to be the one to mend this problem.

Surely this is nothing, I argued with myself. *This signifies nothing, or somebody would have acted. This is not a circumstance, surely, that would depend on me. Surely, not on me.*

Within my chest, my heart lurched and I felt suddenly ill with apprehension.

A baby. 'Tis a baby… It was a fact that could not be got around.

I glanced around at the men—quite distant now—but they were laughing together and entirely heedless of what we women saw, or, indeed, were barely aware of us at all. One would have to be unusually forthright to attract their serious attention. It would take time. I looked back at the girl, now slowed to a stride over by the completed embankment. It was clear she knew this uneven landscape well.

Perhaps she spied her doorway into one of those long, dark tunnels lined with bricks.

'That is not her baby,' I said, at last. 'I cannot see how this pauper girl can have a baby, or at least not one wrapped as it is.' I found myself tapping my fingers against my mouth—made, oh, so nervous, testy indeed, with the opposing desires to be doing something and to be assured that nothing needed to be done.

This is not right. It cannot be right. There must be something done. I knew this to be true.

Sobriety, at any rate, was heeding my concern, and had already started off again, walking fast and billowing out sideways as she went.

Look there, she acts while I merely make conversation. At last, and it was as if pulling away from glue, I pattered off after her, even while pieces of gravel jabbed at my feet through my thin soles.

'Mr Brent!' I called over my shoulder, but it was apparent Mr Brent did not hear. His head was hidden behind a black-clad shoulder; his body bent forward and taut with interest as somebody's hand sketched a conversational parabola.

Sobriety was moving further on, and so I must catch up.

If this wind worsens, we shall turn into kites and fly up across London, petticoats and drawers and all. We might cause alarm to travellers in hot air balloons! I could not help but let out a little huff, a giggle, a spurt of my own excitement (while I thought it absurd to feel so, and it did not sit well with that sick anxiety) but found it difficult to both laugh and breathe, puffed out as I was with the effort of keeping up with Sobriety. My lungs were embattled from the constriction of my stays and from this unaccustomed trotting. I heard Sobriety's own panting up ahead.

We were drawing closer to the girl and her wriggling, blue burden, had nearly drawn abreast of her—though still separated from her by several yards of muddied, gravelled, and rutted ground—when she succeeded in pulling open some manner of door into one of the tunnels, and disappeared.

We stood a moment, each with a hand at a heaving breast and staring after the vanished girl.

'We shall…have to…pursue,' Sobriety said with difficulty.

'Oh, heavens…I suppose so.' I looked back at Mr Brent, who still stood at the edge of the male coterie. I made to slow my breathing, as Sobriety began to pick her way to the embankment and the tunnel opening, arms out for balance, holding the furled umbrella in counterpoint.

'Hi! Mr Brent!' I called, loudly, and then stopped for a moment, startled at myself. I had not shouted in that way since I was ten, if ever. I felt myself redden both with the effort and with self-consciousness, almost hoping none of the men would hear me after all.

Yet that would be ridiculous. Mr Brent ought to be with us. I drew another breath.

'Mr Brent! You must come!' Mr Brent looked around at that, and so I gestured to him to follow and turned to join Sobriety. *Ladies must not go adventuring unaccompanied*, I thought, and felt for a light-headed moment that all had so suddenly become wildly absurd.

While it was not far, the walk to the entranceway was slow with the necessary picking and hopping from dryish patch to dryish patch, and silent with concentration, barring Sobriety's whispered 'oh!' and 'tcha!' as mud adhered to our petticoats and water spread upward in a brown stain. We clutched at our wilful skirts.

We reached the small entrance to the tunnel, a heavy metal door with a large handle, which at first Sobriety tugged, and then I did, and then both of us together, grunting as we pulled. The door opened.

That girl is strong. Or we are weak. And, oh! It is so very dark in there!

We peered in, veils streaming and pulling in the wind behind us, skirts and petticoats snapping like sails; even our bonnets shifted and tugged a little, although securely tied under our chins. The entrance-way was not only dark, but was itself meant for men going about their business, not for ladies in wide skirts, who would have to enter sidelong, tilting our unwilling cages and partly folding them up so as to squeeze through.

Sobriety, adjusting and tilting, was first to enter. She hovered a moment, turned and spoke. 'There is a metal ladder here.' She glanced behind herself. 'But it is not too far to the bottom.'

I believe I was unaware for a second how my mouth hung open. 'A ladder?'

This grows worse, minute by minute!

'Yes. It is perfectly safe. And newly built, after all. You will have to face the wall to climb down.' Sobriety spoke slowly and deliberately—in order, I knew, to impart confidence and dispel fear—as she had spoken once to Cissy when an enormous rat had not only been discovered but had then backed, yellow-fanged and hackles on end, into a corner of the dining room.

And yet she is breathless, too, now as then... It was a little comfort to me to know this of her.

'Face the wall?' I felt myself fixed to the spot where I stood.

'Yes. I will be just ahead. You will be perfectly safe.' I looked at her. 'But we must do it, if that girl is not mother to the babe, as you believe.'

Perhaps Sobriety could do it herself? I took a breath. *No, of course not. Little Sobriety alone in a tunnel with a desperate baby thief? No.*

'All right. I will follow you.'

Sobriety began to sink from sight, her face, colourless against the darkness massed behind her, turned away and downwards.

I glanced around to where Mr Brent, hat clutched to his head and greatcoat bellying in the wind, had almost reached the point where he must pick his way over messy ground to us. He looked across and I put my finger to my lips to prevent his speaking. I then arranged myself, entered and turned to face the descending wall, a hand on each of the metal holds. My heart beat so that I thought it fought to escape my very bodice. I shook a foot clear of petticoat before stretching out in search of a first rung.

Lord, my knees are shaking. And my arms! They quivered with the strain of holding my own weight, were shot through with pain with both the holding and the stretching upward, as I descended. I was so utterly unused to this kind of activity. There was a tension at my seams and the whispered tearing of something giving way at the armsaye. At least my paletot would conceal the disaster to my dress. A drop of perspiration trickled from under my bonnet down the side of my face. *Can I hold on? Will I fall?* I twisted my head to one side and saw Sobriety waiting below, a grey blooming in the gloom.

It did not take long to reach the floor, I suppose, though my arms ached with the weight they had had to bear. Neither was it, when my eyes adjusted, as lightless as it had first seemed; after all, daylight still showed in one direction, where the tunnels were still being constructed, as well as from the open entranceway above our heads. We peered into the shadows the other way, a yawn of blackness whence came the echoing cries of the baby and the receding scuffle of feet.

We have no light to follow. What now?

We began to walk slowly toward the sounds; I reached for Sobriety, who held my gloved hand with a grip both tight and tense. For comfort, I brushed my other hand against the curved brick wall. We had not gone far before Sobriety stopped, and so did I. I realised I heard a crooning, along with the whimpering of the baby, and then we saw a flare of light.

Of course, the girl has her own bit of candle.

A mere twenty feet away, and there she was. Her face was there, of a sudden, in a circle of yellow candlelight dimming into shadow. She was on her knees as if at worship before a small nest of musty clothing and a thin blanket, in which the mauve-wrapped baby kicked and cried. She had settled the babe into its nest, and reached with arms and fingers like sticks to twitch the cloths about him. Her face in profile, thin and so without flesh as to seem very small indeed, bore a look of great concentration. Her eyes were enormous, and her lips parted with the beginnings of a smile.

We moved forward on tiptoe.

I had a sense of being both a part of and witness to this scene: *Dark shadows creeping, the moments inching closer to the point where this poor girl will lose her tiny god. Poor girl, or villain?*

Then there came the heavy footfalls of Mr Brent rushing up behind us, calling, 'Ma'am, what are you doing?' His voice boomed.

Oh, Lord. Shh!

The girl squeaked, and looked around. Her face, blurred in the half-light, held still a moment, before knowledge settled on it of doom borne upon her by our three figures swaying at the edge of light. Then she began her shouting, a shrieking that bounced against the walls of the tunnel and added fear to fear until the whole cavern was filled with her overlapping, clamorous voices. The baby wailed its own cacophony through it all.

'Stay away! Stay away! This is my place!' Her eyes were young and round, but what her age was it was hard to tell: she was so thin, small as a bird. I thought she was like that street boy—these children akin in their hunger—crouching there on the tunnel floor before her little nest. The girl looked from one crowding, vague figure to the other and back, eyes dark and dazzled by candlelight, jutting her small chin at us. Deep shadow drew the shape of bone; her face was like the weather-cleaned baby egret's skull I had once held as a child.

I stepped a little further into the weak light, close to the baby. It did not feel as if I had made any decision to move so, yet I did, and my heart banged once more against the very whalebone.

Gracious, what am I doing!

'Ma'am!' Sobriety whispered, close behind me. The girl made to pick up the baby, floundering forward, but I was there first (to my surprise) and crouched down to place my hand on the howling bundle.

I drew breath to shout above the noise, 'Child, child. This is not your baby, is it?' As I spoke, the infant stopped its noise to draw breath, and *not your baby, is it?* echoed throughout the tunnel, repeated and repeated until there was silence, and the baby began its noise again.

The girl looked away and we watched her face pucker. *See them both, these children*, I thought, looking from one wailing face to another. *Yet* . . . I picked up the infant and struggled back to my feet, one hand on the wall to steady myself. A sharp smell of urine hovered in an unseen cloud over a small pile of discarded cloths. My arms continued weak from unaccustomed use, and the baby was heavy. Fleetingly, I recalled that I had not often held my own babe when he had been one. This child's face was messy from tears and mucus, his eyes swollen pink from crying. The shawl about him was loose and he squirmed a little as I held him. I considered for a moment handing the baby to Sobriety, but it was as if the thought had spoken itself aloud and Sobriety had answered 'no', shifting in haste away in the darkness.

Of course not.

I settled the baby further into the crook of my arm and with that small shock of long-forgotten yearning, felt its snuggled warmth.

'You're goin' ter take 'im away, aincha? 'E's all I got!' The girl was hugging herself now; she swayed, stretched her own hand toward the baby and then pulled the hand back, empty. The candle flame wavered with her movement, and all of our shadows swung looming and shrinking, back and forth as if on strings. I closed my eyes a moment against the giddying, before I could speak again.

'But he is not yours, child. You took him from his mother, from his home, did you not?' The baby coughed and ceased his noise. He moved his head as it lay in my arm, perhaps to look about himself, and took a long breath that shuddered. I glanced down at him. He had pushed his little fist into his mouth and was making sucking noises.

''E's mine, and so I took 'im. She could spare 'im.' The girl half reached again for the baby as I held him, pulled back her hands and wrung them. ''Er life is like a picture, coloured like a winder in a church...' Her voice petered out into a whine and then she was silent a moment, shut her face from us and began to shuffle away, sniffling from the candlelight into the dark.

She called out again, her voice disembodied: ''E loved me, 'e did!' There was a whimpering, which receded. When she spoke again, it was in tremolo, and dry with too much crying. 'And I would love 'im, and keep 'im warm with my own body, and feed 'im before I ate any meself.' Her voice grew yet smaller, seemed made up of echoes now. 'More than you would, you cow, done up all tight and smelling sweet. You couldn't love anyone like I could. You couldn't be 'is friend and 'is—'

Mr Brent seemed suddenly to find his voice. 'Oi! That's enough of that, my girl! You stole this baby, and you must answer for it!'

It made me jump. I had quite forgotten Mr Brent was with us there. The girl's footsteps were very quickly padding away, her 'No!' already distant, and Mr Brent made to rush past Sobriety and me. But his movement stirred air that doused the girl's candle and we were all left in darkness with only a glimmer, grey in the distance at the end of the tunnel. I heard Mr Brent's hesitation.

'Oh, leave her, Mr Brent. She is unhappy enough.' *Have a care, have a care. Why must he insist so, without thought?* There was much, much too much pain in this cold and dusty air.

The baby had removed his fist from his mouth and was subsiding now into hiccups. I thought, *I have no stomach for the punishment of children.* I looked toward the baby's small wet face, though I could not see it. He sniffed.

Sobriety was evidently feeling about for matches in the purse at her waist, realised (of course) that she had none, and smiled at Mr Brent when he handed her his own packet of lucifers. She struck one alight, lit the candle in her hand, the umbrella under her arm. Her small figure was so apparently prepared for all of the surprises of today. *How did you climb down here with that?*

'Perhaps we should walk to the tunnel's end, rather than attempt to climb with the baby.'

I feel as if I have been at the sherry! I giggled, though I felt I had no breath, and did not rightly know which of many emotions was now uppermost. *We have only begun—the police, the child's parents . . .* I took a deep breath. 'Sobriety, you are absolutely right. Lead on!'

Chapter Twelve

It was growing late, dark and clinging-cold, the lights on their poles fuzzy in the moist air when Mr Brent at long last clattered the landau to our door. He was off immediately, after handing us down, for the horses strained toward stables and their feed. Sobriety and I could hear the low rumble of Mr Brent's murmuring to the beasts, their clattering and clopping through a pool of yellow light, and the landau grinding its great wheels into the night. Misted breath—the man's and his charges'—rose and frayed above their heads. We two were both trembling with cold. I assume Sobriety observed of me what I noticed of her: a nose glowing pink and lips paling to blue.

Inside the house were contrasting tempers like crosscurrents of sea or air: Mrs Staynes spoke, through tense and sharpened consonants, of Cook ('Cook could not tell, ma'am, whether to light the stove'), and her gloved hands by turns gripped and patted one another. There were tasks, she said, that had had to be deferred—and marketing, whose details could not be discussed with Mrs Hadley, as would otherwise have occurred, because Mrs Hadley was gone so very long. Mrs Staynes was so out of sorts that she spoke of me in the third person. She could not look at me. The plaint continued, with her report of the arrival in the afternoon of parcels upon parcels and a lumpy shape, which could only be a machine for sewing.

'It is very large, and takes up a lot of space,' she said, and it was clear to me that Mrs Staynes dwelt on the details of this arrival in particular. Her eyes lifted at last to mine—the question in them clear, and perhaps there was a difference in her tone. Perhaps there was curiosity, a little excitement . . .

'Oh, they have come?' I pulled at the knot to remove my bonnet. The movement caused a sharp pain in my upper arms, a stinging that startled me and must have arisen, I realised, from clambering down the ladder earlier in the day. It was a pain I would nurse to myself in secret, my own private harbinger of life and adventure, a noble wound, the mark of heroic gesture . . .

I glimpsed the latest card from Mrs Charles in the dish and felt for the moment curiously disorientated. So much had changed, and yet this former life stepped forward to tap me on my shoulder. *It is as if there were some uncomfortable spectre whispering from another place…or perhaps it is we who are arrived from that other realm.*

'Yes, ma'am. I took the liberty of having them stacked in the morning room.' I blinked and then recalled what it was Mrs Staynes and I had been discussing.

The housekeeper opened the door to that room, gestured at the piles of differently sized shapes in brown paper. 'I felt we could not do more without your direction.' Her hands, having opened the door, now gripped each other once again and I knew myself not yet forgiven.

I am a disturber of the peace, I realised.

The function of this small world, our house, was to travel with reassuring regularity through its cycles, with every person in it accountable and to be found in the proper place at every hour and minute. The calendar and the chiming of the clocks were the measure of the household life, a certainty in repetition, a maintenance of pattern, just so, just so. I had knocked this asunder today and brought the unknown and unknowable here, to our space. I was out of time with everything and Mrs Staynes was made nervous by it. Mrs Staynes was frightened by it. I looked at her hands—gloved fingers around each other in a tight interweaving.

Yet I could not wish to promise never to repeat it. Of a sudden, a fizz ran through my veins. I moved my shoulder and felt its twinge.

Still, I took especial note of where the sewing machine had been placed, for it stood by itself next to my own little side table, the parcel of a shape and size in its wrapping to be a very ill-concealed secret. Mrs Staynes, I knew, had had that placed there herself. I caught her expression.

Really, she is as excited as a child at Christmas, and wishes she were not. Dread of change and now this—all dwelling embattled in the same breast! Mrs Staynes turned her eyes away, as if she were caught out.

There was a movement from above. Cissy crouched on the landing outside Mr Hadley's bedchamber, where she was plainly on sick-room duty, and pressed her face against the banister. Perhaps she thought herself hidden in shadow, as she leaned to catch what was being said below.

'I think you and Cissy might unwrap the machine after supper, perhaps, and put it where you think it would best be kept,' I said. There was movement from the landing, and then some sound escaped from the crouching child above. Cissy slipped back into Mr Hadley's room before Mrs Staynes could properly be aware of her truancy.

I brought my attention back to my housekeeper. 'We will deal with the rest tomorrow.'

Saying this, I handed my bonnet to Sobriety, and was brought back from my own distraction when she at first failed to grasp it. I looked around at her then, whose reaction had been so slow, as if dreaming; Sobriety took the bonnet as if she barely knew what it was. Her skin was waxen. All this time, she had stood there so quiet.

My poor girl, so pale!

'When these things are put away, Sobriety,' I unbuttoned my paletot and Sobriety held it while I slipped out of the sleeves, 'you should go early to bed and I will have something brought up to you.'

'But there are our petticoats to soak else they will stain, and your own toilette ...' Sobriety's voice was like the scratching of dead leaves, and as nearly noiseless, so that I must bend forward to hear.

'A soaking is simple. Leave anything soiled outside your door… Cissy will help me again tonight.' I took her arm and led her to the staircase. 'Go.' Sobriety mounted slowly. I saw that Mrs Staynes watched the muddied hem of Sobriety's petticoats jostle with each step.

'Mrs Staynes, we have had adventures today.' The housekeeper's eyes seemed to set, a stillness that no doubt signalled her foreboding of what tale I might tell. I knew my attempt to jolly her was too obvious. 'And yet you may approve. You are going to the kitchen?'

'Yes, ma'am.'

'I shall come with you.'

In passing the dish on its little table, I thought how Mrs Charles's frequent card-leaving might signify that the woman had nowhere to take her emotion but to our door, but could not yet bring herself within the house itself. And I—who had always taken care that Mrs Charles was not among guests at our dinner parties (it was a small thing I could do, being in charge of drawing up lists and always obliged at some point to perform at the pianoforte and, quavering at the attention, attempt some song. She would not, at least, be in my audience)—was surprised to feel pity.

I could not help but wonder if there had been a true passion of some kind, between Mrs Charles and my husband. I had not considered this before, that passion might be a thing Mr Hadley had harboured—could harbour—for another human being.

Cook was assured there was no need for anything more than a light supper, nor on any account to go to great lengths at this time of night. I sent Albert, who was mopping his own plate with bread, to relieve Cissy in the sickroom, and Cissy, when she came to the door, to carry a plate of cold meats —some left from the servants' own meal—up to Sobriety.

For myself, I sat where Albert had been and felt of a sudden a great draining of my own energies, as if a drawstring had been loosened around a bursting purse and all the pennies poured forth. The kitchen was warm with bustle, of cooking fire and use and people; the muscles of my neck and shoulders gave up their cold-gripped tension. I let out a slow breath.

I had no inclination to pick myself up to dine upstairs alone in the chill, with those tiny pure sounds of silver against china, the slow sip of water, the crystal glass beautiful upon the cloth; Mr Hadley's father upon the wall opposite the resplendent pheasant upon whose dead and hanging neck the feathers were detailed—the sheen and the frothy down—with merciless artistry. No inclination at all.

The fire had been lit in the dining room, no doubt. Well, I did not know if that were so. Perhaps it had. I assumed so, and knew I should feel a responsibility not to waste it, although that room always resisted the best efforts at heating. I did not really care to move. I was beyond caring very much about anything.

'Cook, Mrs Staynes, I am happy to eat just here, at your table.' Cook let out a low exclamation; Mrs Staynes had the look of someone who could not think this time how to compose her face. I smiled around at them, though it felt as if my own features creased against their will. I felt a gathering tightness about my eyes. 'I too shall have some resurrection pie,' I laughed a little, 'and tell you all that we have done today.'

Cissy appeared in the doorway, heralded a moment before her arrival by a *thump-thump* upon the stairs. Sobriety was asleep, she said, and so she had left the plate, with its covering, on Sobriety's bedside chair. She had over her arm the muddied petticoat; I pointed out my own and that both petticoats would need a soaking overnight. The three serving women all bent to look, the room full of the question behind their careful silence.

I looked up at the three faces. In my exhaustion, I felt the rising of a most uncommon affection for them, and was too full with it for a moment before I could speak. *Foolish baby that I am!*

'I shall eat here, and then I will tell you all, and then I shall go to my bed.'

It could not be said that all of the rituals of the house had returned to their pattern, next morning. Cissy loitered at the morning room door, pulled back there as if by a string no matter what employment she had been set to do elsewhere. It was understood—she understood—that there would be no examination of the sewing machine without Mrs Staynes, at the very least; and Cissy must spend her hours with Mr Hadley, and when she was free Mrs Staynes would then take her turn in the sickroom, and Cissy must wait still.

Mrs Staynes, of course, was not so constrained, and spent some time with me and Sobriety, pressing treadle and turning wheel, bending to peer at the needle rising and plunging, the long point vivid as the dagger of an Italian assassin. For the moment, Mrs Staynes kept her hands by her side. Sobriety ventured a finger toward the needle.

'Adequately sharp, I think,' she said, and laughed. Yesterday's alabaster weariness had gone.

'It is a new model,' I told Mrs Staynes. 'Very new, indeed. It is called the *Letter A*. I suppose because of the shape.'

I stepped back, better to view the machine, my head to one side. 'Although, perhaps not.' I smiled.

'We do have a small book to instruct us, and we shall have a man come and show us how to use the machine.'

'That would be best, perhaps, ma'am.' Mrs Staynes crossed one hand over the other.

Finally, my housekeeper smiles for me, at least a little. A small weight, that I had not realised I carried, lifted from my shoulders.

I drew a cloth over the machine to protect it from the dust, and Mrs Staynes and Sobriety left the room. Sobriety returned with coffee for herself and me, and the morning newspaper—for breakfast had been brief that morning and abandoned quickly in favour of an examination of the machine.

Our tale was lavishly described in *The Times* with expressions of horror and exclamation points distributed generously throughout the text. We could not decide (I think I may speak for both Sobriety and me in this) which emotion was uppermost in us—a sense of being laid bare, somehow, or a giddiness at being for the moment famous (at least to ourselves, for, mercifully, our names were not used). We read and read again the tale of our own adventure, (with, oddly, our cheeks the deepest and hottest red) both amused and relieved at the reference to our virtue as "unnamed gentlewoman, her lady's maid and servant"; discovering for the first time the name of the family—that of Robert Farquharson—to whom the stolen baby was now returned. A description followed of the Farquharson family's own virtues, amplifying the details laid out in these pages just yesterday when the theft of the baby had been first reported; of Mr Farquharson's successes in the world of business and the respect with which he was held by both church and commerce; and how his wife, very young and pretty, was prominent already among the charities of London, very glad to condescend to the poor and so on.

Sated with this story of our derring-do, we took my small scissors to the string around the parcels still piled on the rug in their brown paper, and uncovered the various stuffs—much of it in black crêpe and bombazine, Henrietta, some lawn for cuffs, cambric for handkerchiefs—all in preparation for a household in deep mourning. Some parcels I put by to be opened much later, for these were half-mourning colours of lilac and grey, and a smaller parcel of jewellery in velvet boxes: a brooch, necklace and earrings in jet.

Sobriety gathered up the string and brown paper; I folded the newspaper at the page that recounted our adventure, for Cissy and Mrs Staynes would surely wish to see it. We each took our burdens through to the kitchen to be disposed of.

Later, I sat unmoving for some time at my little table by the window in Mr Hadley's room. The stillness brought with it scampering visions of women with parcels and paper and string, and that machine that was both delightful and dreadful, and then of distress—*that poor mad girl, the baby…and Sobriety.* I breathed quietly around it, as if I meditated like some old Indian fakir from my own Papa's youthful adventures. For some time—it was many minutes, perhaps a quarter of an hour—I sat in this way, until I began to rouse and glance at my husband to see how he did. *Well enough*, I thought.

And so, what was your greatness, Mr Hadley? I gazed at him some moments more. *George, what was your greatness?* Then I turned my attention to pen and paper, dipping the nib into ink.

In the evening, Sobriety and I sat for a time before the fire in my morning room, sharing between us the pages of *The Times* and of *The Illustrated London News.* Our empty cups were set aside with their saucers on my little table. We sat together on the little settee, the other chairs providing a surface for the higgledy-piggledy heapings of haberdashery that had not yet a home of their own. It made the room quite crowded, to be sure, yet to my mind there was also a sense of comfortable busyness. To tell the truth, for the moment it pleased me well.

I held open the journal for a glance at the particular items that dealt with ladies' fashion, but then thought there was little point in considering this season's colour and laces, given black would be my covering for another year. I considered this. The machine for sewing would do its part in practical ways until then, once we had all learned to work it. I turned the page.

'See here how the bones of another ancient creature have been found,' I leaned toward Sobriety to give her a view of the article with its illustration.

'They are inevitably of such prodigious size. They say, or at least I understand Mr Darwin to say, that there were no men about when these monsters existed.'

'It is as well. I do not imagine these creatures were careful where they trod.' Sobriety smiled at this. I sat straight once more and read another moment, before looking up. 'Do you know, I think I can well believe there are some people who are descended from apes.'

Sobriety laughed. She folded her newspaper on her lap.

'My uncle James, when on dry land, is a naturalist. Had I told you?'

I said I believed she had done so, some time ago. 'Does he collect?'

'Oh, yes. He has eggs of all sizes, and many kinds of feather, the skeletons of small creatures. But best of all—' Sobriety smiled. 'He has a piece of rock that he found by the sea, with marks upon it of some tiny, ancient creature. It is perfect in every detail, like a sketch with a very sharp pencil, pressed into the stone.'

'How wonderful. I should love to see it. We must attend exhibitions of such things.' I corrected myself. 'That is, of fossils.'

I closed and placed my newspaper next to our cups. 'When I was a girl,' I recalled, 'there was a lady who was very well known for her finds. Great creatures like crocodiles, found on our own beaches. When she died, my mother told me of her, and read to me about her, from the newspaper.' I laughed. 'I would imagine, when I climbed my tree, that some great monster of the sort had once come floundering across the field, and might still do so.'

Sobriety smiled once more, and the silence crept back to settle between us. The fire cracked as a log collapsed; a wind buffeted the window beyond the curtains, and died away.

Gazing a while into the flames, I felt the weight and movement of a world careless of those who survived within it. Monsters lumbered less and were not so huge as they had once been, but were a danger nonetheless, a danger to the young. To girls. Girls, as I had been a girl. Sobriety would have been a very industrious girl, in the field and in the classroom. I thought of myself up high, wrapped in my leafy cover and looking out for those floundering monsters; I thought of Ida, no less a girl than myself, who had been sent sometimes to find me. I thought of Cissy, whose childishness was so apt to burst forth at any moment.

'What age do you suppose that poor girl is, who took the baby?'

Sobriety took a time to answer. 'Young, very young.'

We both were quiet for a time, as the fire died back and the coals began to glow. Beyond the window, the world lashed cold.

Chapter Thirteen

Ladies—what of the world between us all?

By A. Hadley

Mayhap some ladies of education, upon reading this modest article of writing, think to look first outside their window at those busy women of another class out in the world, and then consider a moment those others who serve your needs in kitchen and with polish in hand.

May we hold, for the sake of argument, that there is a community of ours, of women, which dwells within and weaves through and yet, in a way, beyond that of men? For these men function, one might muse upon it, with different purpose, within different spaces—and must, so often, be of a different set of mind—from our own…

I came to this point in my discourse on paper—if such it could be called—and found myself unable for the moment to continue. There was a thread of some thought, I knew, if I could but catch hold of it and pull. It could very well lead to strange, if not dangerous places. Might I ask ladies to step outside their position thus? *Most likely not.* And yet, what was I considering, as my theme? Might folk consider me as one would regard a revolutionary with an incendiary device?

I wiped the pen, put it down and placed my hand over my eyes. *Writing might indeed be considered an incendiary device*, I thought, and then: *Well, I have moved beyond writing about the weather, at least!*

Perhaps I had taken a step. Though I could not be sure of it.

I folded the paper and placed it in my box. *I will think further about it.* Mrs Charles brought herself, at last, to visit. There was no surprise to this, given the dish in the hallway now held three of her calling cards. There was no surprise that the lady came alone, without her husband—a wealthy but thin and vanishing presence who went about Society making very little impression, it seemed—and without any other company but her coachman.

Mrs Staynes opened the door to her, let her in, and went to tell me of the visitor. Mrs Charles stood very still in the hallway, a medley of sombre tones from bonnet to hem—soft greys of two kinds, a charcoal, a sober blue like a painter's notion of distant hills. She looked about herself, just a little, for of course she had never before been to this house. I glanced about too—I could not help it—and thought that it would do; then found myself irritated that how my home appeared to her should so concern me.

I shook her hand. The woman's face was a deal paler than I had ever seen it before; new lines dragged her mouth down, spelling a despondence, I thought. And yet, she held her elegant head high, and still her expression spelled dominion; but she was, undeniably, sad.

'You wish to see George, of course,' I said, for I had, after all, no wish to put Mrs Charles in the position of having to ask. She made a slight bow of her head in assent, and I led the way upstairs and to Mr Hadley's chamber. *To George's chamber*, I essayed to myself. It was Albert on watch by the bed, and I hesitated a moment before calling him away, which I felt I ought to do out of kindness, so that the door could be closed to leave Mrs Charles alone with Mr Hadley. With George. With my husband. With Mrs Charles's lover. *I do not suppose it matters overmuch, in the end, if Albert wonders at this.*

Albert waited on the landing, while I descended to my morning room. In perhaps a quarter of an hour, the bedchamber door opened and closed, and I went to greet Mrs Charles at the bottom of the stair. In silence, we touched hands (it could not be said there was any grip) at the front door, and then Mrs Charles was gone.

It was after luncheon that the men arrived together—the policeman and the very superior gentleman, Mr Farquharson himself. Guests were rare; strangers even more so, especially on my account. Mr Hadley had, on occasion, been visited by men who evidently felt they were well enough acquainted with him to arrive at his front door. I myself knew these friends of his (if they could be called so) not at all when they arrived, and barely when they departed.

And now all these new strangers do wash up upon my doorstep. And on my own account! It was a taxing thing for me, to stand alone and shake the hands of strangers.

Indeed, Mr Farquharson was very much of a type with Mr Hadley's former visitors, though this time come to visit me. This fact in itself was disconcerting. It made me feel, somehow, like an interloper, though I dwelt here. I felt myself a child interfering in adult deliberations, even while I was mistress of this house. A few minutes before, I had been chattering with the women in the kitchen, about the machine and the useful work it could be put to once they knew how to make use of it. Moreover, I had been laughing with them, not like a lady of the house at all, and in this I felt somehow found out by this gentleman and the policeman.

These two, furthermore—and here I experienced a squeeze of irritation, embarrassment at my littlest servant's inept fumbling—caused excitement to Cissy that was very evident, perhaps even to the visitors, as she took hats and coats and Mr Farquharson's cane (mother-of-pearl inlay, and largely ebony, with some exquisite carving of intertwined leaves). The whispering between Mrs Staynes and Cissy, which, while taking place at the darker end of the hallway, was nonetheless obvious, and I was aware of the urgent hissing as if through my very skin. I glanced at Sobriety, who hurried away to join Mrs Staynes in chivvying Cissy back to the kitchen.

What must he think!

The inspector held out his hand to me even as the servants' agitation moved to the nether reaches of the house, and introduced his companion.

'Mr Farquharson insisted, Mrs Hadley, that he should meet the very brave person—' The inspector corrected himself with a glance at the darkened tunnel of the corridor. 'The *persons* who saved his youngest son...'

The larger gentleman stepped forward before the inspector had finished, impatient perhaps at having to wait upon such an introduction by a lesser man. It was an impression confirmed by his failure to glance at the inspector; and emphasized in the cut of his frock coat, and the fine embroidery on his waistcoat, surpassing in quality anything my brother Harry might wear and at least the equal to Mr Hadley's day apparel. *I wonder if he shares Mr Hadley's tailor?*

Mr Farquharson reached for my hand and bent over it, and I underwent another moment of confusion. His very cologne water was exactly Mr Hadley's, and brought to mind Mr Hadley himself, as if he had risen from his bed. I felt that I stood next to myself and watched all of the bravado—*nay, authority*—of the past weeks fall away and leave me once more the child, the perpetual child bride of drooping posture, of drooping character, entirely unimpressive, stupid with uncertainty and incompetence...

Mr Farquharson kissed my hand. 'Dear lady, words cannot express my gratitude.' I murmured something—Lord knows what—in response.

And then of course there was the problem of the household itself being at sixes and sevens after our trip to town yesterday. There was nothing sorted, and this felt monumentally as if we had been found lacking on this occasion of our first proper visitors. *My* first proper visitors. I had not had time to carry through my own plans for a rearrangement. The gentleman and the inspector could not be shown into the morning room, which was strewn still with piles of haberdashery and encumbered by the sewing machine, but into the drawing room, even though it was my intention that this be closed up in favour of my own receiving room. This in itself, I was aware, would be the cause of upset for Mrs Staynes, for the drawing room must always be the centre of the domestic; it was the hearth, the temple antechamber of the moral family. Yet, somehow and despite Mrs Staynes, and any attendant army of housekeepers, matriarchs and patriarchs, and any number of unexpected visitors, I was quite determined it would be closed. I was for a moment very vexed that circumstances had thus caught me out.

I felt myself tremble a little—and my mind to…to wring its hands, as it were—for everything was so out of its pattern, the house so full of oddments. The future for us all was so uncertain and this uncertainty given emphasis the more, indeed, because of all these objects cluttering the house.

And here were these visitors—*all these visitors*—come to witness its irregularities.

I collected a small part of my wits and rang the little bell that stood on the mantel.

As of the day before, Inspector Broadford was not entirely a stranger to me. It was he who had, eventually, resolved the problem of the ladies who had come bearing the stolen child to Hampstead's police station, the child by then hoarse and whimpering, his little face a rough red with high distress.

We had presented an unaccustomed scene—and Sobriety and I had glanced at each other at its oddness, relieved to be amused in this rough and strange environment (and reassured with the doughty presence of Mr Brent behind)—as we told our story over the racket. Several men in uniform stood frowning, hesitant to relieve us of this stolen but animated property. Inspector Broadford was out when we arrived, undertaking some duty or other, but to everyone's relief returned in not too long a time. He sent an officer forth with the baby cradled in a stiffly woollen arm, in search of a wet nurse in the town. The noise withdrawn, the story was told yet again. Yet where it came to the details of the young girl's description, we had both thought it best to be vague, for neither of us, it seemed, could abide the thought of the girl's arrest. Mr Brent followed our lead, stolid and silent. We could not tell what age the young person had been; we were not certain what clothes she had been wearing.

This, the deliberate lack of detail in the story told the previous night, made me shift a little in discomfort and glance every now and then at the inspector. He did not, however, demonstrate any sign of suspicion, I thought. *And how, in any case, would I be able to discern what is in his mind?*

Mrs Staynes, her face so set as to appear done in wax, appeared at the door in belated answer to the bell, and I asked her for tea. *What on earth is the matter with everyone?* 'And would you ask Sobriety to take some with us,' I said. After all, Sobriety, too, was a heroine of the hour, whatever the dramas now being enacted elsewhere.

The inspector and Mr Farquharson sat at either end of the formal settee—Mr Hadley's settee as I was coming to see it, for this was, I felt, his room, with his portrait, the manly hunt upon the wall, and the large, stout and tasselled settee for guests of note. Mr Farquharson had in his cravat an ebony pin, and wore large golden rings on his hands. I was eased somewhat at seeing these: *Mr Hadley would have pronounced them vulgar.*

I thought a moment. *George would have pronounced them vulgar.*

I sat a little straighter at this, watched how Mr Farquharson placed his hands firmly upon his knees. His gaze was a deliberate one—the eyes dark and the muscles just a little tight around them—and he considered every ornament, vase and figurine, landscape by academician, and formal portrait, and halted at one.

'I know this gentleman, ma'am. I have been introduced (a very good style of portrait, too, if I may say). He is your father? Your father-in-law? A fine man; many have heard the name of Hadley in the City.' He raised his right hand in emphasis, as he spoke in an accent that held a memory of the north.

He spoke thus, and my cheeks grew hot. Squabbling and contradictory emotions blended, in a few long moments, into a simple resentment, even while I could not identify to whom this emotion referred. Was it Mr Farquharson that I so resented, or Mr Hadley? For an instant, I saw the face of my father, but I turned from that.

'This is my husband, sir, who lies upstairs very ill.'

Mr Farquharson bowed his head. 'My dear madam, what a great pity. Please accept my best wishes for Mr Hadley's speedy recovery. It is not only his family that has need of him, of course, but I understand his friends, his Party, and the nation, too, have great expectations of Mr Hadley not only in the City but in the corridors of Parliament.'

Does he tell me he knows this because he moves amongst those who feel so? I struggled to know what the man was truly saying. *Does he merely flatter me by saying so, about my husband? Does he tell me that our families are socially allied? Yes, I fancy that is what he does.*

Mr Farquharson's face folded into an expression to encompass, I surmised, sympathy and gallantry combined. 'I am sure Mr Hadley could want for no more angelic a nurse than his beautiful and plucky young wife. Your care must be a tonic in itself.'

I was tempted, but then decided against frankness. *George's passing is our business*, I told myself. *And in any case I do not think I desire that conversation.*

I bowed my own head rather than respond. The inspector nodded and beamed. Small, energetic, ruddy and square, his was an emphatic presence, as if outlined in sharpened charcoal.

Mr Farquharson spoke again, rising as if to take his leave.

'Ma'am, I shall not wait for tea, although that is most kind. I have business to attend to, I'm afraid. Please accept my deepest thanks once again for the rescue of my son and an invitation…' He searched an inside pocket. 'For Mrs Farquharson expressly bade me ask, when she had me come in her stead—for, of course, she has had a shock or two!—to beg you to attend a gathering at our establishment on Thursday next? In the evening.'

He withdrew from his pocket his card of introduction and an invitation (of most elegant production, with decoration and emboss-ing and on quite heavy card of excellent quality), which I took. 'Many of the best people are expected, and this is to be an occasion for building friendships.' He smiled and shrugged as if in self-depreca-tion. 'There will be music and a supper, and perhaps some may care to dance—we have a fine room for it.'

'Most kind, most kind.'

There followed a moment, and then another, before I realised I stared at the two cards as if I had never seen suchlike. My heart thumped as if I were a girl once more (and I set aside any notion for the time being of Mr Farquharson's vulgarity) that my personal attendance was required at such a grand occasion, for it did sound as if it might be grand. I composed an expression upon my face that said I was quite accustomed to such invitations in my own right.

Mr Farquharson spoke into the momentary silence. 'Of course, we were not aware of Mr Hadley's lamentable state of health. We are happy, naturally, to accept with pleasure the presence of any escort you deem suitable.'

I essayed a smile. 'I shall be pleased to come.' I searched my mind for a gentleman who might accompany me, and stayed the panic that tinkled through me like a shower of shattering glass. *Mr Gordon?*

Lord, no… Harry? Save me! 'I am certain my brother Dickie would be pleased, also, to accept.'

Mr Farquharson once more bent over my hand and left there a small wet patch. 'Excellent!'

Do I tremble at this invitation? Oh I hope not!

I rang the bell for Cissy to hurry with Mr Farquharson's hat and coat, and went to farewell him at the door, leaving the inspector for the moment on his own amid the well-polished hush of Mr Hadley's ornaments.

Back soon, to a smiling and repeated bowing between me and the inspector; I was minded of marionettes jerking sadly out of time with each other, and gave him an assurance that tea would be right along.

And still the inspector made no conversation. *What does he wait for?*

There was a short silence, which made itself felt as it sat stubborn despite the many busy noises of the world outside the window—the rumble of wheels, hurrying feet, somebody's raised voice. A young man's, I thought, and wondered if there would be an answer. It all added to a jumble in my mind, which persistently included the *oom-papa* of a waltz…

I felt I must drag my attention back from thoughts of social triumph, the murmur and laughter of gentility, the hiss of gaslight, the waft of cologne, the swing past of many colours… Instead, there was the brief racketing through my consciousness of that young, misery-hardened voice and its despairing contempt—*done up all tight and smelling sweet*, and I flinched from it.

I must, I knew, calm my thoughts, and I took a breath to do so. 'The wind has died a little since yesterday, has it not?'

'Indeed it has, ma'am.' The inspector smiled. The silence settled back into place. I studied him to see if he were as discomfited as I by this, and whether he in turn studied me. I saw no sign of this.

Thinking to turn from dark thoughts to light and from awkward-ness to delightful speculation, I began to compose in my mind the note I would send Dickie directly the inspector was gone. *How surprised he will be!*

Suddenly Sobriety was with us and shutting the door behind her, while the inspector was on his feet until she had sat down. He smiled again, this time at Sobriety, looking from beneath his eyebrows and then dropping his eyes when she glanced up and down.

'I hope you are well, Miss Mullins, and recovered from the excite-ments of yesterday?' I watched Sobriety wave away the inspector's concern with a little movement of her hand.

He has come so very far to pay his call on us. And then I saw, suddenly, as if I were myself the inspector, the shape of Sobriety's face and how it settled after smiling without fuss into its accustomed oval, her eyes steady, aware and stoical; how the smoothed darkness of her hair sat above the dusky grey and rose of her gown, how the bow of her lips had strength and warmth, were soft and curled with ready humour. I glanced back at the inspector, though his attention had turned so completely from me and to Sobriety.

'Ladies, I too have come by especially to thank you for your heroic efforts.' This time he included me in his glance.

I said, 'Oh, hardly that,' and Sobriety and I laughed, self-conscious, leaning toward each other and each slightly pink. I once again regarded myself in my mind's eye and wondered at the differ-ence in my response to the inspector from that to Mr Farquharson. Mr Hadley would have scoffed at the inspector's station in life—and would no doubt have had something to say about the man being seated in our drawing room. And yet, the inspector was likeable and made me comfortable, to confess the truth, in my own house. And something of this sense at least, I realised, was due to relief at Mr Farquharson's having departed, taking his resemblance to Mr Hadley with him, though he had so flattered me with his invitation.

'Nay, if only all of our citizens were as sharp-eyed and willing. Although…' He glanced up at Sobriety again and waggled his head. 'Of course, I would also argue that ladies need take care a situation will not overwhelm them.'

'This was no matter for concern, since there was only one very small malefactor and three of us—and one of us a man,' Sobriety said at last, for he did seem to be addressing her above all. She looked quickly at me, for there was a sense between us—at least I felt it to be so—that we each continued to protect the girl, at least a little. Sobriety's attention then flicked back to the inspector, perhaps lest he interpret for himself our shared glance.

A whisper passed through my head as I watched the play at disinterested conversation between the inspector and Sobriety, for compliment and denial seemed set to continue for a while at least. *I think we have a further complication to our lives here.* There was a jolt beneath my ribs, small but distinct.

At last, Mrs Staynes brought the tea rattling into us.

Chapter Fourteen

Ladies—what of the world between us all?

…One might, indeed, think on how much we ladies hold in common with our men, and how much with those of our own sex, not merely within our own class, but also among those who dwell at every level of our teeming, complicated society.

It is we, ladies, who are designated the gentler of the two sexes; it is we who must look to harmony at home. We keep our hearth warm even while we look to the sterner sex for the means with which to do it.

Since it is we who must regard the hearth as of the highest importance and the welfare of those about us as paramount, and it is natural in us to look beyond and find in ourselves a sympathy for our sisters, who…

I laid down my pen and sank my chin into my hands. I stared a long few minutes at my writing. *Still, I do not know where I am headed.* I sighed and rolled the blotter over the ink. Surely, any reader would find risible my attempt at argument. I was no Ruskin, nowhere near it (my cheeks burned at this), nor yet Mrs Gaskell, nor… I held the paper and read it once more, before placing it back in my box, shaking my head.

Cissy and Mrs Staynes maintained their strained discourse for the next two days; it was difficult not to notice. Their conversations were never so loud nor indiscreet that a word could be distinguished; yet the tone was there in their murmurings—a certain whining, with sometimes a raised insistence from Cissy; from Mrs Staynes, very evident attempts at a strict authority broken by exasperation. Away from Mrs Staynes's censure, or continuing lecture, or reproof—or whatever it was that so exercised them both—Cissy did her work with a downcast air that fell just short of surly.

When these two crossed my mind (seldom as that was) I was as glad, really, that the matter seemed to be between themselves only. It was irregular, and Gwendolyn would have spoken harshly on the matter of servants' disagreements becoming audible to the rest of the house, but Gwendolyn (I breathed gently) was not here. To my question, 'Is everything as it should be, Mrs Staynes?', the housekeeper merely answered, perhaps too abruptly, 'Yes, ma'am.' I left matters there, for the thought of an evening with such superior folk as the Farquharsons, with music and dancing and an elegant supper, had turned me quite giddy, giddy as I had not felt since a girl a-tremble at the thought of my first ball. There was little space in my thoughts for matters other than the choice of gown and of its trimmings.

On occasion, a shadow peeked from a corner of my mind, that girl wrapped in once-gaudy rags, pain seeping from her like cold from ice. That is, it reminded me of the cause of all this, but I would not acknowledge it. *It is not to be helped: there are starvelings everywhere in London, and despite that, and apart from that, this party is occurring and is . . . and this invitation to it is to be celebrated.*

In any case, all the gaiety will be done and gone all too soon.

But stubbornly my mind turned back a moment to what hovered there so doleful and hopeless. I recalled a trip taken once to London with my parents in their carriage. We had become lost somehow and wandered for a time in the narrow, poor, noisome reaches of the great city. Tenements tottered above us and dimmed the light; our wheels lurched in the holes created by stolen cobbles. The stench was rich and coated everything with a rot both fruity and fleshly; we passed an alley where ragged folk had built a fire from refuse and bent over it like lost souls in Hades, their shadows wavering against the filthy walls. We travellers were looking at these ragged few, when hands reached up in sudden supplication at the carriage windows. Some begged, some clawed—a long scratching accompanied by a kind of toneless wailing that seemed to have no source in the dark— and all of us within gasped. Papa said to Mama, 'It is best to pay no heed.' But she replied, in a whisper that perhaps only I, her youngest daughter, caught, 'I am not certain of that.'

The notion of the ball made up (a very little perhaps) for the note sent by Mr Thackeray regarding my short piece about the weather. 'It was very kind of you to forward your thoughts to me. I sincerely regret…' he wrote, and I writhed at the implication of inconsequence. He was scrupulous in his manners; the note was polite, and he could not be faulted on it, I knew. Yet perhaps this made it worse, that here was a sentiment well-wrought—because it was well-repeated to all those other dull folk who wrote about the weather. Foolishly, I had taken my cue from these. Pieces of this kind *often* filled a page or two in other journals, I thought in a flash of pique. On receipt of the note, I had spent some twenty minutes sitting in my morning room. I drooped thus first in dejection and then in what felt like despair. To these already weighty two was added humiliation—Mr Thackeray must have surely thought me some kind of ninny, an empty-headed housewife of no account (though then I realised he addressed me as Mr A. Hadley)—but drifted eventually to notions that were very nearly optimistic. At least, they drifted back to where I had begun, when I first took up my pen these last few weeks. That this was but one instance of rejection, and in any case, he was correct: the weather was no topic at all.

In my thoughts, that shadow—never far away for long—peeped

out once more, thin as a handful of twigs and its scarlet skirt filthy, near hidden by night, but I shook my head to chase it away. For now, brighter things held my attention.

The blue—a light blue silk, modest enough for a married lady but glorious for a fair person, and edged as well as generally trimmed with fine black lace (Sobriety did this fine work throughout her sittings with Mr Hadley, and for many more hours besides). Sleeves to the elbow only, and a cape in black velvet; black lace and blue ribbon to dress the hair, and I would wear jet at my ears. There was a brief argument regarding the waist, for I fancied taking it in considerably, while Sobriety (who in any case always preferred not to tug too tight on laces) disapproved. 'Breathlessness is only attractive in the very young,' she said, and bit through thread.

There was a silence at this, with myself indignant yet unsure whether I had a right to be, until I judged it perhaps a good moment to discuss the evening meal with Mrs Staynes. The housekeeper was just then coming from the kitchen, evidently in search of me for the same purpose. As the door swung to behind her, it was clear that Cissy now murmured urgently with Cook, her aunt.

The business of the house took time enough to distract my mind from what an age it was for Dickie's reply to come. Finally—it was already late afternoon, and but a day until the great party itself—the knocker sounded and Cissy fetched a small envelope from the boy at the door. She dipped as she handed it to me, her face telling me nothing. 'Mum,' she said. The girl's brows were drawn together and she seemed hardly aware of her own gracelessness. I was, again or still, not inclined to discover the problem, while I did consider it may soon be my duty to do so. . . but in any case Cissy had already gone from the room. So I turned instead to Dickie's note.

This was long, considering its message. Dickie explained how he had thought he may be occupied tomorrow evening, but found he was not; and that his household was sufficiently settled for the moment—there were no sick children, for example—so that, yes (*at last we come to it!*), he was able to accompany me, his sister, although it did surprise him that this party should suddenly come to pass, and myself invited, and at such a time.

Thus I sat my turn with Mr Hadley, with George (at whose collapsing face I confess I glanced only briefly), but could not settle my mind either to read Mr Collins, or find any part of a journal still unread, or pick up my pen and write something. George wheezed and rattled gently on. After a time, I did open the newspaper to peruse the fashions that were there, but before long I was sighing in impatience. I ended by moving to the window to watch what small traffic there was in the street below. A fine drizzle, like mist become a slow spray, made men and women shrug closer into their coats and cloaks, and horses to hang their heads in endurance. I wrapped and unwrapped a blue satin ribbon about my finger.

This enclosed life! See how it is at its hardest when we realise what has kept us so…limited…all this time. I stroked the ribbon against my lip. *It is at its hardest when we consider there may, indeed, be some way to leave this behind us, even while we are not certain what that way may be.* I let the curtain drop back in place and looked at the clock on its mantel. *And that, in any case, nothing, when we have reached it, is assured of success.*

I wondered what it was that ragged urchins did on days like these, when rain fell like fine, insinuating silt over everything.

Shaking my head against such thoughts, I imagined, instead, that I danced and danced until lights and music merged and blurred about me.

I was surprised at my own appetite when the roast was served, though it did cool so very rapidly in the chill damp of the dining room.

Breathless—although Sobriety had in the main got her way and the waist had not been very much taken in—I stepped from the landau. This took some time, as vehicles there were in abundance, with all having, as a matter of course, to set down their passengers in genteel fashion at the proper place. Yet for all this, I had not yet quite recovered my breath, nor indeed my equilibrium, for the drive itself had so served to heighten my anticipation that I barely noticed what the other traffic did—either here at the Farquharsons' great house or on the streets coming here. It was just as well, I thought, that Dickie was with me, for I had kept my long story of the baby's rescue and the Farquharsons' gratitude from him until this night. Telling the tale to his exclamations was a very great satisfaction to me as we travelled, and I had had to retrace my descriptions more than once to remove exaggeration.

'But I, too, have a tale involving Mr Farquharson!' Dickie had said, which had the effect of startling me from my chatter.

'No! How is this?' I peered at him in the dark, streetlights jolting past, making with their glow a nimbus of the fine hair of his head. I could neither see his face nor guess his expression. 'What has occurred?'

'Oh, little sister, have faith!' He pinched my arm lightly. 'I am an investor now, and have already attached my small but earnest rope to Mr Farquharson's shooting star.'

'This is not cards, or horses, or some other form of gambling?'

'No, no. No such thing. Already I have put in a small amount, and the accounting has it that there has been an increase of twenty percent.'

'Money?'

'Well, yes, dear.' He kissed me on the cheek and I could tell that he smiled.

'Well, at last something goes well!' The tension fell away that had wrapped me around at the thought of the waters in which Dickie sometimes swam. I had always loved him best of my siblings for his pink-flushed enthusiasms, and yet also feared for him because of them. Still, if it was settled that there had been a real increase of his money, then all was well and all would be well. This was a happy thing, a most happy thing. *What a grand night this is!*

When we finally drew to a halt, I felt the entire vehicle must thrum from my trembling, and was grateful for Dickie's firm hand as I stepped to the ground. My breath misted in the thickened London air, all frostiness merging into foggy faerytale. *Had I but worn glass slippers!* I stayed a giggle.

Every window of Mr Farquharson's great mansion was ablaze, light pouring into the square that it dominated; the shifting, parting fog itself reflected this glory, this spectacle in every tiny droplet. The mansion was like a great, illuminated ship adrift in a mist-cloaked sea; and the carriages, that also parted this shining foam, were barques crowded in welcome about this grand vessel...

It was a few steps to the portico, and then a queue of couples awaited entry at the great door. Mr Farquharson's liveried men stood at attention by the columns at either side, their white-stockinged calves sturdy as posts. Other servants too did duty, dressed in a plain sort of formality—jacketed, and a smart, pressed trouser—with which they were uncomfortable, apparently, for these two or three such-dressed men shifted about in the shadows. One shrugged occasionally as if to make his jacket sit the better, and it was this that drew my mild interest, for otherwise they were for the most part silent. Perhaps they were there merely to keep an eye out.

I had only a moment for gazing about myself, having entered, at last, and reached the top of the first flight of stairs that poured itself to the edge of the cavernous vestibule (*this staircase wide enough, surely, for a public building! Two dozen at least could be accommodated there!*). Colour sprang up everywhere—for every plaster fruit or flower (and there were many) was painted to outdo nature—and gilt glinted from the frames of vast paintings crowded upon the walls. Such scenes there were from the hunt; landscapes so large one could imagine the breeze or count the leaves in the canopy of overhanging trees; portraits in full pomp. Great fronds in heavy arabesques rose from fat pots, and doorways were wide and high as fantastical portals. Everywhere rustled an acreage of skirts of lace or satin, splendid with flounces and laces and bows, coifs with a complication of feather and jewelled combs, and dark-suited gentlemen upon whose chests purred snowy waistcoats beneath intricate cravats.

Dickie sought directions from a liveried footman standing by a wall. Thus I was guided to the ladies' cloakroom, and spent some minutes there in divesting myself of my cape, having my ribbons adjusted, and receiving my ticket. For a moment, I paused in all this bustle and felt myself pale and grow cold. Supposing Mrs Charles were among the throng? I felt myself beset by reactions to this notion—*and what if she is? And she will think me degraded indeed to be thus disporting myself while Mr Hadley lies ill. And what if she does think so? And am I so low…and what of her?*

Dickie waited for me at the doorway when I emerged. 'Shall we find our host?' I could only nod, bewildered still at the cacophony of sight and sound. Mrs Charles was nowhere to be seen, so far at least, as I looked about myself at the sea of feathers and flounces and whiskers.

Mr Farquharson stood very tall in the centre of the landing, head and shoulders above the rest and an echo, indeed, of the dimensions of his own house, though walls and arches soared well above his head. Folk standing nearby waited to bow, and bob, and smile into his face, and ribbons and rosebuds dipped as they bent their heads. He received them all with a distant grace, and with an air a little as if he gathered them to himself. Consequently, it was quite ten minutes before Dickie and I achieved Mr Farquharson's presence.

'Dear lady, how delightful.' He looked about himself then, and gestured to a young woman, whom he introduced as Mrs Farquharson. This was a very small person, barely reaching to her husband's shoulder, whose beribboned head of posies (*perhaps too girlish for a wife*) was fixed firmly to dark hair in a profusion of trembling ringlets. She had a nervousness about her, as if she could never decide if it were best to do this, or that, or step this way or the other. Beside her, her husband's massiveness was as stone.

'Oh, Mrs Hadley!' The young woman spoke inaudibly in puffs (*I wonder for how much longer this young person's whispering will be attractive*, I thought). 'I have waited here especially to thank you, and to tell you how my little Steven does—' Mrs Farquharson's cheeks shone as if stretched. 'For he is right as rain...and all because of you!'

I could barely comprehend more than every second word or so, through a hubbub rising as each guest struggled to be heard above the others and above the efforts of a stringed ensemble playing some-where. The music came, I fancied, from beyond a splayed plant that gestured hugely from its vast brass urn with leaves like great hands, a captive from some heated jungle. *How does it survive?* I wondered, and then thought, *Strauss*, and then brought my unwilling mind back to little Mrs Farquharson. She had just finished with, I realised, '...all because of you!' and waited there with her mouth a little open and her eyes round and shining.

I replied with nods of my head and with graceful phrases.

'In Mrs Farquharson's eyes, there is no greater heroine than your dear self, madam. In which, of course, I concur, for you have rendered inestimable service to the house of Farquharson.' Mr Farquharson's voice was large, as he was large, while his wife's whis-pering was like stirring tinsel. 'Sadly,' he continued, 'I must attend my guests,' he bowed to me and to Dickie, 'and hope we may speak again later in the night. Please enjoy yourselves. Supper'—he indicated with his enormous hand a doorway where folk passed in and out—'is through there.'

Mr Farquharson surveyed his guests and the palace within which they swirled. 'My wife will be happy to acquaint you with some of our friends.'

Mrs Farquharson's own head hesitated back and forth, ringlets and ribbons and posies all bobbing, apparently in search of acquaintances worthy of the introduction. She slipped her arm through mine to guide me, with Dickie following, to a nearby group of persons. Introductions were made—to a deacon and a marquis, a dowager Mrs Grimsby, and a young man whose name I missed entirely.

Each bowed, and *how-d'ye-dos* said, but then silence fell over us all. The music, beyond that great tropical shrub or monstrous fern, ceased and then began again, and I could not help but turn my head toward it a moment. Mrs Farquharson's arm was growing hot in mine (*We all seem to steam in here!*). I made my face pleasant, and thought, *My reward will come.* The silence between us continued and Mrs Farquharson, as well, seemed similarly affected and concerned by the awkwardness evident in this group; but she could do little other than simper and nod as if animated by some form of conversation, though there was none that presently involved her. It is true that two—oddly enough, the deacon and the marquis—did speak with each other, in desultory fashion, although from the profiles presented to us it was clear it was not to anyone else.

'Been watching events in America? That Lincoln fellow, unsettling things with the South.' The marquis leaned into the deacon's white-whiskered ear.

'Well, slavery, you know. Still, interesting. I've investments, you know, in the North.'

'Yes, worth watching.'

Mrs Farquharson, to whom none of this was addressed, smiled and nodded, her eyes darting, and a growing strain evident between her brows.

Dickie raised his own brows to me.

Lapsed now into silence, the marquis and the deacon gazed about themselves, cheeks glowing like new and well-glazed buns. I imagined, behind the murmurous cacophony, the hissing in their brackets of all those lights on all those walls, as they heated the air about them more and more with each passing hour. We all steamed, I fancied. Each member of the group now stood wordless, looking about and searching each passing face for, it could only be surmised, some acquaintance or someone with whom it would be advantageous to be acquainted; for someone, indeed, who would rescue them from the growing social consciousness of this singular lack of conversation.

It gave me, at least, the opportunity to look about on my own account. *Such an array of persons! From high to . . . well, not low exactly . . .* I cast about for faces that I knew, well or otherwise, and then felt hot, embarrassed because that was what all seemed to be about. Mrs Charles, I was confident by now, was not in this crowd. Most of the folk that I could see were intent that their presence be noticed, but beyond this achievement were in the main at a loss as to how to spend their time. It was not, after all, very much different from other occasions I had attended with Mr Hadley.

There was at some distance, a gentleman with a confection of whiskers above his cravat that I recognised from a soirée among parliamentarians—and those who aspired to be parliamentarians. I bowed to him, and he to me, and I confessed to myself some relief that there was little possibility of conversation with him.

Young women in groups giggled past. They were galleons under sail, all swaying and dipping and gleaming, with young men as eager skiffs trailing in their wake.

'Ah. See there, our host!' Dickie murmured into my ear.

Mr Farquharson was weaving, slowly and overwhelming in his confidence—such as a roaming society gourmet might display, dipping into proffered viands or confectionary—in and out of small knots of people. As with my own companions, some of these visitors stood mute, staring about them for persons of note to acknowledge, until such time as they could catch Mr Farquharson's eye. Others chatted like birds in an aviary, and tossed the fronds and garlands in their hair or laughed in hectic excitement. Fashion was insistent at every point upon the floor, and each confection of dress was a burst of hue and shape and frill at violent odds with every other.

Mr Farquharson would stop, I saw, and the person he addressed grow pink and smile, casting a glance about to check that others had heeded their host's condescension. Sometimes the conversation was general, it was clear, and Mr Farquharson, with a genial if watchful nod at others as he passed, moved on like some stately, towering potentate. Other times, there followed something more serious: with questions from the guest, and responses of an evidently intense cast from Mr Farquharson. His beringed hand would rest upon the guest's shoulder, he would nod a moment and look up searching over one way or the other, until a clerkly man appeared, of slight build and with a face as sad as a monkey's. Then Mr Farquharson would bow and move on, and the clerk would stay to write in a small notebook he had removed, apparently just for this purpose, from his pocket.

There is purpose to this ball, beyond the dancing.

Chapter Fifteen

'Mr Farquharson's acolyte that you notice there, sister,' Dickie bent to my ear, 'is Mr Giles, his secretary.'

Curious, I watched Mr Farquharson speak in this way to a bishop, splendid in his apron and gaiters, as well as to a tall woman of middle years whose old-fashioned curls jiggled and bounced with every word, and to the Member of Parliament I had noticed earlier. Each time, Mr Giles, with that look of simian distress that was no doubt merely an habitual expression and not a mirror to his soul, would slip up behind his master, bow, and hold his pen at the ready.

A waltz from Mr Farquharson's large room struck up its three-beat time, and I swayed a little to the music. Dickie, I could see, gazed over several heads, first at the perambulating Mr Giles—himself with his eyes on Mr Farquharson and whomever he might speak with next— and then at the intricate beribboned headdress of a young woman whose skirt held at least twenty flounces. I swayed the more... *one, two, three; one, two, three...* I wished very much to prevail on Dickie to accompany me to the supper room, and realised that I marked time so obviously in order to catch his attention. It was very hot, also, and I realised I had a thirst for iced tea that was perhaps greater even than my desire to dance. When tea had been taken, it would be high time to take to the floor—the crowd being so great—for the ensemble did keep excellent time.

I was about to say so, when Mrs Farquharson touched my arm. It made me start a little, and I thought then that the little whispering woman might have been trying to get my attention for some minutes.

'Would you care to see my little Steven, dear Mrs Hadley?' She looked full into my eyes, and I, who had neither considered nor looked for this possibility, took breath and said, 'I would be delighted, of course.'

I suppose there is some obligation that attends the deed of rescue, I thought in duty, and it was with a twinge of regret that I looked about the twinkling throng. Dickie's attention was still with the travels about the crowd of Mr Farquharson.

'It would not do to abandon my brother overlong, of course,' I said. I placed my hand on his sleeve.

'Eh? Oh, of course, of course,' Dickie murmured, craning still over our heads. He realised only then, it seemed, where my hand rested, and looked, at last, at me. 'You will be anxious to dance, my sister, and have refreshment, if I know you—'

'In any case, I would not be responsible for keeping little Steven from his bed—' I began in the midst of this small confusion, but already Mrs Farquharson had my arm once more in a steamy embrace, and we were off, the two of us a flurry of my own blue silk and Mrs Farquharson's froth of pale tulle.

'Yes, you are quite right.' The little woman nodded her head as she hurried, so that the tiny daisies in her posies lost a petal or two. 'We must be quick lest Nurse has put him…' Her eyes grew wide at this, and her words died away. She seemed unable to both speak and continue our too-rapid swaying toward the nursery.

We rustled thus arm in arm, stopping to bow left and right to guests as we passed. As we swept through doors that closed behind us, the press grew less and then ceased. Corridors were more hushed, the lighting less bright, the shadows longer. Yet, everything here—as with everything in that more public part of this great house—I could see was new, brand new and shining with polish, carved with great intricacy, inlaid so that no seam could be discerned. Everything, from carpet to vase to heavy bureau, sang of the wealth that had bought it…and that not long ago.

At last, the nursery was reached, and its door, finally, closed behind us.

In the silence, where the noise of the grand party was but a murmur so distant it might only be fancy, a single lamp stood subdued on a table next to the large cot, itself an architectural feat of great craftsmanship, hung with netting and bows and satin fit for a princeling. A fire crackled mightily behind a guard to one side of this cot, and beyond that, an open chest that might have passed for a small boat was filled beyond its brim with toys both soft and wooden.

But it was all very quiet indeed, and the signs, I recognised, were not good for a visitation. Very likely, the young Steven was already enfolded for the night. I was still short of breath from the barely dignified rush (*nay, gallop!*) through this house's many chambers, its long corridors, its numerous doors—but whispered in a kind of gasp that it seemed we were too late.

'Oh!' Mrs Farquharson's eyes sprang pink and full of tears. I looked away and hoped the little woman had reserves of self-control from which she might draw—*what shall I say if she does not?*—but then I saw instead the shade in the corner. It moved, and revealed itself as the nurse bearing a small bundle.

'No, see! I was mistaken. We are just in time.'

'Oh, yes!' Mrs Farquharson's voice was a breathless squeak. 'Nurse, may we? May I show—?'

Please do not weep! This was a scene too far, surely, and she far too like the wringing, anxious girl that I myself had been. *I was not looking for this, for this…* My cheeks burned with recognition. My very thoughts themselves were left speechless. Suddenly, away from crowded pomp and splendid condescension and worshipful hubbub, here in hushed shadow and the snapping firelight was a mother pleading for the mere sight and handling of her own child, as I myself had done.

Her child. I looked at Mrs Farquharson. *This child.* I must brush from my mind the notion that there stood that tattered other in this room, as if standing where the light did not reach and watching, rather than shivering somewhere with the rats of this city. The girl, that other child, that took this child and loved him too.

How will this child know his mother? came the thought, unbidden and clear, and the name *Toby*, so that I thrust it away. *I would rather die than be as Mrs Farquharson.* I realised suddenly that this was no melodramatic phrase but the absolute truth. *And yet do I not lack my Toby still?* How much was Mrs Farquharson my mirrored self? I closed my eyes a moment, over the thought. *I would rather die.* I was obliged to clear my throat before I could speak.

'Come,' I said. 'Show me this brave fellow before he goes to bed.'

It was a subdued journey back to the crowd, chatter, music and lights, though Mrs Farquharson still had hold of my arm. Yet I had time to regain something of my dignity, and Mrs Farquharson time as well to wipe at her eye and retrieve her smile. She squeezed my arm, so that we veered a little off-course a moment. 'I think that we shall be the best of friends. I do indeed!'

I could find no words to say, but bowed my head at this clutching at love and regard. *Who is it that grabs at the first smiling face and claims such a relationship?*

'We shall go about together and show off our sons.' Mrs Farquharson tossed her head and laughed. 'What fun!' The buzz, like that of a distant hive, had increased for some minutes as we walked along, and finally the last door from the house's domestic quarters was opened and the chatter of hundreds leapt at us with full, immediate force. *From apiary to aviary once more!* I fancied, dizzied by it.

'See, there is your brother!' Mrs Farquharson nodded toward the crowd, and I did see Dickie standing at a small distance. But then certain guests billowed past, and it was only after they had moved on that I saw my brother was in florid and earnest conversation with Mr Farquharson, who nodded, spoke, nodded again and waved the clerk, Mr Giles, over with his notebook.

'Oh, I see he is in conference with my husband.' I glanced at Mrs Farquharson and understood that the two men were not to be disturbed. *More business, Dickie?* My hostess dipped her head to a couple, and introduced them to me, so that more *how-d'ye-dos* were exchanged and there was more gazing about by these people (whose names I do not recall) in search of a worthier introduction; until, glancing over, it was clear to me that Dickie and his host had finished their discourse. My brother seemed well pleased with whatever business matters had transpired. There he was, adjusting his cuffs and casting his own amiable gaze about. Mr Giles was gone, scurried, I supposed, somewhere into the crowd. Mr Farquharson's back could be seen at a little distance, another set of pink faces tilted up at him.

Dickie saw me and smiled. Describing a hesitant semi-circle around a woman who surged back and forth without discrimination, he arrived at last at my side.

'Adelaide, Mrs Farquharson, how was the young master?'

'Oh, as lovely as I remembered him, of course,' I said. Mrs Farquharson's face stretched into a smile once more, and I wondered if this young woman spent her time swinging like a pendulum from bereft despair to ecstatic gratitude, and thought that this would be a very wearying sort of life.

'So kind, so kind. Thank you.' Mrs Farquharson's smile continued for several moments until the *oompapa-oompapa*—which had halted for a few minutes—began again. 'You will want to enjoy yourselves. I shall be off, to attend… We shall have you to tea, and much more besides…'

We watched her progress away, and I turned to Dickie.

'Dickie! What do you do with Mr Farquharson?'

'Business, my dear sister.' He looked self-satisfied, and drew himself up. 'I have given Mr Farquharson my undertaking for a greater investment, which should render even greater dividend!'

'Dividend?'

'Profit.'

'Ah...' I thought everything that night twinkled like some children's fantasy, everything larger than life. The shadows of the nursery, and those darker shadows in my own mind, were far away. Young Mrs Farquharson, while nervous and apt to cling, was pleasant enough. Her only fault was her youth, really. Acquaintance with her might be a very good thing.

And here was Dickie, smiling, with another part of a tale full of happy endings. *I wonder if my own could be as magical... Ladies, surely, do also make investments.* The very thought of a life that held no uncertainty, that held every day some interest, where every day was guided by myself—this made me breathe fast, and it made my head swim.

'My mind does ring with all this right now, brother. Take me for refreshment and then to dance.'

Chapter Sixteen

My breath frosted even here in my own chamber, such was the time of year. Yet I was content beneath the blankets, worn out with the dancing I had had last night with Dickie—and some other gentlemen also. Still there stayed with me the remainder of that faery-tale twinkle, the glorious bewilderment of lights and movement, a kind of glamour cast on all who attended the Farquharsons' occasion, even while in a dark and ill-defined part of my mind there was also a heavy rankling to do with Mr Hadley. I knew not whether this last arose from an abiding resentment at him for all his past coldness and violence, from his contempt for and humiliation of me—even while he continued his unconscious ebb toward death—or from a guilty pity, in the fact that he must lie, empty, and stare at nothing by day and night. While I, it must be admitted, gadded about from time to time. It occurred to me there might have been some satisfaction, after all, had Mrs Charles been present at the great party. Herself similarly caught gadding . . .

I do, of course, maintain the wifely duties. I do. Did Mrs Staynes, I wondered, make judgement of me, or indeed did Sobriety do so? I felt sure Gwendolyn would, if she knew. *Dickie will not say, I am certain.*

Still, I did hug to myself the events that had shot my life through with interest these last weeks. *And last night, last night.*

'Mr Farquharson is such a man that he will carry us all with him to greatness,' Dickie had said in the carriage as he escorted me home, and I felt and hoped in my heart of hearts that it must be so.

I blinked at the cool light now showing through the lace at my window, and smiled. A warm and sleepy cat. It must be quite late; and what luxury it was, to lie abed in this way. And yet, I must arise.

Dear Sobriety, waiting now to straighten my chamber, would have known to leave her mistress be after such a night, and would therefore need alerting that she was needed. I rang the small silver bell at my bedside.

In my morning room, I stretched my feet in my shoes. There was a certain soreness and possibly a little swelling—I had danced more than I had intended last night—and consequently, some tightness around the toes. I smiled into my coffee at the small discomforts that served as reminder. And despite the sufferings of my feet, exaltation—nay, exhilaration!—had lasted through my exhausted slumber to my waking. Sobriety had laughed at me this morning: 'Keep still! You are like a schoolgirl! I cannot keep grip on your buttons!' *Sobriety is patient with me, it must be said, given how my little Methodist eschews ribbons, bows, and frills. All curls stretched straight; the plainest of buckles and buttons!* I smiled, and my heart was suddenly full of fondness for her who disapproved so, yet loved me.

I turned a page of the journal, meaning to find some news of America's troubles, since I had overheard talk last night. But my thoughts dwelt instead on the swing and sway of skirts, their sweep and rustle as the music gave time, and the babbling and chatter that passed back and forth, ebbing and swelling through great doorways beyond which the hopeful sought magical fortune.

If my adventures had put Dickie in touch with such a very successful and influential man of business as Mr Farquharson, and with his wife (who seemed so intent on developing a fondness for me), might this not herald the end of all my own troubles? I might not, after all, be obliged to nibble my way through a widow's mite, once Mr Hadley was gone. I might not be obliged to fade away from society's sight, banished into the gloom for the sin of not mattering. I might not be obliged to take guidance in all things from Gwendolyn, and Harry, and Mr Gordon, all of them in lieu of Mr Hadley.

Of a sudden, I found I had to breathe in deeply and then out, lest my eyes blur. For there came a rush of feeling; a grief for my mama, who I missed sharply, deeply; the more entirely because Gwendolyn sought so to supplant her. Gwendolyn would fail always to do so, would merely make thoughtless mess of her memory—for Gwendolyn had no banter, did not make a play of anything. It was not Gwendolyn who had gone in search of me one day when the great house was over-quiet and empty, and found me in my candle-lit cupboard; had crouched down to admire peg-dolls and misspelt tales of romance and daring, kissed me and crept away with her finger to her lips in promise to keep my secret. Gwendolyn did not make play with words and names; she did not find humour in anything much. Gwendolyn had not dipped and swirled, laughing as she taught me to dance, taking the part of a young man to my clumsy girl. 'You shall curtsey here, and I will bow, thus, as befits my manliness,' Mama had said, her voice pitched low as a boy's so that I laughed and lost my balance.

I thought, I closed my eyes gently a moment, *I had thought at that time that more would come from dancing, and balls.*

Instead, instead…the memory came and went like the slap of a hand. So like a slap it was to recall how, when I lay still stitched, slow and weak after Toby's wrenching birth, I heard Mr Hadley speaking with the doctor and that it became loud so I could not help but hear what he said. Later, though he held the babe with a large and possessive pride, he had turned from me in a manner so decisive, so…full of meaning that it made me shrink into my sheets. I would not bear him more sons, and he was angered by it.

Too long ago, surely, to affect me so now. I breathed out.

I put down the pages so that they lay like crackling sheets. *Instead of vanishing into a lonely burrow of Gwendolyn's making*, I mused, *I might become a hostess in very high fashion, with the assistance of the Farquharsons, and folk might well be invited to attend my own gatherings to discuss the times and the arts.*

Mr Hadley! And, with stabbing insurrection, *George! Do you see? I might succeed at your game!*

My thoughts were wavelets back and forth against the shore. *Dickie and Amanda will poke their heads out from under that perpetual cloud in which they live. The sun will shine for us all.* I put my head back against the cushion behind me and contemplated the little landscape on the wall, without at all seeing the field of corn depicted there. *We might all undertake a tour of the European places of antiquity. We might go further. Oh, yes…*

The shadow passed through my mind once more—the now-accustomed shadow of that ragged girl—and I frowned, winced as if at some small pain. *My every rising hope makes her seem the more diminished. How can this be my fault? Why do I feel I caused her pain? I did not! I did not!* I imagined that…egret…in her dirty, once-bright skirt as a member of that wailing crowd whose skeletal fingers had once scrabbled at our carriage window—though she had, of course, not yet been born into her pitiless world. *I might,* I thought in reassurance to myself, *take up charitable works among those who dwell in London without a home…*

For some moments now there had been, beyond the closed door, an urgent muttering, a rising and falling of voices. It had moved closer, having travelled from elsewhere in the house, from the landing, to various points upon the stair, and now was so near as to be impossible to ignore.

Lord, what now? Revolution? Beyond my own petty insurrections? I laughed to myself, just as there came a tap at the door at last.

There was a small crowd there in the doorway, it seemed. Sobriety held little Cissy's hand, and Mrs Staynes stood behind Cissy, and each face was pale as milk. I could not tell whether the universal pallor was due to pique, or nervousness or, indeed, fear. *Surely not*, I thought of the last possibility, *for I have never been very frightening. It must be admitted I am not frightening.*

In Mrs Staynes's case, it was very soon evident, the cause of her pallor was pique. 'I do beg your pardon, ma'am. I feel I should say that I was most reluctant to bother you in this way. Cissy has been… difficult…for some days…'

Ah. The cause of argumentation and poor temper is finally to be revealed.

The girl stared at the carpet and shrank against Sobriety. *Perhaps as if to hide in a fold of her skirt*, I thought, and understood by this that Cissy's white-faced fear was of Mrs Staynes.

'In any case, I did want to have it understood—'

'Mrs Staynes did want to leave you in peace, it is true,' Sobriety said. I thought how pallor always made Sobriety's eyes very dark, as they were now.

Mrs Staynes let out a breath, relieved perhaps at this understanding, that whatever was afoot was nothing, any longer, to do with her, and she would not be held to account. 'I must get back to Mr Hadley now. Mind yourself, Cissy.' She frowned at the back of the girl's head. Then, dithering a moment, she said, 'It is my opinion, ma'am, that the girl tells monstrous and shocking tales, most unsuitable to your ears. Her imagination must be curbed, and I wonder at her aunt.' With this rushed jib at Cook, she bobbed once and rustled away to the stairs.

I turned my gaze to the other two and raised my eyebrows.

'I am to learn at last what has so agitated my staff?'

'Yes,' Sobriety sighed. 'I have only been told what ails everyone this morning, myself, and I felt…' She wrapped Cissy's hand in both of hers. 'Cissy?'

Upstairs, Mr Hadley's chamber door was shut with a bang.

Cissy raised her other hand and brushed at her eye.

What is this? What now? I felt as though I was at the theatre.

'There is no call for nervousness, Cissy, though you must do your duty if what you say is true,' Sobriety said.

'It is, Miss. I—' Cissy's voice faded to nothing.

'Sobriety?' I said, thinking: *It is pantomime, with the audience obliged to take part.* There was a moment when I might have laughed out loud. *'Behind you, behind you!'* Oh stop it, I chided myself.

Sobriety took breath, and looked quickly down at Cissy and back at me. 'Cissy is quite certain she has recognised the gentleman, Mr Farquharson, the baby's father.'

'Oh yes?'

'Yes, only from Manchester, and under very different circumstances.'

'Well, yes, he does speak with a very little accent—'

'—Cissy says that Mr Farquharson is the Mr Forster who is a grocer in Manchester, fairly well known as such to Cissy's family...'

Cissy gripped and twisted her apron, her eyes round and fixed on the tiny side table that bore my cup. Sobriety closed her own eyes a moment and drew another loud breath.

'Yes?' I said into the pause.

'That is, this Mr Forster...'—Sobriety began to speak very fast so as to be almost incoherent, and I was obliged to concentrate—'... has a different family, mostly grown, and all living in Manchester, and none so grand as the Mr Farquharson living here in London.' Sobriety breathed out in a deep sigh. 'Ma'am.'

She then perhaps feared the point was not yet made. 'That is, Cissy says he has *two* families.'

I looked at Cissy. I think my mind had completely emptied of all thought at that moment.

'Mrs Staynes felt this may all be a young girl's fancy and its airing would cause too much of a disturbance.' Sobriety patted the child's hand. 'But I felt the disturbance may well be the worse for ignoring it.'

I turned my eyes to Sobriety.

'Thank you, Miss,' Cissy whispered.

Chapter Seventeen

Cissy hovered a moment in Mr Hadley's sick-room, holding the vase. She had dropped three objects to my certain knowledge since the inspector's visit alone. There was a bowl in the kitchen (the baize door had been open and I had heard Cook's shout and then the smash), then in the morning room a spool of thread, which rolled under the small armchair. Afterwards, a day spent at the centre of so much concentrated attention only fed this clumsiness the more. My piece of Sèvres tumbled, as the girl swung the feather duster, but Cissy (*heaven preserve us*) caught it before it struck the floor.

It was clear Cissy had not yet recovered from the strain of so much confrontation, not to mention from the extended fright of being for so many days at loggerheads with Mrs Staynes. *Poor child. She must have expected the tumbril at any moment.*

The girl seemed calmer now, and was perhaps to be trusted with the vase. It held white roses, speckled and overblown at this time of year, cut from our small arbour and placed in the crystal vase every other day. I wanted the vase taken from the little table by the window in Mr Hadley's bedroom. When the roses and vase were gone from there I, Adelaide Hadley, could place upon this little table my writing box and do my writing. As I had done before, but from now on, the roses would dwell elsewhere, and I would lay claim permanently to it. Its height and its size suited me. *This is a thing Mrs Hadley may do. This is a thing that Adelaide Hadley does.* The writing box, up until now an occasional visitor to this room, would take its place here also, always ready and set to one side on the tabletop. Until such time, of course, that this room itself was no longer in use by Mr Hadley.

After all... I breathed out slowly. Our looming circumstances did demand it, and there would, apparently, be no rescue. No gallant on a charger, or, more to the point, no bonds or shares would lift me and mine from penury. My only hero would be myself. I had gone beyond timorousness, gone beyond mere pastime; this hero's permanent place of work was here at this table. Here, at this symbol of my transformation, I may—I must—earn my keep. I must come out from behind the curtain and proclaim my craft…and hope I would be paid for it.

There was, to say the very least, much to think and write about, after the events of the past few days. Shock, perfidy, fraud. High society and base deceptions. Drama on a grander scale than I had ever dreamed of or been visited by in nightmare. Inspector Broadford must frequently witness such things. Was he so much as startled by the message I sent him after Cissy's tale was told us?

'Ma'am…' Cissy said, after a moment of looking around the room. Every surface was covered in Mr Hadley's personal things: his precious little bowls and pillboxes; his hinged containers fashioned in chased silver or with an Asiatic inlaid patterning in polished slivers of exotic timbers; his watch and chain, the silver-backed hair and clothes brushes, the pomade, the tray of shaving brush and blade and towel. And there were the carved busts and carved animals that had been collected or given as gifts. And above it all, Mr Rossetti's painted woman pouted down, robust and forward as a flame on the wall behind the bed of the faded invalid.

Each thing is linked to another. No thing exists entirely on its own. Each person, event, object has something at its tail. Nothing is simply done, ever.

The delirium of Mr Farquharson's party and the ecstasy of hope that attended my sleep and my rising did but last, after all, a moment in time. The descent was rapid, the gloom that settled then was due to disappointment, and, I was nearly ready to confess, to the realisation of myself as foolish and so very, very easily duped.

Nothing is simply done.

'Oh, take the vase to the morning room, Cissy. I will think about it later.'

Cissy left the room, holding the vase to one side so as to see her way past the roses. Petals fell to the carpet; I bent to pick them up, and sat by the sickbed stroking the petals without thinking until they went from satin to a damp, greying bruise. Mr Hadley breathed steadily like a saw in rhythm and stared all unknowing with his pinkened eyes at some point an arm's length before his face. (Things with him these days were very different indeed, from the time of a previous illness caught while away on business, some ague that laid him in his bed and had him calling out or thumping his cane upon the carpet or ringing a little silver bell several times every hour. The household, including myself, his wife, was a-running up and down with hot drinks and cold, bringing foods and taking them away again uneaten, fetching journals and, in my case, reading them to him. Nothing pleased him, though it was a mercy eventually that he had shouted himself hoarse and must sip quietly at his brandy-and-honey.)

Cissy interrupted my reflections, arriving at the door with my writing box in hand. I held it while the girl carried the little table back to the window where the light was best. She lifted away its lace cloth before I put the box down. It was a little like a ritual, a ceremony of dedication. Cissy placed the chair at the table and was about to leave the room when I called her back. I gave the petals, creased now as well as bruised and pressed together, into the little maid's hand. The door closed too slowly behind the girl, for she was attempting not to bang it.

Do I trespass, Mr Hadley? In this corrupt world of yours? George?

The steady rasp of my husband's breathing was again the only sound, bar the ticking of his mantel clock. I listened, suspended a moment: *How time does follow us about.* I rested my hands on the polished walnut surface of the writing box. It was cool, sturdy with its brass edging, and I looked at it as if it were not the writing box I had used many, many times before for letters, notes, and lists. It was as if it was something new, and I would be surprised at what might be inside it. I shook my head the smallest fraction, and rubbed between my eyes. My writing box, in truth, was merely my writing box, I knew, yet I stroked it once more before reaching for the key at my waist and turning it in the little lock. I opened the lid, extracted a stylus and the brass rocker blotter, chose a nib, and selected several sheets of paper.

There I was, my foot upon a path at last. Women such as myself did nowadays take pen to paper and, sometimes, even earn a living thereby. This was both a little shocking and a little thrilling. But in any case, what was left to me after the airy dream of an independent income from investments was blown away on the breath of Mr Farquharson's disgrace?

I sighed. One piece had not been accepted, but the next may be.

I could very nearly smile at this.

The great Mr Farquharson's star was now brought very low, and all respectable people obliged to turn their backs to him. I had rushed yesterday to Dickie to warn him as Sobriety waited upon Mr Broadford's arrival. For this was crime, shocking crime, and I must report it, and did so. Inspector Broadford, by return note, announced his intention to visit in order to interview our little witness. That I had been associated in any way with that man, Mr Farquharson, caused me sick dread, especially as I recalled how nearly I had succumbed to the promise of his investments.

Dickie, when he heard the news, could not form words for a

long time, while florid patches fled across his face, much as painful thought no doubt fled through his mind. Amanda, her eyes on his face while he looked away, placed her hand on his shoulder. She herself had her mouth set firm as if it took some self-control to do so, as if she might otherwise weep, or as if her gorge revolted.

'Of course, one cannot be further associated,' Dickie said at last; yet I thought he struggled, in making the very self-evident statement, to convince himself of this.

I kept my voice steady, so that he could be in no doubt. 'No, indeed.'

'No.'

'And it must be made clear that any understanding arrived at last night between you and Mr Farquarson is no longer so.'

'Yes.'

'Yet, there is still the prospect of a small profit—did you not tell me?—with the sale of your existing investment, is there not?'

'Yes, yes.' Dickie made to straighten his shoulders, though his mind was still so clearly not at rest. 'I must set about this straightway.'

'Yes,' I said. 'And then there will exist no more link.'

'Yes. That is to say, no.'

The quiet that followed was smudged with distant shouts from the children, for Dickie and Amanda's offspring were by nature and nurture boisterous and untamed. Amanda looked across at me.

'May I suggest,' she glanced at Dickie, 'that we need not disturb Gwendolyn with this news. That Dickie…that we…'

'No, no. We need not. Of course not.'

A door banged upstairs and running feet made a racket down and then up the stairs. We foolish adults, meantime, were lost each in a personal world, pondering lost dreams and the appalled recognition of what must be seen as a very close shave with disgrace and penury.

I set up the sloped writing surface, laid new paper on it, unscrewed the lid of my inkwell and set it back in its slot. I would not, I decided, continue with my call to the 'Ladies'. My way was lost there, and all would surely recognise it. I would begin upon another theme. I took a breath and felt for a moment the tension of those tiny voices hissing in opposition within me: *I am too fearful, weak, courageous, absurd, rebellious…foolish, foolish woman…* I had had one lesson already in humiliation. *I have exposed myself to contempt.* The paper sat virginal, white, expectant.

Or is it that I am arrogant, that I assert myself in unattractive fashion…or that I simply do not have the courage of my own arrogance?

I let my breath out.

I have not enough light.

I pushed the little table forward to make space for my rising, pulled the great brocaded curtains open to their furthest extent. I hitched up my skirt so that the hoop beneath should not pinch, sat, pulled the table toward me and smoothed the paper, which was already without a wrinkle.

I dipped the nib into the ink. My hand hesitated over the blank page.

Mr Hadley wheezed and then he coughed. It was a light cough, but it cut through the rasping back-and-forth, back-and-forth of his breathing and the slow tick of the clock.

I held myself still: it was *his* cough, surely, unlike any of the sounds he had made since the day he fell down. Familiar as a memory, the cough of the man who ruled here, not so long ago. I sat, looking at the hand that held the stylus.

No.

I could not look elsewhere, certainly not at Mr Hadley. Was he waking? I was cold—as if a damp shadow climbed my neck and stroked my face with ice—and yet while I felt cold there was the prickling of perspiration across the top of my lip and on my forehead.

He coughed again. A little pair of coughs, and they held behind them a trace of his voice. *Dear God, I can hear his voice*, as with the clearing of his throat on so many mornings—it felt so long ago— between the sip of coffee and the twitch of the newspaper.

No!

I rested my hand on the slope of paper, stared at the clean steel of the nib with its wet tip of ink.

I could not take in air as I listened to his breathing. I was intent on sound and its meaning, listening to Mr Hadley around and behind the tick of the clock, as if there were a small page of sound between the swing of the pendulum, to be read with a fine and concentrated scrutiny. Mr Hadley breathed on; he did not cough again.

Does it sound as it did yesterday, today, half an hour ago?

I was certain, at last, that his breathing sounded as it had done since his illness.

I looked across at my husband. He stared, as ever, at a point an arm's length before his face, his blue eyes innocent of knowledge or passion or power, even of this place and his position in it, his face collapsed in folds and no animation therein to give expression. Still, and unchanged. There was a trickle of saliva just beginning at the corner of his mouth, though Cissy had wiped there shortly before.

My hand, I realized, was shaking, and I put the pen down. I was breathing again myself now, yet it came in gusts with the creasing of my own face, hot now, which I held in my two cool hands until everything calmed—my breathing, the moment of dry weeping, the tumult of panic.

Forgive me.

When all was steady within me, I pushed back the table, rose and went to his bedside. Perhaps the cough merely indicated thirst. I took

149

up his glass and tipped a teaspoon of water between his lips, dabbing with the cloth at the thickened, whitish deposits moist in the creases at his mouth.

I sat again, pulled the table to myself, took up my pen and dipped the nib in ink. I wrote:

The great city is built upon lives in layers, and each life made up itself of layers, these lying in darkness, darker as each covering is pulled aside, like heavy curtains dirty with the dust and motes of generations...

Part Three:

In which Adelaide and Sobriety confront darkness and demons

Chapter Eighteen

. . . Suddenly a shadow flits, as someone runs for dear life away from us. In our eyes, this person may have done wrong. But if we have a soul, we might recognise that in some species of wrongdoing there is a wordless—and perhaps a little or very mad—reaching at happiness. How might, after all, the very wretched find joy? For happiness is something little understood down here, where all is lawless and without mercy. Here, happiness is a thing only ever glimpsed from afar, glowing from a warm-lit window illumining families and beloved babies, love and smiles. To us, this window forgets to tell the whole tale of disappointments and triumphs, of occasional quarrelling or affection. But from afar, all is perfect, happy, lit and glowing from within.

Venturing forth in our carriage, as I so rarely do, I said to my companion that it was as if we were tourists in our own city. The noises grew of so many thousands of working lives, and strands of music laid upon each other until they had lost their melody and were like so many files rubbed against metal. The vast conduit that is the Thames reminded us with some force that Mr Bazelgette is now a-building his own mighty work, and that tourists such as ourselves might visit and wonder at it.

And so we did, that windswept day, and also learned that the misery passed down through generations of the miserable can make its sad nest in the shelter provided by the great tunnel whose construction, in a testament to science and engineering ingenuity, is the very talk and marvel of our modern time. . .

My pen continued for a time until my writing came to its finish. I wiped my nib, and read what I had written. *It will suffice. Nay, it is quite good! Lord!* What a relief I felt, so much that I stretched my arms out wide—as far as the seams might allow—as if I reached beyond myself. *Which indeed I do.*

Mr Hadley lay against his pillows, the cloth beneath his chin and a shawl about his shoulders. Within it, he seemed smaller, somehow.

In the street, Sobriety's skirt bobbed, swung, bounced a little, purposeful and very busy. *A short person will often look very busy, when walking.* I gazed down from the window, arms tight folded, leaning against the curtain. A leaf, curled and dead, skittered to one side as Sobriety passed. Her shawl, not her very best but woollen and warm, was pulled tight around her shoulders, and her breath puffed in balls of mist from beneath her bonnet before she moved through and dispersed them into the air. I watched as she passed under the branches of the tree, where three or four brown leaves still clung, and then out of sight. When she had passed by, one of the leaves fell, slowly in arabesques, onto the space she had occupied.

I counted to twenty, by which time the letter Sobriety held might have been posted, to lie for a short while in the dark before being collected to begin its journey to its publisher.

Its publisher. There. It is done.

I had chosen to send my written piece once again to *The Cornhill Magazine*, because it was very new and much spoken-of. Certainly, it had been spoken of by Mr Hadley, who had on occasion even argued out loud with it, as if it were a dissenting debater. Many new and interesting writers were published therein, some of whom were women. *Women,* I had to admit, *who do not write of the weather.* When Mr Hadley was away on business, I had settled happily to read episodes of Mr Thackeray's "Framley Parsonage", and thought he must be a fair-minded person to have been employed as editor of the magazine. Finding that this latest edition included a piece entitled "Unto This Last", which was listed as Essay IV, or "Ad Valorum" under its general title, I searched about for and discovered the last three editions and settled to reading Essays I to III. I had not yet fathomed much of the argument, beyond that it was critical of what the author called the 'political economy', and I was intrigued as to who the author—given only as 'anon'—could be.

Altogether, what was most clear was that folk in journals did argue much and with each other in these pages, and that this perpetual argument represented so much of the country's mind.

There was risk, of course, in this public argumentation. Attention was attracted thereby; talk was, of course, engendered in parlours, and the writer (himself or herself) become at last a matter of discussion. *I wonder if I do not take the risk—wilfully, even—of setting myself beyond the pale.* I was struck, again or at least more distinctly, by the thought that I did so not just by writing so very publicly, but by seeking publication in *The Cornhill Magazine* itself.

Yet Sobriety's other errand for me was to purchase a simple writing book, a notebook, to serve as my own writing journal. In this I would hide notions meant to be private, or those I was not yet brave enough to declare in public, or ideas of which I was not yet entirely certain. *It will be my thoughts' hiding place*, I decided.

I watched the empty street. A dog entered my patch of pavement, thin and matted, with the bones of its pelvis evident and the skin there balding from illness or rubbing, but otherwise self-assured. Or perhaps this cur was so experienced with the world that it simply knew what to expect. The dog trotted from point to point, sniffed where it discovered emanations of significance, and moved on, its pelvis sawing up and down. The pavement was empty again, for the moment.

Of a sudden, I was overcome by what I suppose was a kind of literary stage-fright. I brought the knuckles of one hand to my mouth and pressed. *Lord. Perhaps I should have read it through just one more time.* I let out a heavy breath. *Sometimes anticipation is very like dread.*

I let the curtains drop back into place. The little table was set once again near the window, for the light and the dozen little distractions of the street, and held my coffee and folded journals. A letter, unopened as yet, rested upon the small pile, with Toby's careful, childish loops on the envelope.

At the other end of the room, where the light was dim, Mr Hadley lay shadowed, probably asleep. His eyes, at any rate, were closed.

Lately, he had begun to emanate a light stench, which arose from the sores that bloomed on his back and legs where he lay against the bed. The doctor had sent his boy over with a salve, and this was applied daily, and the wounds checked closely, though there had been no sign of improvement so far as I could see.

All was still after the energy that had been this morning's complete change of bedding—a flurry that had become a controlled one, now that the household had converted to ritual all the needs of Mr Hadley as a comatose person. These rituals themselves were become enfolded within those of the house, and involved everyone save Cook and Mr Brent. While Albert held Mr Hadley in his arms, the domestic dance worked its concentrated way around Mr Hadley. There were turnings, removals, and replacements—of palliasse, overmattress, and underblanket, as well as the unfolding of well-starched sheets—and Mrs Staynes' quick check (bent close as possible to the seams) for any sign of vermin. Finally, Mr Hadley was laid, long and loose, back down upon the bed and his arms tucked under the counterpane. This was followed by the settling, the patting-down, the carrying away of soiled piles, until the room was quiet and empty again, save for the regular dragging of his shallow breath and the meagre rise and fall of his chest, and the snapping of the fire in its hearth. Dust motes agitated for a while in a shaft of weak light from the window, until they, too, returned to a steady floating. Beyond the closed door, voices murmured across the landing as Mrs Staynes and Cissy heaved at another palliasse and overmattress, and changed the bedding in my room.

I contemplated Toby's letter, hesitated, and reached instead for *The Illustrated London News*. This I opened, tilted the whole with a rustle toward the light, and peered at the wearied, passionate faces; at the arms outstretched in praise of Garibaldi, hero, conqueror, disruptor, creator of a new world entering, in operatic triumph, the coastal harbour of Cape Di Europa, Naples. I lifted my head just a little as the front door downstairs thumped close behind a returning Sobriety, and then lowered my eyes again to the newspaper. Here was tumult and chaos that might speak itself in a foreign poetry, but never in these quiet streets of London. We were never so stirred, our blood not prone to flame. I could not imagine these near-operatic gestures here on Landsbury Street, where carts and carriages clip-clopped and creaked past our windows.

This urgency is foreign to us. I turned to an engraving of the Battle of the Volturno, Garibaldi's victory against the Bourbons. Such opera.

It all brought to mind the time when I was a girl in my private cupboard under the stair, when I had come across Lord Byron's *The Siege of Corinth*. The volume sat on a high shelf where, no doubt, it was hoped I would never venture—since civilised folk liked his poetry well enough but were bewildered at his sensual adventuring. I read it by candle, and remember still these lines:

Many a vanished year and age,
And tempest's breath, and battle's rage,
Have swept o'er Corinth; yet she stands
A fortress formed to Freedom's hands.

I let one page drop and reached for my cup. I looked for a long moment to where the brocades hung at the window, heavy and ready to be drawn against months of cold. The lace behind the weighty, figured material suggested light without struggle, with all sound filtered, calm and distant.

In the shadowed room, one corner of Mr Hadley's mirror, tilted in its polished mahogany stand, caught and reflected the light in a dulled gleam, like pewter. *When he dies, I suppose we shall drape his mirror in black.* I contemplated my husband. *As well as all the other mirrors in the house; as if we cast a shroud over the household life. Should we?*

I shook my head to clear it, took a breath, and reached at last for Toby's letter.

Toby's uprights spread across a very few lines. He had never chattered much to his mother, by spoken or by written word. He began *'Dear Mama,'* and my mind could see the schoolmaster—cousin, surely, to a dark and angular stick insect whose illustration had appalled me once years ago—with hands clasped behind his back, bent over each boy in turn as they wrote at their desks. The schoolmaster would ensure, by this close scrutiny, the proper level of filial fondness:

> *...I shall be home for three days of the Michaelmas holiday, beginning Friday, to visit and pay my respects to Papa. Phillip Miller's Mama and Papa have kindly invited me to stay for the remainder of the holiday, and there was no time to enquire of you, so that I said I was certain you would be pleased for me to go, since things will be at sixes and sevens, as Papa needs so much care now...*

There was a break here—an overlarge space, as if Toby lifted his head to smile at his friend Phillip.

They live in Richmond. Phillip has a pony he wishes me to see.

I glanced again at the window, feeling humiliation and a whiff of outrage at the thought that Toby might make such arrangements without consultation with his mother, whereas he would never have presumed to do so without his father's permission. Then I thought, *Friday?*

Outside Mr Hadley's bedroom door, Cissy thump-hopped down another tread of stair as she rubbed polish into the banister. Next would come the polishing of brassware, and doorknocker, as well as other sundry items and fixtures. These were Cissy's Thursday duties.

Friday is tomorrow! I had forgotten the Michaelmas holiday.

I was uncertain as to whether to claim a hurt disappointment or an abiding relief that Toby would stay but a short time . . . regardless, other emotions shrilled with criticism of this unnatural mother.

I had forgotten.

How could I forget?

I folded Toby's letter and replaced it in its envelope. Rising from my chair, I opened the door and called through to Cissy about the airing of Toby's room.

By luncheon, the heavy hush of the dining room and the cold had joined to became one living thing, almost, and impossible to ignore. Fingers stiffened and there was a suggestion of frost with every breath. There was a palpable damp. I lifted the silver spoon to my mouth. The soup was already tepid in its shallow bowl. The rich carpet in this grand dining room was become a sponge subject to a subtle rot. It smelled thickly of a frosty yet foetid moisture, more and more pungent as the season progressed to chill. The fireplace—since it was hardly worth preparing a fire for the sake of luncheon—sat empty, its blacking innocent of comfort. The fire in this room had, in any case, always proved ineffective.

Sobriety sat next to me at table, as had become the habit since Mr Hadley's illness. She had not removed her shawl upon her return from the post, and was swathed in it as she, too, dipped her head toward her raised spoon.

We would be a deal happier in the kitchen.

I rolled my eyes at myself. *How my standards fall!*

The meal was brief. Sobriety and I were quick afterward—almost running, with short, pattering steps—to the morning room, its own fire and its clean air. (*How is one side of this house damper than the other?* I wondered, my teeth clamped together against the chattering.) The morning room was somewhat transformed not just by haberdashery (now stacked folded on the windowsill) but also, and still, by its newest tenant, the sewing machine, which took up a deal of space. And, in the absence of any other notions as to where it might dwell, it seemed likely the machine would inhabit the room for some time. The footstool had been drawn up to this iron contraption as if the two were a pair. Once again, it was clear how awkward the disposal of this machine had proved—there was nowhere here where one was not obliged to find the space to walk around it.

We two women went straight (but for the negotiating of the sewing machine) to the hearth and held white-gloved fingers to the flames there, each silent until the heat began to be felt and the relaxing of tension allowed for the unclenching of teeth. After some minutes, Sobriety sighed and began to unwind her shawl. She moved away and sat at her accustomed end of the settee, closing and moving aside the copy of *The Englishwomen's Domestic Magazine* with its plates of the latest fashions. She tipped her head back, her eyes closed a moment, before lifting it to examine the lacework she intended to attach more firmly to my engageante.

I laughed. 'I fancy we are not the privileged, when it is we who are forced to eat in such a torture chamber!'

Sobriety might have answered but for the rapping of the knocker at that moment, and so she and I waited, instead, while Cissy thumped her way down to the front door, paused, and then walked more slowly, and with less noise (*blessedly*), to the morning room door. She knocked and said that my brother, Mr Broom—'That is, Mr Harry Broom,'—was come to visit, as he stepped through himself and Cissy was obliged to move, sidestepping in her hurry, out of his way.

Chapter Nineteen

I announce the birth of my latest, a girl, this very morning!' Harry filled the room with this—for the sweep of his arm was meant as drama and the flap of his frock coat, evidently, to be reminiscent of a pantomime magician. His waist was so expanded these days as to threaten the buttons of his waistcoat. It seemed the space where he stood was suddenly all his own, and filled with his presence over and above all else, where a moment ago it had been as benign—as calm, as enfolding—as home.

I began to exclaim at the good news, as one does, though I knew (while I did not mention) that my sister-in-law must be reduced by this birth to an extreme fragility. This was her eighth lying-in and she had never been especially robust. For many years now, she had always seemed, by turns, swelling up or bearing a red-faced child wrapped in laces and shawls from settee to settee. Harry was, I often felt (perhaps unkindly) less interested in the diminution of his wife's strength—nay, her very self!—than in keeping count of his children, particularly of his boys.

Moving further into the room, Harry dropped his arm and wagged his head—as he had always done to his younger sister, and as he had also done, I recalled, to a succession of family puppies.

'—And I come to escape from the army of women intent on wearing holes in the carpet with their scurrying!'

I regarded him who came with such news—the birth of a child—but seemingly so uninterested in it, thinking: *This is unusual in Harry. It would be more like Dickie to present such tidings in person.*

Poor Dickie. I felt a small, familiar mourning for Dickie, the hero of my childhood. He had passed from teasing fondness of his little sister, years ago now, to share hearth and table with his wife, and to raise his children. There had been little contact between Dickie and me in recent years, not just because of our separate parenthoods but also because of Dickie's shrinking embarrassment at his own repeated losses; at his shame, so increased by Gwendolyn's uncomplicated scorn and the onus of her accompanying act of rescue. And, it must be said, his absence from my life was also the result of Mr Hadley's treatment of my brother as somebody beneath his notice. *Poor Dickie.*

And yet, I very nearly smiled at the revival in these last days of my closeness with my favourite, though I did not, since it was not Dickie that now stood and preened before me.

What has Harry really come to say?

For a moment, it was as if I stood to one side and observed (as the ghost of myself) as Harry Broom laid claim to primacy of place by gesture, by the size of his voice, and by his representation of the hard and manly world that prevailed beyond this house and room. We ladies gazed up at him with our soft faces, seated, as we were, in this womanly room embroidered so prettily and curtained away from the world. The very vase on the small table, filled with what few roses and foliage could be found this time of year, gave emphasis to my domestic womanliness. I saw his assumption and it was both sharply delineated and foreign to me, I realized. It harkened back to that time—*both a few days and a century ago, lord!*— before my household and I had been so shaken up and had had to find its own new shape. *Our own new shape.* Before, indeed, I had sought to make my own connection with the outside world.

But I sank back, despite myself, into the so-recent habit of deference. It was with an almost physical sensation that I felt this deeply unwanted slide back into meekness, while all my authority fled away, save that of hostess.

I turned to Cissy, grey as a mouse in shadow behind the guest. 'Sherry, I think, Cissy. The Oloroso. Sobriety will help you.' Sobriety glanced at me. She rolled up her lacework and rose, shook out the folds of her skirt, dipped and murmured a good afternoon to Harry, and left with Cissy, closing the door behind her.

I watched as they left the room. *And are we not also an army of women?*

Some remnant of the person who rescued babies existed still within me, and stamped its feet in rebellion. At least, I saw myself in imagination thus, stamping my feet.

But this too faded almost immediately, in the face of Harry's complete ignorance of any change whatsoever. In my imagination, I was a child who stamped her feet, and now stopped in awareness of her childishness. The past weeks faded and what had loomed large—the musts and must-nots— were no longer important, were paltry and short-lived, colourless and infinitely small. It was all sham, a farce, a pretending to be something it was not. An absurdity. Of no account.

'And how are they?' I said, of my sister-in-law and her own new baby. My voice was without resonance or weight, after the noise of Harry's entry.

I am sulking like a child. Foolish woman.

I closed my eyes a moment over my internal disturbance and sought calm. *So. Is my face now pleasant for him?*

Harry had his thumbs in the pockets of his waistcoat, where there was precious little room for them. He looked around the room—at its small landscapes on the wall, the portrait of Mama, the tables and sideboard, inlaid and brought to a glow with polish, the vases and doilies, the porcelain bowl of some antiquity and my own efforts at decoupage—as if at a marketable proposition. This habit, which had grown after his achievement of the chief partnership of Papa's business, seemed more about behaving in a masterful manner than anything to do with knowledge of the value of things. For in this, he was merely Mr Hadley's apprentice.

I looked at him and knew that Mr Hadley's illness, his wandering in powerlessness and incoherence, gave Harry by contrast invisible inches to his stature.

My brother bent to peer at the sewing machine before adjusting his coat for sitting.

I sat, aware of every rustle, of the very pace of my breathing.

I waited for Harry to impart the real intention behind his visit. *Why am I so very irritated?* I was testy to my very fingertips. *Why is this?* I looked at him, benign with the purring confidence of a figure in the City. *Because we have been remaking our world, and you have come to stamp upon it.*

'Who?' Harry asked. 'Ah. Sarah—sleeping, I fancy. It went on all night. The doctor seemed complacent, so she must be well enough.' He nodded with something like a smile, in something like my direction.

'And the baby?'

He laughed. 'Yes, yes. Very small. Very red! Perfectly well, I'm told. Elizabeth, named for Sarah's aunt.'

He leaned back in his chair and nodded toward the sewing machine. 'That is new.'

I nodded.

'Practical, I suppose, given the circumstances. Good girl. No change with George, I suppose?'

I shook my head, went to speak but found Cissy was back with the tray, on it two small crystal glasses and the decanter of sherry. When Cissy had laid the tray on the table, I poured the wine. I cleared my throat as I handed Harry his glass.

'No change with Mr Hadley, and not likely to be any improvement, Harry.' *That was abrupt, perhaps.* I softened my reply. 'It is a matter of waiting, I'm afraid.'

'As we thought; as we thought.'

His man, I could not help noticing of a sudden, *has doused him with cologne. It will outlast his departure for hours.*

I was still most annoyed, I realised. It was as if annoyance had struggled out from between laces that had bound it and now I, in turn, must struggle to gather it up and contain it once more. I clutched at it while my brother filled his chest and began to speak of family.

'We were discussing your circumstances, Adelaide. We fancy these will be reduced somewhat after George has passed, is this right?'

I could see in my mind's eye my family's heads a-nodding; I could see Gwendolyn rapping the tablecloth with the ebony edges of her black-laced fan until there was silence enough for her considered pronouncement. All of the children would have been sent from the room, and the tea stewed until it was unpalatable in the great silver pot...since Gwendolyn always took a great length of time before pouring.

I no longer know how to speak to Harry. Too much has changed, and he does not even apprehend it.

I sat unmoving, very still with my glass in both hands and staring at the fluid in it, a thimbleful of deep gold that would slide down like syrup. The humiliation of my family's conversation about my circumstances—no doubt put by Gwendolyn as 'the problem of Adelaide', or something like—hung in the room. In my mind, the whole tribe walked in a circle around me, peering, shaking bonneted heads, reaching to prod with gloved fingers.

I do not think I have ever liked sherry.

'How went your interview with Doctor McGuiness? I have heard nothing from him.' This I said, admittedly, with a flash of vindictiveness, which I banished immediately as being unworthy of me.

Harry's glance was sharp. He had little appreciated our sending

him forth to 'speak' with Mr Hadley's medical man. 'It was thought
the prospect of mutiny by the respectable Doctor not worth the risk.
As I suspect you foresaw.'

I think this is some sort of acknowledgement. I shall take it as such. 'I may
have done.'

'You understand, of course, that Gwendolyn's interest is always
that the right thing be done, the proprieties observed and—'

'"One does as one ought",' I said.

'Just so.' Harry paused to glance at me once more, as if not certain
of what he saw there. He sipped at his sherry. 'This is the important
part she plays, and we allow her this.'

I folded my hands in my lap.

'In any case,' he went on, 'Gwendolyn proposes that we all set up
a small annuity for you. And I am in agreement. Something can be
drawn up, when the time comes, through George's Mr Gordon, who
will aid you in making an accounting to us.'

There must be no Brooms too obviously down-at-heel for show,
I knew. I let out a long, slight breath, and sat for a moment more
regarding my glass until I felt I could raise my eyes to Harry.

'Monthly would be the thing, I expect, and special applications
should there be a need for some major expenditure.' Harry sipped,
his attention trailing to our mother's favourite seascape upon the
wall, as he reached into his inside pocket. 'Indeed, I have here a letter
from us both, Gwendolyn and me, that requests details of your
expectations.' He passed the envelope to me. I was slow to take it.
'Another has been sent to Mr Gordon, who will await your direction.'

My mind emptied. I knew not what to say to this—neither *yes* nor
no seemed possible. The one had me packed like last season's fashion
at the back of the wardrobe, forever, while the other would call down
a wrath such as I had never experienced . . . *How may I declare myself
for neither?* I asked myself, with very little hope that it was possible.

Chapter Twenty

Delay! I must delay! It was as if I struggled to keep closed my door while my whole family pressed against it on the other side.

Take three breaths…

I turned the letter over in my hand. 'I will consider this,' I said at last, and placed it unopened in my lap, and patted it as if I knew what I did. I hoped Harry could not see the tremor.

'You will consider it?' Harry had not expected this mode of reply, it was evident. *He does not know if I have given him an answer, or none at all.*

'I will consider it.' I managed a faint smile. 'No doubt whatever is necessary at the time will be done.'

That I had said nothing at all, I realised, was in itself a screen for the many things I had hidden away. I hid my own plans away from my family as if they were a guilty secret, perhaps, but really—I confessed it to myself—because my family would express outrage and mockery. And my plans, my writings, and my venturing forth would be prised from my very foolish fingers, with myself helpless under the pall of an entire family's ridicule to make any protest, help-less and reduced to a childishness even beyond that of my own Toby.

'Just so, just so.' Harry leaned forward to pat my arm, sat back and drained his glass. There continued an air about him of confusion; he could not quite believe what he had heard.

'Well, thank them for their interest in my affairs,' I said.

'Indeed.'

The chair squeaked as Harry changed position suddenly, slapped his hand on his leg. He gave a chuckle and settled against the cushion, crossing a shin over the other knee.

'Here is a tale for you, little sister. Fellow in the City told it me.'

His smile was very broad. 'You are still an avid reader of Mr Collins, I see?'

Mr Collins's book, the third volume, lay on my little table still, for I had yet to return it to the library. My reading, indeed, was a tacit secret among my family or, at least, among my brothers. Neither Harry nor Dickie, it was well understood, was likely to tell Gwendolyn —who would then be forced to struggle with the notion of 'ought'— and neither would have told Mr Hadley, it was certain. As a girl, I had never been without a book and would read novels, poetry, and any snippet of literary adventure that came my way. Mr Collins's much earlier work, *Basil*—that so thrilled with notions of love at first sight and of betrayal—had distracted me mightily when I was as yet unmarried, and caused me to be teased for days on end by both Dickie and Harry.

Harry waited now for my reply; he was positively smirking, though I could not see why.

'Yes, of course,' I said.

'My chap tells me there are tolerably well-known stories concerning Mr Collins and a certain Mrs Graves, though Mr Collins passes her off as his housekeeper, or sometimes as his secretary.' Harry chuckled and fixed his eyes on me, his mouth pursed over his amusement, and his eyebrows raised. He had always looked so when passing on his gossip, some scurrilous scrap that would cause me to look away, perhaps to blush. It was so often about some person of whom I had spoken in admiration, for he evidently felt that the more foolish I felt, the more adorable I became.

I looked quickly away.

Harry had settled into his teasing by now, as into an old and comfortable habit. Yet it was a habit—this chaffing of his sister— that I now set at a distance, the further with every day that my life reshaped itself. I wished, with a sudden and violent passion, never to experience his teasing again.

'These scribblers you spend so much time in reading are certainly a shady lot! You ladies must be on your guard for what goes on behind the pages!' The skin about his eyes crinkled with amusement as he waited for my reaction. I looked a moment at my hands.

'Come, sis, confess! You are shocked! See how you look away!"

'This is to gossip, Harry, while I have more serious matters to exercise my mind, as you yourself have just now pointed out.'

The heat flooded to my cheeks. I jerked to my feet with a whispered shiver from my skirt. Harry came to his feet too, confusion again on his face as if he had lost hold of some minor thing that he had brought with him. He looked at his empty glass, hesitated, and put it down on the table.

'Please give my love to Sarah,' I said.

'Oh, indeed.' He smoothed the gloves on his hands distractedly. I rang for Cissy.

There was a stirring on his face then, a half-formed realisation, a hesitance. 'Oh, and I shall tell Gwendolyn that—'

'That I shall consider your request.'

'Oh. Oh yes.'

Sobriety bent over the lace, back in her seat after the front door closed behind Harry.

'How was your brother at the news of our adventures?'

'Heavens! I forgot to tell him!'

How am I so restless, unsteady even, as if I were excited? I pressed my hand to my chest. *I am everywhere at once. I am befuddled.* I thought of Harry's face as his newly dignified—nay, proud and righteous— sister bade him such an undeniable farewell, coolly polite. Firm.

I smiled and took breath. 'He came to demand an accounting of my finances.' I exhaled. 'I believe I had Cissy show my brother the door.'

Yet, over the next hour, I felt myself diminish as a balloon subsides for loss of gas. For Harry had left me with ghosts, after all, more even than the prospect of a dole, the meting-out of a tiny stipend at the pleasure of my siblings. No, there were also night creatures whose shape and smells I could not bring myself to face: Rossetti's painted woman, over-ripe, luscious, perhaps bursting through the grey-brown carapace of the seemingly respectable housekeeper, Mrs Graves, coquetting as if she loved it; and Mr Collins, whose written words had whispered to me in both the dark of my girlhood cupboard and the shifting light of my climbing tree, degraded to a man of lust and perhaps forever lost to me as an avuncular conjurer of tales, the erstwhile comforter of the silent hours.

During my vigil in Mr Hadley's room, I stared for so long at the painted woman that the lines grew indistinct and wavered in the near dark. After a while my eyes blurred, I blinked and, frowning, looked instead at Mr Hadley. And then away.

My writing journal—that I had begun to think was the repository for darker notions, darker thoughts, the secret gaseous puffings of my hidden confusions—lay in my writing box, and I pulled it out. Mr Rosetti's shameless woman looked at me, and Mrs Charles, also, did brush through my mind with cologne upon her skirts. I was thoughtful, thus, as I dipped my pen:

> *When I spoke of ladies and our community with each other, how came I to forget it is the sensual that divides us, often? How did I forget what tumult of loathing is left when the beast is about?*

On Friday, the house waited for Toby. Although—whatever the pace Mr Brent set in his fetching of the boy—he would not arrive before late afternoon; by late morning his room was fresh, dusted, aired, and his bed newly crisp with the sheet turned down. Cook had stirred herself especially early for a trip to buy (and this not even a market day) cuts that were Toby's favourites. On her return, hints of baking floated even to the second landing.

I stood in the open doorway to Toby's room, the odours of cake and biscuit warm at my back. Within the room, everything stood child-sized. A few books of tales for boys still stood tipped against each other on shelves; there were his tin soldiers, his paints with the colours well-worn down. His paintbrushes. His rocking horse resting up against the wall, even though it had been two or three years since he had ridden it. *Had Mr Hadley entered this room recently, he would surely have ordered it thrown out.* Toby may do so himself, perhaps, but I hoped to keep, for at least a little time to come, this collection that told of a child's twelve years of growing. I stood thus for many minutes, for at last I communed with this...*this Tobyness*...directly, and alone. That is, I stood there without the disapproving intercession of nurse or nanny, or the possessive disapproval of Mr Hadley—for perhaps the first time. I leaned against the doorjamb and wondered whether I may feel close to the life all this represented, or must know myself very far from it.

The room spoke of innocence, yet it seemed to me all the child-ish things in it turned to look at this woman, this mother, with contempt, all—in all innocence—unable to respect and therefore to love her. For Toby had shown no signs of love for me, his mother, since he had been a baby. I closed the door, smoothed the folds of my skirt, and descended the stairs.

The first rap at the door made those within earshot start, for it was surely too early for the boy? Sobriety peered around the door of Mr Hadley's room, her pale face white in the gloom looking down the stairs toward the door. I, too, tipped my head around the door of the morning room. Mrs Staynes hesitated on her way to the kitchen. Cissy hurried toward the front door, and all heads turned with her movement, as if she had them each by a thread. She opened; there was a short conversation, and she turned with an envelope in her hand. Mrs Staynes continued to the kitchen, but Sobriety glanced quickly back at the patient, and stayed on the landing to watch as I rustled through my door to meet Cissy.

I opened the envelope and took out the letter, bade Cissy rejoin Mrs Staynes, unfolded and read for the space, perhaps, of six ticks of the old clock heard from the drawing room. I looked up at Sobriety.

She again glanced back at Mr Hadley, and then moved to the banister and gripped it, patient for my explanation.

'Mr Thackeray of *The Cornhill Magazine* accepts my piece of writing and will send me payment.' I was almost gasping—which surprised me—as though I were running pell-mell along another tunnel. I was dizzied at the very unlikelihood of it all, and gave a shaky laugh—especially since Mr Thackeray continued to address me as if I were a gentleman. Oh, and how odd and somehow reckless, shocking in its very divergence from respectable life, gratifying and perhaps appalling to be employed thus, and be paid, and all of this in the face of the serried ranks of Gwendolyn, and my brothers, and my sisters-in-law, nephews, nieces… I might perhaps have continued thus in my mind, but for another knock at the door.

And so it was that I, the letter still in one hand, and not Cissy, who opened the door and looked down at my son.

Chapter Twenty-one

For a moment, during that morning's visit by Inspector Broadford, I wished that burying my face in my hands and counting to three—or perhaps to five to give the magic longer in which to work—would make everybody vanish, save me and Sobriety. *We would be left here happy with our reading or our sewing and all would be calm. With none of these...these...meanings washing back and forth!*

Toby, quite naturally in the company of visitors, would have been as silent in any case. He would have sat as straight and as still; a good boy, he would not have spoken unless spoken to. Yet to me his face, even while it hardened into something carved and determined not to give animation to his thoughts, nevertheless shouted out the disturbance in his mind. *See how still he is, yet so like an overly stoked engine, alarming all with its restrained energy.*

I glanced around at the inspector telling his tale, at Sobriety intent somehow (*Lord, here is another story*) on the pattern of the rug, though the tale was so evidently being told to her, to Sobriety, as the object of all of the inspector's smiles and inflections.

I observed it all as if it were a drama heightened unto comedy: here were at least three stories at odds with one another, enacted at one and the same time, running pell-mell in as many different directions, lurching like careering carriages with their possibility of disaster in the midst of exhilaration. Nothing of this was evident in the demeanour of anybody in the room, yet to me the clattering of cross-purposes played before me with dread inevitability, with only myself aware.

Well, perhaps only I am alarmed by Toby.

I looked at my boy's face once more, at his immature cheeks, downy and undefined, the childish bow to his mouth, sulky while too young yet to suggest surliness; the dandelion wildness to his curls, however much the brush and comb were wielded; his eyes, wide despite himself and with that blankness that children have that comes from inexperience. That innocence that can be cruel with its belief in absolutes.

He sat with a stillness and lack of expression that declared disapproval; for how had it come about that this policeman sat in the Hadley parlour, drinking from the Hadley teacups? How could it be that his mother countenanced it—nay, was gracious in inviting the man in, placed him on the furniture, put tea in his hand, sat listening to his vulgar speech addressed, apparently, to the maid?

Look how lonely he is, without his father beside him to set it all to rights. There is a fear, I am sure of it. And who could blame him?

'Mr Farquharson,' Inspector Broadford was saying, 'for all his lofty station in life, has now much more of our attention than he could possibly want. Indeed we are studying him closely, for not only has he for some time carried on two wholly separate lives, but the man—or should I say *men?*—he presented to the world in London and Manchester was...' He laughed and held up a finger to signify that he corrected himself. ' ...*Were* of two entirely different types.'

My attention blinked at this (*Heavens! What does he mean?*), and even Sobriety raised her head and eyebrows at one and the same time. But almost immediately, the inspector responded with his eyes smiling full into Sobriety's—an urgent secret there that cried out for her sharing of it, all the louder for the small tinklings of teacups and teaspoons and the room's quiet made heavy with carpet and curtain—whereupon Sobriety ducked her head to concentrate again upon the carpet.

At that moment, I realised Sobriety was steeped in shame and humiliation—felt it as if it were my own. I felt myself pale in empathy, a spasm of pain beneath my own heart in echo of Sobriety's. And anger, pure and vivid, reared so suddenly that it flared through all the channels of my blood. She was admired—by this man and, surely, by all who knew her—yet felt herself made ugly and unworthy by shame. *My monstrous Mr Hadley, oh monstrous husband...look there, look!* I did not for a moment know what to do with all of this stark feeling—I wished vainly to protect Sobriety from that which shook her calm capacities, her very strengths, and left her with such chaos—and, instead, schooled my face and then my limbs, and my hands, and then my heart to show nothing of my turbulence. *Shh... shh...shh...* I did not look at Sobriety, but I felt her there, wounded when the world thought her whole.

Yet then these thoughts dragged back to my silent Toby, staring by now at the inspector but with an air of someone unsure of where he was.

Last evening, after his arrival, Toby had had command of his voice, had greeted the servants with his portmanteau, his coat, and his gloves and *how-d'ye-do* for Mrs Staynes and Sobriety. He had stood aloof with his cheek tilted for his mother's kiss. And I had kissed him, bent over before him—*see, I am the minion of some small emperor*—while he stood impassive, eyes averted. He had sat for a quarter of an hour with Cook's fresh biscuits, formal and straight-backed, awaiting each of my questions while I sat before him, hands wrapped about themselves in my lap, the pauses frequent and long.

'My masters feel I am progressing satisfactorily, especially in mathematics. I particularly like mathematics.' *See how my little emperor boasts.*

'Your father would have been glad to hear this, I am sure.'

Toby had looked at me then, with a small compression about his eyebrows.

'He *will* be glad. I shall tell him myself.' He brushed a crumb from his lap. 'I would go to him now, Mama.'

He had risen, and I rose with him. Looking down at my boy, I thought his imperiousness absurd, to be sure, yet caught from Toby a current of sadness that he struggled to conceal thereby, even from himself. *It makes him look very small indeed.*

At Mr Hadley's door I laid my hand on his arm for a moment so that he must turn to me. 'You must be prepared, Toby. He will not know you...'

Such a very different conversation from that with the inspector now, who had come, first of all, to advise that young Cissy may be required to testify in a week's time when Mr Farquharson was taken for his committal proceedings. Witnesses were being gathered together in Manchester, it was true, he said, but circumstances could turn against them and cause delay. There could be illness, or indeed the weather might make travel impossible, so that Cissy would have to be summoned. Cissy was called to be advised of this, and turned voiceless and pale as a result.

Inspector Broadford was then invited to settle into a comfortable armchair (another of Mama's, this one full-cushioned and covered in a faded pattern of autumnal leaves) to tell the tale of the Manchester constabulary's enquiries into their version of Mr Farquharson—Mr Forster that was—and his modest life as a moderately prosperous but unassuming merchant. His family possessed all the stolid virtues as well as the accent of the town, and thought nothing at all of Mr Forster's—London's Mr Farquharson's—frequent trips away for, he told them, the sake of his business.

'Of course, they have had from me a very different description of the man,' the inspector said. 'By telegraph, you understand, and we all a-scratching of our heads over the strangeness of this whole story.' He chuckled in Sobriety's direction and sipped at his tea.

'How alarming that a man could deal so mendaciously with all about him and nobody the wiser,' I said, especially since—and even though it was she whom the inspector addressed—Sobriety continued as silent as Toby.

Then I felt myself conscious that Inspector Broadford may very well find some slight in my comment (for should not the police and others in authority have been aware of Mr Farquharson's duplicity?), while Toby was likely all the more perplexed that his mother could be part of such a conversation.

Yet what other surprises can he have, poor boy, than to discover his mother and her maid were, of a sudden, so changed from retiring modesty as to dash about rescuing babies...

Toby's world at home was now a very different place, to be sure, and this he was coming, at last, to comprehend.

There was, I felt, the smallest tick of hesitation when my boy had stood with his hand on the doorknob of his father's bedchamber. But then some decision was arrived at behind those childish eyes with their habit of contempt—perhaps that he would not believe me, or that while his father chose not to know me, he would know his only son, or simply that I could not be deemed to be competent to judge Mr Hadley's illness.

In any case, Toby turned from me and opened the door.

Dropping my hand, I then watched the inevitable shock to my son of the truth: that his father lay crumpled and insensible, much smaller somehow and with all of his power gone. That he who had been tyrant, lord and ally did not, indeed, know Toby at all.

With the boy looking down on what had been his father, I murmured, 'Kiss him, Toby. I'm sure he would feel this as a comfort somehow, though we may not see it.' But my voice died away to a whisper, for Toby flinched and retreated from the bed.

There was silence but for Mr Hadley's breathing, the fainter disturbance of my own breathing and of Toby's, and the mantel clock stepping on and on. I tensed with everything that was unsaid. *This cannot continue, it must not continue.*

'Mr Hadley,' I spoke, finally, after several long moments of searching for the solution to this hiatus that did not know what to do with itself. 'Mr Hadley, here is Toby come to us at Michaelmas.'

Toby's face was in shadow, for evening had been darkening as we stood, the light at the window losing its colour, the clock blindly tapping out the seconds, and even Mr Hadley in his bed losing shape as if he may not be real after all. My boy said nothing.

'Toby is doing very well at school, Mr Hadley. Particularly in mathematics.' I glanced at my child. *What drama am I putting voice to?* 'His masters have mentioned this especially. The mathematics.'

Look at him, standing there. I must bring this to a close.

'I suppose Cook will be nearly ready for the evening meal, Toby. Say goodnight to your father; he will have a drink of water soon, and Albert will settle him for the night.'

I reached then for Toby's arm and he moved away from the bed, though he said nothing still, either to me or to his father. In the shadows I heard Albert stir, ready to take his place back at Mr Hadley's bedside. I had forgotten he was there.

And here Toby sits now, listening to this stranger, the inspector, as if it is my boy who is the stranger come wandering into the wrong place, fearing that this, his own place, has melted away while he did his mathematics and parsed his Latin… If I close my eyes, will everything be changed?

For a moment I had a sense of Mr Hadley and Toby standing there fully robust and pink of face and myself ghostly and grey, flitting at the edges of their most important lives…

And so if everything changed, what would it all change into? Toby, Toby, your wish and mine are very different things.

'Mr Forster, they tell me, prospered in his business and was helped in this by inheriting a sum of money from an uncle—forty thousand pound, they say. He began to be admired for his acumen, so that—' Inspector Broadford reached for his cup, which must by now be quite tepid. He put it down again. '—so that the local businessmen invited him onto the committee of a small finance company and he even became the loyal treasurer for the local Tory Party.'

The inspector's inflection brought about murmurs from we two, Sobriety and me, like the cooing of pigeons, which he appeared to take as encouragement. Indeed, even Sobriety had by now raised her eyes from the carpet. He smiled and leaned a little forward.

'Mr Forster had so established himself, it seems, that even when the finance company collapsed he was not linked to any prosecutable activity. He continued to prosper, and took to travelling very frequently, telling his wife and friends that this journeying was for the purpose of his grocery business or on behalf of the Tory party. But we have found out otherwise.' The inspector looked up. By now all eyes were rounded and fixed upon him, half-empty cups and saucers forgotten in our grip.

'And so he began his double life, for he was travelling frequently to London and had established, as Mr Farquharson, the Southern England Credit Foncier and Mobilier, of which you may have heard—'

I nodded. I had not, in fact, heard of this company but did not like to say so. Sobriety glanced at me and then back at the inspector.

'—which financed the many investments he had begun to promote, such as railways, public utilities and so forth. Indeed, we have begun to look into his accounts and, while much of it appears to be written in cipher and we are still searching for missing ledgers, they do explain some of his other suspected activities—'

I held out the plate of cakes to him—without thinking, I suddenly realised—and now felt it to be something of a non sequitur. The inspector paused in his recitation and a small confusion disturbed his face, but he reached for a slice and I was able to replace the plate. He put his cake on the saucer next to his cup and continued.

'—activities, which included the hiring of Irish thugs, men desperate for money to send home to their hungry wives and children. He used these men to silence shareholders who had begun to ask questions at meetings.' Mr Broadford reached for his cake.

'And he married, of course as we know, the young and only daughter of a wealthy naval hero. So that he was truly arrived in society and able to influence all with the wink of an eye.' The inspector sat back, took a bite of his cake with his other hand beneath to catch the crumbs.

'There you have it, ladies.'

'Inspector, this is astonishing. This is…' I could not for the moment think of an adequate epithet. 'This is appalling.'

'It is appalling, Mrs Hadley, but it is not, I am sorry to say, astonishing.' There was a pause, during which Mr Broadford finished his small slice of cake.

'What a very bad man, with perhaps worse to be discovered,' Sobriety said.

The inspector looked at her as if she were the cleverest student in class. 'Perhaps, indeed.' He smiled at her, while this time she looked away.

Chapter Twenty-two

The inspector was thanked for his visit and his information, a duty he had again travelled unnecessarily far to fulfil, though we understood well enough why he had done so. There was quiet after he had left, after the thud of doors and Cissy's receding rustle and patter. My boy and Sobriety gazed into different corners of my morning room, and I looked wordlessly first at one and then the other, unable to speak either with Toby in Sobriety's presence, or with Sobriety in Toby's.

Sobriety, finally, rose to her feet. Holding her face—pale still from illness perhaps, but also, I felt, most certainly from the chaos of her thoughts about herself—from my sight, she said, 'I must go upstairs…I must go upstairs to, to fetch…something.'

She was gone then, with myself left staring at the closed door, my own unfinished thoughts chaotic as a crowd of kite-ribbons in a contrary wind: *What is the answer? George leaves his sin upon Sobriety… who could forgive him? But Sobriety… What does Toby make of all this?*

I took a breath and sighed it out, realised as I did so that I had held myself for many hours as clenched as any fist, and turned to Toby. He had not, apparently, paid attention at all to Sobriety's stammering, and now was instead grasping the publisher's letter to me, left open since yesterday on the small table.

If I could close my eyes and wish this all away! Would I?

He stood up—*Oh, what now?*—and drew himself to his full height, although this did not as yet amount to very much. He looked down at his seated mother with a frown that only lacked the steel-and-snow show of his father's eyebrows to be an exact imitation in miniature. His little chin was raised, his fist on his hip with the flap of his jacket drawn back, the letter held forward like an accusation in his other hand.

Today has been so full of mime.

Thus we regarded each other, and I felt once more that I watched us—Toby and I—doing so, from shadows, like an audience witnessing melodrama. Once again, I felt myself part-audience, part-player, indulging in a constant mental commentary: *This is a farce full of misunderstanding, full of overplayed gesture.* I made no effort to break the silence, to be the first to make excuses, and it went on overlong until Toby dropped his arm, perhaps because his stance began to seem ridiculous even to him. *After all, he is not well practiced in playing the ageing tyrant. Poor mite.*

'What is this, Mother?' He was a little gruff, for he had not spoken at all for some time.

'It is a letter, Toby, from a gentleman who will publish something I have written.'

Still, my detachment continued, as if I had handed on, or put down upon a table, all of the anxiety of the last few hours. I was interested, merely interested, in what was here unfolding in my morning room.

As soon as one part of life peels itself from another and moves on, see how many explanations are demanded! Somewhere in my mind I found this amusing, but took care not to smile as I gazed at my son.

'And he will pay me.' I believed in being thorough.

Now I did venture a small smile, as if I expected Toby's congratulations, while knowing, of course, that these would not come. My detachment played as if in a game, for I knew that Toby would behave as he would behave. *He will behave as he believes his father would behave and would want him to behave in his stead.*

'Mother, how long has this been going on? What of Papa?'

I regarded my son a moment. *Remember he is a boy still.* I sat a little straighter, for now I knew, a little wearily and bored with the necessity, that I must gather energies, gather myself back into this scene, and explain.

'Toby, it is something that I can do in the circumstances—' he took a breath to speak, but I forestalled him with a raised hand '—which are that your father, when he passes, will leave most of his wealth to you, as is right, of course, but very little to me.'

Toby did not answer, though he clearly had meant to. He simply could not. I watched his face as all his cloak of pomposity finally fell away—and my own detachment with it—and he dwindled to a frightened, pale-faced child. It was evident that all he had truly heard of my speech were the words: *when he passes*. His eyes were hot and his mouth shapeless with unwept and unspoken grief. 'No, do not say that!' he burst out. 'How can you say that? You, who adventured while he suffered!'

Toby was gone through the door, his feet rapid on the stairs, up two flights to his room, with a slam at the end of it all.

Left alone, I looked around the room, my morning room. It was, despite the theatrics of today, just as it had always been: pretty, presentable yet informal, filled with the things and the furniture that I loved. There was the sampler whose embroidered *Bless this H...* had not proceeded far since I had first begun it.

When was that?

Not long ago, yet so very long ago.

I fancied this quiet room was relieved that all that trouble had gone from it; but with a weary exasperation, I sent my mind beyond, to each of the house's storeys now nurturing a different tragedy in discreet rooms—Mr Hadley's, Sobriety's, Toby's. I sighed and rose to say what I could; in Toby's case, probably through his closed door, for, since the day twelve years before that Mr Hadley had first taken the red-faced bundle from me, Toby had learned never to allow his mother to comfort him. Rare tears had been for Nurse, and the display of control and manly accomplishment reserved for his father.

'Toby, all of this bespeaks your grief—' Upstairs, I crouched and murmured through my boy's keyhole, to silence inhabited by a muffled sniff. I began again, 'Toby, I am your mother—' but felt I had no conclusion for this statement that could reach him, and rose to my feet. I was about to creep away, but paused a moment, bent again to the keyhole and said into it, 'Remember that I love you, Toby.'

Matters were similar at the door to Sobriety's small chamber. I opened it a chink to venture, 'Sobriety?' but I addressed only my maid's back as Sobriety lay clutched to herself on her narrow bed.

Sobriety's voice came strained and a little cracked. 'I am sorry, I am not fit to talk right now. I shall be better soon…' and I said, 'Of course, of course,' and closed the door.

Chapter Twenty-three

We Speak of Children

We speak of children and the joy they grant a household, filled thus with a life that runs in little steps, and calls in little cries, and holds out its little arms for love. And this is so; it is the truth on many days and in many homes, where such is expected, and welcomed, and countenanced.

But there are such homes that are not so, and we (who speak of children) tend not to speak of this. We do not speak of the hopes that mothers have of such a thing—of homes made bright by infants and children who laugh and play, and raise their eyes with trust and love; hopes that are dashed when the babe is taken, wrapped tight, and trained to be old before their time by fathers and governesses and tutors in schoolrooms, all creaking their sour disapprovals.

We do not tell that, in these many, many cases, the little gentleman, stolen thus from she who would love and teach him, is taught instead to look askance. When next this boy gazes at his mother, it will be to disdain. He, the child, will turn the wheels about and it will be the mother reduced to meaningless chatter and fumbling, to childishness.

And, yea, there are others in this land with bodies God has prepared to bear new life, who are betrayed by those placed above them and then cursed—at first for a failure to resist when resistance is beyond possible, and then for either of the only two outcomes likely thereafter: to bear a babe in disgrace and both condemned to shame and penury, or to seek the alternative...

I blotted the pages of my journal and read again what I had written. It was a note, a message, a thought described to myself, and never likely, I knew, to see the light of public gaze. *A thought, nonetheless, about we mothers whose children are stolen…* It filled me with dreariness; a lassitude that had pooled deeper and deeper during all the long, long days gone by spent at a distance—as if perpetually in another room—from the child who did not love me. I thought of myself, and Sobriety, and little Mrs Farquharson. I went to close up the writing book. *It is near unbearable to think on it, yet it surely not to do so cannot itself be borne.*

And yet to have written this—and it did come close, very close to an accurate expression of my thoughts—was a relief, a satisfaction in itself. *All these years, without the words to say what ailed me. How did I bear it?*

I sat quiet for the remainder of my time with Mr Hadley, my hands folded and the clock filling the silent void with its ticking, until its chime.

'Mrs Hadley, my dear, poor Adelaide!' Mrs Courtney, Edith, entered like a gush of damp air. I saw that Sobriety had an eye on the ornaments as Edith ballooned past the Chinese snuff bottles clustered on lace by the door. My sister-in-law reached me without mishap, grasped me by the shoulders, and kissed my cheek. She turned to Toby, who was at his drawing, perched on a chair pulled up to the small table and surrounded by pencils and paper. He was still pale with misery and offence, but had recovered enough after luncheon in the dining room (he had forgotten his apparent resolution not to speak as he sat shivering over the soup, and agreed with me that the room was indeed as icy as any ancient Hebridean dungeon) to seek out my company and that of Sobriety in the morning room.

'Toby!'

Toby rose and stood, resigned to his aunt's advancing attentions, while yet his hand still rested on the pencil with which he had been wrestling with the foreshortening of a knight in armour.

Poor Toby. You know she will never notice either the drawing or that you have been busy doing it.

'Toby, poor boy.' Edith Courtney pulled him to her own armoured bosom and hugged him tight for such a time, rocking the small boy from side to side, that Sobriety and I exchanged glances. It seemed unlikely that the boy had enough breath in him to withstand his aunt's embrace.

'Oh, Toby, Toby, Toby, what a sad, sad time for you. You have been up to see your poor father?' Toby's answer was muffled by his aunt's shawl.

'Oh, my poor, poor brother. Oh, George.'

Of a sudden, Edith held Toby at arm's length and bent to look into his face. 'Of course you have, poor lambkins. And you have been a brave boy, too, haven't you?' Toby managed to agree that he had. She turned him around and held him close to her side, where he stood at an awkward angle, more on one foot than the other, while she continued, 'Look at you all, so very pale. What a tragedy this is!'

'We are all very tired today, Edith, from the emotion, I believe. It has been a strain.'

'Oh, my dear. Of course. But I have come with an invitation for you, Adelaide. Such a thing! You know that I have encountered a wonderful, most marvellous person. A spiritualist of extraordinary talent, Madame Drew, in London only these last few months and yet already the darling of so many who matter, and now at the very centre of my life, and…you would have been amazed, my dear Adelaide… She speaks to me of poor Mr Courtney's enduring love. Because, you know, he comes to her especially when she is in trance.

He is waiting for me from Beyond. It is so very moving!'

I had heard very little before of the spiritualist, yet this revelation came as no surprise. Edith Courtney had long been apt to take passionate fancies to this lady or the other, who were often described as 'prescient, you understand', and she would lower her voice and raise her eyebrows with 'she *knows*, my dear…' This new acquaintance with a world of spirits was a thing of great value, I could see, that my sister-in-law held to herself, that was entirely her own, even while she had dared not speak of her beliefs in Mr Hadley's presence.

Edith's voice faded into a tearful whisper, though rallying as she spoke, all the while searching out her handkerchief from her reticule. 'It was so very comforting. I really thought of you, my dear, most particularly, and how comforted you would be…'

I marshalled myself, watchful, even suspicious of a sudden. Edith, surely, had come to encompass me in some way. She would make me complicit in something, God knew what. *A spiritualist now? Lord. Mr Hadley would have scoffed both loud and long.*

'I do not understand. It would be fine to hear of Mr Courtney's love for you, but the comfort is yours, surely?'

Mr Hadley, it was well known to all save his sister, had never held Mr Courtney in high regard. 'That whining milksop' was the usual descriptor, which rang now in my head. It was a business to keep a straight face, though I imagined for a moment the combination of Mr Hadley's scorn for spiritualists and his contempt for the Courtneys. *Surely he would cry: 'Why would anyone wish to call the milksop back?'*

'No, no, no,' Edith's voice regained strength. 'I meant that she might speak with Mr Hadley's soul for *you*.'

Oh, Edith.

'Mr Hadley is not yet passed on, my dear sister.'

Edith, Edith.

'Yet my dear, it does so seem to me that his soul hovers, does it not? It hovers outside his body—overhead, as it were—and he would be glad, would he not, glad to have you know how he is, of his love…?'

Edith was stopped by tears for some moments, her face in her handkerchief and shoulders shaking, the seams in her bodice straining with each breath. I stood with my arm about her, head averted from the trembling bonnet. My own sensibilities, flayed as they had been these past two days in particular, were aware now as never before of Edith Courtney's loneliness and her determined grip on continual grief as her only companion. I understood that she pleaded today for—positively grasped at—my companionship in this other world she had found for herself.

See how much comfort she needs, and what she will grasp to find it. Poor Edith.

'It has been hard, for my Mary is of a singularly narrow mind on this and will not see Madame Drew as the miracle she is. But I knew in my heart that you would be glad…' Edith's voice quavered once more.

Poor, sensible Mary—but what on earth does Edith step into? Lord, where does she invite me?

'If you wish it, of course, I will come with you, Edith. Yet we should be prepared for the possibility that she cannot speak to Mr Hadley.'

She has leapt upon me as a fellow sufferer. She cannot even wait for my widowhood!

Edith raised her head from the sodden handkerchief. 'I really do believe it may happen, Adelaide. His soul…' Her eyes were puffed and lined with a raw redness, her face blotched. I sighed a long, quiet breath.

What can I say?

'Well, you may be right. Of course I shall come.'

She then visited a few moments upstairs with her brother, bending over his bed with a loud whisper, 'We shall speak soon, I know it!'

Downstairs, Edith grasped my arm and was as earnest as she could be. 'Sister, Madame Drew will impress you as strong and upright, and able to lift your hopes and spirits as would surprise you, truly…', and departed in a swirl that left the vase in the hallway teetering on its stand until I stilled it with one finger.

The morning room returned to peace; we three glanced at each other, and after a pause, I said, 'Poor Aunt Edith.'

Sobriety and I sat once more, with all our silken sibilance and adjustment; Toby drew his chair back to the table. Soon, I would go up to Mr Hadley for my hours at his bedside with my writing box and papers; Cissy would receive instructions for the evening from Mrs Staynes. Delightful odours from the kitchen, conjured from the list of Toby's favourites expressed by him at holiday intervals, would begin to reach to us.

All was quiet, made the more so by the comfortable noises from both within and without the house, and the light through the window that wavered a little with the breeze shifting the branches outside.

It is like—very like—any domestic scene with the adults and children in companionship, going about their separate occupations.

Look at him. He is a child, after all.

'Mother,' Toby said, lifting his head from his drawing. 'What was Mr Bazelgette's tunnel like, on the inside?'

Chapter Twenty-four

Toby touched his father's head at the end of his own visit to him the next morning. I stood aside to allow him the door, and nodded to Cissy to return to the bedside. It was Sunday, and Toby and I were both dressed for church—a medley of sober blues in the pattern and trimmings for me, and Toby in a dark suit and waistcoat, a pin in his cravat like a memory of his father.

Sobriety waited at the foot of the stairs. With her, cradling his hat in his long, thin, black-clad arm, stood Mr Gordon, attentive to the very tips of his out-bent elbows to both mother and son as they descended.

'Ah, my dear Mrs Hadley, and Master Toby! So grown! So much the image of your father, and of course your dear mother!' His face contorted with the effort of expressing both gladness and sympathy at the same time, his long black frame bent in a solicitude too much like crouching.

For an instant I saw Mr Gordon in my mind, nibbling at cake with his mousy mouth, blinking at me with his tiny, mousy eyes. I glanced away from him even as I spoke.

'Good morning, Mr Gordon.'

He took my arm as the group descended the steps at the front door, but Toby very soon tugged so hard at my other hand that I must stop.

'I must speak with you, Mother.'

Mr Gordon moved on a few paces and waited, his Sunday smile fixed beneath his projecting nose. He bowed and tipped his hat to a couple clad for church, strolling on the other side of the road. His angles dipped and rose as if he danced but had little notion of the music.

I looked down at my son, whose eyebrows pulled together and whose breathing came in puffs. *What now, Toby?*

I knelt as if to adjust Toby's cravat.

'What is it?' I reached for the cravat, but he pulled away.

'Why is he here, Mother?'

'Because he comes to accompany me to Church, Toby. It is kind of him, I suppose.'

I could not help a small rise of impatience, and looked into Toby's face. About to reprove him for risking a scene here on the street, I suddenly understood. Blood rushed to my face. I felt of an instant as if a steaming kettle had doused me. There was Mr Gordon standing, too, his long hands in dark kid resting on the knob of his walking stick, his long body pale and thin beneath the dour propriety of his well-pressed cladding, no doubt redolent with his personal smells and perfumes. There were his black eyes waiting with their tiny points of light, his little nibbling mouth, his breath that might smell of stale tea or sherry…

'Oh, Toby, no! I am not looking for… Oh, no!' I turned my shoulder so that Mr Gordon could not see our faces thus agitated.

How could I not have thought! 'Toby, no, no. Absolutely not.'

I put my gloved hand to Toby's face a moment before turning to join Mr Gordon, glancing back to meet my son's eyes. *Absolutely not!* It was a revelation. It left me shocked—aghast! Appalled!—at the thought that I must watch for such manoeuvring even before my widowhood, and embarrassed at my own naivety before my own son, and a recurring notion, even as my mind recoiled, of violation only narrowly averted, that this was my own fault.

What a dolt I am, did I not know? I am the child, a child! There is no hope for me!

Though at his side, I walked to the church at as great a distance from the lawyer as could be deemed polite. I looked around to see if I could read speculation on the faces of others strolling to worship, in twos or small groups, more numerous now as we neared the church.

Lord! Who else might suppose it! Does the whole world muse on this?

Chapter Twenty-five

Tristram James

By A. Hadley

Tristram James sat with all the gravity of his twelve years, his hat upon his knee, while all around him the women fussed about. His early arrival had caused a deal of excitement among the servants, and for his mother, under whose eye everybody save Tristram bustled— cleaning, straightening, setting the fire, carrying the young master's bags to his room. Great skirts swung and rustled, heels pattered on the flags. Yet in the midst of all this busy work, Tristram's face held no animation. It was as still as a pond, and as cool as the pebbles beneath water. His mother halted a moment, the keys to the linen cabinet in her hand, and wondered if there were melancholy there. Tristram had good reason for sadness, for all that the towering rock that had been his father had worked to make a stone of this boy...

I rubbed the back of my neck. *Good gracious! I begin as spinner of tales!* I chuckled, softly, though only Mr Hadley was there as audience. *The greatest obstacle is this consciousness of display! One writes alone, yet imagines all those who will make judgement. An invisible crowd, so to speak...* I rolled my eyes and shook my head at myself. The room, indeed, was silent but for the small clock and Mr Hadley's shallow breath. Some small sounds came from somewhere in the street—a child's voice, a little sharp. Perhaps commanding an animal; perhaps disobeying a governess.

I read over what I had written.

I was self-conscious; I was not certain if I would ever let another read this tale, let alone publish it. I could not discern whether I was guilty or merely shy. I was uncertain whether I should explore further this child who was, of course, Toby. It was the portrait of a child, a boy, that I was building, and I began with my own son as its cornerstone. The child in this story of mine had Toby's arrogance, which placed him more distant from she who loved him than the furthest stars; he had such untried innocence as to make his mother ache for his frailty. This story was an exploration; it was a stroll down a path that grew less familiar, that split into other paths that were, in turn, sometimes more and sometimes less familiar.

While the room continued silent, and the voice outside had ceased, I was clutched of a sudden by an emotion somewhere between excitement and fear; there was something of anticipation in it and yet something that was very like a need to hide oneself away. My heart, I fancied, might be beating fast, beneath the layers of my clothing. It was time to take a breath, a slow and deep one, and close my eyes to gain the comfort for a moment of a personal darkness.

Then I was ready to bend over the paper once more.

Somebody laughed in the street outside the house, and there may have been an answer as the small sound moved seemingly from one side of Mr Hadley's room to the other, carried perhaps on the travelling rumble of a handcart. Indeed it was a handcart, undeniably, for it I guessed that it struggled—from the scraping of the wheels and the grunting of its owner—with the large cobble I had often noticed standing up a little loose from the rest.

Otherwise, within Mr Hadley's room the only noises were the scratching of my nib, and the faint, dry rasp that came from my husband's bed, so faint and so regular as to have become a part of the room itself and therefore almost forgotten.

I paused, the ink drying in the air. I had been writing for an hour already and my back ached from leaning over the writing surface. The lines drawn through unsatisfactory phrases had become less frequent upon the page, I judged, within the last half an hour or so, and the penmanship more confident. Enough for now. I was content with it. I thought that it would do very well in serial form, if Mr Thackeray could be persuaded to publish it.

Hush! For it is she, Adelaide Hadley, the lady novelist! I smiled.

Blotting the last line written, I wiped at the nib with my cloth, straightened the papers and placed them inside my writing box, in company with the bottle for ink and my pens, the cleaning cloth, the blotter. I closed the lid and regarded my husband, his hair, soft as any baby's, spread upon the pillow.

His neckcloth was wet through, I could see, and so I rose to him and took it, placed it on the tray that sat by the bed for just this purpose, and picked up a dry cloth that was folded there.

Lord. Mr Gordon. It is droll, I suppose, all of it.

I wiped Mr Hadley's mouth and chin, and tucked the cloth at his neck. *Droll, even that I should have been unaware. Can I have been so unaware?*

It dawned on me then that more was changing, and would continue to change with Mr Hadley's passing. I was to become a woman alone, with all that may betoken speculation, by gentlemen, about me. I felt, of a sudden, exposed and expectant, all at once. And then, with that prickling at my cheeks, I thought that some of that speculation might be mine. At which I recoiled, for the physical presence of Mr Gordon had reared itself before me.

Oh! 'Tis too much!

Mr Gordon had for so long been the whispering stick figure who arrived sometimes to be closeted with Mr Hadley in his study for an hour, two hours, once for almost half a day. Afterward, Mr Gordon might be invited to stay for luncheon or the evening meal, and he would crouch over his soup or his viands and agree with Mr Hadley at the correct moments, bowing to me and bending his features into some semblance of smile, all of which would require him to look up, as it were, from his crouch. I recalled Mr Gordon's mouth moving around his food, and the dabbing of his lips. The papery rasp of his voice seemed to insinuate so, and made the listener yearn for a cough. I considered my forthcoming position as widow, inheritor of a widow's mite. *He would be the only man, surely, of my husband's acquaintance, to imagine (if indeed he does) that he would benefit socially from marriage with me. Perhaps marriage to your deceased client's wife is to rise in the world...*

I pulled my mind away from further thought of Mr Gordon, his person, his ambitions, the very notion of his creeping to my room in his nightshirt. I shuddered, surprising myself with the violence of it.

Then, as I returned to smoothing both cloth and sheet, I considered that there had been one small advantage as a result of this absurd misunderstanding with Mr Gordon. Subsequent events may well pull me down in Mr Gordon's eyes. Sadly, this small advantage arose from the note that came from Dickie, which said only:

Alas. Too late or I was misled—there was no profit, only loss. I am chastised by fate and my own foolishness.

On reading this, I was, most naturally, pensive for a time, was sad indeed for my brother and Amanda, who must learn another harsh lesson through financial loss. I had sat with the paper in my hand, thinking. *How can this be? Was Dickie mistaken, and there had never been a profit? Was there no profit, and Dickie simply misled into believing there was?*

But sad as I was for my brother, a burst of a thought had then occurred: how little I knew of Mr Hadley's own investments! Would he have been so remiss? How well had he known Mr Farquharson? Was he vulnerable to grandiosity and overlarge gestures, whether Mr Farquharson's or anyone else's? Could this be the case, I wondered, even while he himself (I had often witnessed) could persuade through flattery any fellow from his uncertainty. *Surely Mr Hadley would have known better!* Then I blushed to think how close I had, myself, come to falling in behind the knave, Mr Farquharson.

It is a thing of which I must be certain. I closed my eyes at the thought of Mr Gordon nibbling in his rooms. *I suppose.*

The thought of a visit to Mr Gordon was discomposing enough, but then came the notion that Toby might misunderstand my purpose entirely. This washed over me like cold brine, and was so mortifying I must catch my breath. I cringed still to think that Toby had ever considered I might look on any possible advances by Mr Gordon with favour. Sitting thus, my eyes closed and slowly—as Mama had always dictated—filling and emptying my lungs, I formed a plan.

This might do. Yes, this might do very well.

Thus, I would seek out Toby in his room. He might accompany his mother to enquire of Mr Gordon whether their life had in fact been exposed to Mr Farquharson's dubious practice. Here was a plan that covered many needs. There was time still before Toby left for his friend's place.

My son looked up, when I tapped, very gently, and entered. He saved his place with his finger in the book he had been reading. It looked, from where I stood, like a volume that had always been his favourite and, while I could not think why, this very fact closed my throat with emotion so that I must cough a little in order to speak. *We all find comfort in the things of our childhood.* He listened with his wide-eyed gaze on me, with that innocence that could speak equally of love or of contempt.

'It is right that you should have some little involvement in your father's affairs, for they will be your own when you are a man.' I folded my hands at my waist. 'And—' I was most serious with him. '—your company as chaperone would be most fitting.'

Toby was my small and serious companion, then, seated very straight all the way in the landau to Mr Gordon's chambers. I could not help looking long at him, for here was my son travelling with me for my own sake, and on business that affected us both, and my pride in his presence was all undiluted. *His father*, I must be frank with myself, *is not here to declare possession and leave me bereft.* My head swam a little to think of all that was being enacted here, while Toby and I sat in this cocoon as the world passed by, and it made me smile. So near to this boy, who was my own and yet a stranger. Whose eyes may yet, one day, turn to me and see me.

In the end, there was little time spent with Mr Gordon.

'No, no, all seems to be in order,' he said, bending his long, black-clad body over his desk and leafing through papers and bound documents. The scraping and shuffling echoed the dry crawling of his voice. 'There is nothing outstanding nor, indeed, about which to be concerned.' He looked up at me with curiosity.

I smiled and was gratified that, for this moment at least, I appeared to Mr Hadley's solicitor to have some small grasp of finance.

Or at least, of the import of some influences upon it.

'There is no reference to a Mr Farquharson?'

'No, no. Mr Farquharson, Mrs Hadley?'

'He is a financier and broker in the City, Mr Gordon, whose dealings are being uncovered as quite questionable.' I knew I appeared to know of rumours—pertaining to Mr Farquharson—of which Mr Gordon had not heard. Yet, although there was a deal of satisfaction to be had from this, I could not help the heat that came and went on my cheeks (though I was annoyed by this betrayal of myself), for really I did not believe myself to have been particularly clever. I felt I lied in concealing the depths of my actual ignorance. *And yet lying is what all this has been about, with Mr Farquharson-Forster, his life and his promises.* How much of business was, I wondered, a performance. A ruse. A trick. A sleight of hand.

And then, it came to me with a start, Toby himself might now take either the road that declared his mother an unwomanly meddler in men's affairs, or the one that declared her to be plucky and sensible for a woman. *What to do, if he despises me even for this? For this knowledge does come from experience, where a gentlewoman is normally innocent of such.* He may rebel, again, at one more sign that I abandoned my rightful place at the hearth, at the bedside, to venture into business none of my own. It was quite possible that no way could be found to marry, as it were, his esteem and my growing capacity in my own affairs. *And yes*, I decided, *my capacities are growing.* Yet would he thrust himself further from me because of it?

I threw a secret glance at him, but there he sat gravely by the desk, looking from one adult to the other. He listened, it was evident, and although he did not understand, he strived to do so.

Look, he is flattered, it came to me, *child that he is, to be included in such talk.* Perhaps, in this, he had forgot his disdain; he had forgot to put on his look of Mr Hadley, just this once. *There may come a time when he will forget to do so altogether.* I felt I floated with relief, as I smoothed my gloves and drew the veil back over my face.

A pale sunshine hesitated through cloud as we descended Mr Gordon's stair, and light glinted from new puddles upon the road. Two gentlemen passed by at a fast walk, and one clapped the other on the back and laughed.

Mr Brent awaited his mistress, horses clattering one step forward and another back on the cobbles, ready for the drive home. Toby turned to me.

'I am glad you brought me here today, Mama,' he said, and I smiled at his young dignity. I delighted in it.

'And I—' he cleared his throat. 'I assure you I understand you must involve yourself in some little way in these matters, but that I will be proud to care for you in all things when I am older.'

I regarded him, the smile still on my face, while my delight faltered and sank. *It is a dance—one step closer, one step further away.*

'We shall see what must be done when the time comes.' I swung the small hand that I held in mine. 'Would you care for an ice before we leave town, Toby?'

He looked up at me and took his hand away. I had never in his life before behaved so lightly with him, had certainly never swung his hand.

'It is not so unusual, my love, for a mother to take her boy to have an ice.' Instead, I patted his shoulder. 'You might tell me about Phillip and his pony.'

He ate his ice in a small shop with me, and spoke of his friend and his pony, for all the world as if he did indeed wish his mother to know and enjoy what he so enjoyed; and I thought that I might later search in my great cupboard for journals put away from many years gone past. I fancied I might find there Mrs Gaskell's excellent tale of ghosts, *The Old Nurse's Story*, and my son might shiver in delighted dread to such lines as had affected me, too, when I had been a child:

> As winter drew on, and the days grew shorter, I was sometimes almost certain that I heard a noise as if some-one was playing on the great organ in the hall.

Reaching under Mr Hadley's head and neck to support him the better, I held to his lips a teaspoon part filled with water. I held my breath as I did this, for he exhaled in feeble gusts a moist and foul stench. My reaction—my holding my own breath—was now what I did as a matter of course, with barely a thought.

Indeed, my thoughts were elsewhere, and that vexingly frequent heat came and went on my cheeks. For this last Sunday I had pretended to a slight cold and so had put Mr Gordon off rather than attend church with him, since Toby was gone and I still feared the man's advances, or at least that he may plan to make some. I had sat inside near a curtain as if I considered hiding behind it (perhaps I did), while Cissy made her apologies to the lawyer standing at the door in his Sunday best and his hat in his hand.

I had done something very like, I recalled, when at the height of my coming out. There had been a young man, not favoured by many of those giddy girls and certainly not by an Adelaide drunk on music and admiration and late nights, who I left standing while I swirled off with another, despite having permitted that poor boy to mark my dance card.

Imagine thinking of that now. Poor boy, poor boy. He had stood, so unhappy, striving not to look it at the edge of a laughing group of young men, all fevered and animated in their arrogance. I caught glimpses of him in snatches as faces and feathers swept past, and the music played on.

What a coward I am and always have been. I pressed my cool hand to my face a moment, then bent back to my work.

In any case, it was not long after that all my headiness was silenced. By Mr Hadley.

I looked at my husband, tilted my head away to take a breath, and reached with the spoon for more water.

My mind wandered down another path: *The sewing machine takes up too much space in the morning room. We are perpetually having to find our way around it.*

I tipped the smallest sip of water to Mr Hadley's mouth so that it would slip between his lips without choking him. Lowering his head a little at just the right moment, I had discovered, would enable him to swallow and the water not dribble out and onto the cloth.

Mr Hadley's study. I tipped the spoon again. *Else there is no use for the room at all.*

I reached for more water.

We should put the drawing room under sheets. I will spend days in flattering Mrs Staynes; she will be persuaded that though things change, there is no wrong in it. The morning room does for all occasions, I fancy.

I stood for a moment, teaspoon in hand.

Judging that Mr Hadley had had as much water as he needed, I sat once more and glanced at the clock on the mantel. In the hearth, the fire was burning low, though Cissy would be along soon to encourage it. Luncheon would be served, once my husband's fouled cloths and sheets had been changed and Cook's gruel—whose thickness was now become so well judged—fed to him.

Lord. The dining room. The very thought of it made me draw my shawl close and tight.

Chapter Twenty-six

I think you should speak, Sobriety.'

The maid's silence, in the days after Toby's departure for his friend's house and horses, had hung about the house like a doom-laden wraith in weeds. *Our inescapable passenger,* I considered it. It accompanied us from room to room, from meal to meal. It sat with us as a third at luncheon, a presence cold as the room itself, and the gelid soup, and the fish lying yellow in its congealing sauce before us.

It had wrapped itself around the little woman like a shawl, some-thing knitted from the yarn of a deep despondence. When Sobriety paused in the hallway to regard the dish with its few visiting cards and notes, the inspector's topmost, and turned away without expression, I knew the very claylike emptiness of her face held meaning. This meaning spoke in its very stillness even while she watched Albert carry the sewing machine to the study, while Cissy followed with the heavy piles of folded material that had these past days taken up so much space in the morning room.

Sobriety sat now and stared unmoving at the mending in her hand. The light from the window fell on the whiteness of her face and it glowed faintly, for sadness fed a lingering physical weakness, and both lent her translucence.

'Please speak to me, my dear.'

Sobriety looked at me, slowly, as if she were not inclined even toward this much movement. There was a small flicker pinched about her eyebrows, and I fancied she was about to speak, but instead she shook her head and looked back down at her sewing.

She cannot find the words.

'You know I will persist.' I drew the small footstool up in front of

Sobriety and arranged myself upon it.

'I know you will.' She slid the needle into her work for safekeeping. She smoothed the cloth with long strokes.

And still there was nothing but wordless emptiness, through which travelled a distant rattle on the road outside, perhaps of some rickety vehicle come lurching back from a long trip to market. Sobriety sat with a frown, her fingertips to her lips, then looked again at me, with a slight wave of her hand.

'I'm sorry. I cannot think where to start.'

I took her hand between mine.

'Is it that you like Mr Broadford?'

'To tell the truth, I do not know.' She considered a moment. 'Although he is presentable. And intelligent. And passably amusing.'

She drew a deep breath and her mouth pinched together.

'And for all that,' she said, 'he is a simple man, and straightforward, and that is a good thing.'

See, she has been considering him.

'No, it would be difficult…delicate enough if it were only that. But it is not…'

I waited.

'You know I am not quite well yet, after…after. And it is so hard, so very hard for me to have a man pay his attentions—' She glanced quickly into my eyes, and then away. 'For he *is* paying attention to me.'

'It is very evident, Sobriety.'

She flushed.

She is annoyed with me, I thought, a little guilty. *That was out of place.* 'I am sorry. This is not a time for levity, I know that. Please tell me what troubles you.'

Sobriety closed her eyes a moment, then with the smallest of movements nodded her head, before speaking again in a quiet rush, as if to get the words out before her own confusion refused to let them see light.

'I do not know my own feelings in this, but I have been thinking that it does not matter what they might be—it is immaterial what they might be—because I am not worthy in any case. I am sullied. I am lost. My body testifies to this…' She halted, and let her breath out in a long sigh that left her still once more, as if only that breath had animated her.

'Your body is wounded, my dear, and will rally —'

'My body is wounded because I…because…'

What can I say?

Sobriety's face was by now wet with tears, washing down her face in sheets. She wiped at them with her handkerchief, roughly, as if her weeping had come only to distract, to try her while she found the will to speak. I remembered my own handkerchief and searched in my sleeve for it, and without speaking exchanged it for hers, which was bunched into a wet ball.

'I cannot see what option you had, Sobriety.'

'And yet, I must carry the sin, all of the sin; for what I show to the world, to God, represents what I am…' Her voice had lost its own cadence; she intoned, nearly chanted as if from a remembered text.

'Blood may expiate, or it may condemn…'

This is her father speaking. I cast my imagination to the small man, hard with labour, taut and brown, his face massed with sharp pleats thin as razor cuts from decades of squinting into God's weather as it slashed or shone; who gathered together his sternest powers to preach by night, driven by belief. By candlelight wavering in the shadowed hall, he would address the gathered folk of their small hamlet, his eyes black and fathoms deep. His voice would rise to a shriek that could pierce the ears and conscience, until some soul was overwhelmed and fell down in agonies of guilt, delivered thus on the floor of the sin of self-will, of independence of being, of pride. Wailing, sweating and quivering with it, curled in fear like a child.

I recalled this story, which Sobriety had told to me as one of many. This had been before Hope was victim to the cholera and also after she had died, so that Sobriety's tales grew darker and the chill of moaning winter nights and desolation could be felt in them. In the telling, she had whispered an admission, as if her father might be lurking near to hear it. She may, she said, privately have been repulsed by the self-abasement of her father's self-confessed sinners. This was not something she had ever thought to herself at the time, but now she fancied there had always dwelt in her mind some germ of this repulsion, and this was in itself a thing that haunted. For here was betrayal, was it not, of the respect which one ought to pay one's father? Of the commandment—was there not a commandment?—not to doubt the preacher, for this itself was pride.

'The Lord sees what I am and it must be this...' The tears trickled more slowly now and she sat with my handkerchief gripped in both hands, her eyes nearly closed. 'And it must be that it was always evident, that I had perhaps the sin of pride, of self-sufficiency, and it was for this reason that Mr—' She halted, as if she could not say the name.

'Mr Hadley,' I whispered.

My Sobriety closed her eyes a moment and took a breath.

'It is for that reason—because what I am was evident—that he... that he took...and he retains...because I am spoiled for all else, and God can see this, and that then, though I tried to put it away from sight, He could see my sin, which was great, it *is* great...'

She hugged herself close, rocking back and forth, while her voice sank lower and lower, her eyes closed, and her mouth barely moved. She was murmuring fast, as if at prayer.

'...Mr Hadley was the instrument and has taken and he keeps... I am fit for no man, and no man would accept me, for how could he when I am thus used and thus spoiled by another...'

I was moved to grip Sobriety by the shoulders, to hold her still.

'Stop!'

'If I were good, if I knew I had grace, I would yearn to die, to be joined to the Lord. But I cannot, for I do not deserve it…'

'*Stop!*'

She stopped, panting, her eyes swollen as if she had fever, her face blotched and wet with water that had run to the end of her chin and dripped to her chest. I tweaked my handkerchief from Sobriety's clenched fingers and wiped my friend's face.

'You speak as your father would have spoken. And yet you have not always—you have told me this—been so absolutely convinced by his preaching.'

She will make herself ill, or mad, with this. What can I say? Sobriety's face was white with a trance of exhaustion.

'Are you listening to me?'

There was a pause, before she nodded slowly. I took a breath and spoke. 'Mr Hadley owns the sin, my dear. All of the sin. You must know this. I know what he did to you, for after all it was like what he did to me. But what he did to you was worse, far worse, for he knew all that could befall you as a result of…what he did. And…' I paused for more breath. 'And how can he possess any part of you when that would make him a bigamist?'

I am inspired! Though he has done his best—his worst—she must not be permitted to believe in her own ruination.

Sobriety looked up at this, her eyes wide, for the moment. I looked into them—the red rims and the eyelashes wet and clumped into spikes, the puffiness that gathered now in the soft flesh around the eyes—and myself also felt shock at the word, the notion itself, the linking of ourselves in this iniquity, that I had pronounced it in some headlong giddiness that propelled all along with it. My mouth moved a moment before sound would issue.

'Like the abominable Mr Farquharson.'

There was another moment's pause, until we both laughed, high-pitched, Sobriety's giggle harsh and desperate, and in the end only an avenue for more tears.

'And yet, I cannot ignore my own sin and ruin—'

'This is your father again, Sobriety. You have no end of quarrelsome relatives with argument to counter his, you have told me their stories.' *This is such hard work.* 'And I have always thought it made you weigh evidence with a great objectivity.'

'But—'

Look at her. I must not fail to make her doubt her own damnation.

'Remember your Uncle James.' *Oh yes, James!* 'He would argue with your father on anything, but most about sin, you told me. And what did he quote that you recalled to me from your childhood, that Mr Thomas Spence the Jacobin had written at the very beginning of this century?'

Sobriety closed her eyes. I could barely hear her speak. 'I do not recall.'

'Oh yes, you do. It began, "What is the significance of great reforms..." No, that is not quite it...'

Sobriety sighed. Depleted though she was by the tyranny of her wringing emotion, her glance said that she recognised my ploy to make her recite these words.

'It was: "What signifies Reform of Government or Redress of Public Grievances, if people cannot have their domestic grievances redressed?"'

'Lord, Sobriety! The stuff of revolution! Mr Hadley would have fetched the army!'

Look, she smiles a little, at least. As she ought, for I have apparently turned politician in order to save her!

'And yet—'

'Do not judge yourself more harshly than you would others, Sobriety.'

Sobriety shook her head slowly side to side, and opened her mouth to answer. *Still, she persists!*

'Sobriety, did you ever think that I deserved Mr Hadley?'

The maid's eyes opened wide at that. 'No, no, of course I did not!' *Bless her, my only friend!*

'Well, there! Mr Hadley has committed his own sins, and we are left to survive them.'

We women were still. A dog barked outside in the street and a child shouted at it. Sobriety took a breath that wavered, stopped and took another before she whispered: 'Did you ever hate me for it?'

'Hate you? Why?'

Yet, for an instant I recalled a resentment that had indeed swept over me and left its trace, come from knowing that my husband took his needs to my maid. He had chosen to enter Sobriety, forcibly, while I listened and was thus shamed, humiliated, reproved, I supposed, for my inadequacies. And set aside in this way, with this demonstration of my inconsequence, even while he would nevertheless continue to visit me without notice. Yet then I would think of Sobriety's little body pressed in this way, and know that his thrusting at me crashed my own bedhead against the wall so that Sobriety, in turn, would know…

The very memory turned me cold. I took breath, and with that knew for certain that Mr Hadley had intended in his brutality thus not merely to take possession of both, and humiliate both, but also to tear us one from another as beings who lived a life in friendship when he was not in the house.

I kissed Sobriety's hand.

'My love, no. I could not hate you. This was his sin, and he sinned against both of us.' We looked away from each other, until Sobriety sighed and I relaxed at last.

I sat back on my stool, my head swimming with the concentration I had brought to this conversation; I felt myself powerful with it, triumphant somehow, as if I had been doing battle against such demons, in armour and with sword and shield, on behalf of both of us. And then there was a sense of revelation, to know that I had spoken nothing but the truth, that somehow the truth had declared itself in all of this discussion with Sobriety.

I do absolutely believe all that I have said. I do.

Sobriety's breathing had calmed; she sat thoughtful, the salt crusting around her eyes and on her cheeks. But I felt Sobriety's thoughts, perhaps, turn with mine to the farm kitchen, dark with stone and smoke. I pictured the too-hot fire in the hearth and the cold needling from cracks in windows and door, the press of bodies around the great, thick table grooved from a century of scrubbing. There were the silent children with their elbows upon the table listening again to the two men raising voices in a perpetual battle of credos which contradicted yet were nonetheless born alike in opposition to the corruption of power, of State, and of Church.

And I felt Sobriety's knowledge, an awareness leached by sadness, that a Sobriety violated and changed by Mr Hadley, and driven thereby to seek a miscarriage, could find no welcome or comfort at that hearth if her secret were ever honestly divulged, though that violation itself was enacted out of the very corruption that had fed the wrath and guided the oratory of Farmer Mullins.

Her secret separates her from her family. It is the secret itself that is the change in her, and it is unbearable.

Winding between us there was, too, that knowledge of Mr Hadley in his bedroom above, his own power evaporated, his body ebbing toward death.

If we are both his wives, then we will soon be widows.

I closed my eyes. *Perfidious woman! It is my own self-will that speaks, as if it were a separate thing! Wrong, wrong, to wish for his death!*

I had another thought. *And Mrs Charles. Do I count her in our widowed band? No, no. She is of a different case.* I shrugged a little, and shook my head clear of thoughts of Mrs Charles.

I opened my eyes. Sobriety had been staring at the window where a small bird was an agitated shadow beyond the lace. We women now looked at each other. In a long moment, looking thus into Sobriety's face, I came to know that this woman would never dress the facts of a case in anything but its own plain clothing. Her task was first to confront what Mr Hadley had left her, and then to accept that it was a story that could not be told without disaster to herself, to family or indeed to spouse—should Mr Broadford press his suit—no matter what affection lay there.

'If Mr Hadley had thought to make us both friendless, he has failed,' I said at last.

Sobriety reached to touch my hand, and took breath.

'While I fear God's grace may have gone, yet all I can do is find what is best to do for duty on my path,' she said. 'And, besides, I must find this path so that Mr Broadford can know my mind, for otherwise there would be sin also in allowing an understanding that may not exist.'

In a half-dream that night, I felt that I floated in the eddies of the night air, wrapped in my quilt and sheet which made a tail behind me as I travelled, and my hair flew behind me too, loose as I had worn it as a girl. I slid close to rooftops and chimneypots, gliding as fish glide, for the air had a thick feel to it, like water, and gently glided as watery currents do. I passed Sobriety's bedroom window, but all was dark within and I could not tell how Sobriety slept. The shadow that was my maid moved once, but there was nothing to tell if Sobriety's dreams were good or bad.

I glided on.

Elsewhere, sometimes there were lights in the mounded darkness of buildings, and lamps left circles of dim gold, but beyond these were doorways of ink or black shelter behind carts where breathed huddled bodies—of children, perhaps, or young girls—murmuring in sleep.

Chapter Twenty-seven

I had on my mind a great crowd of womenfolk, ones that I knew well and others that I did not. There were those of my household, those whose very character—I came to feel it in a rush—gave shape to both myself and this house. There was Sobriety; there was clinging, fearful and now lost little Mrs Farquharson; there was that girl, that shadow of the street. That nameless soul.

To this crowd I chose not to add Mrs Charles nor, indeed, the sensual woman who even now hung her fur-clad flesh on Mr Hadley's wall.

I drew out my writing, that entitled 'Ladies, what of the world between us all?' and dipped my pen:

> . . . *those who have not our good fortune, who have none to care for them, and for whom misfortune, indeed, has led to despair and perhaps madness.*
>
> *Think on it, ladies, how the fairer, gentler sex can be exalted or cast down, by others or merely by fate! And then understand how, at your own hearth, without a word you are yet bound in a deep companionship with those women who are about you, whatever their station.*

I read the addition, with the whole, and could not help but raise my eyebrows at myself. *There! 'Tis true, I am cousin to the Italian revolutionary! Or some such.* I sighed—or subsided— and put the paper away. *This ladies' revolution of mine will be a private one, I fancy.*

'Sobriety and I will take luncheon in the kitchen, Mrs Staynes.'

This was sudden, said just at the close of arrangements between me and my housekeeper to do with the sewing machine (with the man coming from the emporium that afternoon to demonstrate its use) and the time that might be taken by each of us to practice. That is, today perhaps Albert might spend additional time with Mr Hadley, so as to enable the women to receive their tuition with the machine, while, later, time for further practice must be set aside, despite household duties. Further, arrangements must also be made for the next day, when Cissy may yet have to testify in committal proceedings against Mr Farquharson, who was also Mr Forster, the Mancunian grocer. Poor Cissy—to whom we all were now speaking especially kindly, while keeping an eye open for danger to vases approached by the affrighted girl.

It had seemed a complicated thing to Mrs Staynes. In addition to disliking change in the way things were done, she quite evidently disliked the indignity of seeming to struggle with newness itself. Any disturbance to the everyday, ever-repeating tasks of the house, to its deep and reassuring patterns, was a disturbance to Mrs Staynes, and disturbance was by its very nature unsettling and apt to play upon the nerves. Earthquake and pestilence would, I felt, have had less effect on Mrs Staynes than this disturbance to domestic organisation.

I had written the plan down so that Mrs Staynes could be satisfied that all had been taken into account in an orderly way, and she was about to leave the room. Yet there was a rigidity now clamped upon her figure and her features that indicated she had yet to accept the changes. While she knew these were inevitable—Mr Hadley's study turned into a ladies' sewing room (at last, my morning room would be rid of that machine!); a strange man coming to teach us the uses of this contraption; the cessation of work while he was here; Cissy's upsetting of all our rituals while she (possibly) spoke in a public place about terrible things—there was certainly something about her eyes that spoke of someone lost and afraid, despite all assurances. One knew, after all, how to nurse a sick person—this was simple duty—but the tumbling down of one's ordered world about one's ears was a very different thing altogether. Mrs Staynes clung to word-less and frozen dignity as her only option, given the circumstances, and turned to face the unknown armoured thus. Her hand was upon the door handle when my announcement tumbled out at her feet.

'Oh, Mrs Staynes, I meant to say…I have decided that henceforth Sobriety and I will dine in the kitchen.'

Mrs Staynes appeared to freeze on the spot. *That was not done diplomatically.*

It tumbled, abrupt and rude, though I had essayed various intro-ductory speeches to myself that morning over coffee. I knew, what-ever was said to lessen the effect of such a statement of revolution, Mrs Staynes would be shocked: the house disrupted once more, upstairs brought downstairs, domestic relations set in flux, with the whole placing its foot onto untested ground.

I cleared my throat. It gave a moment in which to slow my speech and to regain an authority I felt had left me with Mrs Staynes's arrest, statue-like, at the door.

'I think it would be best at least for the rest of winter.'

Mrs Staynes turned slowly, dropping her hand from the handle, and stood, holding her face so without movement that the distress within was evident.

She hopes she will end by comprehending some other meaning in my words. Poor thing! Think of the relief were this to be so— 'Oh ma'am, do you know what I thought you had just said!'

'Ma'am?'

'We are so very cold in the dining room, Mrs Staynes. It is so very uncomfortable and cold that even the food is never warm—'

'I'm sure we do our best.' Mrs Staynes was become marble—she was as pale and as unmoving—and her gaze was directed over my head.

*Now s*he *struggles even for resignation.*

'Oh, Mrs Staynes. One could not hope for better. You are my helpmeet in all things domestic—' The housekeeper had moved her hand to her waist where hung the household keys, though she still stood perfectly erect with offence, and perhaps with irresolution. 'But it would be beyond the best of servants—as you are, absolutely—to overcome the effect of that room. The fault lies somehow in the building of the house itself, I believe.' I looked at Mrs Staynes's face.

She strives so hard for dignity because she fears the ground shifting beneath her feet.

'Do you think the problem lies with the house?' I gave this a lilting appeal, that which I had always used for my elders, aside from Mr Hadley, in circumstances like enough to this. It was an appeal that relied on the older person's indulgence. It paid a compliment; it asked for patronage.

If she answers me, we are nearly arrived.

Mrs Staynes's set lips parted to mutter, 'Perhaps it has to do with the lack of windows.'

Ah, she replies.

'Indeed, indeed, I think that you are right. But in any case, it does mean that we are never comfortable there, that food never tastes as it should, and...' I hesitated.

'Yes, ma'am?'

'As things are, Mrs Staynes, with Mr Hadley ill and unresponsive as he is and all of our work in consequence to establish our pattern of life—and you and I have worked together to achieve what I never might have done alone—it feels like banishment at mealtimes to preside over frozen discomfort, as I must in there.'

Gazing at Mrs Staynes, I kept my eyes a little wide, conscious that my own cheeks still held the fullness of a woman not yet thirty, almost a girl next to Mrs Staynes. I allowed my mouth to fall softly, hoping there was something of a pleading pout about it, with nothing overdone but just enough to assure the housekeeper's authority as the elder.

Mrs Staynes looked at last into my own face, and I felt tightness ease from my shoulders. *She returns. She has collected herself.* There was a gradual smile of condescension there, affection creeping with the small nest of wrinkles about her eyes. It was not a full smile; it was a little sharp for that. I understood that she was allowing herself to be won over, and perhaps that only to avoid impasse.

'Well, ma'am,' Mrs Staynes said. 'You know that I do not like disturbance to the right way of doing things.'

I nodded, my face still upturned.

She said, 'But I can concede this, for that is not a pleasant room at this time of year.'

I kept my gaze still.

Mrs Staynes turned back to the door and reached for the handle, 'I shall send Cissy to put the room under sheets.' She paused a moment to speak over her shoulder.

'It should be said, ma'am, that you have shown a mettle of late not many would have suspected, and—' She looked directly into my eyes and tipped her head just a little to one side. '—an uncommon capacity for persuasion.'

Soup was taken in almost complete silence, as if the hush customary for the rest of the house had travelled here and taken root. Cook essayed some quiet stirring at the stove and lifted the lid on the beans very slowly so that steam billowed out in a noiseless cloud. In the unnatural quiet—where normally all would be clattering and banging, and the door swinging on its hinges with the to-ing and fro-ing and the sweeping of skirts, the tapping and sliding of feet on the flagstones, and the giving of orders and the chattering asides—Cook then lowered the lid slowly to the pot and achieved this with no noise whatever.

When Sobriety and I had entered the kitchen, it was as if we were somehow strangers. Everyone stopped work to watch us approach the table. Two settings had been laid, with silver and crystal and cambric, and set at the end of the big table so that we sat in a space apart from the rest, who did not sit but stood about—except for Cook, who could resort to a flourish with the poker at the stove's fire—as if they had forgotten their lines in a play.

Albert—who might normally take his luncheon at Mr Hadley's bedside but had exchanged his turn with Cissy, so that she might be present later to learn the mechanisms of the sewing machine— slipped outside to the courtyard, with a pair of boots and blacking in his hand for an excuse. I wondered whether these were Albert's own boots, for Mr Hadley was beyond soiling his own.

Mrs Staynes advanced a step to hover between the table and Cook's stove, and Cook, swinging the black iron door closed on the fire, leaned slowly toward her cooking pots and ministered to us in near-silent pantomime.

By the finish of soup, the tableau was infinitesimally less stiff, even though every movement was hesitant and stilted still, for I praised the taste and added, 'And it was warm, ladies, as are we, which is clearly how luncheon is meant to be, had we but known it!'

Mrs Staynes swayed a little on her feet like a soldier on parade. She blinked at an overloud hoot from Cook, who flushed at herself and said, 'The heat brings out the flavour, that is certain.' Cook set herself to ladling out portions of herbed stew whose gravy steamed so that the kitchen smelt of it, and Mrs Staynes laid it on the table with a murmur that Cook had been very particular with this meal, since she would be audience to its eating.

Cook clasped her big arms about her middle and watched the play of knife and fork, and the lifting of forks to mouths, and nodded when comment was made. Sobriety had to blow to cool her morsel down, and I said to the rest, 'This is a rare problem for the two of us,' and Cook laughed.

It was clear that Cook paid especial attention to Sobriety's eating for, while she strove to eat it, and though it was more palatable for the heat, she did not take much. For some time, weeks perhaps, this had been the case—everyone knew of the empty plate and the half-empty plate that descended to the kitchen thrice daily. So now, when Sobriety laid down her fork, Cook had ready a hot concoction in a cup, and trotted past Mrs Staynes to place it before Sobriety, saying, 'I know you've been peaky, Miss Mullins. This is my auntie's brew and is sure to pick you up.'

Sobriety had no option, evidently, and sipped while all the women watched. There was a pinkness gathering about her eyes.

Look, she will weep soon.

I turned away and raised my voice. 'Cook, you know that the man comes today to demonstrate the machine for sewing? Would you care to observe our efforts and perhaps take your turn?'

Cook must now look away from Sobriety. 'Oh, ma'am, yes.' And the conversation turned to how very interesting it would be to learn to sew with the machine. Sobriety lowered her cup.

At the finish of the meal, our chairs were drawn out for us and, nodding to the servants, we rustled from the room; it could be heard repossessing itself behind us, with noises and movement and a sense of the return of familiar purpose.

Chapter Twenty-eight

The Emporium's young Mr Dinsdale, the centre of female attention, appeared to grow taller in the assertion of his maleness. He had so forgotten himself after half an hour that he wagged his finger in Cissy's face and, it must be said, flirted with Cook. All had, at first, listened to his explanations, each craning to observe his finger on the pages of instruction open on the desk. Our skirts ballooned and pressed up against the bookshelves of the small room, the smell of books and papers and cigar smoke now overlaid with that of new machinery and its oil.

Sobriety had, with this audience shuffling to make way, taken her turn at the machine first of all, for she would have most of the care of my personal sewing. The clatter and whirr of the machine, the crumpling and entangling of the material and the several attempts at an easy rhythm on the foot pedal—all had the effect of setting Cissy to giggling. Cook was no better, her low hoot oddly schoolgirlish even while she clicked her tongue in reproof; and Mrs Staynes drew closer to me, disapproval lending rigidity even while her entire body tilted the better to see, for she was curious and also obliged to know what the rest of the household knew.

I found myself observing the housekeeper. *It is as if she needs a name for her feelings in such a situation, else she does not know how to comport herself!*

Next came Mrs Staynes's turn. She sat with an unmoving glare at Mr Dinsdale, apparently in case he should forget himself into familiarity with her, and proceeded something like a marionette through her lesson. She made rushes at the pedal, darting to pull material away from the plunging needle, with all the time her lips pressed tight. It was evidently no time for levity, and so Cook and Cissy fell into silence until it came to their turns, which they took with whispered encouragement of each other.

Cissy, finally, held up an object very like a handkerchief, that she had hemmed with the machine, and it was then there came a knock at the door and she must rush off to answer it, while the rest pressed back to allow her through. She was back soon—she must have run, indeed, in her eagerness to be back in the room with its machine of absorbing interest—and held out a letter to me. I opened it and read.

Mr Dinsdale, his package of instructions under his arm, accepted an invitation to a cup of tea with Cook before he must take his leave. The hallway, crowded and a-chirrup for a moment with all those spilled from the study, emptied and quieted as Cook took Mr Dinsdale off to the kitchen, Sobriety gathered herself to climb the stairs to the morning room, and Mrs Staynes accompanied her up one flight to the linen cupboard with scraps of material salvaged from our afternoon lesson on the machine.

Cissy, too, while rendered slow with the anti-climax now that the sewing demonstration had come to an end, was about to mount the stairs to relieve Albert at his post by Mr Hadley's bed, when I called to her.

'Cissy, it is a letter from the inspector, Mr Broadbent. In a way it is for you.'

'Oh, ma'am, perhaps I don't have to—?'

'No, my poor girl. It says that you must attend the court for the committal case of Mr Farquharson.' I folded the letter. 'There is a difficulty with the trains, it seems, so it is not certain the other witnesses coming from Manchester will be there in time.'

Cissy stopped still and opened her mouth, though no sound came for a moment. Of a sudden, now that there was no reprieve for her, the girl looked small, like a child's toy, and very alone, standing on the first tread of the complacent Hadley staircase as if at the gaping mouth of some monster.

'Although, I understand the police are certain the witnesses will be present for the trial itself,' I said. 'So it is just this visit you must make. That is all.'

'Yes, ma'am.' The child's voice had disappeared.

'Poor Cissy,' I said to Sobriety that evening. We were in the morning room with the curtains drawn and the world reduced to ourselves before the crackling of the fire, light and shadow shifting on the walls. Outside, beyond the thick curtains, a fitful rain fell, and there must have been an equally uncertain wind, for occasionally there was a moaning while rain spat at the glass. I held my novel, fetched from the library, so that the light from the fire would illuminate the pages.

'We shall be there, and it will be over quickly enough, I suppose,' Sobriety said.

My eyes drooped a little. The words upon the page danced about and blurred, and must wait for a better light. The flames would drop soon, from great, lapping hot tongues to darting fingers and then to secret, thrumming embers. *So tired*, I thought, and wondered at this until my mind ran over all of the things that had happened today, new things in my life, and would happen tomorrow, and had happened thus far after Mr Hadley's crisis. And would continue to happen, for now there was no stopping at all if there were to be a place for me and mine in this world so unstable and unaccountable.

There were times, many times, when an anchor of some sort would be of enormous use, for my world swung about and changed so that I felt I had no purchase on it, no firm grip at all.

I let myself sink into the warmth, watched the hectic flames, placed a marker in the book and closed it, drew my shawl close at a smattering against the windowpane.

We were alone, yet the chaotic dance of light and shadow across the walls and ceiling might imply, if one were so minded, that this was not so. *As if,* I thought, *a conclave of spirits fidgeted and played.* I allowed myself to consider it.

'Shall you come with me to see Mrs Courtney's spiritualist?'

'Certainly, if you wish.'

There was snap from the fireplace, and a small log disintegrated.

'I had an aunt like that,' Sobriety said. 'Well, to be precise, she was a fortune teller.'

'This must have been a subject—another subject—to liven the dinner table.'

'Indeed it was.'

The rain outside settled into a steady drenching.

Sobriety said, 'Cook sometimes has an inclination that way, I believe.' 'You do not say that, surely, because she offered you a cheering concoction?'

'No, of course not. She reads tea leaves. She read Cissy's.'

'Poor Cissy.'

Sobriety understood my meaning perfectly.

'It will be over soon enough,' she said.

Chapter Twenty-nine

The crowded gallery was oppressive with chatter and shuffling, movement bending back and forth and restive; hands and kerchiefs waving, hands clutching and pointing, sudden laughter. All were compressed between the plain, unadorned ends of the seating, polished by countless hands over countless years, and lit by windows four panes wide and very tall and square. The light coming into this room from the grey day beyond was flat, unforgiving, and lent no colour to the faces around me, though the brass chandeliers declared pomp even while this paying public contradicted it. Gaslight hissed in brackets upon the walls.

I attempted not to appear as if I gazed about myself.

The mahogany table in the centre of this room lent the weight of authority to the lawyers, who arranged their papers upon it. Their place, however, was humbler than the raised bench of the judge, whose seat was of leather and edged with studs. And all of this impressed all the more with false columns and the carved canopy that bore the coat of arms of the court and realm.

The man pressed against me on the public's bench was too large for his clothes, his hems threadbare and grey with grime, the buttonholes on his food-spotted waistcoat fraying from the strain of containing his great, pressing gut. He shifted suddenly from time to time as if bothered by a travelling itch, and stirred up a concoction of smells from himself, of ancient sweat and of drink—soaked, apparently, into his very being—and an ammoniac presence to make the eyes water. At Sobriety's side sat a woman equally large, whose overblown arms spread in sleeves like wings, so that Sobriety must tilt very slightly toward me.

Sobriety and I had worn our veils into the courtroom and would, by tacit agreement between ourselves, keep them over their faces. We held scented handkerchiefs to our noses. We knew we gave an impression of separation from the press of common folk with this veiled anonymity and felt a small sense, however imaginary, of safety because of it. We had drawn the veils over our faces almost as one, after descending from the carriage, and whispered courage to Cissy and squeezed her shoulders. We assured her, before she went into the building by her own witness's entrance, that we would be near her in the courtroom as she testified. Nonetheless, there was a tension in us as we sat side by side, and I became aware after a time that my jaw was clenched. The crowd, meanwhile, restless as if suffering delay at a theatrical event, began to call out to each other, and this loudly, either in abrupt and rude language or in jest.

The pause between hearings came to an end, at last, and the court officer's stick sounded against the floor. The chattering noise settled to a sibilant humming, a coughing and a shushing, and all eyes swung to the front. Mr Farquharson (or Mr Forster) was led into the dock, where he stood with the jury on his right. He faced an empty space, raised so as to be easily visible to all, what I supposed must be for witnesses, of whom Cissy would be one.

Poor Cissy.

I recalled Mr Farquharson was a tall man, but was surprised none-theless by the breadth of his shoulders and a girth solid with the consciousness of power rather than over-easy living. From the dock he loomed over the court. He was unmoving and watchful, the cut of his coat perfection and fresh-brushed as though his valet stood just without the door (*perhaps he does*), his waistcoat a medley of greys and an embroidered intertwining of leaves whose every detail spoke of wealth and the hours spent by his tailor's apprentices on his behalf.

Poor Cissy.

When last I had seen this man, he had been in supreme command of himself, his polished mansion, and of the great crowd of folk who came to fawn and pay him court. What stirred now in his brain? Was there shame, or apprehension at the slide of all his expectation?

I had wondered in like fashion this morning to Sobriety. 'There are folk who cannot see fault in their own actions,' she had said. 'They lay blame anywhere but at home for what befalls them.'

Mr Farquharson now surveyed the humming room with an air of cold anger.

Safe behind my veil, I regarded him and how he stood tall still, and surveyed all, as if, despite everything, he were the powerful one and entitled, absolutely, to that power. He had met Mr Hadley once, he told me that day in Mr Hadley's drawing room. It must have been a meeting of like to like, their handclasp joining two souls of similar intent, who likewise cleaved to control as their machine for living life. *They stood eye to eye and saw this in each other.*

The murmuring began again to rise in pitch as individuals around the court discussed the wealthy gentleman caught out in bigamy. Two heads in front of me leaned bonnets into each other, nodding and agitating, although I could not hear what was said. Mr Farquharson's marriages were clearly the cause of a vast interest. I supposed that such a crowd was not usual in the courtroom, particularly at a committal.

'Silence!' came of a sudden from the court officer, who this time struck his stick with a force upon the floor that caused both Sobriety and me to jump. There was a gasp behind us, something rattled to the boards, and the crowd grew quiet. At last, the gas could be heard once again to hiss.

'Be upstanding for His Honour!' The voice was overloud now in the newly quiet chamber, and its owner glared at the gallery as

227

all struggled to their feet and filled the ancient space with creaking, shuffling and the clearing of throats. The magistrate entered and clambered to his seat. I recognized the Lord Mayor, for I had shared a table with him on more than one occasion of formal dining at the house of some acquaintance of Mr Hadley's. I wondered if he would also preside as judge at the trial proper. It was not unheard of, I understood. His Worship had, that evening, bent close over his soup in much the same way that he now bent over his counter, or desk, and the gavel that lay before him. Oddly, I recalled the few white hairs that sprang in haphazard style from his freckled, balding head. The wig, I surmised, must scratch.

The crowd subsided, creaking and shuffling once more, back into its seats.

The first to speak as witness was Inspector Broadford, which he did in a manner to assure those present of his authority, even though he was not tall. He stood erect, but was neither stiff nor self-conscious, so that an idea of that authority settled about his person. I sensed the slight turn of Sobriety's veiled head, and a tilt of Sobriety's shoulders, with the attention she was giving him. He gave his answers in a firm voice so that there could be no doubt about it, and Mr Farquharson's lawyer seemed to me, indeed, uninterested in placing any doubt there.

I became aware—as this lawyer paused and bent to touch a paper on top of the pile at his desk, so that he could read something there—of sensations in contradiction to each other. Once again I felt both visitor to and a partaker in proceedings. I was a stranger and yet so deeply involved, while nothing was familiar. *I have never been in such a place*, it occurred to me, regarding the spread of my skirt pressed up against my noisome neighbour, who twitched once more and suddenly shifted his leg. *Yet it is as if the inspector were a friend whom one wants to do well.*

My other neighbour, Sobriety, sat very still. Though she, too, was veiled, I knew that Sobriety's gaze was direct upon Mr Broadford, and Mr Broadford, somehow alert to Sobriety's concentration, looked up for a moment at the small woman hidden behind dark gauze.

Look there. He is a determined man.

Mr Broadford's time as witness did not last long, for he was only paving the way for Cissy, the true link between London's Mr Farquharson and Manchester's Mr Forster. The murmuring began again as the inspector stood down and then Cissy entered by the witness door—ashen, clumsy as she crossed the floor, looking about herself as she came. She nearly halted in so doing, bewildered for the moment as to where to go next until the prosecutor touched her elbow and directed her to the witness stand.

She cannot see us here.

I thought to lift my veil, just for now, so that the girl could see that she was not alone, and Sobriety did the same. Cissy, upon climbing to the stand where she stood very nearly engulfed by it, looked about and saw us, replied to our smiles with a small one of her own, breathing out—it was evident—in some relief.

The officer's stick thudded and everyone jumped once more. It was then that Cissy raised her eyes and beheld Mr Farquharson immediately ahead of and above her, for he was such a large man, and the eyes in his impassive face directed so pointedly at her. What had been left of colour in her face now faded utterly, and she stared at him as if she had no will to do otherwise.

I recalled that Cissy was often hard to find when Mr Hadley was at home, perhaps for fear of him, too.

'Miss Cissy Smithson?' said the prosecutor.

Cissy did not appear to hear. She stared at the man in the dock as if he might strike her, like a snake, should she look away.

'Miss Smithson?'

She turned her head and gazed at the prosecutor, with dark eyes in their bloodless background, pale and fragile as bleached muslin, in what I knew to be a desperate concentration to block out Mr Farquharson's concerted glare. The little maid barely blinked.

Chapter Thirty

*Y*our name is Cissy Smithson?' the prosecutor asked.

'Yes, sir.'

'What, what? The child is whispering! Speak up, girl!' The magistrate, leaning forward and held his hand to his ear.

'Yes, sir! My name is Cissy Smithson!' Cissy nearly shouted at the start of her response, then faltered and faded and bowed her head, now turning red as a new brick. Some folk in the gallery tittered, and the officer bellowed: 'Silence!'

But the prosecutor put into his voice a fatherly purr and a brief chuckle, such that all would recognize a kindly patriarch in him. Several members of the gallery smirked and nodded, raised their eyebrows at each other. I glanced around. *Such theatre. Everything is theatre.*

'Thank you, Cissy. No, there is no cause for nervousness. We are here only to find the truth.'

Cissy nodded, and kept her eyes on the prosecutor as he bade her tell her story, of how she recognized Mr Farquharson as Mr Forster the grocer (who had served her mother for many years in his Manchester shop), when he had called upon her mistress after the rescue of the baby.

Several heads began to turn in search of any other person from Cissy's household, and we twitched our veils back over our faces. Each of us felt the turn of her neighbour's head. Beside me the portly man breathed so that a waft of old smoked fish and of even older rot stirred the gauze of my veil. Some others also guessed that these two women were the rescuers of the Farquharson child, nudged each other and pointed, but turned their heads back to the court after only a few moments, with a stirring of musty clothes and a creak of old timber.

Cissy calmed after a little while of sympathetic questioning, but then it was the turn of Mr Farquharson's lawyer. He had been making notes all the time that she was speaking, and came up to the witness stand with his papers clutched in his hand. He stood gazing at the papers for some moments before he looked up at Cissy and smiled a long, vulpine smile. He had colourless eyes beneath black brows, and whiskers rich in greys and whites, and he clearly knew well how arresting was the overall effect. He pushed back the folds of his black gown with his unoccupied hand and, with a smile once more at the maid in the witness stand, made to consult the silver watch that hung on a chain from his waistcoat. There was a cough from the gallery that ceased, and the unending hiss from the lights. Cissy's fingers gripped the edge of the stand.

'Miss Cissy Smithson,' the lawyer said after what seemed to have been a very long time. He paused so that the sibilant phrase itself seemed loaded with insult, perhaps to imply the absolute unreliability of the name's bearer.

'Yes, sir?'

'My learned colleague would have us believe that you are a devastating witness against Mr Farquharson's good name. Yet is it not so that it was *not* you, in fact, who first told the fantastic tale that Mr Farquharson, respectable merchant of the City of London, is Mr Forster, grocer of Manchester?'

Cissy looked at him a moment, her eyebrows pulling together.

Earnest child, she is worried that his meaning eludes her.

'But, sir. It *was* me, sir.'

'I put it to you that it was *not* you, but a Mrs Staynes, housekeeper, who first told the tale, purportedly on your behalf.'

'But I first told it to Mrs Staynes, sir, and Miss Mullins, sir, and then it was Miss Mullins told the mistress, and wrote it to the inspector for me, and then he came and said I must tell him—'

Poor Cissy. A truthful girl, so anxious to be believed. Of a sudden, I was wrung with fondness for my littlest maid.

'Hah!' the prosecutor said. He stepped back to gaze around the court, until lunging—it seemed to me—once more toward where Cissy sat. 'I put it to you that you meant to spread this tale, but to make it seem true what was needed was intercession. Yes, Miss Smithson?'

'Sir,' Cissy voice was husky and she wiped quickly at her eyes. Her voice rose until it was a plaint. '*What* was needed, sir? I cannot understand your question, sir. I cannot answer it.'

The magistrate leaned over toward the girl. His chin very nearly touched the edge of his table.

'Intercession, my girl. It means that someone spoke for you.'

'Oh. Thank you, sir. Your Honour.' Cissy looked back to the lawyer, and opened her mouth, yet no sound came from it and it was evident that she had forgotten the rest of the question. The lawyer raised his voice, and Cissy shrank back into her seat.

'I put it to you, Cissy, that someone had to speak for you because you knew it to be a tale—'

Cissy's mouth fell open. *Poor child!* I was swept over with the desire to rise to my feet and call out 'Desist!' even though I knew I could not. Indeed, the notion of actually doing so then made my cheeks hot.

'No, sir, no!' Cissy's voice had found a loudness to go with her most obvious indignation. 'I asked Mrs Staynes and Miss Sobriety to speak for me because…because…' Her voice lowered now to a whisper.

The magistrate made a sound like 'tcha!' and leaned toward Cissy once again.

'Child, you must speak up.'

We both also leaned forward, a little.

'Yes, sir. Your Honour. I asked them to speak for me because I was most frightened to speak in front of the gentleman, sir, because I am a frightened girl, sir, and most shy...'

The gallery and all in the courtroom had been silent, holding its breath with this interchange, but now all sat back from the edge of their seats where they had crept. There was a burst of laughter, for there could never have been a clearer picture, surely, of an honest girl made tongue-tied by having to speak to strangers. Cissy added to this impression by gaping about the courtroom. The skin on her forehead crumpled and her face was now patched in white and raw pink.

The lawyer, speaking over the titter and rumble from the gallery, did make claims that no proofs could be believed of any alias of Mr Farquharson's, because Cissy must have made it up, but the continuing murmuring and stirring plainly showed that his attempt was in vain.

The gavel sounded several times, the Lord Mayor calling out 'Silence!' with no result until the court officer stepped forth with his stick and his bellow. Even then, he had to shout his order several times. The crowd, it seemed, was exercising itself after having held its breath, and surged back and forth, side to side, tilting heads and raising laughter. Sobriety and I were jostled from one side and the other.

At last, the crowd chose to obey the officers of the court, and there were no more than a few whispers and a little giggling when the Lord Mayor permitted Cissy to step down from the witness stand. She nearly ran to the witness door in her haste, her cheeks suffused and hot, glancing up to where we two veiled women bent our heads in acknowledgment of her and discreetly twitched our handkerchiefs in encouragement.

Sobriety touched my gloved hand. I turned my head in surprise. With the slightest of gestures, so as not to be noticed by another soul in the crowded court, Sobriety pointed with her own gloved finger to where, standing straight and raised above the sea of people in his prisoner's dock, Mr Farquharson had his eyes directed at one spot.

His face was sunk into a look that spoke—with an intellectual force concentrated and palpable, and aimed with deliberation—to one person in this room. It spoke, in glacial waves, of hate, perhaps; of power, certainly; of blame, it seemed... I thought of blame, for the person whom Mr Farquharson held with his gaze was the girl who had stolen his child.

Certainly, I thought, my mouth dry, *contempt is there, and...what?* He stared at the girl, who gazed back with a look upon her starved face of such loss, such yearning, that tears like pinpricks started in my own eyes. These two, the man well-dressed and stout with wealth, and the girl who hungered for everything in this life, held each other's attention across the room in this way as if there were no others about, as if the crowd and the lawyers, the officers and Sobriety and I were simply shadows, or less, all merely the fading elements of imagination.

Here was this girl, at last, who had herself been a shadow so often in my thoughts these last few days and weeks.

Sobriety's hand sought mine, and I thought for a confused moment that Sobriety meant thereby to emphasise our existence in the warmth and strength of our hands' grip, but then it was clear that Sobriety trembled. I looked from the profile next to me, where it puffed slight breath against the gauze of the veil, and thence to the face in the dock, hatred carved into its pale folds, and was afraid. I recognized this man's species of tyranny; I had met something like it in Mr Hadley. I had met the destruction that was the expression of mastery such as his, that crushed and used others simply so that he may stand the taller. I felt all of this, moreover, on Sobriety's behalf, as if in concert with her.

It seemed a long time that the two, the man and the starveling girl, held each other's gaze. Indeed, the magistrate had begun to speak during those stretched moments, committing Mr Farquharson to trial, but I barely heard him and the two who gazed at each other also seemed unaware that he had uttered anything at all.

Then the ragged, hungry girl of a sudden broke the hold of Mr Farquharson's glare, with a grimace that made a torture of her face, and she was away, pushing past knees and the shoves of complaining people, away through the door to beyond the courtroom, with a flick of the dirty red skirt before she was gone.

But she was not alone, for another person detached himself from anonymity, from the bench just behind where the girl had sat. The man pushed and pressed himself past the knees and the whispered exclamations until he reached steps, to clatter down them, through the door and beyond, with just a glance at Mr Farquharson as he went. It was a thin man who left, slight but with the strength of twisted wire, his face intent, tight and gaunt, his mouth a down-turned line.

At first I hesitated, but then was certain. There was about this man, the set of his shoulders, perhaps, that was familiar. He had stood, of this I was sure, in the shadows watching the guests enter Mr Farquharson's house, the night of the party.

She has had time to vanish, surely. She has had time to get away? We gripped each other's hand for some minutes more.

And how did Mr Farquharson come to know her?

The house was dark and silent but for those squeakings and scrap-ings for which there is never any answer—winds in the eaves, perhaps, or a general easing of boards. I lay with my eyes wide. The events of the past day paraded before me, and would not settle in my mind.

It was in the wee hours that I arose and scrabbled with matches and candle, wrapped my shawl about my nightdress and took myself down protesting stairs to my morning room. Now that that machine had found its place in George's study, and that room was apparently become the sewing room, I felt my morning room was more settled. It had gathered itself to itself, and it was more my own. I wondered a moment if, on Mr Hadley's passing, I should resolve to take his chamber for my work, or if I would come home, as it were, to this familiar place.

I had brought my journal down to read, earlier, and I searched about now for the elderly pen and a very little ink I knew still stood on the mantel. In the murky and uncertain light, I sat at my tiny coffee table, unscrewed the ink pot with great care, and into it dipped my pen.

> *Every day is a performance! I am astounded over and over at those who place themselves on Society's stage. They use us all—we who speak all unrehearsed and honestly and do not comprehend that these people, these actors, have about them a script. They have their lines ready prepared. Everywhere are the prevailing themes of hope and fear, where ordinary folk seek love and comfort and wish only to see their way ahead and to comprehend it. And into this these demon kings stride, masters of all, for only they know that the play has been written and all of us but minor parts.*

> *How they do use us all.*

At last, my toes were too cold to stay longer. And, in any case, I had written what was in my thoughts and could sleep at last.

Chapter Thirty-one

I opened my eyes, with very little inclination to do more.

In any case, it was still very early. There had, I fancied, been a scattering of feet down the alleyway behind the house that had awoken me, though the runner was gone now. Beyond the curtained window all was thick and quiet with the dark of a coming winter, greying dawn showing indistinct around the curtain's edge. The furniture of my chamber stood in black shapes hunched and heavy around my bed, yet familiar as sentries. Among my bedclothes, warm from the night's sleep, I felt myself cupped, safe with the door closed against a world become bewildering in its glories and cruelties. My brows were drawn together as if they had an anxious life of their own; and I recalled, in vague fashion and as if my sleepy imagination was bedded in cloud, those medieval tales of the basilisk—that pitiless, scaly head of mythology turning to expel its poisonous breath upon the innocent. The world, somehow, was first become like Mr Hadley, and then, even worse, like Mr Farquharson…basilisk monsters, both. With a distant, sad interest, I realised a tear was travelling across my cheek into my hair. The world, I thought, like Messrs Hadley and Farquharson, bedecked itself, scented itself, and congratulated itself upon its success, and yet on a fine day would sweep past the huddled urchins of the street, or on a cold and howling day might stop to kick the unfortunate in order to hear their very bones snap.

I turned toward the window and fancied there must be frost outside, for my breath was faintly misting in the near-dark. I blew gently, as I used to when a girl, and imagined the ragged cloud of my breath merged with the cold stillness of the room.

238

And who is Mr Hadley? I wiped away the tear. *Is he akin to Mr Farquharson, with his every word a falsehood, his home but walls around grim secrets he keeps even from his family?*

These were quelling notions, I felt, as I burrowed more deeply beneath my bedclothes. There was a cold trickle of air blowing in at my feet from some tiny uncovered spot. It was a frightening thing, this world, and I felt myself to be childlike, humiliated by my own ignorance. *How much I do not know!* And what I did not know loomed dark and solid, all the more as I became aware of it.

And it was an odd thing that while I had so often in the last few weeks thought of the theatre and the stage as the various dramas had played themselves before me, in fact… *In fact, what has happened is that I discover that I have always been on the stage, saying my lines in this predesigned setting, and this has always been make-believe. What is real, what is not make-believe is far from bright and perfect, it brings to the ugly and the cold and miserable no justice, in the end.*

I sought once more for that moment of joy last evening on our arrival home, when *The Cornhill Magazine* greeted us with my own written piece therein, and my own name printed there, at the head. But even so, beneath my triumph, I believed myself to be a charlatan, pretending a knowledge I did not have and yet seeking to profit by it. The thought stirred confusion as to how I ought to feel, when my authoring brought both shame and pride. I backed away from it.

I closed my eyes and tried for sleep, which came eventually, but only after thoughts, not quite a memory, of darkness and the giddy swinging of a lamp, a whisk of red skirt and the diminishing thud of running feet, one pair behind the other.

Later, I woke again and watched through half-closed eyes as Sobriety entered, walked with skirt swinging quick, first to pull open the curtains to the flat light of broad morning, then to lay a cup of tea on the chair next to my bed, and then to the fireplace to scrape a match to the kindling and coal laid last night by Cissy. Sobriety waited, still crouching, until the little licking flame gained strength, and pops and crackles lent dancing energy to the room. I turned onto my side and drew up my knees, like the bundled child that I had been all those mornings of years ago and since, watching a fire being lit in my bedroom to chase away the chill. The bedclothes pulled up over my cheek and ear, I tilted my head to follow Sobriety's movements.

She stamps about this morning as if she has found her lost confidence, of a sudden. She is busy and practical as if she had dealt with a question and has put some uncertainty aside.

Sobriety went to the airing frame and picked it up to set it in front of the fire, to warm the clamminess from chemise and petticoat.

'Are you awake?'

'Not at all.'

Sobriety smiled, pinched and pulled at the clothes to spread them the better on the frame and then left the room, pulling the door to behind her, while not closing it entirely. I heard her on the stairs, a tap-tap-tap, light and fast, that faded and left me with the snapping of the fire and some man outside in the laneway calling in language blurred by distance and masonry. My eyelids drooped.

There was a slower tramp on the stairs until Sobriety pushed the door open again, with the large water jug held in both hands and a folded towel over her shoulder. She elbowed the door closed and went to pour the hot water—the steam in a sudden cloud—into the flowered basin on the washstand. Sobriety tested the water—overhot as yet, by all accounts—and laid the towel over the back of the other plain chair.

There was something like satisfaction in the set of Sobriety's mouth. Or perhaps not satisfaction, exactly. Watching her, I thought more on how to define Sobriety's aspect. *She has the bearing of someone who knows where her path is and where it will take her.* Sobriety opened the door to the wardrobe and stood a moment, while I felt loneliness spread and contract, fleetingly, like an opening and closing hand. And worse, for while Sobriety so evidently was settling into newfound certainty, I could not imagine that any observer would think the same of me.

I knew exactly at what point this firmness, this serenity, this confidence in what was coming, first appeared in Sobriety's expression.

We had all three—Sobriety and Cissy and I—been standing outside the courts in the City, waiting for Mr Brent and the landau, its sections of roof in place against the sharpening weather, and blankets folded upon the seats, with Inspector Broadford standing with us and casting his reproving eye at any who might stare at or jostle the small group. He said, 'Well done, well done,' to Cissy, who was by then much the happier with her ordeal in court over, and craning with too high an enthusiasm at the bustle of the street and the road. He folded into her hand a sweet in its wrapping.

'Tell no one, now, lest I be accused of bribery.' We three adults laughed while Cissy's face fell blank with incomprehension.

Remarks about the weather done with—for a yellowing fog had lifted itself that morning, which might descend again in the evening if there were a frost—there was a pause among us until Sobriety said to the inspector, 'There was a girl in the court whom we—' She glanced at me. '—whom we have seen before, and who left, in a hurry it seems—'

'Ah, yes. I did observe that.' Mr Broadford smiled, not asking more, though he must know where it was we women had come to see the wraith of a girl, and in what circumstances. He waited, head tipped and the crinkles about his eyes speaking of understanding and warmth, most deliberately, I thought. Further, his mouth curved with expectation that was patient of fulfilment.

Sobriety took breath and looked up full into the inspector's face and I fancied there was the pause of a very long moment, though in fact there was none. Sobriety did not glance away; she and he looked direct into each other's eyes, and it was done.

Then, it was then, that Sobriety's mind and decision stepped toward him, and he greeted her, with never a word, the conversation continuing all the while about dreadful things, dreadful and strange things, while the speakers came to their private conclusion about themselves. *See how the play continues,* I thought, *while another story unfolds in the wings.*

'A man left too, immediately after the girl, and it did seem to us he may be attached to Mr Farquharson, er, Mr Forster.' Sobriety had smiled at this confusion brought about by this man with two names.

'Mr F—shall we call the gentleman thus?—has a man by the name of Seamus Spillane, devoted to him and ready, we suspect, at a moment's notice to do any work asked of him by his employer.' Inspector Broadford bowed. 'And it was Mr Spillane who left the court, it is true.'

'And it was he who, with others, silenced the shareholders at Mr… Mr F's meetings?'

'We believe so.'

'With violence?'

'Indeed.'

He and Sobriety both nodded, apparently in comfortable agreement. *Though the comfort lay in the fact of agreement and not in the subject of that agreement, of course.* I understood, while I had felt I should look away from a discourse between them that was so very private, yet had not actually taken place.

I stretched in my bed and encountered again that trickling cold that made me draw myself together again. *Or should I say,* I amended in sudden realisation, *the agreement is there that there shall be an agreement. Ah yes.*

But there, yesterday on the street—where the world was at its busiest point of the afternoon and folk pushed into the crowd until their backs receded from view amid the noisy, coloured chaos, and faces had a hardened distraction that was sometimes, I could see, almost a desperation to get done what must be done in the day—I had had another realisation.

'But that girl, Inspector...' Both the inspector and Sobriety turned their now complacent faces to me.

'Oh yes. My own man did think to pursue Mr Spillane, ma'am.' Mr Broadford chuckled, turning his head to Sobriety to share the joke. 'And although Mr Spillane is apparently adept at spotting a pursuer, much to the chagrin of my man, I must say, it did mean that he was—that is to say, Mr Spillane was—diverted from any more vicious purpose and obliged to turn his feet elsewhere.' He beamed at Sobriety. 'And the young woman did scamper off alone.'

He and Sobriety each wore a smile of reassurance, the echo of the other, now that the inspector turned his face back to me.

'And we must also wonder at how complicated has become this nest of acquaintanceships,' he said, and I saw that he too pondered Mr Farquharson's recognition of the girl.

The relief was such that we were almost festive with it. It made us all chatter, babble almost, in a most uncharacteristic fashion. Sobriety—so unlike her! So pink about the cheeks!—then took the conversation to other things, to Cissy's impossible growth lately that had made Cook search out garments that might fit her niece if cut down and refashioned, to the tales that Cook would tell over tea leaves, to—inevitably—the impending visit by me to the spiritualist Madame Drew. Mr Broadford here raised his eyebrows and I assured him I had no desire to fly about and cause flashes of light, only to placate poor dear Mrs Courtney, my sister-in-law. We all smiled at this.

When I took my turn with Mr Hadley, I spoke in my mind to him: *Mr George Hadley, your wives are leaving you.*

Then I remembered Mrs Charles.

He lay there helpless in his bed, he who had been monster to my mouse. I thought to myself how it had not been long since—perhaps two or three months only—when he had come home and to my bedchamber, pulled back my sheet and pushed my legs apart to receive him, and I had smelt a woman's scent still on his shirt and cheek, faint as he grunted into my ear. Did Mrs Charles reach there to kiss him goodnight, as he, the gentleman, bent his face to her? *Was I used thus in her stead? Were we, Sobriety and I, used thus in her stead?*

Chapter Thirty-two

There letters lay in a line on Mr Hadley's bed, and I regarded them. I rubbed the skin on my brow and reached for the cup of coffee by my little writing box, sipped and placed it down.

The first contained a cheque for my published piece of writing, and signed by Mr Thackaray himself. This and the letter that accompanied it lay unfolded so that I might revisit them. And I had already done so twice this morning.

Next to these was a note on Gwendolyn's writing paper—so very much her own, with its printed rosettes upon the paper and the sealing wax on the envelope, and her monogram impressed upon it; letters from her announced their sender before ever the subject of the letter were known. Gwendolyn's note was to the point.

> *Your family is distressed and perplexed at reading the piece that bears your name in a magazine. Harry was, besides, unable to discern a clear response from you to our request for information about your financial circumstances. This is all most alarming, and I am certain you will understand, on sober reflection, that good sense must prevail. You will meet with us and discuss what is to be done, at my home Sunday week at 3.*

How little sense there was in this, since Gwendolyn could not claim the power to undo my very public writing. In thinking so, I put my hand to my mouth, for I had never before, not in all my life, deliberately done what I knew my family would not like.

And I did know this, I did. And look where I have put myself.

I must now defend this little hill that I had reached, and a spurt of laughter something like a smothered shriek escaped through my fingers. Perhaps I had evaded any direct thought of my family in my taking up of the pen thus, for money, in order to put myself in this very position so that there could be no retreat and I must defend what I had already done.

They will have to surround me and starve me into submission. I smiled. *And yet, they cannot.*

In truth, they could do very little, I supposed, and yet the familiar marching of discordant instruments began again in my blood, for I was afraid of my family, and they would be ranged all together against me. They would try to prevent my continuing with the writing, and my receiving payment from it, and I would say *no*—yes, I would simply say that, and repeat it, and pay no heed to what might be expressed to me.

I sighed. What might happen next at this meeting was lost in shadows in my mind, gesticulating shadows that wore first a lacy cap of the old school (Gwendolyn) and then a heavy topcoat (Harry), and crouched as if to hiss into my face, and thereafter barked in muffled sentences—muffled because I could not yet imagine what might be said at this unimaginable meeting. *See, I fear them yet.* I passed a cold hand across hot cheeks.

The third letter was from Toby. He enquired after his father's health and mine. He had enjoyed himself at his friend's house and he was applying himself to his schoolwork. It was a dutiful letter, although he did spend some time writing of Phillip's pony, how tall and its colour, and how he had ridden it for quite a long time. I pictured my boy, but at first could place him in imagination no closer to me than the other side of the room, with his hands folded before him or in his pockets, his gaze passing over and beyond me, perhaps on its way to something or someone who better held his affection. Then my mind took up the picture of my Toby a-gallop on the pony, with his eyes wide and his breath coming in gasps and his cheeks whipped hectic by wind. But soon into my imagination there flooded a sense of his small boy's loneliness, of the lost boy's wondering what he must do or be, now or next, to be seen to have done his duty either as son or man, to be seen to deserve affection.

I returned to Mr Thackaray's letter and cheque, by way of comfort. This was not complicated, at least. Except, and here I smiled a little, that his invitation to attend his office and discuss my work was addressed to Mr A. Hadley Esq., and I would perhaps surprise him by not being a gentleman.

I folded my letters into their envelopes, and finished my coffee before opening the writing box and pulling forth pen, ink and the sheaf of papers on which my tale of Tristram James had been begun.

The novelist, Mr A. Hadley, Esq., at work, I thought. I chuckled, though it came a little shaky still.

Cissy stood in the hallway, waiting to open the Hadley front door and then close it behind Sobriety and me. We were, as a favour to Mrs Courtney and reluctantly—most reluctantly—to attend a gathering at Madame Drew's establishment. Sobriety, already bonneted and wrapped against the cold, stood with my bonnet in her hand and my shawl over her arm. I, however, was now bent over the dish of visiting cards, which stood on its little stand in the hallway. I sifted through the cards with one gloved finger—I would remove those that had been there longest when we returned, I decided—and then stopped to pick out another. It had been given me, and I had placed it there. I knew exactly when. So long ago; before the exultation of sparkling lights and dance music; before my education in evil worldliness.

'Good heavens! How very peculiar!' It was Mr Farquharson's card I showed to Sobriety.

'Madame Drew is his neighbour! This is most strange! How very droll!'

I went to drop the card back into the dish, thought better of it and instead tore it in two. I considered a moment and reached in for Mrs Charles's cards, and tore them in two as well. I placed all these shreds in Cissy's hand and turned to face Sobriety, who set the bonnet on my head and drew together the ribbons at my chin.

'If Madame Drew has chosen that neighbourhood for its respectability, she must be disappointed.'

Sobriety laughed.

In the carriage we fell silent, listening to the steady ticking of hooves, the creaking leathers and chink of metals, watching how the black shadows moved across our space as we passed streetlamps or, where there were no streetlamps, filled our space like oil, thicker than the dark night outside. I felt my earlier mood settle back over me. I was waiting for news, I realised, with a dread I knew to be unfair. And yet it was there, and I struggled against a sense that this news would finally tip up my world, overturn it utterly like the ill-made vessel that it was, and all that I knew would fall out and bob around like debris, pointless and aimless, to sink dwindling into the depths or float away out of reach.

Eventually, Sobriety's voice came out of the dark.

'I have decided, about Mr Broadford, should he ask for me.'

There. You see.

My voice came out at first as a whisper, so that I must clear my throat. 'As he will. What have you thought?' *I know what you have thought.*

'He is a good man, and steady, and he looks to offer a good home and certainty. And so I will accept.' There was a short silence. Sobriety spoke then as if to excuse herself. 'I can be a helpmeet to him. I can make his home and life orderly. I shall make a home.'

I wondered, but could not ask, where Sobriety's family lay in all of this, who may or may not approve of this marriage. It did then occur that Sobriety might push the farmer-preacher away now, for how else to deal with the secret of the sin that had been inescapable but for which she could not forgive herself? Obedience to her father, the tenet knit into her very soul, would struggle, surely, with the secret that had also settled into place there. She must, simply, not tell.

'But...' she said.

'Yes, Sobriety? What question can there be for you?' *What question can there be? I have no claim, I have no claim...* I thought of nights to come, lying in stillness made absolute by the lack of companionable creaks from above, the movements of Sobriety's small ministerings to her own dress and undress in that small, plain room that was her own. No more. *Dear God, I feel so alone, and she is not yet gone, even.*

'Oh, none, really. But I will give him no answer until after Mr Hadley is gone.'

The carriage lurched a little and settled, and the horses clopped on as if keeping time in the silence that followed.

'I understand.' *I have no claim, I have no claim.*

'Yes. But even so, I do not intend to leave until you are prepared for it.'

My eyes filled and I scrambled a moment for a handkerchief.

'And it seems to me we may continue as friends.'

There was a rustle as Sobriety reached for my hand.

Chapter Thirty-three

Sobriety and Mr Brent had both, quite separately, miscalculated the distance to Madame Drew's establishment. We were early, consequently, and quite clearly the first to arrive. Our vehicle stood alone in the silent street in its empty square where great houses stared dour and stately at each other across the dark and paved expanse. In our self-consciousness we chose to place the carriage in the shelter of a spreading street tree, seemingly merging with it as a puddled, shadow-like shape, next door but one to Madame Drew's house. The landau lurched as Mr Brent descended, but I whisked my gloved hand at him. 'No, no. Not yet, I think.' I looked out. Great spills of black from trees were patched with moonlit greys. There were yellow puddles of light from streetlamps. Mr Brent nodded, and we felt the jerk of his re-ascent.

'We shall enter when there is company. They may not take long,' I told Sobriety.

'I hope so. Have you enough of the rug?'

Sobriety leaned over to ensure my lap was fully covered with the rug. She glanced up into the night, past my bonneted head. Something was agitating, apparently, at the edge of her vision.

'Look there! How extraordinary!'

I followed Sobriety's gaze to where Madame Drew's front door had opened of a sudden, so that there was a dim golden oblong against which a figure stood out in bell-skirted silhouette, swinging a large fringed shawl about her shoulders.

Madame Drew's door slammed. The figure, head down and arms clutching her shawl close-wrapped about her person, headed along the wide footpath past the houses of the great. The figure ran, *absolutely ran* (extraordinary!), with her tolling shadow swinging, looming and shrinking past the streetlamp—whose light revealed her as tall and stoutish, and the gathers and ribbons on her house cap sweeping back as she went—across the end of the square. She reached that heavy mansion, three houses wide and three storeys high, with which I was already acquainted. Almost no light showed in the tall windows stationed regularly across the frontage, or at the double doors nearly lost in the shadow cast by the portico and stolid columns, or in its bay windows blind in the darkness by the entranceway. Everything about the house spoke of absence, save for a very faint glowing as of a forgotten candle, or a night lamp turned right down and left, perhaps, in a corner on the ground floor.

And where was that little whispering wife, the small Mrs Farquharson who wished so much for companionship? She, who grasped at friendship, apparently, from the first person to show consideration? Was she hid in those dark and silent rooms, or gone back to her bemedalled father to puzzle him, indeed, with her tenuous position and a child who may be seen as fatherless? Her fortunes tied, helpless, to those of her husband.

So much falls along with that base man.

'Is that Madame Drew herself, I wonder?' The woman had reached the Farquharsons' door. I whispered in Sobriety's ear, for now Sobriety sat back in her seat the better to see from her own window, and I leaned across her, with my cheek brushing a tiny ribboned rosette in her bonnet. In turn, Sobriety moved her own head to one side a little to evade the edge of my headwear.

'It may be.'

There followed three heavy raps at the door of the louring mansion, and the sound echoed around the street. Madame's shadow jerked back and forth in little impatient steps, while her figure was itself hidden in the dense, still shadow of the portico.

'That is Mr Farquharson's house.' I slid the rug from my lap and held my hoops and skirt up to step the awkward space across the landau, crouching to avoid the roof but stepping upon Sobriety's hem because I could not see it—so that I could sit opposite her. The carriage tilted and bounced on its springs until I had settled. We two peered into the dark to see if the woman had heard the jiggling and the creaking of the springs, or had observed the inch back and forward of the wheels—but we could see no sign of her noticing. The presence of Mr Brent, patient in thick overcoat with collar up to his ears and hat pulled down to them, did not attract the woman's attention either, we assumed, his shadow and that of the carriage merging blackly and fortuitously with that of the tree.

Instead, there was a further rapping at the door, a pause and then the woman stepped down the two entrance steps to see if there were any sign of habitation. Madame turned her head to left and right, old fashioned curls like well-sprung sausages swinging beneath her cap, and then began to call out.

'Mr Farquharson, Mr Farquharson!"

Sobriety murmured to me, 'Surely she must know he is not there—', when, as if we had been overheard, Madame Drew called out: 'Mrs Farquharson, you must respond!'

The woman's voice was so loud now as to be straining. Distress had dried her throat, it seemed, so that she was quite hoarse. Around the square, shadows were appearing at many windows; something even seemed to shift in the one faint-lit window of the Farquharson house, though I could not be sure.

Does someone in there listen, even as we do?

I whispered, so that the words barely stirred the air, 'If I were Mrs Farquharson, I would also be elsewhere. Away from those who would bang upon my door.'

Sobriety's eyes were round, concentrated on the drama in the street. 'Yes. Mrs Farquharson is not there.'

I touched her sleeve. 'Do you think she might be American?'

'This woman on the street? Oh, yes. Possibly.'

The woman let out something like a bark. She paused a moment, her head turned upward toward the faint glow at that one window, and then she walked quickly, stamped across so that her skirt positively bounced, and shouted at the infinitesimal light. 'Mrs Farquharson, it is outrageous! Where are my investments? What has your husband done?'

There was no response, and the woman stood for a long moment until it was clear she listened in vain. There would be no response, whatever that small light represented. Madame Drew—for it must be she—then stepped back some paces and raised her voice to a wail, while the great façade continued all stony aloofness and jutting shadows. *See, no longer a ship of hope.*

'Spillane, he promised me, he promised me! Mrs Farquharson, Mr Giles, Spillane, answer!'

This last seemed to echo, but all then fell away into silence and Madame Drew stood looking up at the house, paced rapidly this way and that a few moments, her skirt swinging violently with each turn. She paused once more just where the feeble light shone, and called, 'Again and again, I shall return. I assure you!'

But the house and its faint light continued silent and at last she stamped and swung about, scurried along the edge of the square back to her own house, with her shadow billowing and shrinking once more past the streetlamp. Her door opened, there was a moment of dim light, and then it closed behind her.

'She must be very anxious about something, to display herself so,' I said, when the night's silence had returned to the square, with nothing more notable than a thin cat purposeful across a pool of lamplight.

'She has lost investments.' Sobriety rustled a little on the seat opposite. I could see, beneath the night-grey florettes of the bonnet, Sobriety's profile painted silver by the moon.

'The inspector will not be surprised, I dare say, that there should be another such loss,' Sobriety said. Looking across at my friend—so compact as she was there in the dark, a feature here and a fold there lined with hushed moonlight—I felt again a moment of separation, a sting that came and went like the stab from the finest of blades.

See, she refers to him already. It is done.

'Poor woman, I suppose.'

I realised Sobriety still gazed into the street. 'What are you looking at?'

'The cat…see the cat? It has a friend.'

I squinted. And indeed there was a slight movement, ill-lit and grey, undefined so that one must blink to keep the image in the eye, at the entrance to the small laneway next to Mr Farquharson's house. I fancied a figure there did, as Sobriety thought, cuddle the cat.

'Look what we do to pass the time, spying on all the night's goings-on! Poor Mr Brent must be chilled.'

'Yes.'

'Yet I am even more wary of knocking at Madame's door by ourselves, with no other of her clientele yet arrived. A most peculiar and overwrought person!'

'It does seem her second sight has failed her.' We giggled together softly, and the carriage wobbled a little with it.

The night fell silent again, weighing on all three, I fancied, with we women inside the carriage squinting through windows misting over from our breath, and Mr Brent atop, his own breath surely frosted puffs in this chilly night, like that of the two snorting horses shifting from haunch to haunch. One of the horses shook his head, and the clanking together of metallic pieces was crisp in the cool air.

Sobriety rubbed at the window. The cat continued for the moment its mutual caress with the figure at the mouth of the alleyway next to the great house, and then apparently tired of it and jumped down. The small figure stepped out a small distance onto the footpath; the cat danced away as if to tease. Sobriety drew in a sharp breath.

'What is it?'

'It is she! It is the girl!'

'Girl?' I rubbed at my own window. 'Oh! The girl!'

As we watched, the girl—she who had stolen Mr Farquharson's child and had poured out her wordless yearnings toward him as he stood in the dock, and lurked and run through my imaginings as the most desperate of suggestions—stepped back into the alleyway. The shadows fell across her as a heavy curtain. We women sat a moment in silence, watching where, unseen, the young girl breathed alone next to the great, grand house, all of its windows empty and blind but for one, with its faint but steady glow, there, on the ground floor.

'She should not be here,' Sobriety whispered, finally. It was as if the girl's vulnerability poured on misery-poisoned air from the alley in which she hid. We sat and gazed more, as the cat stepped back whence it had pranced, its own shadow stretching to a point behind it. It sauntered back down the street and slipped, ink into ink, into the alleyway. I shuddered as if from the stroke of an icy finger.

'She should not be here,' Sobriety said again. I reached for the handle of the carriage door.

Chapter Thirty-four

Mr Brent was left by the carriage, standing by the horses with his hand awkward upon a halter. His eyes were on the black space of the alleyway, toward which we had gone—slowly, and with the air around our faces in a billowing and fading cloud from too-fast breathing. We drew close and the cat, slipping from the heavy blackness, an inkblot detached and animate, scampered away to lick itself by the streetlamp.

'Child! We know you are there! Speak to us.'

I held close to Sobriety, arm in arm, for the courage that it gave as she stared into the inhabited blackness, and for the warmth, since a little fear had set us both to shivering.

And why are we afraid? We are not a poor, mad child with no bed but these cobbles and no roof at all.

If only we could see…

We held our breath a moment for the silence; and it may have been, I thought, that the tiniest movement—a scuffing against stone or brick—sounded from the lightless cavern of the alleyway. We breathed again, and the mist that came from our mouths joined into one small, ragged cloud.

She sees us, two wrapped women entwined and alien, utterly foreign, utterly, as if we stepped from a painting—some kind of fantastical image of light and warmth—into the real world of cold and pain.

'Speak to us, child. We have not come to hurt you. We would not.'

There was a sniffle from the dark, and it seemed we could see movement in there, where some part of the darkness shifted. The very air here was not as the air in the great square with its trees and its flagstones; the laneway exhaled foulness from urine and faeces and rotting matter, which may have been either vegetable or animal.

'Child?'

'You.' The voice was rough, without the music of a training in gentle cadences, yet it was very young. So far, the voice came steady and quiet. 'You were there, before. In my tunnel. You took my baby.'

'You know that was not your—' I began, but the answer came back before I had finished, louder, with the beginnings of a metallic shrill.

'You took my baby, and then you had them take *'im.*'

'Child, child…' There was in the girl's words and tone a loosening of despair that wrung in me a desperate pity in reply: *poor girl, poor girl*. I stepped into the darkness of the alleyway, hand in hand with Sobriety, toward that unquiet, thrashing spirit. *She is mad with her delusions*. But the girl by now was not listening, and continued with a voice stripped from loss and lack.

'You had them take 'im, and 'e blames me! 'e blames me! Did you see how 'e did look at me, when I was 'is, 'e knew I was 'is…' The girl took breath. 'And 'e loved me. 'e did love me.'

We stopped. My eyes were wide now and my belly, beneath the stitchings and the whalebone and laces, queasy with a slow-growing understanding. To have so misunderstood what this girl had told us in Mr Bazelgette's tunnel. Knowledge prickled, settling into outrage that was as yet uncertain of its target—Mr Farquharson, of course, was more monster than any had imagined; he had used this girl for his lusts. But what of this girl, despoiled and now ruined? I had an urge to turn from the girl as something made unworthy and unclean, and then shook my head against such a thought. I took breath, and with it came pity interwoven, hopelessly, with a kind of shame that suffused everything, even though I could not say why. The childish voice continued.

'More than ever that woman in his 'ouse, I am 'is wife, more than she is. She'd sit there dressed up like a doll, noddin' and smilin', noddin' and smilin'…' she said in a sing-song, with a sneer, perhaps, on that small young face dim in the dark, her facial expressions blurring the more I squinted to see. 'Stoopid. Feathers. Lace. But 'e came to *me*, 'e would find me where I waited for 'im, and 'e would cover us in 'is coat till I could 'ardly breathe under 'is great weight, and push until I thought I would burst, and 'e would whisper to me—'

'Dear God,' Sobriety murmured.

'—"Mine, mine, mine", and strike me 'ard to leave 'is mark—' The rusty voice broke off and began again, '—and then when my belly grew, 'e knew what it was, 'e did, and 'e brought me bits of food and money, and once a blanket.'

We stood stock still, our breath puffing and vanishing, puffing and vanishing. We felt our faces paling in the cold; the stench reached out from the dark and wrapped around us.

'And still I was so surprised, I was, when the pain came—I thought it would never stop…' The girl's voice trailed away, and the only sound for a minute or more was of the breathing of three people, broken eventually by sharp barking from somewhere nearby.

''E took the baby away. 'E gave it to that woman to look after, so she could wrap 'im up and feed 'im. I saw through the winder, many times.'

The girl began to cry quietly, her voice wavering. 'But I just wanted to smell 'im, my baby. I wanted to wrap 'im up myself.'

The nearby dog paused, then barked twice.

'I took my baby. But everything went wrong after that.' She sighed. 'Everything went wrong.'

She took a breath. 'Mr Farquharson, 'e—' She stopped and took another breath. ''E was that angry, 'e wouldn't talk to me. And then they took 'im away, and now 'is scent's on me no more, and 'is marks all faded, and I 'ave no shillin' to say I'm 'is…'

'Child—' I could barely make sound. The girl's crying had become a drone, hopelessly repeating, with the hollowness of a wind. We stood and listened, for we were appalled and our minds empty of any way to help. I raised a hand, I think perhaps to touch the girl, and perhaps to link the three of us together where no words or actions could do so. Perhaps…though I could no longer say what my own actions meant.

Suddenly, behind us at the mouth of the alley, there was a man's shout and the thump of booted feet. The dog began to bark again, hysterical. Sobriety and I turned, falling in our haste against the brick wall, and saw two figures struggling, stopped still for a moment as each strained against the equal force of the other, and then broke away. The smaller ran off, his scraping footsteps receding and ending with the heavy slam of a door. The larger turned toward us, his features blurred in the moonlight, concentrated on peering into the black where we stood. The dog's barking began to slow.

'Ma'am?'

'Mr Brent?' He stood amorphous in his coat and hat, blasting forth foggy breath from his exertions.

'Ma'am, it was a man come from this house.' He indicated the wall of the alley, which was also the wall of the Farquharson mansion. 'But clearly he was not the master, ma'am, and he was creeping like he might have no good on his mind—'

There was a rapid scuffling then, from behind us women (and a *woof* from wherever its source stood listening in the night) and we turned our heads back toward the girl, but her voice sounded from much further away now, receding even as she still spoke.

'You bring me no good, madam. You bring me no good.' The voice grew smaller and more lonely. 'Go away. You bring me no good.'

I felt myself paralysed. I was beset by scattered, incoherent thoughts wrung with guilt, then of uncertainty that I was guilty. *What have I done? What might I otherwise have done?* Nausea shifted within me at the thought that I might indeed be to blame, for something or for all of it. I could not say.

I bring nothing but confusion. Was it I that brought this confusion? I have been careless; I have been clumsy. Oh Lord, clumsiness makes such misery… I was swamped now by loneliness brought about by this nausea, by a sense of being closed in by heartless, grinding forces—like the heartless, heavy walls of the great Farquharson house—with no pity for the small, the hungry, the rag-doll playthings of monsters.

And here, heaven forgive me, was a plaything whom I called delusional, but was not. Poor child, she was not.

I felt that I had broken something, but could not put a name to it, and was sorry, with a depth and desperation that took my breath.

'Has she gone, the girl?' I knew the answer, and could not have said why I whispered, except, perhaps, to speak as one might tiptoe—in order to do no more damage.

So much damage, so much…

I stood and stared into the dark of the alleyway, overwhelmed with a cold that shook me in its grip so that I quaked.

'Come away, my dear, come.' Sobriety took my arm and we followed Mr Brent back across the square, as a brougham, its lamp yellow against the black box of the vehicle, creaked and clattered its way to a stop just behind our own carriage. Another, less grand, was rounding the far corner, also headed now for Madame Drew's establishment.

Chapter Thirty-five

We were slow in stepping across the square, myself with the sense of travelling from one country into another in the space of a few moments. The night was still, and all of its shapes—the shadows in overlaid black and greys, the steady furze of lights from streetlamps—seemed painted. A mist was gathering to hover over the ground, thickened with the gathering smoke from London chimneys on a cold night. I looked about without comprehension; I could not for the moment remember how to comport myself. There was a feeling that there was much that was important left undone, and that there was indeed something very important that must be done.

If I could only think what that could be.

Sobriety, too, was looking about herself as if she had just stepped somewhere strange. She, too, glanced back to the black mouth of the alleyway, where the mist gathered to blur the cobbles, and then to the newly arrived carriage, the brougham, where now a door had been opened and steps let down. A tall figure leapt to the ground with a lightness utterly at odds with the misery that dwelt by the great dark house on the other side of the square. The gentleman was proffering a hand to someone still within the carriage when that other vehicle slowed and came to a stop behind the two vehicles already stationary.

It was an awkward moment, for it was clear we had no acquaintance with these new arrivals, at least not with the gentleman we could see, and could not linger in the street where each group must ignore the other. I grasped at this reminder of manners, come at last to give shape to an evening become so confused and shapeless. I took Sobriety's arm and paused a moment to thank Mr Brent—*poor Mr Brent, who believes his mistress must be rescued at nearly every outing*—and

261

then moved in the direction of Madame Drew's house.

I looked at the front door, at the end of its short path and rise of two steps.

In fact, I am not ready for this either.

I bent to Sobriety.

'How vexing that Mrs Courtney is not yet—' But I was arrested in this by a low call: 'Mrs Hadley, Miss Mullins!'

It was a startling thing, for a moment ago there had been only one gentleman in evidence, and that a complete stranger. We halted, both turning to see who had called and ready, in self-defence, to summon a regal coldness to our rescue. Each had a tight grip upon the other, for circumstances were such, and untoward events tumbling over one another at such a rate, that it was difficult—a struggle almost distressing—to arrive at some form of behaviour that would be fitting.

It was Sobriety who was first to relax—her grip loosening of a sudden. She whispered, 'It is Inspector Broadford.'

'Ladies, I am pleased to have caught you before you entered!' He came toward them, wading through the mist at his knees.

'Inspector, what brings you here?' Sobriety said.

'I have come to see that fraud is not committed, to be frank, ladies.'

'Fraud? This night will make us dizzy, Sobriety!' I took a breath. 'Fraud, Inspector Broadford?'

Lord! There are predators at every corner!

'There is every possibility. Indeed.' The inspector stepped a little to one side. 'I should introduce some people to you before we knock at Madame's door. Mr William West, and his sister, Miss Josephine West…'

I, with my mind full of incomplete sentences like querulous puffs (*how much more? Much more? More?*), turned to regard two tall figures who now stepped into a pool of light diffused by the mist. Mr West—

he who had handed a companion down from the brougham—wore a loose, dark velvet coat, unbuttoned, and a copious fine-woollen scarf tossed about his throat and shoulder. I raised my eyes until I met those of the man himself: dark, heavy-lidded, languid and steady. He stood at his ease in a way that those in thrall to the clocks of industry are never at ease, I thought with a shrinking self-consciousness.

What is it he sees? I blinked to bring Mr West and my own attention the more into focus, and saw his face then—pale, with full lips smiling slightly, shadows cupping cheekbones, and the tiniest curved flick of a shadow from eyelashes black as this night. These eyelashes, I considered, were what gave the eyes such intensity. They were pupil-less eyes now, though the gleam of streetlamp reflected from them. He wore a large-brimmed, soft hat perched a little to one side, which threw heavy shade on his face as he moved, and black hair hung to his velvet collar.

Mr Hadley would dislike him intensely, I thought, and knew I had never met any man so evidently artistic in my life. I felt some physical response, disturbingly somewhere between revulsion and fascination, at what manner of subjects this man might discuss in drawing rooms.

The inspector was still speaking. ' …Mrs Hadley. And Miss Mullins, Mr West, Miss West…' And I found—though I must have placed it there, when I ought simply to have bowed—my gloved hand clasped in Mr West's and then, his impression and warmth still upon me, I likewise greeted his sister, pulling my gaze from one to the other, while aware still that the first stood, warm and breathing, close by.

Miss West, too, had a pale face and dark eyes. She looked down at me from nearly the same height as her brother, from under a bonnet that was very plain while well made. She looked very long indeed, clad also in what looked like dark velvet beneath a loose cloak, while the mist swirled about her skirt…and I understood of a sudden that the woman wore no crinoline.

Does she wear stays?

It was a very good thing, it crossed my mind, that it was much too dark to see me blush. It was said, too, that those who adopted the dress favoured by the Aesthetic Movement, such as this, were acerbic regarding the wanton display of those who did not; while I myself could not help for a moment thinking of Rossetti's painted woman—she, of ambiguous relation to the artist and, possibly, acquainted with the Wests themselves (assuming Mr Rossetti himself to be acquainted with them)—draped in sensuality upon Mr Hadley's bedroom wall. Miss West was not so clad, of course, but the plainness of her dress seemed a disguise, where something disturbing lay beneath while, at the same time, I felt myself to be trussed and encased and slightly absurd.

What is absurd, I told myself, though my thoughts still swam, *is that I am thrown into this state, by ambiguity and…and knowingness…and…*

And the woman was so tall.

That is it. She is so very tall. I took a breath.

And one does not know how she thinks. I let the breath out, and memory stirred amid my mental confusions.

'Miss West, the poetess,' I said. 'And Mr West, the artist?'

The artist. A man full of notions which are discussed in galleries and, sometimes, reviled in parlours…

'Indeed, indeed,' Mr Broadford said. 'But also, the Wests whose young relation, a cousin dependent upon Lady Florence West, is threatened with penury because the lady—in all good faith—promises to make over the bulk of her estate to Madame Drew.'

'Ah.' There was a pause, for I did not feel I could say more, this night being so full of stories, each too large for comprehension.

'But Inspector,' Sobriety spoke, and the inspector turned to smile at her. 'Inspector, that is calamitous, but is it fraud? Necessarily?'

'We think a case can be made.' Sobriety, the inspector and I all turned heads to look up at Mr West. *There is a languor even to his speech, a drawl,* I noted, that spoke of the Wests' childhood (I had read in a journal) spent amongst the unhurried aristocracy, whose elegant salons echoed with the wit of English intellect and the murmur of amusement at the stodgy display of the English middle classes, of which I was a member.

Mr West raised one dark eyebrow. 'Madame may not be entirely who she says she is, after all—that is to say, she is neither Madame Drew nor able to summon the spirits of anyone's dearest. It is because Madame pretends to fulfil Lady Florence's desire to be reunited on a fortnightly basis with her late husband that she—Lady Flo—proposes to make her bequest.'

He looked around the group, and smiled a little when his gaze came to me. 'So, you see.'

'Yes,' I said, because I felt I ought to say something. Despite the chill of the night, my cheeks heated again. A thought occurred. 'Is she American?'

'Oh yes,' the inspector said. 'Her fame—or notoriety, if you will—first began in a small town in the United States. She had some quite exalted followers later, in New York.'

There was a pause, during which I fancied the Wests regarded me closely and Mr Broadford looked from me to Sobriety and back.

Oh! They think...

Sobriety suddenly spoke into the silence. 'It should be mentioned, perhaps, that Mrs Hadley is here herself, and I with her, because Mrs Hadley's sister-in-law Mrs Courtney is also admiring of Madame—'

'Oh, yes, yes. She wanted our company.' I looked around at the others. 'And I was concerned at the degree of her devotion to a spiritualist.'

I experienced some discomfiture, when I had finished speaking. My very breath puffed in foggy spurts. I wondered at this; perhaps it was the embarrassment at so suddenly being flung into the centre of a closely listening group such as this, of people I scarcely knew. It made me aware even of the sound of my own voice, and this awareness itself made me falter. Perhaps also it was that I had felt such a need to explain myself, making excuses like a child.

I have not felt such a child for—for weeks.

This night! It is too much!

Miss West began to speak, during which I took pains to slow my own breathing. I counted in my head, and fancied it was something like a slow dance...

'We believe, and the inspector also suspects it—' Miss West inclined her head toward Mr Broadford. '—that Madame has done this before. She has encouraged other bequests on the basis of her unlikely gifts. I think you do well to be concerned for Mrs Courtney's welfare.'

'It would certainly account for Madame's ability to lodge in such a neighbourhood.' Mr Broadford chuckled, addressing himself at first to the group in general and then, at last, to Sobriety.

'Oh.' The thought had just occurred to me. 'It is possible Madame is financially distressed.' Mr West's face was all attention, I supposed, although I did not feel I could both look to see and speak sensibly at the same time. 'She may have made some rash investments with Mr Farquharson.'

'How so?' said Mr Broadford, whose surprise was evident, and the others murmured too, and so I was able to smile my own small smile of satisfaction at having added something important and unexpected, while Sobriety took up the story of Madame Drew's frantic outbursts across the square.

Chapter Thirty-six

The inspector was not to be acknowledged as the inspector, it was agreed, until came the time of arrest or similar declaration.

'It is *Mister* Broadford, I must emphasise.' He smiled widely at Sobriety. 'This is most important.'

'Certainly, Mr Broadford.' Sobriety returned his smile.

She flirts with him! Deciding for the moment to regard my own reactions with circumspection, I noted how instant, every time, was the faint stab I felt whenever Sobriety and Mr Broadford communed, or even when Sobriety merely mentioned his name.

Indeed, these two—Mr Broadford and Sobriety—continued to murmur together at the back of the group as Mr West took up the brass knocker to tap twice at Madame Drew's door. There was a wait of a few moments, during which it was clear to me that my maid and the inspector discussed the waif in the alleyway by Mr Farquharson's great house. I heard, 'Mr Spillane, I believe—' and in reply, '—yes, yes, very likely.' The two glanced twice toward the now befogged alleyway and returned to their hurried discussion until, at last, Madame Drew's door was opened.

How the stage is set! Inside the crowded vestibule it was evident Madame much preferred the dimmer character of candlelight—mainly within glass flutes—and small oil lamps, to that of gas, and that drapery of all sorts was for her a favourite form of furnishing. There was velvet and brocade, especially, very rich in plum, deep green and maroon, and in parts heavily embroidered with fleur-de-lis in gold thread, hanging in thick curtaining in doorways (as well as over windows), from great brass rods fixed where might otherwise have

267

been a picture rail. It gave to the whole room, and no doubt to the rest of the house if all was similarly draped, a deadening hush, where every word and sound fell heavy and dull, and all felt as if wrapped in fog.

We divested ourselves of hats, cloaks, coats and shawls (taken by Madame Drew's very small maid, who nonetheless seemed able to receive this pile with a practiced efficiency that Cissy might do well to emulate) and moved through into Madame's front parlour.

Mr West looked about himself as he took his hands from his gloves, and held these for a moment in long, white fingers, absently stroking the leather before slipping them into the pocket of his jacket. His sister, too, quietly observed the room, and I followed her gaze. There was a small and sinking fire in the hearth beneath the marble mantelpiece, which itself bore two candles, these without glass covering, and a collection of silver-framed daguerreotypes of Madame Drew with various folk familiar to Society displayed on the cold, mottled surface. There were two small tables laden with lacquered boxes and a weight of pale peonies, and a larger, rectangular table pulled to the side of the room, with an oil lamp on it and several chairs pulled up around. Oddly, several paintings—severe portraits too dark to identify in this light, and three feathery landscapes—also hung from the brass rods, against the drapery.

The pale oval of Miss West's face, observing the room, showed no expression beyond dignity, and the simplicity of her belted and uncrinolined dress lent her a nun-like composure. It was all of a deep blue, with a simple lace collar at the neck. She caught my eye and smiled a little.

Miss West and Mr West. They share a look of intellectuals—what did Mr Hadley say of intellectuals? 'They do not think straight.'

Madame Drew stepped into the room behind the group, her hands folded before her waist and her small mouth curved in welcome. She was quite calm now, after her hectic running about in the street, her demeanour one of a great, quiet confidence.

It is thus we recognise her performance. If she but knew we had witnessed.

While not as tall as Miss West, Madame Drew was taller than either me or indeed Mr Broadford; she wore much black jet beads and lace of a very good quality, and equally wore an air of self-possession that knew the impression she made even on the very sceptical.

'I am so pleased to see you all,' she said, and we all bowed. 'You must be…' she began with the Wests, and continued through the group until she had identified each, and then, capably and with much practice in evidence, formally ensured that everyone was introduced to everyone else.

'There are two more guests to come—there is our very dear Viscount, and Mrs Courtney. She is your sister-in-law, is she not, Mrs Hadley?' I murmured that she was. '—And they are quite my regulars.'

Madame Drew took breath for what was evidently an oft-repeated lecture for the sceptical, or for timorous clients who still harboured doubts. 'So it remains for me to observe to you, as I do for all my guests, and quote the very wise Mr Rymer in his wonderful pamphlet, who said these words: "Many of the truths of this day, however familiar they may be to you, were the ridiculed but of yesterday. Three centuries have scarcely rolled away since the man who dared to say the world went round, was adjudged by the scientific and the learned to be impious and profane…"'

'Such a wise man,' Madame Drew said. She looked from one to the other in the assembled group, a comfortable smile upon her face as of some wise aunt of elevated stature. 'And so it is this I would ask all to keep in mind, for a thing can be most wonderful and true at the same time. And wonderful things do happen in my parlour.'

There was a short pause here. Madame looked expectant of a

response, and so Mr Broadford obliged by saying, 'Indeed, indeed. I have heard many reports of the wonderful things that happen here.' He tipped his head to one side. 'It is, of course, what has brought me. The seeking of answers.'

Suddenly, there was a knocking at the door, and Mr Broadford brought his hand to his smiling mouth as Madame Drew turned toward the sound. Sobriety and I heard a busy rustling through the open curtain leading to the vestibule, and a familiar 'Oh,' and Madame Drew excused herself—hurriedly, it felt, after her composure of a moment ago—to greet Edith Courtney as she entered.

Sobriety turned to the inspector and murmured, 'Really, Mr Broadford, you test us all!' But I was intent instead on the rapid conversation taking place past the curtained doorway, where Madame Drew's words were muffled and could not be discerned. Edith, on the other hand, could be heard in reply, 'No, no, my dear, you know that I will see you through…'

Oh, no no no.

I must have made some sign of my reaction, for Miss West glanced at me. I looked away—deeply annoyed, I found to my surprise, and examined this feeling. My annoyance was only partly due to the notice I had drawn from Miss West, I decided. In the few minutes before Madame Drew was to come back into the room, with Edith and the faithful if stony-faced Mary, I discerned in myself exasperation, chiefly with Edith, of course. I recognised the prickling of a kind of angry helplessness at this woman who would never, never listen long to a sensible word, but would drag all about her into danger where all her friends must be responsible for her as she leapt into…Lord knew what.

I closed my eyes and breathed deeply. I had to admit that, as far as I knew, I myself was the only one now under obligation to be responsible for Edith, save Mary, whose remonstration had been rejected so often, by Edith's own report. I wondered if this knowledge helped my feelings, which I continued to examine.

It is, I was surprised to note, *that Edith depends so utterly on me, did she but know it, while calling up worshipful visions of George, who cared not a jot for her, or for me either... And none can tell her that. One must compress one's lips around this knowledge. Which is utterly vexing.* I breathed out.

Ridiculous woman, I thought, and then felt myself foolish with Edith's own failing—that of being a woman alone. *This is to come, this is to come.* The time was coming when I would take my place in that crowd of ridiculous, ageing women seeking meaning for their lives, in lives whose meaning had been withdrawn. A prey to all those who would feed my fear for their own benefit.

I opened my eyes. Madame Drew was entering, her arm through Edith's. She placed a kiss on Edith's cheek and patted her hand. Mary was obliged to stand to one side. She had her lips pressed very firmly together, I thought.

'We have some folk here tonight with whom you are acquainted.' The two women bowed their heads at Sobriety and me. 'And some with whom you are not yet. Allow me...'

As the introductions were made, a knock came again from the front door, and in a moment was ushered through a small man, deeply unhappy, by the look of the colour of his face and the heavy pouches beneath his eyes. He was very thin. His collar, though it topped a fashionable and well-cut assemblage of jacket and waistcoat whose tailor knew what he was about, gaped from his neck, and his jaw was a sharp line beneath the loose, hanging flesh of his face.

He was introduced as the Viscount Balder, and the party was complete. Madame's maid entered a moment to put out the candles, except for one upon the mantel, and to light the lamp upon the larger table. She then withdrew noiselessly, pulling the curtaining to behind her. The fire in the hearth was sinking so low now as to cast almost no light.

It was gloomy, nearly entirely dark in all the corners of the room. All sound seemed swallowed, all faces deeply shadowed. It was unearthly.

Chapter Thirty-seven

We all sat around the larger table, with Madame before the much-draped wall, not quite opposite me, and—a thing that made me too shy to look in that direction—Mr West sat upon my right. The Viscount sat at my left, a small man made smaller again by his very evident misery. He seemed made of saggings, from the flesh on his face to the clothes upon his person, within which covering he appeared to shrink.

The room had a heavy, waiting air about it and the only illumination was very little: the small oil lamp upon the table, with a curious dark-blue glass body to it, and one thin candle, with no covering and glowing very faint, upon the mantel across the room.

There was a silence when we were all seated. Averse to staring at Madame Drew and the others and at the extraordinary appointments of this room, or what I could see of them, I tried to keep my eyes on the dim lace of the over-cloth on the table, while a prickling began between my shoulders as if a crowd of wraiths whispered there. I took a breath and straightened, whereupon Edith, whose perch at Madame Drew's right hand seemed to indicate a certain possessiveness of the spiritualist, caught my eye and smiled kindly, as if to reassure a younger woman made nervous in the presence of the otherworld. Next to her, Mary sat with face tilted away in what some might take to be haughtiness, but what I knew to be a deep disapproval.

Suddenly annoyed once more, I looked away to where Miss West, very straight and shadowy at Madame's left, sat watchful and apparently expressionless.

'Are we ready? Are we composed?' Madame Drew asked. 'I will

call now on my spirit companion, whom Mrs Courtney and the dear
Viscount have already met,' she said, and these two murmured in
reply as if they made the responses at a service. 'My spirit companion
passed to his spirit world many hundreds of years ago, but here on
earth he was the leader of a great tribe that roamed the plains of the
United States of America.' She breathed deeply. Mr Broadford and
Sobriety, the one at the head and the other at the foot of the table,
set eyes upon each other a moment.

It is as if they already presided over dinners of their own.

'Please, we must all clasp the hands of our neighbours.'

There were hesitations around the table as each glanced at the
faces of those on either side, or at least at their hands. I myself
glanced to Mr West's hand, elegant and absolutely composed, as I
thought, lying there a few inches from my own. I was bound by
embarrassment and reluctance—and something else that regarded
the well-buffed glow of his fingernails and the faint, pink flush beneath them—knowing that I must hold his hand and that it was usual
at séances to do so, when of a sudden my other was taken by
the Viscount. His hold was as limp as his demeanour, and his hand
dry and so thin that the skin seemed barely attached to the skeleton
beneath, and I was for the moment distracted, and in no position to
object.

'May I?' Mr West then murmured on my right side, having turned
his hand over so that it lay slightly cupped and awaiting my own to
rest in it.

'Oh...yes,' I said, and my face burned as I placed my hand in his.
My thoughts were a jangle and I closed my eyes briefly in an effort
to quieten myself.

*Nothing has happened. Nothing...and yet disturbances clash against each
other both without and within this place...yet again, see how the others sit calmly,
if I could only do as they do...*

The candle on the mantel blew out.

'Running Warrior is here,' Mrs Courtney whispered.

My heart pulsed, and cold washed through my body.

The table rose. There were gasps; everyone save Madame Drew reared back just a little, as their arms and hands rose with the surface. The table twisted a little this way, and then that, and sank to the floor.

'Are you there, my friend?' Madame Drew breathed. There was nothing but silence and stillness. The room in all its abundance of brocade and velvet seemed to wrap around me from head to foot. I felt I could barely breathe.

Madame Drew appeared to sigh, then subsided to the table with even her arms dangling down. It took a moment or two for Sobriety to ask, with some hesitation, 'Is she all right? Is this part of —?'

Edith replied, with a placid expression of patronage, 'Oh, yes. The spirit enters her, that is all.'

See how she draws confidence from this. From being a part, she believes, of its secrets. An initiate. Oh, Edith. How are you different from those who fancied themselves in Mr Farquharson's inner circle, even as he emptied their pockets?

Madame then moaned, sat up slowly and took back into her own the hands on either side. She spoke. 'Are you there?'

Of a sudden, there was a thump behind us all, which made everyone start. Heads turned to see, but nothing stirred there in the thick shadows. Madame's breathing could be heard, deep and long.

I thought I could hear something else then, a shuffling perhaps, although it was not loud enough for that…when there was a creeping, a flapping at my left, and a gloved hand, it seemed, reached over the edge of the table. I could not help but shriek, just a little, and the hand withdrew.

'Outrageous,' whispered Mr West, and squeezed my fingers lightly.

''Tis nothing, I am all right,' I said to them all—for several had exclaimed both at the appearance of the hand and at my reaction. I felt my voice was both breathy and childishly high; my heart beat as if it laboured to escape.

'It means that he is here,' Madame murmured, and sat very still a long moment so that everyone was obliged to do likewise. My heartbeat slowed and settled, though I was conscious of a continuing tremor in my own hands as they rested in those of my neighbours.

'There is a soul here,' Madame Drew finally spoke, but in a guttural, jerking sort of way and very much lower than her normal tones. *Running Warrior, I suppose.* 'There is a soul here who calls for another —' Madame breathed so rapidly she almost panted. 'She calls for Bernard...Bernard, she cries...'

The Viscount of a sudden jerked his head upright. 'Winifred!'

'Yes. Winifred says, "Bernard, you must not weep. Weep no more, Bernard..."'

'Winifred!'

'"Bernard, you make yourself ill. You must take care..."'

'But Winifred, there is no life without you!'

I shifted a little on my seat and sank my head, embarrassed at the man's exhibition. *How can he display himself so?* I felt overly warm. Mr Broadford cleared his throat nearby, as if he too were in need of distraction from the Viscount's very public declarations.

'Winifred says it is not your time, Bernard, and you must not make it so. She says that others have need of you, and they expect you to do your best.'

'Winifred, that is cruel, I cannot...' The Viscount's head sank. 'I...' he began, and at several places around the table there were audible sighs. *It is like being present at a domestic dispute!*

'Winifred says you must take care.' Madame Drew's tone took on a finality at this, and there followed another silence, during which the Viscount sniffed several times. I looked at the man's profile, sunk now with his chin almost at his chest.

The man lives on misery. I corrected myself. *Madame Drew lives on his misery.*

After a few moments, Madame's breathing once more became rapid, was like a light panting.

'There is another, but he is not quite of this realm. And yet—'

Something like a breeze blew across the room, while yet it was too dark to say from whence it came. 'And yet—' Madame, or her spirit companion, began again. 'And yet he yearns to contact a loved one, even while he hovers between one state and the next...'

At this point I caught the flicker of something from the corner of my eye. Slowly, I began to turn my head, the skin upon my face now damp and become very cold, my breath shallow (*Foolish! There is nothing there! Of course there is not!*), when all of a sudden I beheld a glowing, gauzy apparition of a man—clearly a man from the shape of his whiskers, which were snowy white, as was his face. He held white hands before himself, perhaps in supplication—indeed, he did seem to be suffering some emotional perturbation—and came swooping up to me (*Nay! Not me! Why does he come to me?*), whereupon he moaned, 'My dear!' and passed his face close to my cheek, so that I felt a puff of breath, or it may have been a kiss.

Immediately, he was gone.

Chapter Thirty-eight

Where he had gone for the moment nobody stopped to ask, for all were distracted by my very evident distress. I could say nothing for several seconds but, 'Oh! Oh! Oh!', wiping roughly at the spot on my cheek that the apparition had kissed.

Others, too, seemed unable to finish their sentences. 'The devil! What…?' cried Mr Broadford, and 'Mrs Hadley! How…!' repeated Sobriety. Mr West veered between 'Appalling!' and 'Water!'

The Viscount sat huddled with his head bent and his hands clasped in his lap.

Eventually, Miss West herself took up the appeal for water to Madame Drew, to steady my nerves, and it was fetched, while Edith rustled around the table, past Mary and the inspector, to me, and pressed my hand. She kissed me, and murmured to me, 'See, did I not tell you? George has been waiting to show his love.'

I, who had been sipping at my water and taking shaky breaths that were now steadying, looked up at this and glared at Edith Courtney. I closed my eyes a moment (lest I do something to be regretted), before turning to the others.

It is not her fault. We must finish this properly. Remember why we are here.

'Thank you, all of you, for your concern.' I tried to smile, but it was a very feeble one and made the muscles in my cheek twitch, so I gave it up. *To be…used, yes, used thus! It is beyond…* 'It is nothing, really. I was merely taken by such surprise. I would not like to think we had had to stop the…séance…because of it.'

I took a deep breath and let it out slowly. Thoughts muttered across my mind at each other: *For a moment there…but if it had been, oh! The gall! How, how appalling…but yet, of course, it was not…*I was faintly nauseated, I realised, and closed my eyes a moment over a sense of being soiled, and…of the presumption here, the very presumption by that woman (I took another deep breath) about Mr Hadley (*who would never, in any case!*) and myself. But most of all, I was shaken by a fury on my own behalf.

She presumes very wrongly about me.

I sat up and set the glass down.

Very wrongly.

'This is too important, I think, to everybody here. We had best continue, had we not?' I looked at Mr Broadford, who sat back in his chair, the dim light giving his face great intensity.

The inspector and Sobriety, regarding me from each end of the table, both had such looks of unsmiling acuteness, with such tension about their shadowed eyes, as to appear quite similar. Through nerves quivering still from shock, I felt another anger that was almost vindictive, that made me frown so that my brows momentarily pinched together.

'If you are certain, ma'am?'

The moment faded. *See how I summon anger to supplant confusion.* I breathed. 'Oh, yes.'

The rest, though there was an air of hesitation still, sat down once more, one by one, where they had been. Slowly, they took up each other's hands again, and Mr West bent toward me to murmur, 'Absolutely certain?'

'Yes, thank you.'

'May I say what a very plucky lady you are?'

I was able to bow a little and give a small, but steady, smile at this, when the Viscount spoke.

'It may be, it may be Winifred may likewise come to me. Running Warrior…'

Madame Drew replied, but she was testy. 'Running Warrior waits for us to quieten and call on him, sir. And if Winifred wishes to come to you today, we cannot know.'

'It would only be fair—'

'She cannot be obliged. Perhaps she may be ready to come to you next time.' Madame's speech was quite clipped now. 'Yes, yes, I am certain she will be prepared to come to us next time. In the meantime…' She looked at the Viscount, whose chin hung a little closer to his collar in acceptance of his delayed conversation with the dead. 'There are several here who wait to hear news from beyond. But now we must steady ourselves. Please.' Madame Drew's face wore exasperation, and it seemed in her brusqueness that she forgot for an instance the skills of gracious host and conjuror. 'I must have quiet.'

There was silence again. I glanced around the darkened room, sensitive now to any movement. But there was none, and I looked instead at the others, and then at Madame Drew.

The spiritualist sat with her eyes closed. At least, they seemed, in the near-dark, to be closed.

At last, all was quiet. The flame in the small oil lamp began to gutter.

'He is here. He takes hold of me.' The pitch of Madame's voice rose and the flesh crept upon my arms.

With a last flicker, the flame went out. The lightlessness and silence, packed about with that stifling weight of velvet and brocade, was as if a cocoon or a coffin held us all buried and airless deep in the earth.

'He takes me, he takes me.' Madame's voice seemed to move from its place at the table and to rise, physically, toward the ceiling. I found I was gripping Mr West's hand, and that he too had a tight grip on mine.

Miss West suddenly exclaimed, 'Oh heavens. There is a foot upon my shoulder!'

'Oh, hallelujah! She levitates!' cried Edith. 'Praise the—'

But then it was that Mr West withdrew his hand from mine, and apparently Mr Broadford, too, chose that moment to slip his own from Edith's. Each of the men struck a match against a box taken with a rattle from each of their pockets.

In the brief and wavering light could be seen how Madame Drew stood on her chair and leaned for balance against the curtained wall, and how one foot was raised and rested upon Miss West's shoulder.

Chapter Thirty-nine

The rest was farce. *It is something that might have enlivened the music hall,* I thought, though I had never attended at such a performance. *Such a performance, indeed! Though not quite the one Madame had in mind.*

I repaired with Edith, Mary, the Viscount, and Miss West to the other side of the parlour, while Mr Broadford—declared as the inspector, at last, and blowing hugely on his whistle (somebody shouted outside in the street)—struggled without success with his matches and the oil lamp upon the long table. Sobriety brought a candle to the table to be lit, and then rustled across to other candles standing on the mantel and smaller tables to light these also.

Mr West, standing behind Madame Drew, had a strong grip on the spiritualist's arms. She wrestled a few moments with him, and their shadows played looming and jerking across the ceiling like monsters dreamt by the Brothers Grimm.

There were some moments before the inspector gave up the struggle with the table lamp. 'Tcha! It is empty!' he said, surprised.

It seemed right that the rest of us should stand to one side while the drama was played through—a crowd though they made with me, Edith, and Mary pressed into a corner, skirts ballooning against chairs and small tables, and the Viscount, and Miss West standing like something biblical and full of judgement. In any case, Edith had need of some restraint and a great deal of talking to. Keeping a strong hold of one of her elbows, while Mary had hold of the other—for she showed signs of wanting to fly to Madame Drew's rescue (while Madame herself was showing signs of wanting to fly the house itself)—I spoke firmly.

'Shh, shh, Edith. This must be done. Tell me, what was she

expecting from you?'

Miss West, cradling one hand in the other and regarding the activities of the men and the Madame as if she too were at a performance, turned at this.

'Mrs Courtney, too?'

'I believe so. Edith, what was she expecting from you?'

'Look how he grips her. The monster!'

'She does not deserve your sympathy, ma'am.' Mary nearly hissed, it seemed to me, as if much exasperation had been pent up for too long. 'You must tell what she was expecting.'

Mr Broadford was now walking about the table, pulling aside the chairs and lifting the cloth. Sobriety held up the candle, and together they bent to peer underneath.

My sister-in-law wailed, meanwhile, 'Oh! Outrageous! Adelaide, Adelaide—when she had brought George to you, from the very brink!' Mary and I both stared at her, neither with the words to answer.

Calmly, the inspector's voice came muffled from beneath the table. 'See, Miss Mullins, such interesting engineering. She would press here...' The table jerked a little. 'Ah yes.'

Mr Broadford tugged at something from beneath the table. At length, he pulled up a quantity of gauzy material, white and scattering a white powder. He sniffed at the material, and showed it to Sobriety.

I turned to Edith. 'Not Mr Hadley, I think, Edith.'

Mary breathed out a long time, as of someone finally vindicated. 'No. Indeed.'

Sobriety handed the candle to the inspector, and looked closely at the material. 'Cheesecloth. It is coated with something, I think, Mr Broadford. Is this a kind of paint?'

The inspector chuckled at this. 'Oh, I do believe you are right,

Miss Mullins. Mrs Courtney, here is what was worn so that we should all think a spirit descended upon us.'

One of the inspector's policemen entered then, having caught an elderly fellow, or, I decided while peering from across the room, simply a fellow with the remains of a heavy powder upon his face, hair and beard.

'Oh, yes. And here we have the spirit himself,' Mr Broadford chuckled. 'And you see, Madame—' He raised his eyebrows at the silent spiritualist. '—how my reinforcements have been waiting without all this time.'

I shuddered.

I glanced at Edith, whose face was become slack, was without focus and older, as a result, by many years. The flesh was thick, colourless, drooping in pouches outlined without mercy by shadow. She shook her head slowly again and again, perhaps to deny what was occurring, to give this betrayal no chance to grip and bring her down.

Edith, pray remember: the betrayal is not mine.

Edith's eyes were lowered, her hand raised to her mouth. She breathed as if she laboured uphill, puffing. She leaned into me, drained of any spark, murmuring in such monotonous, low tones that I was shocked.

'Adelaide, you do not know. What have you done, what have you all done. This was her calling and I, her acolyte. And we witnessed such miracles. Nay—' And here Edith's voice rose a little. 'Nay, we created miracles. We unlocked truths—we were respected by those who came to speak with us...' Her voice faded. Mary produced a handkerchief from where it was tucked into her sleeve, and Edith began to weep silently into it.

See, she does not distinguish...all the world is responsible. It is simple. She is hemmed in by betrayal. She is bathed in humiliation. And she has lost...well,

284

she has lost what she thought she had helped create.

The inspector, meanwhile, scraped a finger against the new captive's cheek and smiled at Sobriety. 'Flour.' He turned to the policeman who held the man fast. 'Into the vestibule, for the moment, I think, where—' There was the sound of rustling and an angry grunting from the open doorway. '—I fancy the maid is also being held.'

The policeman said, 'Come along, then, you,' and led the floury man away. Madame Drew now stood still and silent in Mr West's tight hold (with his full mouth very stern), while her breast heaved and she watched, unblinking, first as her henchman was taken through the doorway, and then as Mr Broadford bent once more to look beneath the table, holding aside the cloth while Sobriety moved the candle forward.

I placed my hand over Edith's.

'Edith, what had you promised Madame Drew?'

Edith Courtney looked toward the spiritualist, but Madame Drew turned her face away so that only her profile was visible, shadowed as grey stone.

Mr Broadford, down on his knees, was by now feeling about beneath the table. With some huffing and heavy breathing, he soon began to back his way out, and then sat on his heels and grabbed the edge of the table to help himself to his feet. He turned to the group gathered across the way, and, watched by Madame Drew, still unmoving in Mr West's firm grip, held up his hand. Those regarding him—with the exception of the spiritualist herself—each could not help a small gasp, which we uttered almost as one. For a moment only, it seemed like horror had truly visited us, for what Mr Broadford held in his hand seemed like another: a ghastly hand detached from its arm. But soon it was evident that it was merely a glove, stuffed with something so that the fingers stood stretched just like a person's. The breathiness throughout the room became titters and giggles for a moment, each pitched too high and quivering with the release both of fear and relief.

'See here,' Mr Broadford said, poking at the end of the glove, which was oddly wide and quite long. 'I believe Madame slipped this onto her foot, when we were all thinking she had gone into a dead faint. It is probable...' He smiled, thoughtfully slapping the gloved fingers against the palm of his hand (*I do wish he would not do that*). '... We will find a slipper down there when next we look.'

Edith, who had stood very still now for a long time, now turned to me. Mary lifted her head, alert to her employer's final defeat. Edith's face was wet, though she seemed scarcely to know it. She had ceased to dab at it with her handkerchief some time ago. She did not look at me when she said, 'I had redrawn my Will in her favour—'

'Edith!'

'Mrs Courtney!'

'And I was about to give her a large sum—I had not decided how much—as an advance, because that odious Mr Farquharson had cheated her.'

She kept her face averted while she dabbed at her tears.

'Women must do what they can on their own for their own good,' she sounded petulant, and I was sure she quoted Madame. 'And men such as that think nothing of cheating women who must fend for themselves.'

Well, that is certainly true.

'Edith, it seems to me that Madame Drew was intent on cheating *you*,' I murmured, my arm across my sister-in-law's shoulder.

Edith Courtney twisted away, and snapped in a fierce whisper that drew another succession of tears. Her face shone with them. 'You cannot understand, Adelaide. She gave me what I needed!'

I dropped her arm, and felt it best to say no more for the moment than, 'I am sorry, Edith.'

At the table, Mr Broadford shook the oil lamp and held it up to scrutiny for a moment, by the light of the candle that Sobriety held. 'I see now. Timed, I suspect, to go out and add full drama to Madame's levitation,' he said, and replaced it upon the table. 'She must have worried that the Viscount's argument would land us all in darkness before she was ready!'

He then took the candle from Sobriety and crossed the room, to twitch at the curtaining at the wall until he found space behind it. It was soon evident to all that another doorway stood behind. Mr Broadford walked through, and within a moment was back with what looked like an apple on a piece of string.

'Bump!' he said.

Edith whispered, very quietly so that I was obliged to tip my head to hear. 'What now? What do I do now?' But it seemed a very private thing that she was expressing, and so I made no answer. I thought instead of Edith sitting the long nights, through the long years of her widowhood alone in her house but for Mary, watching the flames twist in endless, tedious repetition in the fireplace. This, where once she would have wrapped her shawl about herself and called the carriage for her weekly visit to Madame Drew, for that reassurance that the late Mr Courtney, at least, still held her to be central to his being, wherever he dwelt. Such visits being all the more of a comfort, I pondered, because the late Mr Courtney in life was in truth a flawed gentleman, prone to peevish outbursts that demanded his wife's anxious pandering. I peeked at Edith, whose agitation shook her plump cheeks with little tremors, and thought that, more than anything, these séances—this fantastical world hushed by velvet and dressed with empty incantation—were a creation by these women and fearful men, where everything and everyone was just as they should be, where loved ones yearned for them now as they may never have done in life. There was the illusion of power; they could summon noble savages, great men and wonderful, wonderful beings.

The Viscount pulled a cloth from his own pocket, and likewise pressed it to his eyes.

Suddenly, there was a banging on the front door, the sound of its opening, and some hurried male voices. Into the parlour rushed another policeman, a young man all out of breath and with the cold of the winter's night about him.

'Inspector Broadford, sir!'

'Constable! Where have you been?'

'Sir! Sir! I…sir!'

He was a boy, his face gone white—this much was evident even in this weak light—and his hands waving inside their overlarge sleeves as if they were themselves seeking words to speak.

Mr Broadford put the apple upon the table and clasped the young policeman's shoulders.

'What is it, lad?' It was a little as if he dragged the boy to him, downward, for the young man was the taller by far, though slight and gangling. The young policeman opened his mouth and closed it, looking about himself as if lost, and Mr Broadford grunted 'Lord!' in exasperation, and shook his constable roughly, just once.

'Look at me!'

The boy looked at him.

'What is it? Tell us, boy!'

The youth reared back an instant, as if aware of his superior's face for the first time, thrust up into his own.

'Oh! Murder, sir! Actual murder, sir! And I gave chase—' It was very clear to all those in the room listening, with their breath held fast for the moment and their eyes unblinking on the white and sweating face, that the young policeman was as innocent of any real experience of violence as anyone here.

His voice twisted. 'But I lost him, and when I got back—' Mr Broadford's hold upon the shoulders gentled at this. '—she was dead.'

The boy's face contorted while he struggled for a breath to calm himself. It came with difficulty, wheezing as if his throat could not relax around it. Mr Broadford turned first to Sobriety and then, silently, to me.

Of course, of course.

We left her alone out there.

Unaware that I did so, I opened my mouth and keened in one long note.

Part Four:

In which Adelaide and Sobriety make ready for what is to come

Chapter Forty

The folk we do not see

by A. Hadley

London thrives, we know it. The world knows it also, and sends its goods for trade in mighty ships, and we sleep each night well satisfied with England's might and England's Empire. We are certain of our place at the centre of things, and certain that our emissaries and soldiers do make of this world a better, more British place. We are certain that London's industry and London's business is a beacon to the rest.

Yet in powerful London, think on it, there are poor creeping folk whose home is found in rookery or alleyway and is shared with vermin, and who live, perhaps, by the sale of our waste. Speak to them of 'the world' and they will believe you speak of London alone, or that small part of London that they know well, for this is where they scrabble, this is all they know and hear of, and this they will never leave.

It is a wild place, this London, and it is not kind.

I was content with this. It had flowed onto the page and settled there. I even fancied there was an authority to it, though it made me sit with hands folded, thoughtful for some time. I fancied—and it left me with a nausea almost, at the very idea—a teeming of thin, homeless children such as that dead girl, all brown and hunched and scurrying as rats through the streets of London, all left without shelter because Mr Mayhew's report had caused where they had used to live, those rookeries, to be torn down. Slums, yes, but homes, and all ripped away because London felt disgraced by them. *Is this how she came to shiver in alleys and tunnels, each meant not for shelter but for the passage of wastes?*

I drew my shawl more tightly about my shoulders.

I wondered then at the Madame Drews of the world, and of that awful concoction of a séance that pretended to reach the dead when all the time, outside… In any case, how was Madame Drew herself made? She who was the pair to Mr Farquharson in many ways, each conjuring false solace or hope in order to make gain, shamefully, from those who are perplexed in these ungentle times.

And Madame Drew, I thought, *made a further pretence—to be fey because it is often thought it is women who are fey, or who even are witches. People expect it, and so she gives it to them.* I smiled at this a little. *Since there is no hope of her pretending to be the purchaser of railways!*

I thought how last evening, when Sobriety and I, suddenly and unusually both restive at home, had set out to walk together for perhaps half an hour—we had decided to reach the new house a-building not a great distance away, before turning back—and Sobriety had said an odd thing: 'Women are expected to say and do what is comfortable to others. And all of us prefer to be thought wise.'

Sobriety squeezed the arm that she entwined in hers. 'I think of my aunt who read fate in cards, especially. I do not know if she believed in her own foretellings, but certainly many flocked to her for the comfort, and sometimes paid her for it.'

To which I had felt I must exclaim, 'But it is so wrong to take payment for a lie!' And Sobriety had said, 'Of course it is. Very wrong. But people do pay, or make gifts, because they receive comfort in some way, and the fortune teller receives it knowing people believe they have paid for comfort.'

She paused, and I watched the mist puff into the air from our breath. 'Besides, my aunt believed she was wise.'

We walked along in a silence of whispering skirts while a carriage clip-clopped by. 'And it must be remembered,' Sobriety said at last, 'that fortune-telling, that I know of, leads to very little violent death.'

I smiled. 'You are grown remarkably forgiving for a Methodist, my dear.'

Sobriety laughed. 'Oh no, no. To mislead others is always wrong!'

But with these thoughts my mind had swung, without her willing it, back to Mr Farquharson and violence, to the despised and lonely wife grasping for love, and to his littlest, most frail victim.

I passed a hand in front of my eyes before packing away my pen and papers.

'Do you not wonder, Sobriety, who she was, or at least what she was named?'

'Yes. Yes, I do.' Sobriety knew, of course, to whom I referred, though I had spoken without preamble. Sobriety stopped her rubbing at the silver on my brooch. 'I wonder what we will do to remember her when time has passed and we cannot recall her face, or the sound of her voice.'

'She will fade to nothing.'

'It is not right.'

'No, it is not.'

That this child would vanish into the very air, as if she had never existed, set each of us into a silent pondering on disinterested fate. All had stood among the stenches and fog of the alleyway that night as the inspector's young policeman raised the girl in his arms from the cobbles. The small head fell back and swung a little, lolled where life was gone that could have supported it, until the young man steadied it with the crook of his arm and a trickle of blood scribbled thick and black from the mouth across her cheek. The soft skin of a child was crusted with dirt behind her ears and at her neck, and the childish soft lips were loose in death, and the patches of wet glistened still beneath her eyes and at her reddened nostrils. Scrapes and bruising showed dark and ready to bleed, the blood halted because the heart was stilled. Here was the small face, individual in death, that I could yet not have described in life, for fearful flight had always intervened. I had never even seen the living girl properly, could only ever have described her by her trappings: the strands of her dark hair, her youth, her red skirt.

Fled, always, before anyone could come close.

Outside this comfortable dwelling now, the weather moaned, its insinuating fingers seeking out any in this great city who shrank for protection into the rat-filled crannies of alleyways, the rotting bales upon the docks, those places where the stinking Thames lapped refuse up to the shore where the mudlarks waited to search out small broken treasures.

We sat, each wrapped against the cold despite the struggles of my morning room fire and each with a cup of coffee cooling beside her, until the conversation began again.

'Do you know what I would like now?' said I.

'No, indeed. What is that?'

'I have a yearning to play some tune, perhaps sing a little. Will you join me?'

Sobriety turned her plain-dressed head to look at me, and raised her brows a little. 'What would you sing? I do not—'

'—yes, yes. I do not propose popular songs or prepared pieces for Mr Hadley's unsmiling set. We are of a quiet mood, and we might sing some thoughtful hymn of your liking.' Sobriety seemed uncertain, for it was not the Sabbath. 'Oh come, it would do us good,' I said, and rose to my feet.

The drawing room was now like a field of tossed snow with its furniture and the ornaments under sheets. So the pianoforte must be uncovered, the sheet folded back, and the stool pulled out. I essayed a few minutes to find the chords for accompaniment, and sang a descant to Sobriety's choice until my fingers grew too cold to play:

Jesus my Shepherd is,
'Twas he that loved my soul,
'Twas he that wash'd me in his blood,
'Twas he that sought the lost,
That found the wandering sheep;
'Twas he that brought me to the fold,
'Tis he that that still doth keep.

Then, the stool pushed back and the sheet drawn over the instrument, we returned to the morning room fire. The flames licked and played, as they did not in dark alleyways where the rain dripped chill and unchecked by any ceiling. We held our hands out to the warmth.

It was thus that Sobriety came to ask her inspector for his help and his authority, and he approached the governor of the prison, and we three—for Mr Broadford did insist on accompanying us—went to visit Mr Farquharson-Forster in his room therein, where he passed his sentence. We watched while the turnkey twisted at the key, his lungs bubbling rot with each breath.

It was ill lit, to be sure, for the window was tiny and let in a niggardly light. Yet there was evidence again that Mr Farquharson's own will had made him wealthy—his determination to pursue riches and power whatever the means or consequence for others—and that his will now provided furnishing about which other prisoners, no doubt, could only dream. His bed was draped in figured brocade with a burnished fringe; there was a fine piece of embroidery framed on the wall, perhaps Chinese; he had a desk that was small but well-crafted and polished to a glow that smiled in the feeble light; indeed, he had a light, a crystal fluted lamp. A small Turkey rug lay upon the floor. There was a chair, and this, too, was made by carpenters and upholsterers who knew their own worth, and I was ushered into it.

Look at him, I thought. *Who would think that he is in disgrace?* For Mr Farquharson-Forster stood as straight as ever, his cuffs as neat as ever, his waistcoat with a satinate embroidery, and in his cravat the pin of sterling silver glinting in the muted glow of lamplight. The image of a gentleman, as ever.

Mr Broadford spoke first, from the shadows it seemed, for the lamplight barely reached where he stood. 'Mr Forster, you will recall these ladies, Mrs Hadley and Miss Mullins—' Mr Farquharson-Forster glanced at me but not at Sobriety. '—and they visit today to ask a question of you.'

The tall man took breath and seemed to expand, to loom over us all as if we came cap-in-hand and he were not a miscreant. 'You will address me as Mr Farquharson, sir,' he said in his great voice. 'And madam. It is my name.'

He looked down at me and folded his arms.

'Folk make a grave mistake in questioning my business, madam, if that is what you have come about. Though I recall of your family only your brother had investments with me.'

'No, no, I—'

'He is a foolish man, like others. I cannot regret their failure, since nervous fools cannot be countenanced in business. I shall not have truck with them again—'

'Indeed not,' began Mr Broadford. Sobriety laid a hand on his arm, for it was clear irritation was growing. Nonetheless, Mr Broadford continued. 'I fancy your sentence will not be so short when the truth of your financial fraud is uncovered.'

'You know very little about business yourself, Inspector, it is clear.'

Mr Farquharson smiled a little at this, as if there were some secret of which the others knew nothing. 'You have worked to bring me down, but I have my servants and admirers still, and this sojourn here will be a short one.' He looked into the dark where Mr Broadford stood. 'Rest assured, there will be no proofs held against me.'

I looked up at him and believed, at least, that he believed this. I wondered if it were true that Mr Farquharson would rise again from the ashes he had made of the fortunes of others, and never be brought to book. *All things, sadly, are possible.*

'You have not the foresight, Mr Broadford, Mrs Hadley,' the man made a mocking bow to each, 'to see what an intellect such as mine can bring about.'

'I have begun lately to think on money and the getting of it,' I said at last, my voice wobbling a little around the exaggeration. 'And it seems to me, as I have read recently—"No man ever knew, or can know, what will be the ultimate result to himself, or to others, of any given line of conduct. But every man may know, and most of us do know, what is a just and unjust act.'"

Mr Farquharson looked at me fully now, and in the poor light it seemed the lines were deep and shadowed with contempt. For the moment he said nothing. Instead, he reached for the watch hanging on its chain at his front. He opened it, looked at the time (*he makes as if he had an appointment*), and clicked it shut. His hands, I was reminded, were massive, but deft and confident, cared for with creams and manicured well. His hands, certainly, had no doubt about the future.

'Madam, I suppose your innocence of the facts behind business does you credit as a woman. The truth is more subtle: that there is art to the making of money, and that success rests with he who tells the best story. And I always tell the best story. The making of money has nothing to do with justice. However, I am come to the end of my patience with this.' He stepped to the wall and leaned against it, his arms folded once more. 'What are you here about? Not the child, surely?'

We all three looked at him, not certain of which child he spoke.

'Not the baby, taken off by my silly chit of a wife to her parents, as if it were hers to take?' He lowered his brows to look at us, the shadow falling across his eyes. 'He will be back with me, soon enough.'

I opened my mouth, about to defend the poor young woman, Mrs Farquharson, whose life would truly never be the same again, wreckage created as if by afterthought. But I thought better of it, swallowed what I knew now to be rage, and said instead, 'No, sir. I speak of the other child. The mother of your baby.'

My face heated at this, this intimation of the foulest abuse and the basest of animal lusts, and I knew it to have turned the deepest red. I felt queasy, as if I smelt his sin. Here was this prison cell bedecked as if it were the miniature of a gentleman's chamber, and here was this man, who behaved as if the very dust of the streets would move aside for his sake…and yet. *And yet*—here my eyes pricked—*he flounders—nay, he revels—in the sewer, and drags all down with him.* I looked at the corner of the bed, near where Mr Farquharson stood, breathed in for courage (while my breath shook) and blinked so that I may face the man himself. He looked as if he had no idea of whom I spoke, and then the set of his face changed with realisation.

Yet surely there must be some tender place still for the girl with whom he—

'You have come here for that?' He looked at Mr Broadford. 'She wastes my time with talk of flotsam and jetsam? What were you thinking, Broadford?'

The inspector spoke from the shadows. 'We were thinking that this girl has been murdered, sir, and by your man.'

'Which man?'

'Mr Spillane, and he has run off.' This was from Sobriety, her voice no more steady than mine. There was movement from the two who stood there in the dark, and I felt that the inspector patted Sobriety's hand, which still rested on his arm. I myself felt such a flood of revulsion at Mr Farquharson's evil that would have me flee from this presence. My body clenched in resistance.

'Did he now. Did he.' Mr Farquharson nodded, as if he were thoughtful, and then as if he acknowledged something, was admiring, or approving, or simply appreciative of his henchman's blind loyalty. 'Well, now.'

There was a silence, in which we three waited, until Mr Broadford said, 'The man killed the girl, Mr Farquharson.'

'That girl barely lived. If that is all—'

'No.' I felt unable to sit longer, and rose suddenly to my feet. 'We come for her name, Mr Farquharson, for she had one.'

He straightened at that, looked at me with a surprise on his face, his eyebrows raised, and laughed.

'Her name? Good God, madam.' He went to the door and banged upon it. 'Turnkey!' he called, and spoke to us as the lock rattled from outside.

'She was a little night animal into which I planted a seed. There it begins and ends.'

'Her name, Mr Farquharson.' I felt both cold and ill, my stomach roiling at his statement of loveless appetite, my mind flinching from an image of his great-coated presence hunched over her tiny form, heaving in a cobbled, stench-filled corner…

But here he only walked, in silence, the few steps to his small desk, drew out the chair there and sat with his back to us.

'Her name. Please.' I wished, unbearably, to go and shake the man. I swallowed against the desire, and my own queasiness, and knew that I had never before felt such a rage as this.

Yet he did not speak, and neither did he move, and the door was by then opened, with the turnkey standing in the doorway, his keys clanking still and the foetid air in his wet lungs bubbling back and forth.

Sobriety went to speak, but had to cough before she could make a sound. 'Come. This man only proves once more he has no human feeling.' She took my arm. 'Come.'

We heard him chuckle as we left. 'You could call her Flotsam...'

Chapter Forty-one

Tristram James

By A. Hadley

. . . Her boy, his mother felt, had had to learn much. Fine feeling dwelt in his breast after all—for his cheeks were wet with tears— despite his father's attempts to instil heartlessness therein. Tristram's soul could melt, she could see, in what was a truly manly sensitivity toward another's need. His stricken silence at the fading of this ragged girl told her all of that.

Yet, what of this realisation that not all was gentle and just in this world, that the poor and helpless could be trampled thus and no rescue snatch them from pain and death? Would this knowledge of sad injustice slow his feet along his path? Which way would that path lead?

Tristram put his hand to the young girl's hair, and the girl opened eyes already shadowed as the light within dimmed, and tried a weak smile for him.

'Young master, do not forget me. And dry your tears, for you have brought some brightness to me with your presence, and I do not die alone.' Her eyes drifted shut and she sighed. 'God takes me now, to my rest.'

There was a hush, which Tristram filled with a quiet weeping, until he turned his face to his mother. This new knowledge was a weight upon them both.

'Why, Mother?' he asked. 'Why must it be so?'

I sat at my post by Mr Hadley's bed, my writing box open before me. The fire snapping behind the grate made no difference to the cold. Outside, a wind had picked up. My thoughts occasionally wandered there, to the savagery that both drew and repelled with each rattling fling of cold temper. I sat wrapped to my neck in my woollen shawl, and watched Mr Hadley's face.

That is, I had my eyes fixed there, since in reality it was only occasionally that I was aware of him, for my mind was alive with shadows, of which only one was his. The writing here before me, which did not yet give me that sense of completion that always told me when a thing was well written, was itself born out of the uncertain shapes and shadows of my mind. I could not help the feeling those shadows were yet to show themselves as beings that convince. Uncomfortable with what I had penned but uncertain as to what was amiss, I stared at the page before me, then raised my eyes in escape.

For a moment now, Mr Hadley came into focus and I gazed at the skin draped so loosely over bone, the shapes of his skull asserting themselves as the flesh fell away. The stench of his sores (or perhaps they could be called ulcers by now) remained, but over it lay the scarcely less unpleasant smell of the doctor's salve.

His very character had long ago faded from sight, and what was left was barely reminiscent of him. His circle would scarcely know him; his colleagues would not recognise the imperious regulator of others—this characteristic so unnervingly like that of Mr Farquharson-Forster.

Arrogance and evil, both so very well tailored for it. I know it now, George.

I hesitated in my silent soliloquy, for I was aware that there was much I did not know of him, and never would. Of Mr Hadley. Of George.

You must have had occasion to whisper to Mrs Charles things you would not whisper to me. But then, she did not know what you did to me, and to Sobriety, and so she did not know you either.

George Hadley's presence barely made an impression even upon the bed and pillow, where his hair floated like so much inconsequential silver fluff, now so thin and fine that his pate showed yellow and flaked through it. These last few days his breathing had diminished to the merest suggestion, with a light clatter behind it like the tremor of raffia. I waited, with the barely breathing body of my husband, for the visit of Doctor McGuiness, to be told what I knew already to be the case: Mr George Hadley would soon slip from this world, with a barely audible sigh.

There in the silence of home, with the great noise of angry nature without, I thought of the small face, individual in death, that I could yet not have described in life, for fearful flight had always intervened.

Fled, always, before anyone could come close.

I reached now for the page of writing before me and tore it across and across. False, insincere. A mere imitation of life itself. *All is invention. All lies.*

I looked at the paper torn in my hands. *It is not so easy to do justice to tragedy.*

Now, certain that these events must have some worthy record made of them, I took out another piece of paper, thought for a time, and dipped my pen into the ink. I wrote:

> *The girl was still for a time, and it was clear that she was gone. The two young faces were lit by lamplight, the one flushed with knowledge, the other empty of all that she had ever known. Tristram's mother felt it as a deep ache that her son should have come by such hard knowledge at such a young age, but then this girl was as young, and had had hard knowledge, and too much of it, and nobody had cared to keep it from her.*

There, it was done. I exhaled deep and slow, surprised to realise I had been holding my breath for so long. I considered how characters change under the nib; there was the suggestion—more than a suggestion—of Toby and the dead girl in the red skirt, and myself (I supposed), yet…yet Toby and Tristram were not the same, and this girl on the page was but a cousin to the one I had known in the dank streets of London.

And Tristram's mother draws closer to her son than I am to my own. But perhaps…perhaps. Toby swam into my mind, licking his ice yet refusing my hand. My throat closed for a moment on the thought and my eyes blurred.

Gathering up my inky cloth, I began to clean the pen, sniffing a little. Then I gazed at the paper again, for the dead girl—my own, very real dead girl—rose up in my thoughts and I, as an offering perhaps, conjured what must have been nights sleeping in tunnels or alleys on rags, knees pulled up so far to leave little exposure to the winds. The knock of other boots against the cobbles, passing close by her vermin-ridden head where it rested. If there were no overhanging eave, the rain must splash cold and trickle to the warmest crevices, past the ragged collar. There must have been, before sleep were taken and chased away, a struggle with others or with animals for bones or crusts or the mouldering mushed remains of fruit. The hunger, always murmuring, sometimes clutching and roaring; the threat, always looming, from poor man or rich man alike.

Child, child, child. I wiped away the tear that fell.

After the interview the next day with the lawyer, Sobriety had said, 'Poor Mr Gordon. He seemed hardly to recognise you.' For I had been brittle—nay, abrupt—nay, contemptuous of small talk and parlour politeness. No, not even that, for I had not cared enough for his opinion even for contempt.

With the briefest of greetings, I had said, 'I want funds, Mr

Gordon, for a small funeral and gravestone. No, no, of course I do not speak of Mr Hadley,' for Mr Gordon paled and opened his mouth and eyes. 'It is for a person to whom I feel I owe this much.'

'Madam, does this person not have family who should—'

'No, she does not.'

He straightened his black-clad shoulders. 'I cannot see why you should feel you need, madam. If this person has no means, if she is a pauper—'

See him bobbing and pursing his mouth.

'You did promise, Mr Gordon, that funds would be forthcoming when requested.'

I was unsmiling and had lost for the moment all softness, was impatient with delicacy, and he was taken aback, it was evident, and lost the argument with no shot fired. For a moment, as we ladies left his office, Sobriety looked around and read pale distaste upon his face, his hand upon his breast as if he suffered from shock and sought to protect himself from further alarm.

Sobriety later remarked to me, 'I fancy you are now safe from him as suitor.'

These vanities do flit about on the outskirts of life, a smile here, a demurral there. A present of a nosegay; the promise of a home. They do not matter. They do not matter. Who could think they did?

Yet it was clear that Sobriety felt they did, for there were times when I glanced her way and caught the stillness of her face. I knew that Sobriety had packed away her secret, put it right away and would never refer to it more, for the sake of a home some day with Mr Broadford. I, at these times, would myself acquire a little of that stillness, for my own secret was kin to Sobriety's.

And then at other times I would regard Sobriety's small and matter-of-fact face and know that nosegays bore no part in the little woman's reasonings, and that it was fear, fear of a world that would leave innocents floundering in treacherous sand that led to her decision. Sobriety, both practical and fearful behind the secret that she carried, reached for the safety of rock.

I looked at this woman who slipped, these days, from maid to friend. *We each effect our own escapes*, I thought, and unwillingly followed the thread that suggested that, in her transformation from minion, Sobriety also escaped from me. *To return as my friend?*

I looked at George Hadley's face, at this thinking about secrets. *You had secrets, I am certain, terrible ones perhaps. We will never know what they were.*

My George, Mr Hadley. After all these years, I know less about what you have wrought out there in the world than I do about Mr F. I leaned forward and put my finger to my lips. *And George, Mr Hadley, perhaps it is best I do not know all.*

It was drawing close to the end of my period of watching over him, and I took up several of my papers, today's writing and some from days gone by, and folded them into an envelope. I contemplated this a moment, tapping my finger against the paper, and then opened it up, unfolded and looked through the sheets, took one from these and read it over again, pressing my lips together. Once I made to discard it, and then again, and then I folded it once more with the others and replaced them in the envelope. Once, as I enacted my nervousness, I did smile at myself.

Then, with luncheon over—a simple haddock with a white sauce, had there in the kitchen while clanging, wiping, and the footsteps of busy women played beyond where Mrs Staynes held her self-imposed post next to me and Sobriety—I hurried into bonnet and shawl, crying, 'Make haste, Sobriety! I must be there by three o'clock!

Where is the envelope?'

Sobriety had the envelope in her hand ready, since I had given it her but a minute before (for safekeeping lest sauce fall on it), and said, 'Here it is. Not lost, do you see?' And I thought once more to take a deep breath, as Mama had always advised. 'Yes, yes. I do beg your pardon.'

In the hallway, I stilled myself so that Sobriety might tie my ribbon at my chin. 'Oh, Lord.'

Then it was into the landau for a trip—*a business trip!*—into the city to the rooms of *The Cornhill Magazine*. It seemed a journey of inordinate length, though the traffic did flow smoothly. Three more times I opened the envelope and spread out my papers upon my knee, until my sheets were become creased and perhaps a little soiled. I put them back and set the envelope aside on the seat, to stare at the life in the streets. There was colour, there were smells and the coming and going of noise; it was all a jumble, and myself but one of the many pieces that made the busy whole. I could see the bonneted and hatted heads of those in other carriages, as they passed but an arm's length away. These faces were a little grey, seemingly, there in their shadowed boxes. They turned sometimes toward the street, and sometimes bent away toward each other.

Then Mr Brent pulled into Cornhill Street itself and stopped. The carriage lurched as Mr Brent descended to let down the steps, open the door and present a hand to help me down. My own hand shook, I knew, and I very nearly forgot to pick up the envelope where it lay on the seat.

Mr Thackeray, when I was ushered into a room full of stacked papers and a desk that knew no order, seemed all angles, being tall and himself put together in haphazard fashion. I was surprised by his voice, which was high, and by his very first statement to me: 'Madam! We had thought you were a parish curate!'

I laughed at this, and shook his hand, relaxed suddenly from relief, even though a few minutes later there was a tremor still as I opened the envelope and drew forth the papers from it.

Chapter Forty-two

$\mathcal{D}$ays seemed taken up with dark shapes, with the hushed shiver of skirts in black. Two dresses were dyed; Cissy and Sobriety sat serious at the clattering machine for sewing, with ribbons and fringing, and Sobriety bent over a blackened bonnet with trimming and new netting. This busyness was a harbinger of that to come, when George's passing would call out all of the mourning stuffs, that great fuss of brooding, heavy blacks, to be added to these small things now being made ready for service, folded and waiting in the sewing room that had been his study.

'I shall spend more hours by Mr Hadley's bedside, for he slips away, I think,' I said to Mrs Staynes. 'You will have much work between you in preparation.'

The other women moved about the house; perhaps they glanced at me, I did not think of this until much later. They were made quiet by my very pallor, I suppose—I caught sight of this in a mirror in my darkened morning room, stared at my staring self as if at a stranger and thought somewhere in a still-wondering part of my mind that all would do well to be afraid of this face.

For I am afraid of it myself, of what that face has seen.

I saw there were dark patches beneath my eyes, for these last days I had not always slept well. I had wept for a short time, then.

The occasional murmuring from behind doors or burring faintly from the kitchen was a sign that Sobriety had told the story, as I made my wordless way about the house, my hand a moment upon the banister, the boards creaking beneath the carpet. At mealtimes in the kitchen, I lifted the spoon to my lips and down again to the bowl. Mrs Staynes stood at attention to give orders, but there was that look about her of uncertainty, particularly in the tension lined upon her forehead, that had settled about her lately. All about her had changed and she had been powerless to arrest it, and George Hadley's passing would set such change in place profoundly, perhaps permanently. I had begun to look away from the bewilderment that Mrs Staynes carried with her now from room to room and duty to changing duty.

Sobriety undressed me in the evenings and brushed my hair. Once, I took the brush from Sobriety's hand and held her close, for I had been overcome that moment with a rushing fear. I felt in the first instance that this had been Sobriety's story and the danger had been to Sobriety, and that I could not bear this; and then I felt that Sobriety would be gone from me soon enough, gone to her own home and Mr Broadford, with me left in the world without my own Sobriety there at all times, and I could not bear that either.

Sobriety herself was checked a moment at this, evidently surprised. She returned the embrace and crooned as if to a fearful person *(and that I am!)*, 'No, no, I will not be gone far…'

I sat now by Mr Hadley's…George's…bed and pinched the skin between my brows. There was a slight headache and also a confusion at all of those shapes during all of those past days: the slow clop of horses' hooves and the small, very small group about the girl's grave that merged somehow with the dour, unsmiling erectness of that other small group, my own family who had called me to be reckoned with. The one group that had stood quiet and bowed at the graveside, with faces so pale *(surprising still—the Wests, both of them, and Edith. How came they there to the graveside, and why?)*, thinking on the vanished life of a young girl; and those others, that had sat amongst rich curtaining, polished mahoganies and china, with eyes sharpened and aimed at me, and with a fine wrath so refined and glinting emanating from Gwendolyn in all her dour bombazine and jet, as ever shivering and terrible in her displeasure.

My family had seemed not quite as strangers, exactly, but at least as folk remembered from long ago. They were inhabitants of a place that I had left, somewhere remembered but dimly. The memory was of authority that threatened by the bat of an eye or the rap of a fan, and I expected to be affrighted once more as I entered by Gwendolyn's great door. I wondered at this, that I had no sense that I must struggle against fear, that the fear itself was replaced by impatience—*fancy, simple impatience!*—to have done with this nonsense.

I looked about me with, it must be said, a little trepidation (*but not fear*) at this small crowd of faces, milling about somewhat in Gwendolyn's hall, for everyone had arrived at once. For everyone was summoned here—siblings, their wives, their children—to face down my rebellion. *My rebellion!* I thought, and this time my heart did beat the faster. Then, surveying the unsmiling party, I almost began to confuse them with the other, that pale and sombre group that had stood by that small, nameless grave. Bella, indeed, gave me a start as I stood thus with my mind drifting, for she was thin, so thin, like... For a moment, I had thought...but now my face was of a sudden cold and damp. And Bella, of course, was thin because she chose not to eat. I glanced at Gwendolyn, whose waking agony, everyone knew while none dared notice, was to plead with Bella to take food.

Bella. Will she too die in her struggle to refuse food from Gwendolyn? She never eats! Would Gwendolyn permit her to visit her Aunt Adelaide? Would I be able to speak, in any case, to this girl, to advise her? And am I, in any case (I thought this with a spasm that made me draw sharp breath), *one to advise young girls? Or anyone?*

I thought for a moment of Edith Courtney, certain that there had been no other recourse but to unmask the charlatan, Madame Drew, but uncertain that Edith was left at all the better for it... I sought to catch Bella's eyes, and perhaps I did exchange a glance with the girl, yet I could not be sure of it.

Gwendolyn's maid stood by for my bonnet, but I hesitated, and then decided. 'No, I shall not. I do not intend to stay long.'

I looked at Gwendolyn's face, now paled with offence. 'I must not be long from George's side. He is fading fast.' I gave my sister a sad smile. 'I shall sit with you all a few minutes, and then I must be gone.'

With my every fibre pulled as tight as could be so that my very skin seemed to hum, I climbed up Gwendolyn's stair and to her parlour, behind the sussurating crowd and directly behind Harry's broad back. Dickie and Amanda's brood came up behind me, hopping and nudging and whispering. I had forgot, perhaps because so much had occurred of late to separate me from this place and these people, that above the mantel Gwendolyn's husband's portrait loomed portentous, with its dark background of writhing trees—or perhaps figures, or drapery; I could never quite tell which—his face swimming pale with the consumption that eventually took him. He challenged forever every visitor's entry, his eyes unrelenting and searching for frailty, such was the painter's aim as directed by Gwendolyn. *She is forever her John's self-appointed lieutenant.*

I sat and looked about me with my smile fixed firm, while my sister's servant brought the pot and tea things, and Gwendolyn began to pour with an irritation that rattled the cups because it was an awkwardness that all were to take refreshment except me, the subject of this very gathering.

All around the walls, seventy paintings both small and large—though none so large as John's portrait—jostled and leaned a little forward. Once, when Mr Hadley and I had felt obliged to visit, I had counted them all.

I glanced across at Dickie and Amanda and smiled, most particularly because it was only they who were the more likely to smile in return. They each were quick to do so, and then glanced at Gwendolyn.

I understood, but could not blame them for their timidity. Gwendolyn herself was deliberate and slow with the tea things, for slowness of movement was her habit and her virtue, and all watched as she poured and handed a cup to Amanda. The group sat straight, patient with the years of this ritual, but Gwendolyn chose then to stop a long moment, lowering the pot as she sought once more to reason with me.

'I think you will find there is much to discuss, Adelaide. Please take off your bonnet and take tea.'

With a hush of starch all in the room turned to witness my reply. Seventy depictions of trees and mountains, alien landscapes and Brooms of the past, leaned forward from the walls to witness my reply. I stilled the thrumming in my veins, breathed out long and gentle, and began.

'Harry came to see me the other day, at your request—'

'Oh yes, we were all most—'

'And I have my answer for you now.'

The clatter of teaspoons against cup and saucer, which had begun again in almost surreptitious manner, ceased. I saw that Harry had his tea almost to his mouth, but now looked at me from beneath his brows, with one raised in query.

I turned to Gwendolyn. 'I think I will manage my own affairs, dear sister, and so I do not feel it right to give you details of what these may be.'

'Adelaide! You have not the experience! It is not done! You are not bred to—'

'I will learn. And I have Mr Gordon's help.'

'I cannot agree. And we have other matters as well, that are most serious, to discuss—do you see why this will be no short conversation?'

Here Gwendolyn remembered her duty and raised the pot once

more. Conversation ceased while she poured and distributed cups and cake, and there was no sound but a clatter on the road outside, the ticking of the clock and the occasional whispered 'thank you'. When finally all this came to an end, Gwendolyn put down the pot and set her shoulders and back straight, and turned to me.

I, however, felt I must first make my answer. 'I do not believe Mr Gordon is likely to discuss my business unless I permit it, and so that is the end of it.'

'Reckless girl!' Gwendolyn was loud, her modulated dignity undone for the moment. Those who held their cups flinched and then checked that nothing had been spilled.

'There must be something seriously awry—' Harry began, and Dickie and Amanda murmured to each other, and then to their children, since two of whom fidgeted and two, the older two, had realised the battle before them and its drift, and had begun to giggle. They settled to silence.

'I have decided this. And of course, the question of my writing—'

'Indeed! Scandalous!' Pink patches were coming and going on Gwendolyn's cheeks, and I recalled how my sister, and of course Dickie, had always been the two in the family who could not fudge their emotions, for these they wore always upon their faces. And I too, I had to admit, often shared this tendency. And now I saw tears begin in my sister's eyes, and could hear them in her voice. My own eyes began to prick in response, and I was surprised at the pity that poured into my chest, even while I struggled against this and annoyance grew at the very thought. I knew that I picked up Gwendolyn's ordered world and shook it, and the frustration to Gwendolyn was both physical and truly frightening. In Gwendolyn's view, I had come to throw this world into the path of those whose business—*as with Gwendolyn's own*—was to examine, take apart, comment upon every part and hold it up to ridicule, as a lesson to others who would stray.

'Not scandalous, sister, no. Women write, and are respectable, and are paid—'

'Paid!'

'Yes.' I let out a long sigh. 'I have visited with Mr Thackeray of *The Cornhill Magazine.*' I knew that here I boasted, and certainly knew that I sought to place myself beyond my family's reach. *See my bridges burning!* 'And we are agreed about what writing I might produce.'

Gwendolyn stared.

'I see there is a chasm between us.'

'You have met with a publisher!'

'Well, no, Mr Thackeray is the ed—'

'You receive payment! This is worse than I thought!'

I found myself of a sudden tired of all this—*more theatre, more theatre*—and impatience flooded throughout my body unto my very fingers and toes. I began, almost without noticing what I did, to arrange my shawl and straighten my gloves. I looked at the faces about me, and at Gwendolyn whose forehead creased as if she had headache. *In the end, your claims upon me are a chimera.* And these faces swam and blurred in my mind; they and their loosening grip upon me were fading, losing their importance. For somewhere in the world the murderer Spillane ran and ran around a dirty broken brick wall into night, into day, with his thin jacket pulled tight against the whistling cold and his own guilt. What was all this, compared with that?

It was as if all present held their breath; even Bella seemed spellbound, swinging the huge eyes in that famished face from her aunt to her mother and back.

'We will not agree this day, I think.' I stood. 'I intend no hurt, I hope you believe, or at least will come to believe. I know this is a disruption to you, and I am sorry. Will you ring?'

Gwendolyn face wore the heat and the cold of a dozen emotions crying out to be named. She was silent in her confusion, and instead of speaking picked up the silver bell to ring for the maid to see me to the door.

'Thank you. And Gwendolyn—' My sister looked up, the bewilderment on her face evident as she could not bear, apparently, to bring her eyes to me. 'Gwendolyn, this need not make you ill.'

Gwendolyn spoke at last, in a whisper that made an old woman of her. 'Adelaide, Adelaide. We must not question—'

'Ah. It is there we disagree, you see.'

I stood at the portico and awaited Mr Brent and his horses, the cold air of the world blowing at my face, a small trembling running through my limbs in this aftermath of battle. *I snap my fingers, and they are gone.* I closed my eyes and breathed in the filaments of odours that spoke of a thousand lives, joys and anguishes. The trembling eased.

Of a sudden, that new emotion rage ripped through me, rage at the murderers of that innocent, or at the murderers of my own innocence, or at my very helplessness to do aught about it or at my failure to stay, to stand against evil in that benighted alleyway, and that weeks ago I had robbed that child of her baby, without a question.

Without a question.

Chapter Forty-three

The clock on George's mantel tinkled, and was answered more darkly from below by the grandfather clock in the drawing room. The doctor would be here soon.

Mr Rossetti's painted woman looked down from the wall, but she was now no more than painted pouting, for this old and dying man was beyond the vanities of sensuality, and I had larger things to fear than fur and perfume. *It may even be this woman is not happy*, I thought, *despite the clarion of colour and the bold assertion of her body, though Mr Rossetti and George both did think so. As they would, for the idea of this woman was created by them, painter and buyer both.*

My eyes were drawn to the letter open on my husband's counterpane. It had come from Miss West some days ago and invited me to an evening at the Wests' residence, a Christmas gathering, apparently, and I carried it with me from time to time because it seemed so odd somehow, slipped into this…this netherworld of mine, as it was for the time being. *This waiting life, this waiting until life.* Slipped like bright satin ribbon tossed among a jumble of widow's weeds. Its very oddity made me smile a little. Sobriety had looked as if she may make comment, but did not.

This on my own account? Think on it!

Was I of any special interest to the Wests, and why, or was I part of a crowd only, made up of acquaintances put together for their wit, or because they had occupation, taste, wealth or association, or some other such thing in common?

I have no wit! I have nothing in common with anyone! Nor wit, nor taste, nor wealth! I felt ill with self-consciousness and a leap of panic. *I may as well be asked to stand and account for myself before a crowd of frock-coated*

317

arbiters, I thought. I realised immediately that there may in fact be few frock coats present at the Wests' gathering.

I had mentioned this, that the Wests' gathering would include folk I would find unfamiliar personally and perhaps by their manner, and Sobriety had answered, 'Worldly people, I fear,' and I had flushed hot.

Well, but now I am begun to visit the world! I thought this, but said nothing aloud, and indeed felt foolish for it and not a little ill-at-ease at my own innocence and, yes, the Wests' worldliness; and this although, or perhaps because, the Wests drew me so. *Something like the Tree of Knowledge*, I thought, and blinked at myself.

Sobriety had been bent over all last evening stitching the bodice of the new evening dress for the Wests' occasion; it was of rose pink silk taffeta and had a narrow black, woven stripe, and black lace was to trim the neck and puffed sleeves, and goring at the bottom of the skirt to increase its fullness. This lovely thing would be worn once, and then be put away for the duration of my black widowhood.

Indeed, I essayed a play with Sobriety, about how I would doff my butterfly colours and enter a black cocoon, but Sobriety forced me to laugh at my own expense. 'That would be to do the thing in reverse, surely, for you would emerge a caterpillar!' she said, and shook out the skirt draped over her lap.

In my imagination I contemplated the Wests' front door—beneath a wide porch no doubt, beyond the sinking of light snow-flakes, and heavy, probably, with an elegant knocker just below a wreath of ivy—from behind which would float the thin notes of a violin being tuned, and beneath that would hum the deeper notes of viola and bass.

I pictured the people themselves, then, and fought with a humming doubt that set itself against a certain light-headedness. For if all the ladies were as Miss West and stood about in Aesthetic dress, and if all the gentlemen were as Mr West, leaning and lounging in loose dark velvet and scarves, then I would stand conspicuous, over-trimmed and bright and, it suddenly occurred, the very epitome of vulgar display as complained of by Mr Ruskin in his social comment. The display, indeed, that Mr Hadley always insisted upon, because it demonstrated his wealth, his position, and his young wife.

They will be kind. Surely, they will be kind. I several times felt my hot cheeks with cool fingers, and was angry for a considerable time when Sobriety said, 'This will be entertaining, and a little strange, and I know you will not entrap yourself by supposing you are returning to the girl's life that Mr Hadley took from you.'

Yet I knew myself to be irritated only because it was true. These people brought back the dizzy brightness of those few moments when my eligible maidenhood had been on display, years ago. All those young women, bedecked and over-sweet as marzipan, and those young men, alight, handsome as they would never be again. Yes, again—as I had done at Mr Farquharson's party—my heart yearned for what could not, I knew, be regained.

The Wests were beautiful, as things and people had seemed beautiful when I was young. *But whatever was on offer then is not now. These are strangers; I visit them, as with everything recently,* I sighed, *as I would visit a foreign land.*

I admitted, at last, that the languid Mr West, the artist, did bring to mind those days of faerytale balls when I boasted to my giddy friends that I would kiss that boy with dark curls, he whose mouth was suggestive as fruit. The idea did, of course, bring that Broomish heat to my cheeks, while I confessed privately that I was no longer that girl and he may not be so harmless as that boy...and that now I must encounter him and put such a picture from my mind. Such a thought was not real. Real life was here before me.

And yet, I could not help but think, *it is as if I am to begin my second coming out. I am a debutante once more, of sorts.*

Mr George Hadley. I now looked at the man who was once king—nay, emperor—in this place, and had sought to raise himself to power in other places, and now was diminishing by the hour, at last approaching nothingness. *Power such as yours is based on corruption, George.* And then, as if he argued—*No, 'tis true. I cannot even say you are so far removed from Mr Farquharson, since you have kept me in ignorance about all that you did. Corruption flourishes in the dark, George Hadley, and tyranny is furthered through ignorance. You were tyrannous, and corrupt.*

He, frail, continued unknowing on his bed, but Sobriety came to my mind, and this man's use of her and the bloody consequences of that, and Sobriety's own fear, her struggle with the mantle of guilt. I sat forward with sudden fury, and spoke so that the words hung about the silent room: 'Oh, God, George! Perhaps it is that you wither from the shame!'

I was passing judgement on this man, I knew it, while he was so reduced now, was so nearly insubstantial, was ready to pass into dust. I paused, surprising myself with this thought, that I had so stepped away from him, he who had considered himself master. I took a deep breath, and then another.

I would do much better, George, to recognise both tyranny and nonsense for what they are. We would all do better for that. What nonsense we fashion to conceal our fears! I put one hand on top of the other and was aware of the life within my own flesh and the bones that moved within it. It was myself, and I recognised it.

The story of the past weeks, husband, is about what I have learned. Taken with this thought, I smiled a little. *I carpet my way ahead with knowledge.*

And George, I will walk along that path on my own account. There was a small thrill of fear at this, which passed along my skin like the velvet stroke of a finger.

I thought of Mrs Charles. She had come to farewell the still-living man and would no doubt come to see his body to the ground. *And then that will all be done, George*, I thought, and marvelled at my own hardness.

Toby would be home soon, poor child. I closed my eyes, but my memory held the image of a small, lolling head with the new, perfect skin of the young beneath freckles and smears of dirt, and it caused me to open my eyes with a start. *Will Toby come to me this time? What can be said to a boy who does not know he is loved? How to protect what runs away? Is there a way back from such disdain? What have you taught your child, husband?* I wiped at the tear that had started, while the thought encroached that gifts must be got for Christmas, even though the celebration would no doubt by then be muted by mourning.

'A toy theatre,' Sobriety had suggested. 'Or a magic lantern.' These represented pastimes that could be spent both alone and with, say, his mother, she pointed out, and snipped at a loose thread. I smiled a little.

Sobriety smoothed the material where she had mended. 'He would find the goings-on at the séance amusing, I fancy, particularly the thought of Madame Drew on the chair.'

O Lord. When did my boy ever laugh with me?

But thoughts of the séance were apt, of course, to lead back to death. And that child's passing, alone in the filth of the street, must always—like the turning of a great wheel, over and over returning to the same point—draw up a comparison with Toby. Toby the child, Toby the innocent, Toby the imperious.

'If I tell him a little—' I thought of all that that tale implied. '—a very little of that child's tale, perhaps—'

Sobriety had placed the needle into its little box by now, and packed it away in the sewing case. 'He cannot be as Mr Hadley forever, not altogether.'

I sighed. 'Not altogether.'

We will jog on, my son and I.

I had a notion, for a smiling moment, that my boy might smile and laugh as I had at Mrs Gaskell's story, that little 'Christmas Storms and Sunshine' that my own mother had read to me, the boys, and to Papa so many year ago, at Christmas. *I will read it to Toby*, I thought, *if he will permit it. Perhaps there will come some group of chorister children to the door and sing, as in the story:*

> As Joseph was a-walking he heard an angel sing,
> 'This night shall be born our heavenly King.
> He neither shall be born in house nor in hall,
> Nor in the place of Paradise, but in an ox's stall.
> He neither shall be clothed in purple nor in pall,
> But all in fair linen, as were babies all:
> He neither shall be rocked in silver nor in gold,
> But in a wooden cradle that rocks on the mould.'

I would invite Edith to dine, of course, on Christmas Eve, and coax her, if this were possible or even advisable, from her new enthusiasm for mesmerism.

And then in the silence of thought there was a small pinprick, again, to my conscience and, again, I felt the anxious, steamy clinging at my arm of little Mrs Farquharson.

'I will seek out where Mrs Farquharson now lives, and leave my card for her, I believe,' I said, and Sobriety glanced up with her brows a little raised.

Cissy passed by the closed door, causing a stair to creak, for she always stamped too hard.

She goes to clean grates, I suppose.

Mrs Staynes and Cook were out still, as they had been since soon after breakfast, filling the carriage with a very long list of items—I had insisted they take the carriage for this endeavour—and Mr Brent with all his silent forbearance along as well, and the bill afterward to be sent to Mr Gordon.

I wonder if we can keep Mr Brent after all? It did not seem likely.

Albert sat below in the kitchen, no doubt, with a cup of hot tea and perhaps spelling his way through an old journal, overly robust, even as he sat there, with that breath of surliness that always made a lurking of his presence. He had been absent more frequently lately, had been careless about seeking permission for his outings, though none had commented, not even I, for it was presumed he went in enquiry about future employment.

The fire snapped; the clock tapped its way through the seconds and minutes. The wind had ceased and now a rain fell, heavy and monotonous. George's breath continued a mere suggestion from his bed, and I thought a moment how its absence would soon change the nature of the silence in this room. I thought how altered the house itself had become, with all of its functions, all movements to and fro, the relation of one person to another, and how on George's passing it was to absorb this chamber into itself, its use and its very meaning. The house, so upturned, had settled differently around me, and me within it.

See, George Hadley, how the order of things changes—even the domestic— when you are no longer at our head?

The heavy curtain did not hang straight; its hem had buckled back on itself. I stood to shake it out and then stood for a moment to re-gard the material, a tapestry in elegant chandelier-like design, in blues and pale yellow against a green background, from France. It was fine work, without a doubt, and I realised I had not before spent any time in examining it. Somebody wielded a needle for hours in its creation, and perhaps did damage to eyes and health in earning a pittance thereby. There is so little we notice of who or what is around us.

Opening my eyes, I sat up, lifting the lid of my writing desk and taking out a clean sheet of paper. I cleaned the nib of my pen with a rag, for I had one more task to undertake, since the masons awaited direction and a tombstone must be inscribed. I gazed a long time at the paper and finally dipped the nib into ink. I wrote:

This child who lies here
Was gone too soon
To tell her name.
Wild and a stranger, yet we loved her
For what could have been,
And in love address her thus:
Grace.

I looked a long time at what I had written. *Do I take or do I give, with this? For whose sake do I name this girl?* I thought on this but could not find the answer; or perhaps I knew the answer but did not wish to dwell upon it. *Do I think of thriving from her calamity?* I wondered at this world to which I had fought so hard to belong, and at myself for having no wish to leave it alone.

Acknowledgments

My thanks not just to my sons Tom and Alan Bell and to Alan's partner, the artistic Emerald Buller, but also to my best fan Max Costello; the deeply talented and nurturing members of my writers' group (Alison Goodman, Jane Routley, Chris Bell, Janette Dalgliesh, Steven Amsterdam, Christine Darcas and Mat Davies); painstaking mentor and excellent author Kim Kelly; my sisterly friends Louise Craig and Jo Giles; my cousin Michael Crozier (who knows everyone in London!); Clare Allan-Kamill, author and assessor who saw something worthwhile in my earlier Victorians; and the lovely Christopher Ayling…all of whom have very patiently loved me and my ever-developing novel over the years. Deep appreciation too to Jaynie Royal and Michelle Rosquillo for steering this book so ably, and to the team at Regal House for their work and always-cheerful encouragement.